P9-DMA-219

MARGARET TRUMAN'S

ALLIED IN DANGER

BY MARGARET TRUMAN

Souvenir

White House Pets

Harry S. Truman

Women of Courage

Letters from Father: The Truman Family's Personal Correspondence

Bess W. Truman

Where the Buck Stops: The Personal and Private Writings of Harry S. Truman

First Ladies

The President's House: A First Daughter Shares the History and Secrets of the World's Most Famous Home

THE CAPITAL CRIMES SERIES

Murder in the White House

Murder on Capitol Hill

Murder in the Supreme Court

Murder in the Smithsonian

Murder on Embassy Row

Murder at the FBI

Murder in Georgetown

Murder in the CIA

Murder at the Kennedy Center

Murder at the National Cathedral

Murder at the Pentagon

Murder on the Potomac

Murder at the National Gallery

Murder in the House

Murder at the Watergate

Murder at the Library of Congress

Murder in Foggy Bottom

Murder in Havana

Murder at Ford's Theatre

Murder at Union Station

Murder at The Washington Tribune

Murder at the Opera

Murder on K Street

Murder Inside the Beltway

Monument to Murder

Experiment in Murder

Undiplomatic Murder

Internship in Murder

Deadly Medicine

Allied in Danger

MARGARET TRUMAN'S

ALLIED IN DANGER

A CAPITAL CRIMES NOVEL

DONALD BAIN

A TOM DOHERTY ASSOCIATES BOOK  NEW YORK

This is a work of fiction. All of the characters, organizations, and events portrayed in this novel are either products of the author's imagination or are used fictitiously.

MARGARET TRUMAN'S ALLIED IN DANGER: A CAPITAL CRIMES NOVEL

A Forge Book
Published by Tom Doherty Associates
175 Fifth Avenue
New York, NY 10010

www.tor-forge.com

Forge® is a registered trademark of Macmillan Publishing Group, LLC.

The Library of Congress Cataloging-in-Publication Data is available upon request.

ISBN 978-0-7653-7990-0 (hardcover)
ISBN 978-1-4668-7064-2 (ebook)

Our books may be purchased in bulk for promotional, educational, or business use. Please contact your local bookseller or the Macmillan Corporate and Premium Sales Department at 1-800-221-7945, extension 5442, or by email at MacmillanSpecialMarkets@macmillan.com.

First Edition: February 2018

Printed in the United States of America

0 9 8 7 6 5 4 3 2 1

For Renée.
Thank you for thirty-three years of love, compassion,
encouragement, and being my wonderful writing partner.
I miss you so!
Love, Don

PART ONE

CHAPTER 1

WASHINGTON, D.C.

Robert Brixton and his paramour, Flo Combes, stood with Mac and Annabel Smith in a suite at Washington's iconic Willard Hotel. Brixton had decided that "paramour" was a classy way to refer to Flo rather than "girlfriend" or "sweetie" or "partner." He was too old to have a girlfriend, he felt, and "partner" sounded like they ran a business together. But "paramour" had a nice ring to it, sort of literary. Of course, marrying Flo would solve the question of how to explain their relationship but he wasn't ready for that, nor was Flo sure she wanted to legally commit to the occasionally volatile, mule-headed Brixton. He wasn't known as Robert "Don't Call Me Bobby" Brixton for nothing.

Their attention was focused on the strikingly beautiful woman who'd been encouraged to take center stage by one of a dozen "suits" at the gathering, attorneys of the international law firm of Cale, Watson and Warnowski. Walter Cale waited until conversation had ebbed before saying, "I propose this toast to Elizabeth Sims, our newest partner." He glanced at a note in his hand

and added, "Take a look at our other partners and you'll agree that she adds a needed dose of beauty to the firm."

There was laughter. "Here's to Elizabeth—although if you get to know her well enough she might allow you to call her Liz."

"To Liz," the gathered said in unison as glasses were raised. "To Lizzie," a man who'd had too much to drink slurred.

"Thank you so much," Elizabeth said, lifting her champagne flute.

"She's beautiful," Annabel commented.

"And obviously smart," her husband, Mac, said. "There aren't many female full partners in firms this size."

"It's the law firms that are getting smart offering partnerships to women," Annabel quipped. "They've been missing out on a lot of talent. How is your friend David Portland?" she asked Brixton. "We haven't seen him in a while."

"David's in London," Brixton said. "They call him back frequently to report to his boss. That's why he keeps his flat there. He'll be returning in a few days."

David Portland was a member of the security staff at the British Embassy to the United States on Massachusetts Avenue, N.W., along Washington's famed Embassy Row. He also happened to be the ex-husband of Elizabeth Sims, the attorney at the center of attention that evening.

"Do they find it awkward living in the same city?" Annabel asked.

Brixton chuckled. "No," he said, "David's pretty cool about it. They talk from time to time but not often. He says she wasn't thrilled when he took the job at the embassy and moved here, but they're grown-ups, live busy separate lives, the way it should be. He called me from London. I'll pick him up at the airport."

"It was tragic what happened to his son," Annabel said.

"David's never gotten over it," Brixton said. "Not that you ever do. He told me that he's come up with new information about what happened to Trevor."

"The boy's death goes back a long way, doesn't it?" Smith said.

"Not that long," Brixton said, "maybe two years. David has never been able to let go of it. I understand where he's coming from."

Brixton's empathy was fueled by having lost an adult child of his own, a daughter who was slaughtered in a terrorist bombing in an outdoor café not far from the State Department, where he'd been employed at the time.

"Trevor was Elizabeth's stepson?" Annabel said.

"Right," Brixton said. "David's wife Trevor's birth mother died when he was a little kid, and his grandmother raised him until she died, too, from cancer. He was eight or nine at the time. That's when David met Elizabeth. He'd been bringing up Trevor best he could, considering that his work had him constantly traveling. When he met and married Elizabeth in London she took over the job as Trevor's surrogate mom and continued even after their divorce. David says she was terrific at it."

"How long were they married?" Flo asked.

"A couple of years," Brixton replied. "David is—well, he's tough to get along with at times."

Flo's laugh was wicked. Brixton gave her a stern look. She raised her hand, still laughing. "I didn't say anything," she said, still laughing.

They were interrupted by a tall, angular man with the look of an Ivy League professor. Despite the Harris Tweed jacket with brown leather elbow patches, pale blue button-down shirt, regimental tie, and highly polished ankle-high brown boots, Brixton knew that he didn't spend his days in a classroom. He was Cameron Chambers, a retired Washington, D.C., cop who headed up the law firm's investigative unit and who'd recruited Brixton to augment his full-time staff on an as-needed basis. Brixton had been one of two private detectives in the city who'd signed on as contract employees, available when Chambers needed help on an investigation for a client.

He apologized for breaking into the conversation and said to Brixton, "Spare me a few minutes, Robert?"

Brixton followed him to an unpopulated corner of the lavish suite. "What's up?" he asked.

Chambers looked across the room to where Elizabeth chatted happily with other attorneys. "She's a knockout, isn't she?" he said.

"No argument from me."

"I understand that you're friends with her ex," Chambers said.

"We know each other."

"You stay in contact with him now that he lives here in D.C.?"

"We're friends, only we don't get to spend much time together," Brixton said. "Why?"

"His reputation is—well, let's just say that he has a penchant for making trouble."

Chambers's pinched-nose way of speaking grated on Brixton. Chambers had never been a cop who'd dirtied his hands working cases, had never walked the mean streets of Washington's less genteel neighborhoods. A Maryland native, he'd gone off to college at Dartmouth, where he received a degree in sociology. Upon returning home he was pursued to help flesh out a growing intelligence unit within the Washington PD and eagerly accepted the job. He went on to get his Master's Degree in psychology from Georgetown University under MPD's tuition assistance program, and after six years was tapped to run the intelligence unit, which he did until his retirement. Although not a lawyer, he had the self-assuredness of one, a man without any doubts about his views and conclusions. He'd been married twice and had two sons by his first wife, one of whom lived in Los Angeles, the other in Boston. His second marriage fell apart after a brief run.

"Making trouble?" Brixton said. "What sort of trouble?"

"I've done some checking on him, Robert. He wasn't a stranger to getting into scrapes around the globe, personal *and* legal."

Brixton laughed away the comment. "You're talking past

tense," he said. "David *was* on the wild side when he was working as a security pro for hire, but those days are behind him. You don't get hired by the British Embassy unless your background check comes up clean."

"That may be true, Robert, but my sources tell me that he enjoys sticking his nose in where it doesn't belong."

"I don't follow," Brixton said, although he thought he knew where Chambers was going with it.

While Portland hadn't been specific when he'd called, he did say that he'd been doing some "nosing around" into XCAL Oil, the company for whom Trevor's geological surveying firm had been working in Africa at the time of his death. XCAL was Cale, Watson and Warnowski's biggest client, generating almost half of the firm's sizable income. And Elizabeth Sims, who'd gone back to using her maiden name following her divorce from Portland, was the lead attorney on the XCAL account. A small world indeed.

"I received a call from London," Chambers said. "It seems that Mr. Portland has been asking questions concerning XCAL's possible involvement with his son's unfortunate demise."

Portland had shared what had happened to his son with Brixton over many dinners, lunches, and drinks. After receiving a degree from West Virginia University in geological surveying, the young man had gone to work for SealCom, a geological survey company working in the Niger Delta under contract with XCAL.

"All I'm suggesting, Robert, is that if you hear anything along the lines of what I've just alluded to you let me know," Chambers said.

"Sure," Brixton said, anxious for the conversation to be over.

"That would be helpful, Robert, very helpful. I see that your glass is empty. Mustn't ever allow that to happen, must we?" He slapped Brixton on the back and walked away.

Brixton watched Chambers move gracefully through the crowd in the direction of Elizabeth Sims. Chambers was a smooth operator, no doubt about that. Washington, D.C., teemed with smooth operators and Brixton tried to avoid them whenever possible.

"What do you say we get out of here?" Flo said after Brixton had rejoined her and Annabel.

Annabel's husband, Mac, had drifted away to speak with an attorney for CW&W whom he knew from practicing law in Washington. Smith, like Brixton and Portland, had also lost a child, a son, who'd perished along with his mother in a crash on the Beltway years before he'd met Annabel. That event, and the relatively light sentence the drunk driver of the other car received, had shaken Mac's faith in the law, at least as a practitioner. He closed his office and became professor of law at George Washington University, where he stayed until recently when he again put out his shingle and reentered the combative world of trial advocacy. Annabel, too, had been an attorney when she and Mac met but had abandoned her matrimonial law practice to open a successful pre-Columbian art gallery in Georgetown.

"I thought you'd never ask," Brixton said to Flo.

"You two run along," Annabel said. "I have a feeling that Mac is in for a long conversation."

Flo, who mirrored Brixton's disdain for stuffy D.C. cocktail parties—Washington parties of any sort for that matter, especially those populated by lawyers and politicians—happily took Brixton's arm as they headed for the door. He considered seeking out Chambers to say good night but decided to not bother despite knowing that it would have been politically correct. The retainer with the law firm's head of investigations would pay plenty of bills.

They did stop to congratulate Elizabeth, who graciously accepted their good wishes. She, of course, was aware that Brixton and her former husband were friends, and her infrequent conversations with Brixton were always with that knowledge and the restraints it placed on what was said.

Once back in their apartment on Capitol Hill, Brixton and Flo fortified the party's finger food with bowls of pasta and a salad.

"I get the feeling that you don't particularly like Mr. Chambers," Flo commented after they'd changed into pajamas and sat in front of the television, their meals on folding TV tables.

"He's a type," Brixton muttered.

"Everyone's a type," she said.

"Right, but there's good types and bad types."

"And he's a bad type?"

"Maybe he falls somewhere in between," was Brixton's response. He filled her in on the conversation he'd had with Chambers at the party.

"I'm glad you didn't get into an argument with him," Flo said, speaking from experience. Brixton's fuse was notoriously short, especially when it came to someone like Cameron Chambers. "It was good of Mac to set you up with him," she added. "We can use the money."

"Yeah, I know, it's a good deal getting paid to be on tap in case they want something from me. With any luck they won't."

As they carried their empty plates to the kitchen Brixton said, "David's due back in town in a few days." He recounted what Portland had said during his phone call from London.

Flo winced as she filled the dishwasher. "Your friendship with David puts you in an awkward position with Chambers," she said.

"Chambers is just blowing smoke," Brixton replied. "David's been around, working all those security jobs in every corner of the globe. So maybe he got into a few hassles along the way. Hell, so have I."

He didn't add that he knew of a few assignments that Portland had undertaken over the years as a soldier of fortune that resulted in his taking of a life in order to save his own. He ended his defense of Portland with, "David's a straight shooter."

"Like you," Flo said.

He put his arm around her. "I accept the compliment," he said.

"You know, I kept wondering while we were at the party with all those high-paid lawyers whether the rumors are true about the law firm."

"What rumors?"

"About them helping launder money that some Nigerian scam artists raise over the Internet from suckers who buy their pitch."

"Where did you hear that?" she asked.

"From one of Mac's clients whose father got scammed by the Nigerians. Mac's trying to come up with a legal path for the son to take, but there's not much he can do. Enough about that. Let's catch a movie."

They returned to the couch and debated which film to watch. After coming to a consensus they ordered their choice with a few clicks of the remote. As the opening credits crawled down the screen they settled back for another evening of domestic bliss, Robert "Don't Call Me Bobby" Brixton and his paramour, Flo Combes.

CHAPTER 2

WASHINGTON, D.C.
A FEW DAYS LATER

Brixton drove to Dulles Airport to meet David Portland's flight from London.

They'd first met a year ago when Portland arrived in D.C. as part of a security detail for an Arab potentate who was to meet with the American president in an attempt to salvage a long-standing rift between their countries. Brixton had watched a press conference with the two leaders on television and came to the conclusion that with all the empty talk of human rights and an equitable justice system, the only thing that mattered was oil. We needed it; the Arabs had it. Business as usual. End of any cozy fireside chat.

Portland had bailed out of the assignment when the Arab leader left Washington. The money was good and the assignment easy, and he could have continued working for the security firm that had the contract to keep the potentate and his sizable entourage safe. But he'd had enough of the hypocritical robed dictator and his circle of so-called advisors, and eagerly jumped ship.

Timing had been right. Portland had been accepted into a

government-sponsored program that brought British security professionals to the United States for an intensive hands-on two-week CIA-sponsored boot camp at which they were immersed in the latest anti-terrorist techniques. The camp was held at the Pentagon's training grounds in Virginia, and participants were housed in a nearby hotel.

Brixton and Portland had met in a D.C. bar the second night of Portland's training. Both men were alone. Brixton was in a foul mood. Portland's outlook wasn't any brighter.

"You from here?" Portland asked.

"Not originally. I'm from New York. Where are you from?"

"London."

"Never been there."

"You should visit someday," Portland said. "London has its charms, or so the tourist guidebooks say."

They drank before Portland asked what Brixton did for a living.

"I'm a private investigator," Brixton said. "You?"

"Security," Portland said. "I hire out to security companies around the world."

"Sounds a little like what I do," said Brixton. "Hiring out, I mean."

By the time they were on their second drinks they'd bonded, at least professionally. It was when Portland mentioned that he'd had a son who'd been murdered in Nigeria that Brixton shelved his previous reluctance to prolong the conversation.

"I lost a daughter to a terrorist attack here in D.C.," he said.

"How dreadful."

"You ever find out who killed your son?" Brixton asked.

"Depends on who you talk to. My son Trevor was in the Niger Delta with a geological survey company doing work for XCAL Oil. He could have gone elsewhere with a different company, but he chose Nigeria. Turned out to be a bad choice."

"How did you find out?" Brixton asked.

Portland snorted. "I received a call from the CEO of the

security firm hired to protect workers at XCAL. The guy is a pompous type, the kind of chap who keeps clearing his throat while he talks. He told me that Trevor had been killed, his body discovered by someone from SureSafe."

"The security firm?"

"That's right. He said that Trevor had been killed by rebels. He called them 'savages,' which I suppose they are if they slaughtered a peaceful young man just doing his job. Trevor was an easy target for those rebels who are fighting XCAL's rape of their land, sucking out the oil and raking in millions in profits while the native population starves. What a bloody evil world."

"Must have been a tough call to take," Brixton offered.

"Like a knife to the gut."

"I didn't learn about my kid's murder from a phone call," Brixton said. "I was there with her when some young Muslim woman blew herself up and killed a dozen other people, including Janet."

"How did you—?"

"Avoid getting killed, too? I'd walked out of the café just before it happened and tried to get Janet to come with me. I had a feeling, you know, a hunch that something wasn't right. Janet stayed behind for a moment." Brixton swallowed hard. "I wish it had been me." He downed what was left in his glass.

"At least you know what *really* happened to your daughter," Portland said.

"You don't buy that your son was killed by rebels?"

"I had to buy it," said Portland. "I had no information to counter it." He paused. "But I've never fully accepted it."

They were silent.

"Another drink?" Portland asked.

"No. You have dinner plans?"

"No. You? You have a missus?"

Brixton managed a laugh. "I have what they call a 'significant other.' What yahoo came up with *that* term? At the moment we're on the outs. She's gone back to New York."

"Sorry."

"It happens. Yeah, let's grab dinner. You can tell me what the CIA is teaching you about fighting terrorists."

"So far nothing I didn't already know," Portland said. "Dinner sounds good."

Their friendship was cemented that night over drinks and food, and lots of talk about their parallel experiences. Both worked in risky businesses that put their lives on the line, and often resulted in wondering when the next check would arrive. Both had lost a precious child under barbaric circumstances. And both were divorced men.

Brixton's ex-wife, Marylee, had come into his life when he was a uniformed cop in Washington years earlier, and had delivered two daughters during their brief fling as a married couple. Portland's former wife, Elizabeth, who had almost single-handedly raised his son, Trevor, as his stepmother despite her abbreviated marriage to Portland, was now a top lawyer at a prestigious Washington law firm with offices around the world. Ironically, she was the lead attorney for the firm's biggest client, XCAL, the same multi-national oil company that had employed the security firm whose CEO had broken the news of Trevor's death to his father.

Lots in common.

CHAPTER 3

As Brixton sat in his car awaiting the Brit's emergence from the terminal on a chilly, overcast day he reflected back on that chance meeting with David Portland.

During Portland's initial two weeks in Washington he and Brixton had often gotten together, and by the time Portland departed for London a solid friendship had been forged. Brixton was delighted when Portland called a month later to announce that he had been hired as part of the security force at the British Embassy and would soon be moving to D.C.

But David Portland wasn't the only one whose life had taken a new turn. Much had changed in Brixton's life, too.

Flo Combes had returned from New York and they'd settled back into their apartment, determined to make the relationship work this time. So far it had. Brixton had gone into business as a licensed private investigator thanks to Mac Smith's urging. Things were good, although for Brixton Washington, D.C., would always be a sump of double-dealing and lies, crawling with politicians whose only motivation was to stay in power and get rich in the bargain. Mac and Annabel Smith, and Flo, had learned to never bring up politics with him, especially Congress. When they did they were met with what had become almost a mantra: "Congressional approval ranks even lower than root canals, colonoscopies, and cockroaches," he would spout. "Hell, they just manage to beat out the Ebola virus, Lindsay Lohan, and North Korea." But they decided that his curmudgeonly views, as skewed as they might be at times, were part of his charm.

He'd also found a kindred spirit in David Portland, whose views of politics in Great Britain weren't any more sanguine.

Portland's return to Washington had been welcome news to Brixton. The private investigator had few people in his life whom he could label as close friends, and Portland had joined that short list.

Brixton saw the Brit walk from the terminal carrying an overnight bag. He was surprised at how casually Portland was dressed. For some reason Brixton always thought of the British as being more formal—"a proper Brit"—obviously a cliché. Portland was dressed in low sand-colored sneakers, well-worn jeans, and a navy blue sweatshirt covered by a lightweight white Windbreaker. Brixton had always been impressed with Portland's slim, fit physique, and watched as the Englishman walked with purpose and a bounce in his step as he nimbly skirted knots of people.

Brixton got out of the car, waved, and yelled, "David! Over here!" Portland navigated traffic to reach him. They gave each other an awkward man hug before getting into Brixton's Subaru and driving from the terminal.

"Good flight?" Brixton asked.

"I wouldn't call it that," said Portland. "The airlines squeeze every bloody seat they can into that cigar tube they call a plane and charge a king's ransom for a bag of cashews. Other than that it was delightful."

Brixton laughed. David Portland matched Robert Brixton's general view of things, including air travel.

"And how is Lady Flo?" Portland asked.

"She's fine. The shop is doing well. She's there now. Flo is good people. I don't deserve her."

Portland patted Brixton on the shoulder. "I'd say she's lucky to have you, chum."

Brixton didn't know whether he agreed so didn't respond. Instead, he asked during the ride into the District how Portland's time in London had gone.

"It went well, Robert. The meetings drag on forever, the higher-ups all wanting to hear themselves talk, but other than that it was productive." He fell silent for a few minutes until he said, "A remarkable thing happened a few days ago. I was in a pub, a favorite of mine, when I encountered this Nigerian gentleman who—" He forced a laugh. "I'd prefer to go into all the gory details over a proper drink if it's all the same to you."

"Suits me fine," Brixton said. "Let's swing by my place before I take you home. The Brixton Bar is always open."

He pulled into his apartment building's underground parking garage and minutes later they were settled in the living room, a martini for Brixton, white wine for his guest. They touched the rims of their glasses. "Welcome back, David," Brixton said.

"I see that you're still a martini aficionado," Portland said.

"As long as it's made with gin, not vodka, is cold and dry, and shaken."

"A man of principles," Portland said. "There are too few of them these days."

After tasting their drinks Brixton asked, "Time for me to hear the gory details?"

Portland's face turned grim as he reached into the pocket of his Windbreaker, removed a slender gem-encrusted bracelet from its pocket, and handed it to Brixton.

"Beautiful," Brixton commented as he turned it in his hands.

"Yes, it is," said Portland, "but its beauty is irrelevant. It's what it means personally to me that matters."

Brixton's cocked head said that he was waiting for more.

"As I told you on the telephone, I was in a favorite pub of mine in London and . . ."

CHAPTER 4

David Portland had enjoyed being back in London even though it was only for a few days of meetings at the Ministry of Foreign Affairs. He'd extended his trip for two days and spent his free time becoming reacquainted with the city he knew so well but that was changing, it seemed, every day. While he enjoyed living in Washington, D.C., and liked his job protecting the hundreds of men and women assigned to the embassy, London was home, and he absorbed as much of it as possible before flying back to his new, albeit temporary, life.

He liked the comfortable familiarity of his small two-room London flat, as spare as it might be; his apartment just off the British Embassy grounds in Washington was decidedly more modern—"more American"—but his London digs represented a welcome change. He frequented favorite pubs for his meals; one not far from his flat was where he had dinner this night. He ordered what he usually did, steamed cockles and leeks, and bangers and mash, accompanied by a glass of Chardonnay, typical pub fare that suited his pedestrian palate. He contented himself with that single glass of wine, something that would have been unthinkable when he was in the midst of an alcoholic binge that started upon his learning of his son's death. It had been a year since he'd emerged from that whiskey-fueled daze, two years since Trevor's murder in the Niger Delta.

Portland had conquered his heavy drinking through willpower, eschewing friends' suggestions that he seek help at the National Health Service or some private facility where he would be locked away for weeks at a time to listen to lectures on the virtues of sobriety from ex-drunks, and boring psychologists who would benefit from a proper drink now and then. It had seemed simple to him—just stop getting drunk!

"You've stopped everything," Elizabeth, his ex-wife, used to tell him in her best New England accent following Trevor's death. "You're dried up inside. You were always away. How many of Trevor's birthdays did you miss, or forget, because you were somewhere else—*killing people*?"

It was like a record of her greatest hits, the loving stepmother, mistress of all that was good and decent, self-righteousness personified. But although he railed against her accusations, especially when the whiskey shaped his words, he knew that she was right. If she intended to punish him for his son's murder she needn't have bothered. Trevor's death possessed him like a malignancy; he had every reason to believe that it would kill him one day.

That thought consumed him while he sipped his wine. As he did a large black fist and wrist jutting from the sleeve of a crinkled yellow leather jacket came to rest next to his plate. His eyes went to a multi-colored patch on the sleeve, the emblem of SureSafe, a security company for which he'd once worked, an experience that had not ended pleasantly. A second patch beneath it featured the outline of a country with "Nigeria" spelled out within it. *Nigeria!* Where Trevor had met his end. *SureSafe!* The global security firm that was supposed to have protected him.

His focus shifted to the bracelet digging into the wrist's flesh.

It was distinctly feminine, crafted by a British silversmith with a light touch, Victorian in style.

It couldn't be.

The gold, woven around small red and white precious stones like a snake, was brighter than its dull gray metal setting.

Could there have been an exact replica of the bracelet that Trevor's grandmother, Portland's mother, had worn, commissioned by David's father from a jewelry shop in Somerset? It was unique, a one-of-a-kind custom piece of jewelry handcrafted by a master artisan. It had to be the bracelet willed to Trevor by his grandmother.

It had to be!

Trevor had adored his grandmother, who'd brought up the boy until she'd died. Portland had deposited his young son with her while he traveled the world, and if he never succumbed to his guilt to the extent of staying home it was always with him. His mother's death from cancer had been harrowing for Trevor. With his beloved grandmother gone and his father absent most of the time, he'd been packed up and shipped to America with his stepmother, Elizabeth, who'd entered the boy's life after falling in love and marrying the handsome, globe-trotting David Portland.

The cockles and sausage churned in his stomach as he looked at the profile of the bracelet's wearer, whose deep voice ordered another round of whiskey with beer chasers. The stranger's voice was not only deep; it was also loud; his manner was demanding.

The man's skin was ebony, his wide, pockmarked face gleaming as though automotive wax had been applied. He was over six feet tall and thickly muscled, his arrogant pose matching his voice. Even without the company patch Portland would have pegged him as a security type, tough, cold, and had probably killed a few.

It took one to know one.

The big man carried the beer glasses in hands the size of

baseball mitts to the table he shared with two others, each as black and leathered as he was. He returned for the whiskeys.

"Excuse me," Portland said.

The man turned and looked at Portland, who'd remained seated.

"That bracelet you're wearing," Portland said. "Where did you get it?"

"Why?" the man asked in his baritone.

"I know that bracelet," Portland said. "It—or one just like it—was especially made for my son's grandmother. When she died—"

The man turned away without a word and carried the whiskeys on a warped metal tray to his friends at the table. The three men talked loudly in an African language that Portland didn't understand. They'd had plenty to drink; they'd passed over the line into drunkenness.

Trevor had been working in the oil-rich Niger Delta when he was killed. Did these men work there, too? Trevor's death, the bracelet, the Nigerian, the *questions*, consumed Portland. The world at large had disappeared. There was now only the bracelet that filled his thoughts and emotions.

He picked at a piece of his food but abandoned it. The pub's owner noticed and asked whether he was unhappy with it. Portland shook his head. "It's fine," he mumbled. The owner continued wiping glasses, satisfied it was just Portland's mood that evening.

There really wasn't any question about the bracelet, the gems glistening in the pub's overhead lights, the gold 24-carat well worked, his father's early anniversary present to the wife he adored. He had owned and managed a small factory in the Black Country. When he sold the firm he and his wife retired to Somerset, where they spent idle, pleasant days until he died, leaving his widow to eventually and willingly assume the responsibility of raising their grandson. When Trevor's grandmother passed away it was Elizabeth who stepped in and took over his upbringing—until her decision to leave her enigmatic husband and take his son with her to America. Portland hadn't objected. It was the best thing for Trevor and that was what counted, as painful as it was. Portland's visits to America were infrequent, but he always made time to spend with his son and marveled at the strong, handsome young man he was becoming.

The pub was filling up; the scent of food was heavy in the air. Although smoking was now banned, the once white ceiling tiles were tinted nicotine brown from years of cigarettes, pipes, and cigars. Portland watched out of the corner of his eye as the big Nigerian raised the whiskey tumbler and downed what was left in it. Portland decided to approach the man and again ask where he had gotten the bracelet. But as he prepared to leave his seat at the bar the big man wiped his mouth with the back of his hand, stood, and weaved in the direction of stairs leading up to the restrooms.

Portland slipped off his barstool and fell in behind the unsteady swagger of the leather jacket, moving along the narrow corridor and up the flight of stairs. The man disappeared inside the men's lavatory. Portland drew a deep breath and pushed open the door. The leather jacket was stretched across powerful shoulders as the Nigerian hunched over the urinal. Portland closed the door and entered silently.

He had to do it. The man, whoever he was, wore the bracelet treasured by a dead young man whose beloved grandmother had let him touch it, play with it, slip it onto his slender wrist. Thoughts of those tender moments flooded Portland but were replaced by more pragmatic needs. He would ask the question again: Where did the man get the bracelet?

The Nigerian's posture dwarfed the urinal; he stared at the ceiling as he urinated. The restroom was small, a square box, three urinals, one closet, a hand dryer, two washbasins, a single window looking out over an alley into the February darkness.

"Excuse me," Portland said.

The Nigerian turned his head and looked at Portland. "What the hell do you want, man?" he growled.

"That bracelet you're wearing," Portland said. "It once belonged to my son. He lost it in Nigeria and—"

Portland's defiant stance, and the tone of his voice, triggered nerves in the man. His antenna went up and told him that he was about to be mugged by someone who wanted the bracelet on his wrist. He pulled the knife out of the leather jacket in a single move and lunged clumsily, his sneakers squeaking on the tiled floor. Portland caught the big arm above the wrist, pulled the knife hand toward him, and pushed his opponent off-balance. He stretched his arm away from the shoulder, twisting it so that the knife dropped to the floor, the noise of the shoulder being dislocated louder than the knife hitting the tiles. The man's cry of pain was animal-like.

Portland stamped on the African's right foot and head-butted him as the man clutched his dislocated arm and slid down the wall, his eyes glaring at Portland, black and hating.

Portland now operated purely on adrenaline. He picked up the knife and placed it at the man's throat, just above the tight neckline of his white T-shirt. Simultaneously he removed the bracelet from the man's wrist and dangled it in front of his eyes.

"Where? How?" he demanded. "Where?" he snarled again. "How did you get this?"

The African's eyes were wide with fright. The knife pierced his skin.

Portland slid the bracelet into the pocket of his multi-pocketed vest with his free hand.

"Where, damn it?" Portland asked, again pricking the neck with the point of the knife.

A red, wet blot stained the neckline of the T-shirt.

The man snarled. "A card game," he rasped. "Poker."

"Where?"

"Where you think, man? In the *delta*, man! You don't know where it is? Nigeria, man!"

He'd gained confidence despite the pain of his arm. Shock had sobered him; Portland knew that he could become dangerous. The others would look for him.

"Who?"

"My boss. . . . Frenchman, he didn't have the money to see me . . . he put up the bracelet. . . . I won the hand."

Trevor had to have been dead, or helpless, for this Frenchman to have removed it.

"Name? Not you, the Frenchman. Who was he?"

The Nigerian resisted the knife's pressure with a regained confidence.

"Name?"

"Fournier. Alain Fournier."

Christ!

Portland didn't debate his next move. He banged the man's head against the porcelain edge of the nearest urinal and let the unconscious body slump back onto the tiles. He quickly descended the stairs. The other two were still at their table. He threw money on the bar and said good night to the owner, who eyed him questioningly. He had to get out; he trembled. There hadn't been time for more questions. Alain Fournier, working for SureSafe, a nasty company to be sure.

The noise of traffic replaced the chatter in the pub. Gerrard Street was busy. Drizzle in the air was moved by a frosty breeze. No one followed him. Headlights and lit shop signs glared as he walked blindly toward his flat.

SureSafe. Scum! That wasn't just his opinion. Mercenaries in every place he'd been where SureSafe was employed to do the governments' dirty work—freelance kills, oil security, and site protection—agreed. Don't work for SureSafe, and if they're operating near you give them wide berth. So went the mercenary mantra. London, Paris, and Washington, D.C., offices. They were big and effective. And brutal.

And Fournier still worked for them, in the Niger Delta.

His hand touched the bracelet in the pocket of his jacket.

Trevor!

He wouldn't be put off any longer. The shop window against which he leaned was shuttered, protesting his weight with a jangle of its roll-down metal covering. The bracelet had ended up nothing but a trophy won in a goddamn card game. He should have stayed with the Nigerian longer to find out more no matter what the risk.

Pedestrians hurried past, careful to not get too close. Someone would call the police and he didn't feel up to explaining. He walked unsteadily away from the shop. A young man avoided him and snickered to the girl he had his arm around; Portland heard the words "old sot." Streetlights and headlights were a messy blur as if he were walking into a haunted castle ride at a fairground from his childhood.

A quiet glass of wine and some pedestrian food in his favorite pub had resulted in being recalled to his former messy life, a life he'd been determined to relegate to the past, to his own personal dustbin of history with its year of alcoholic confusion and another year of lying awake at night wondering what might have been. Trevor had been laid to rest in his mind, a sad memory.

But that memory had now come back to life in a very personal, volatile way.

CHAPTER 5

Brixton listened intensely to Portland's story, interrupting only to clarify a point. When the Brit was finished, Brixton shook his head and said, "That's one hell of a story, David."

"I wish it were only that," Portland said, "a story. But I'm afraid it represents painful reality. It's the same bracelet that my father had handcrafted for my mum, the same one she willed to my son just before she died. He wore it constantly, never took it off." His expression turned hard. "Christ!" he said. "To think that it was won in a bloody card game. My question at the moment is how the Frenchman Fournier came to own it."

"Tell me about him," Brixton said.

"Fournier? A smarmy lowlife, Robert. He's been working for SureSafe for years, most recently protecting XCAL Oil's employees from Nigerian rebels."

"And your son Trevor worked for the same company?"

"No. Trevor worked for a survey company that has a contract with XCAL. After Elizabeth brought Trevor to the States for a proper bringing up—my lifestyle certainly didn't provide

that—he enrolled in one of your American colleges, West Virginia University, where he gained a degree in geographical surveying. That degree landed him a job in Nigeria with SealCom. I wasn't happy with his decision, nor was Elizabeth, but Trevor has always been headstrong." A smile crossed his face. "I wonder where he got that."

"I'm sure your ex-wife can provide a quick answer to that question," said Brixton, also grinning.

Portland fell silent, his glass clasped in both hands, his attention focused on it.

"What's on your agenda now that you're back in D.C.?" Brixton asked.

"I called Elizabeth to see what she knows about the possibility that XCAL played a role in Trevor's murder."

"Flo and I met your ex the other night," Brixton said.

"She's her firm's lead attorney on the XCAL account."

"Which puts her in a tough position," Brixton said. "If she *does* know about some complicity on XCAL's part she'd have a hard time going public with it without losing her job."

"If it turns out that way she'll just have to deal with it," said Portland. "My timing is good or bad depending on how you view it. I'm having lunch with her tomorrow before she gets on a plane for London."

"She travels a lot?" Brixton asked.

"Quite a bit. XCAL has a sizable presence in London. So does Elizabeth's law firm, Cale, Watson or whatever."

"Your son is buried in England?" Brixton asked.

"No, here in the States. I arranged for his body to be sent from Nigeria along with his belongings. I never even looked in the box that accompanied him. I assumed that the bracelet was among those belongings. I was obviously wrong."

Portland spent the next half hour talking about Trevor, and Brixton lent a sympathetic ear. He remembered how much he needed to relive his daughter Janet's life to those willing to listen,

including a psychotherapist whom Flo had encouraged him to see. That need to speak aloud about her had waned, but he still talked to her when sitting alone with a drink on their small balcony, or driving by himself.

The discovery of the bracelet had jarred Portland into action from his painful, albeit peaceful, reverie about his son's murder, just as Brixton had been forced to pursue his daughter's killer, which led to his shooting a U.S. senator's son who'd been complicit in the terrorist act.

"Well," Brixton said, "I don't envy your lunch with your ex. I'm sure it will be contentious."

"Which is all right with me," Portland said, clenching and unclenching his fists. "Let's talk about something else. What have you been up to?"

"Things have been slow at the office, but Mac Smith, my attorney friend—friend? Hell, he's my mentor and benefactor—he has some clients waiting in the wings. He's also doing work for another client that might interest you."

"Oh?"

"Ever hear of Borilli Industries?"

"Can't say that I have. Should I?"

"No reason you would unless you follow the women's clothing industry. Anthony Borilli owns—I should say *owned*—a string of ladies' fashion outlets up and down the East Coast. Made a ton of money from his stores. He had a reputation of being a really nice guy, treated everyone who worked for him with respect, paid salaries that were higher than average. Anyway, according to his son, Anthony Jr., who runs the business today and is Mac's client, his father started exhibiting signs of dementia."

"Alzheimer's?"

"I guess. His son says that his father was losing it, forgetting important names, fouling up his personal checkbook, stuff like that. Of course the father denied it. I suppose I would, too, at least until it became obvious even to me."

"You said that this client of Mac Smith's would interest me. How?"

"The father got caught up in one of those Nigerian money scams."

"He *must* have been demented to fall for something like that. Those Nigerian scams have been around for a long time. I thought everyone was wise to them."

"Not everyone, David, at least not Anthony Borilli Sr. According to his son, his father started sending sizable sums to some con artist in Nigeria who claimed that he was sitting on millions of dollars that were being held by the corrupt government. You know how the pitch goes. If this guy in Nigeria has the money to pay to release his funds—a couple of hundred thousand bucks or even more—he'll share the millions with whoever helps him out."

"And Mr. Borilli bit."

"Yeah, he took the bait. From what the son told Mac Smith the father damn near drained his personal checking and savings accounts dry. On top of that he siphoned off money from the business."

"The son, no one else in the family knew what he was doing?" Portland asked.

"Evidently not."

"How did it get resolved?"

Brixton hesitated before answering. "The father put a revolver in his mouth and blew his brains out."

Portland sat back in his chair and exhaled.

"Nigeria sounds like a great place," Brixton said.

"It's a proud country, Robert, with a seemingly inexhaustible amount of oil and other earthly treasures. The Niger Delta is its oil center. According to what Trevor told me, the natives live in absolute squalor while the oil companies make billions. They pollute the land without even attempting to right the wrongs. Government officials are paid handsomely to look the other way and stuff their pockets with cash while their citizens go hungry." He threw up his hands. "Enough maudlin talk! Do we have plans for dinner? My treat."

"Your British pounds aren't good here," said Brixton. "We'll swing by your apartment before picking up Flo at her shop and joining our friends Mac and Annabel at a restaurant. Work for you?"

"Splendid," said Portland.

"It's good to have you back, David."

CHAPTER 6

While Brixton, Flo, the Smiths, and Portland enjoyed dinner together, Elizabeth Sims contented herself with Chinese food delivered to her D.C. condo. She'd canceled a dinner date after receiving a call from her ex-husband insisting that they meet.

"There's something I have to discuss with you," he told her.

"Discuss with me? About what?"

"About Trevor."

"*Trevor?* Trevor is gone, David. He's been gone for two years. Let it go."

"I have let it go, Liz—until now. Look, I've come across something in London that raises a question that has to be answered."

Liz sighed, sat back, and directed a stream of air at an errant lock of bronze-colored hair on her forehead. In the months immediately following Trevor's murder in Nigeria, during which David had sunken into the depths of alcoholism, he'd called her with regularity, ranting about how Trevor had been killed and who had possibly been behind it. Elizabeth had practiced patience during those calls, which hadn't been easy. With Portland's blessing Trevor's body had been sent to her for a proper burial, which she arranged with the help of her parents in Massachusetts. His personal belongings had also been shipped to Elizabeth, a sizable box wrapped in brown paper. Portland had urged her to open it; "You should have the bracelet my mother gave to Trevor," he'd said. But the thought of wearing it was anathema to her and she'd left the package unopened, giving it to her parents, who'd placed it among other boxes in the attic of their Beacon Hill home.

"I'm leaving tomorrow afternoon for London," she said.

"Then we can have lunch before you go. This is important, Liz. Name a place and I'll be there."

She relented, but only after doing some quick mental calculations. She was certain that he would not be dressed appropriately for the high-end restaurants at which her law firm had accounts—the Occidental in the Willard Hotel or The Lafayette in the Hay-Adams—and where there were likely to be people who knew her. Instead, she chose a modest French bistro not far from her apartment. They agreed to meet at noon.

That evening, after some halfhearted nibbling at the Chinese food, she made last-minute preparations for her London trip. It took little for Elizabeth to get ready to travel. She had a suitcase with basics always packed, and consulted a checklist to be sure that nothing additional was forgotten. She reviewed files that she would take with her, sat at her desk, and reflected on David's phone call and her life with him, as abbreviated and tumultuous as it had been.

CHAPTER 7

Elizabeth Sims had been a model daughter and student during her teen years, although she had exhibited an occasional youthful rebellious side, nothing for her parents to be concerned about. Following high school graduation she'd enrolled in Georgetown University, where she earned a degree in geopolitical science. She'd dated often while an undergraduate, and a relationship with a male classmate during her senior year threatened to become serious. But her father intervened and persuaded her to put off any marriage plans until she'd gone to law school and passed the bar. She broke off the relationship, which fulfilled her promise to her father. But she also elected to put off law school for a year, much to his chagrin.

"What do you intend to do with your year off?" her mother asked.

"Julie has invited me to stay with her in London," Elizabeth replied. Julie was a Georgetown college chum from Great Britain who'd returned home following graduation and urged Elizabeth to come to the UK and spend time with her and her parents.

"What will you do in London?"

"Oh, I'll find some sort of job. I need a break away from school, call it a well-earned sabbatical. The break will do me good and make me a better student when I start law school."

She traveled to London despite her parents' objections, moved in with her friend and family, worked odd jobs, and enjoyed London's vibrant club scene, where she met many attractive young Brits—including the handsome, intriguing David Portland. She was taken with his good looks and self-assuredness and they quickly fell in love.

"Mom, David and I are getting married," she excitedly told her mother when she called with the news.

"I'll put your father on."

"You don't know what you're doing," her father said. "You've only known this man for a few months. This is nonsense."

"But I love him," Elizabeth said, "and he loves me."

"What does he do for a living?"

"He's, ah—he works in security. He's a widower and has an absolutely delightful young son, Trevor. He—"

"Look, sweetheart, don't do anything rash until your mother and I get there."

"Daddy, I—"

"This is nothing but a schoolgirl's impetuous act! You're only twenty-two years old. How old is he?"

"Twenty-six."

"We'll be there tomorrow!"

Her parents' last-second trip to London failed in its mission. Mrs. Sims ended up being taken with Portland's easy charm, and was impressed with his son's demeanor and behavior. Elizabeth's father, however, was not impressed by Portland, although he did find Trevor to be a bright and courteous young man. Her parents flew back to the States and did not return until the wedding of their only daughter, a trip made after Elizabeth's pleas to her father were reluctantly heeded.

The marriage of David Portland and Elizabeth Sims was a low-key affair held in a small village church outside of London, and attended by only a few people, including Elizabeth's parents.

The newlyweds settled into married life in an apartment they leased in a working-class neighborhood in southwest London, and Elizabeth threw herself into her new role as stepmother to Trevor while David continued to travel the world as a journeyman security operative. At first his frequent absences were viewed by Elizabeth as part of the unfortunate but understandable nature of his work. It also gave her unfettered influence over Trevor, which she enjoyed, a relationship that Portland heartily approved. But after six months Elizabeth tired of the lonely existence she led during her husband's travels and it became a topic of conversation whenever he returned from his latest assignment. She also felt very much an outsider in the close-knit village where everyone spoke English, of course, but were, well, different.

But it wasn't only loneliness that plagued her. She'd promised her father that she would attend law school, and his dream had now become her own. After a number of serious conversations, Portland, who acknowledged that his lifestyle didn't lend itself to being a hands-on father, agreed that Elizabeth should take Trevor to the United States, where she could begin her law school education, and where her parents would provide a semblance of routine and solidity in the boy's life.

Her parents welcomed Elizabeth and Trevor into their Boston townhouse, and Trevor easily adapted to his new home. With her mother's help Elizabeth was able to attend the Harvard University law school full-time, knowing that Trevor always had someone available to nurture and love him when he returned from a day of classes. She graduated with top honors and was hired by the large, prestigious law firm of Cale, Watson and Warnowski, a coup among that year's graduates.

CHAPTER 8

Like Portland, Elizabeth had difficulty coming to grips with Trevor's murder in Nigeria. Visions of him came to her in the dead of night, wakening her from what was already a fitful sleep, seeing his smile (he had his father's smile) and hearing his laughter (also reminiscent of his father). On nights like this she would sit bolt upright in bed and gasp, call Trevor's name into the darkened room. Earlier, not long after having severed the marriage, she'd found herself calling out for David, too, although that need abated as the months passed, as had her nocturnal cries for her deceased stepson.

She dreaded lunch with David the following day. He sounded obsessed with what he claimed to have discovered in London, and when David Portland became obsessed he could be intolerable. She wanted both David and Trevor to be past tense. She needed to move on. She was immersed in her legal career now and enjoying it. Too, she hadn't been without male companionship. Tall, leggy, and with flawless bronze-colored skin, she'd turned plenty of admiring male eyes and invited a few to share her bed. But there was no one on the horizon who represented what might be termed a steady beau. The truth was—and she admitted it to herself only in her most introspective moments—none had the charisma that had attracted her to David Portland.

CHAPTER 9

WASHINGTON, D.C.

Elizabeth prepared to leave her apartment for her lunch date with her ex-husband. She loved where she lived, and its color palette and choice of furniture reflected her tastes. Although she'd been brought up by parents who'd decorated their home with antique American furniture and who leaned to muted, subdued colors, Elizabeth responded to more contemporary styles, including vivid hues on the walls and in floor coverings. Her furniture was sleek and modern, much of it white, with red and yellow throw pillows adding splashes of color. She was a foe of clutter; the apartment could almost be considered Spartan, its decorative touches kept to a minimum, her books artfully displayed in their white floor-to-ceiling bookcases. A second bedroom was configured as her home office and was as pristine as the rest of the apartment. She was rearranging items at her bedside when the phone rang.

"Hello, Elizabeth," Cameron Chambers said. "Hope I'm not taking you from something important."

"I'm getting ready to leave for London later this afternoon," she said, "and I'm about to go to lunch with—with my former husband."

"The infamous David Portland." He forced a laugh to soften the comment. "How is he?"

"I wouldn't know, Cameron. We don't keep in touch."

"Even though he's now living here in D.C.? Is reconciliation on the horizon?"

"We—is there something I can do for you? I'm in a rush."

"I just thought that while you're at the London office you might check on inquiries Mr. Portland has made regarding the death of his son."

"What kind of inquiries?"

"He contacted the London office of XCAL. Probably nothing to it, but I like to stay abreast of things."

"I'll ask about it," she said.

"Can't ask for more than that," he said. "Enjoy your lunch. The Willard?"

"No." She gave the name of the bistro before wondering why he cared where they were meeting. "Anything else, Cameron?"

"You owe me the pleasure of getting together when you return."

"Yes, of course. I look forward to it."

CHAPTER 10

Portland was standing in front of the French bistro when Elizabeth arrived. He watched her approach, tall and lithe with a certain awkward gait that for him was part of her charm.

"Hi," he said.

"Hi. I'm on time."

"Noon on the button," he said.

"I thought you'd be inside at the bar."

"I don't hang out at bars anymore."

She walked past him and entered the restaurant. He followed. She gave her name to the maître d', who led them to a table. Portland went to hold out her chair, but she handled that action herself.

"I don't have much time, David," she said, glancing at her watch. "You look well."

"So do you, but then again you *always* do."

"How do you like working at the embassy?"

"I like it fine, dull but peaceful."

A bottle of Perrier sparkling water served as their pre-lunch drinks.

"Congratulations on being made a full partner," he said.

"Thank you. I've worked hard to earn it."

The menus they were handed put an end to the opening chit-chat. She ordered a salad; he opted for steak *frites.*

"So," she said, "what is it that you found out in London that we have to discuss?"

He reached in the pocket of the tan safari jacket he wore over a black T-shirt and handed her the bracelet. She examined it, twisting it in her long fingers tipped with crimson nail polish before saying, "It's the bracelet your mother gave Trevor before she died."

"Right."

"Why do *you* have it? You said that it was in Trevor's belongings that you had sent to me. You urged me to take it from the package and wear it."

"Right again, Elizabeth, but I was wrong. I *assumed* that it was in that package. It wasn't. It couldn't have been. I'd like to know what else was in that package."

"That won't be a problem," she said. "I'll have my mother FedEx it to you."

"I'd appreciate that," he said.

She handed the bracelet back to him quickly, as though to hold it longer would stain her fingers.

The waiter brought their meals, but neither lifted a fork.

"Where did you get this, David?" Elizabeth asked, nodding at the bracelet that now rested on the table between them.

"It's too long a story, Elizabeth, but let me just say that it was on the wrist of a Nigerian who'd won it in a card game."

"A card game? He gave it to you?"

Portland laughed. "Let's just say that I convinced him that I deserved to have it."

Elizabeth picked at her salad, and Portland chewed on a French fry.

"A card game?" she repeated.

"Yeah. According to my generous Nigerian friend, he won it in a card game with a guy named Alain Fournier. Know the name?"

"No. Why would I know him? Who is he?"

"He's a Frenchman who heads up a security company in Nigeria called SureSafe. He and his buddies provide security there for your prized client, XCAL Oil."

"I know nothing about that."

"Why don't you? From what I'm told you're the lead attorney for XCAL. It seems to me that . . ."

Her lip curled, a signal he'd come to recognize that what he'd said had angered her. Her words confirmed it.

"I'm a lawyer, David," she said. "I don't get involved in how XCAL finds oil and pumps it into barrels to be sold to motorists. I deal with more esoteric aspects of the company. I have no interest in how the company uses security companies where it drills around the world. You say that this bracelet was won by this Nigerian from a Frenchman in a card game. So what?"

It was his turn to feel anger. He leaned closer across the table and said, "Doesn't it pique your inquisitive legal mind, Liz, as to how this Frenchman happened to have possession of the bracelet? The official line was that Trevor was murdered by Nigerian rebels who've waged war on oil companies like XCAL because those same companies make their billions while the natives suffer. If that's true then some Nigerian rebel would have taken the bracelet from Trevor, not a Frenchman who works for XCAL."

She started to defend XCAL but thought better of it.

"So," he continued, "this Frenchman Fournier, who's in charge of keeping XCAL's workers safe, has possession of Trevor's bracelet instead of the rebels who allegedly killed him. How can that be unless . . . ?"

"Maybe he came across the rebel who killed Trevor, killed *him*, and took the bracelet not knowing who it originally belonged to."

"Interesting plot," Portland said, "but I don't buy it. Try this. Maybe the Frenchman killed Trevor and ripped the bracelet from his wrist as a souvenir to use as collateral in a card game."

Elizabeth sipped water as Portland sliced a piece of steak. The restaurant had filled up and conversational buzz at adjacent tables made it necessary to speak louder. It was Elizabeth who finally said, "This is all very interesting, David, but what is it that you expect me to do?"

"Aside from having Trevor's belongings sent to me, give me the name of someone at XCAL I can talk to about Fournier and the work his security company does for XCAL in Nigeria."

Another glance at her watch, less furtive this time, preceded her saying, "I don't work with people at XCAL who deal with security. I work with the company's attorneys on legal issues."

"If a security firm like SureSafe, the one Fournier works for, is killing innocent young men like my son and your stepson that sure as hell *is* a legal issue."

She said nothing.

"Who's in charge of XCAL's overseas security? Is he at the company's Maryland headquarters, or in the London office?"

She answered by pushing her barely touched salad away and extracting a credit card from her purse.

"No need to pay for my lunch," Portland said.

"Happy to do it, David. It was good seeing you again. Thanks for showing me the bracelet. I'm sure that there's a perfectly logical explanation why your Nigerian friend had it in his possession. I really have to run. I have things to do before my flight."

David would have liked the lunch to continue. Sitting with Elizabeth reinforced why he'd fallen in love with her in the first place, although he recognized that the mature professional woman sitting across from him was no longer the star-struck young college grad whose views of the world, especially men, had been charmingly sophomoric. He'd loved her bubbly youth, and continued to love her in her maturity.

They shook hands in front of the restaurant; he wanted to kiss her.

"Thanks for lunch," he said. "It wasn't necessary for you to pay."

"The firm will pick it up," she said.

"Of course."

"If you find out anything else about Trevor's death you'll let me know?" she said.

"Yes. Travel safe, Liz."

His using her nickname brought a smile to her face.

"I will," she said, and walked from his sight.

CHAPTER 11

LONDON

Elizabeth Sims's promotion at Cale, Watson and Warnowski not only carried with it the coveted title of partner and a sizable salary increase but also provided perks available exclusively to partners—first class when traveling by air, small suites while out of town on business, and a hefty expense account. This trip to London was her first since her elevation in status and she looked forward to it. Her first-class seat in the British Airways Airbus 380-800 jumbo jet was spacious, and provided a fold-down feature should she decide to nap. The drinks were top-shelf, and a skillfully prepared dinner was served on a white linen tablecloth with silver flatware. The choice of entertainment features was impressive; she decided to watch a recently released motion picture after dinner.

But while the ambiance was relaxing, a welcome respite from her day-to-day legal duties, she was anything but relaxed.

The lunch with David had started her thinking, and hard as she tried she couldn't switch off her thoughts. During their lunch she had come up with the possible scenario that the Frenchman had taken the bracelet from the rebel who had killed Trevor, not realizing to whom it had initially belonged. It was a reasonable explanation, she felt, as plausible as the one David had concocted—that Trevor had been killed by the Frenchman, or people working for him, and he had obtained the bracelet that way.

While her possible explanation made as much sense as his did, something told her that his story probably rang of greater truth. She had little to back up that belief, her own defensive what-if coupled with an appreciation of David's instincts.

She struggled with those conflicting thoughts across the Atlantic, her attention to the movie constantly interrupted by recollections of the lunch conversation. Visions of the delicate, gem-encrusted bracelet kept replacing the image on the screen. Trevor wore it every day that he lived with her and her parents in Massachusetts. On occasion schoolmates chided him for wearing a woman's bracelet, called him a sissy and worse. But he never allowed their jeers to keep him from putting it on in the morning as he prepared for school. There were times when he physically struck back at those who taunted him and had suffered a black eye and split lip from those encounters. He stood up for what he believed in—like his father—and took the blows that standing on principle sent his way.

Tears filled her eyes; she was glad that there was plenty of space between her and other first-class passengers. When the captain announced that they were cleared to land at Heathrow Airport she breathed a sigh of relief. What should have been six hours of comfortable escape from the rigors of her work—and an escape from her cell phone and other technological intrusions into her life—had ended up an unpleasant journey, and she was happy when the doors to the jumbo jet opened and she was free to leave.

The London cabdriver took her to The Dorchester Hotel in the center of the city, overlooking Hyde Park. It was the luxury hotel in which ranking members of the law firm always stayed, whose restaurant, Alain Ducasse's, was the only restaurant in London to receive three Michelin stars, although Elizabeth preferred taking her meals in The Grill.

Her Park Suite, with its view of the fabled park in which speakers of every stripe and persuasion gave vent to their passions and beliefs each Sunday morning, was beautifully furnished and appointed, the fabrics specially commissioned, the furniture antique, and the white marble bath featuring the deepest baths in London, or so it was claimed. She unpacked and looked out over the park. It was less busy in winter, but there was still a sizable number of men, women, and children enjoying its lovely expanse. She checked her watch. Her dinner date with Sir Manford Penny, chairman of XCAL UK, was in forty-five minutes.

Penny was the only remaining descendent of a family mining dynasty that had become wealthy leasing valuable mineral rights to other companies, including the first XCAL sites in Nigeria. XCAL had its origins in the 1940s in California, where an enterprising pair of brothers had leveraged its potential—with substantial government aid—to form what had emerged as a major player in the oil industry, perhaps not on the scale of ExxonMobil, Shell, or Chevron but nipping at the heels of those giants in the never-ending quest for world domination as a provider of the precious black gold. It had drilling sites and refineries in a number of countries, but its major operation was in Nigeria's Niger Delta.

A much-decorated British officer, Penny had traded in his military insignia for a civilian suit and tie with a start-up firm whose foray into the IT world had all the promise of becoming a success. Money he'd inherited from his family got the company off the ground, and there was a period when it appeared that the investment had been a wise one. His partners at the firm urged that they take the company public, but Penny had resisted those efforts and the firm remained private, which meant, of course, that its financial health was not available for public scrutiny.

Anonymous insiders claimed that Penny had been "cooking the books" to cover up the precipitous decline in its fortunes, including his own sinking financial situation. Was he nearly broke when he bailed out of the firm to take the job as chairman of XCAL UK? He denied it, of course, and as far as Elizabeth knew the rumors of his financial demise were just that, barbs spread by his detractors. She found time spent with him to be pleasant and educational when it came to the inner workings of the oil industry.

But their dinner dates whenever she was in London had recently begun to turn too personal for her, and she learned that wags in the company had concluded that she and Penny were having an affair. It wasn't true, but the mere floating of such scuttlebutt gave it substance in certain quarters.

She was about to leave the suite to meet him downstairs in Alain Ducasse's restaurant when there was a knock at the door. She opened it to see a young man holding an elaborate bouquet of flowers from the hotel's in-house florist.

"For you, Ms. Sims," he said, "compliments of Mr. Penny."

He refused a gratuity. She took the flowers from him, added water to the vase in the bathroom, and placed it on the desk. It wasn't the first time that Penny had preceded meeting her with a delivery of flowers, and on one occasion he'd presented her with a lovely, and obviously expensive, sterling silver business card case with her initials etched on it. Her initial inclination was to not accept the gift, but at the same time she was aware that it might offend him, something to be avoided with an important client. Manford Penny wielded considerable clout in the XCAL hierarchy as chairman of its British subsidiary, someone whose opinions were highly valued. The XCAL account was the cornerstone of CW&W's client base. It would have been bad politics, to say nothing of a foolhardy business decision, to alienate such a person. Her understanding of this did not extend, of course, into having to act upon his amorous advances. His marital status was murky. Although he was legally married, he and his wife lived distinctly separate lives, in different houses in the UK, and were free to pursue other romantic interests, a modern setup that was anathema to her. Penny's overtures were subtle, of course—Penny was good at subtlety—but the signs were there and Elizabeth was quick to pick up on them.

Penny stood at the entrance to the acclaimed restaurant when Elizabeth came downstairs to join him. Reed-thin and over six feet tall, he struck a sophisticated pose as he leaned casually against a pillar. He wore a double-breasted blue blazer—Elizabeth had never seen him wear anything else—a white shirt and pale yellow tie, which matched the color of his lank hair with just the right touch of gray at the temples. He saw her crossing the lobby, smiled, and held out his hand. "Ah, Elizabeth," he said, "how stunning you look tonight. You must bottle whatever it is that allows you to look so fresh after a long plane trip."

"Thank you," she said, "and thank you for the flowers. They're lovely."

"Nothing like fresh flowers to brighten a hotel room, especially when it's occupied by your law firm's newest partner."

"I was flattered when they promoted me," she said.

"This calls for Champagne and the best that Mr. Ducasse has to offer."

They were escorted to the table at which they always sat when dining there; Penny was enough of a regular to command a prime one. After he ordered the Champagne, which Elizabeth wasn't particularly fond of but would sip nonetheless, talk turned to the situation in Nigeria.

"The new negotiations with the Nigerian government have become testy," Penny said, introducing the topic. "Their leaders are flexing their muscles and threatening all sorts of stumbling blocks as the talks go forward." He laughed. "Of course, we all know that our esteemed partners in the Niger Delta have their hands out. They always do. But they've become even greedier of late."

"I've just begun to dig into the background of those negotiations," said Elizabeth.

"Good for you. As you'll discover, they're complex, and often nasty."

"As the lead attorney on the account I need to get up to speed on every aspect of XCAL's operations, including our presence in Nigeria."

"Expanding your horizons. I like that, Elizabeth."

They ordered from the menu. D'été, duck *foie gras* for him, Scottish langoustines for her. His compliment about how fresh she looked after a long flight didn't represent how she felt. She was exhausted; his voice became a drone as he talked of recent setbacks that XCAL had experienced in the Niger Delta.

". . . and those bloody rebels from MEND have attacked another of our refining facilities, costing us a fortune in lost oil and revenue."

He was referring to the Movement for the Emancipation of the Niger Delta that had been waging war on foreign oil companies in Nigeria for years, including sabotage, theft of goods and munitions, property destruction, guerrilla warfare, and the kidnapping of foreign oil workers.

"They kidnapped two of our British workers just a few days ago," he said.

"Yes, I saw the report on that."

"They issued the usual statement that the Nigerian government can't protect our workers or assets, and that we should leave while we still can—or die." He guffawed. "How many times have they issued that empty warning?"

"How big a force is MEND?" Elizabeth asked.

"It gets bigger every day," he replied, "and they become more sophisticated. XCAL's not the only foreign oil company in their sights. The Dutch, Norwegians, Italians have all been victims of their wrath." He shook his head. "It's a shame that so much oil is in a place like Nigeria. It would make things a lot easier if XCAL could drill in a more civilized nation."

As he continued to express his dismay at the situation in Nigeria, Elizabeth had to struggle to remain alert and to express interest in what he said. Much of his rant about conditions in Nigeria was certainly not new to her. It was the subject of what seemed an unending flow of reports from the company's operatives on the ground there.

But there was also her more personal interest in that African nation of 191 million, Africa's most populous country and seventh most populous in the world, Africa's largest economy. It was where her beloved stepson had lost his young life under brutal circumstances, snuffed out either by rebels at war with the oil companies and their employees or, as David Portland conjured, by someone involved with those same oil companies, perhaps even her client XCAL. Try as she might—and she worked on it—she could not slam the door on his suspicions.

They passed on dessert and finished off the evening with coffee, a splash of Cognac added to his.

"This has been a lovely evening," Elizabeth said.

"It's always a lovely evening when Elizabeth Sims is in town. You have a busy day lined up tomorrow."

"Which reminds me I'd better get some sleep. But before I do I have a question I promised someone I'd ask you."

His arched eyebrows invited her to continue.

"You're aware that Trevor Portland, my stepson, was killed in the Niger Delta."

"Yes. A very sad story."

"His father, David, my former husband, is now living in Washington. We had lunch before I flew here."

"I know."

Now it was Elizabeth's eyebrows that went up.

"How did you know?" she asked.

"Oh," he said pleasantly, "there aren't any secrets in this day and age, Elizabeth. I trust it was a pleasant lunch."

Her mind raced. As far as she knew, the only person who knew that she and David were meeting—the only person with a connection to XCAL—was her firm's security chief, Cameron Chambers. But why would he—?

She decided to not pursue it. She said, "David, my ex, came into possession of an item that belonged to Trevor. It was given to him by a Nigerian who said he'd won it in a card game, and that the person who used it as collateral in the game was a Frenchman involved with security for XCAL in the Niger Delta. The question is—"

"The question is, my dear, why your former husband would believe that something nefarious had taken place. When your stepson died I was given a complete report about the matter. Those who tendered the report were on the scene when it happened. Its essence was that your stepson was killed by members of MEND, that vile paramilitary group whose only goal is to drive us and every other oil company out of Nigeria. The young man happened to be in the wrong place at the wrong time. While that doesn't ease the pain, it makes perfect sense." When she didn't respond he added, "Doesn't it?"

She felt helpless and vulnerable at that moment, like a schoolgirl being lectured by an older, wiser person.

He continued. "I imagine that the so-called Frenchman your husband mentions is Alain Fournier, chief of security in the delta for SureSafe, the company charged with keeping our people safe. I know him personally. He's a dedicated man who does his best to secure our citizens against murderers like those in MEND."

"Unsuccessfully in Trevor's case."

"Unfortunately so. I should tell you that your ex-husband was recently in London and raised this ridiculous notion with one of my staff. I suppose that the loss of a son can do strange things to a father, which seems to have been the case with Mr. Portland. I'm sure that he's a fine chap and all, but he's obviously misinformed."

She said nothing.

"This has been a wonderful evening," he said, "a fitting celebration for your promotion into the lofty echelons of Cale, Watson and Warnowski. I suggest that we continue at my club, where the barman is an expert at—"

"Oh, please, Manford," she said, forcing a wide smile, "this new partner is about to fall on her nose."

"And what a shame it would be to mar that lovely nose. I understand, of course. See you tomorrow?"

"Yes. We have a meeting scheduled at eleven."

"And you'll be suitably rested to take charge at it."

He waited with her at the elevator, and kissed her cheek when the car arrived. "Sleep well," he said. "Until tomorrow. Ta-ta."

As she prepared for bed she kept going over what David had said at lunch about having gotten possession of the bracelet. She'd phoned her mother before her flight and asked that she FedEx the box containing Trevor's belongings to David at his Washington address, which her mother agreed to do.

She climbed into the king-sized bed and stared at the ceiling, wondering whether all that was on her mind would keep her awake. It didn't. Within minutes the mental turmoil of the past day was erased by the arrival of blessed sleep, and she didn't awaken until her wake-up call was delivered the following morning by the ringing phone.

CHAPTER 12

WASHINGTON, D.C.

Brixton looked out his window and saw a swirl of snowflakes whipped into motion by a stiff wind. It didn't snow often in Washington, D.C., but when it did even a modest snowfall could bring the nation's capital to a halt.

"It's snowing," he said to Flo, who sat up in bed rubbing her eyes.

"That's nice," she said.

"No, it isn't," he said. "Everything will stop. Government offices will close—not that that would matter much—and packages won't be delivered."

"Are you expecting a package?"

"No, but that's not the point. I hate snow."

"It's not like you're from Mississippi or Louisiana," she said. "You're from New York, where it snows a lot."

"But they know how to deal with snow in New York," he said. "These clowns in D.C. haven't a clue."

"Put the coffee on, Robert. The snow won't keep the Keurig from working."

And so started another day in the Brixton-Combes household.

Flo was the first to leave that morning. If the snow squalls continued it would cut down on traffic at her Georgetown dress shop, Flo's Fashions, which would give her time to catch up on paperwork.

"What's on your agenda today?" she asked Brixton, who accompanied her to the door.

"A meeting at ten with Mac Smith. Anthony Borilli, whose father got caught up in that Nigerian scam and shot himself, is coming in."

"Should be an interesting meeting," she said, kissing him good-bye. "You'll be home for dinner?"

"That's my plan. Have a good one, Flo. Sell lots of dresses."

Brixton went to his office, where his receptionist, Mrs. Warden, was in the process of rearranging files. Flo had worked with Brixton until she left to open Flo's Fashions, and had personally hired the middle-aged Mrs. Warden as her replacement. Brixton had resisted at first, accusing Flo of having deliberately dismissed other applicants because they were too young and attractive. She denied it, of course. The gray-haired, germ-phobic, but efficient and aptly named Mrs. Warden replaced Flo in Brixton's reception area and ran the office with an iron fist. She and Brixton had gotten off to a rocky start, but he'd eventually come to appreciate the woman and was glad he'd hired her. So was Flo.

He settled behind his desk and was reading that day's newspaper when Mac Smith poked his head through a connecting door.

"Mr. Borilli's here," Smith said.

Anthony Borilli was a chubby fellow with a bald spot from which a few tufts of hair grew. Brixton decided that he was probably younger than his appearance, a guy with bad genes when it came to externals. At the same time he was pleasant and forthcoming, shaking Brixton's hand vigorously and saying what a pleasure it was to meet him. A likable guy.

Smith's secretary delivered a tray with coffee and the usual accompaniments, and a plate of homemade sugar cookies.

"Does she bring you cookies every day?" Borilli asked.

"Not every day but often," Smith said.

"I'm already overweight," Borilli said, laughing. "If she worked for me I'd look like a sumo wrestler."

Smith pointed to an exercise bike in the corner. "Every time she brings cookies from home I hop on the bike. Have a cookie. She's a good baker."

After everyone had tasted a sweet, Smith said, "Let's get down to business. Losing your father the way you did is tragic."

Borilli nodded solemnly. "For a long time my mother and I couldn't accept that dad had been hoodwinked so easily. If we'd known what was going on we might have been able to intervene, but he kept what he was doing from everyone. In going through his papers we learned that keeping the transactions secret was part of the deal. You know how it goes. They warn that if word gets out, the alleged millions of dollars at stake will be jeopardized."

"Your father wasn't the only person who's been caught up in such a scam," Smith said. "There's plenty of them, including a congressman a while back who fell for it, too. He even raided family members' bank accounts to keep sending funds overseas. We can sit here and be smug about how anyone could be so stupid to fall for such a blatant fraud—especially after it's been exposed countless times in the media—but people do strange things."

"My dad had become paranoid," Borilli said, "probably due to his increasing dementia. He was convinced that he wouldn't have anything to leave his family when he was gone and saw the Nigerian offer as an easy way to beef up his finances." He slowly shook his head. "As bad as it was—and let's face it, what he did was foolhardy and wrong—it wasn't so shameful to justify taking his life."

Brixton directed a question to Smith: "Is there something in the law that Mr. Borilli can take advantage of to get back some of the money or at least punish those responsible?"

Smith's nonresponse said it all.

"However," Smith said, holding up a hand, "if a connection can be made between Nigeria and an entity connected with its government here in the U.S. there might be a basis for a suit against that entity. But that's a long shot. I've been doing research into whether there might be a private offshoot of the Nigerian government here in D.C. that's involved with the scams."

"Connected with the Nigerian Embassy?" Brixton asked.

"Not in an official sense, I'm sure," Smith replied, "but I did come across an organization in Washington called Bright Horizons."

"Fancy-sounding name," Brixton muttered. "What's their game?"

"They claim to raise money for Nigerian orphanages and other humanitarian projects."

"They're legit?" Brixton asked.

Smith shrugged. "Hard to tell. I haven't had a chance to delve deep enough into their operations."

As they talked, Borilli leafed through his briefcase. "Here," he said, handing a sheet of paper to Smith. "I knew that name rang a bell."

"Interesting," Smith said after scanning it and giving it to Brixton. It was a series of handwritten notes the elder Borilli had jotted down regarding Bright Horizons.

"Maybe that's the entity you're looking for," said Borilli.

"Could be," Smith said, "provided it was involved in some way with the scam your father fell victim to. We'll have to learn more about this Bright Horizons agency. That's why I asked Robert to join us this morning. He's a skilled investigator."

"Will you be leaving the paperwork you've brought?" Brixton asked Borilli.

"That's my intention."

"I'll do some checking into Bright Horizons," Brixton said. "I wouldn't be surprised if Will Sayers knows something about them."

Borilli's questioning expression prompted Brixton to add, "Will is a journalist here in D.C. He used to be the Washington editor of the *Savannah Morning News*, but now he's freelancing and working on a book about private security firms and how they operate around the world. He's done a lot of research into Nigeria and organizations involved with that country. I haven't spoken with Will in a while. I owe him a call."

"Do you think your pal David Portland might be of use?" Smith asked Brixton.

"I don't know that name," Borilli said.

Brixton gave Borilli a capsule background on Portland, including that his son had been murdered in Nigeria, and that he was part of the security contingent at the British Embassy in Washington. "Hi ex-wife, Elizabeth, works for a law firm, Cale, Watson and Warnowski, that represents the oil company XCAL. XCAL is a major player in bringing up Nigeria's oil and selling it around the world. Rumor has it that her law firm might be involved in the laundering of money that's raised through Nigerian financial scams."

"That's all it is, Robert, a rumor," Smith cautioned, his index finger elevated for emphasis.

"His former wife is an attorney?" Borilli asked.

"That she is," Brixton said, "and a damn good one from what I hear."

"If her law firm is involved in laundering money I—"

Smith quickly interrupted. "Let's not jump to conclusions based upon unsubstantiated rumors," he said, giving Brixton a stern look.

"I only meant that—"

"Here's what I suggest," Smith said. "Robert and I will see

what we can find out about Bright Horizons. When and if we come up with something useful we'll let you know and meet again. No promises. As I said when we first met, trying to use legal channels to recover any of your father's money isn't promising. Knowing that, do you still want to proceed?"

Borilli smiled. "If you mean do I still want to pay the fee you've cited, the answer is yes. I assume it covers Mr. Brixton's fee, too."

"Yes, it does," said Smith.

"Even if nothing tangible comes of it," Borilli said, "I'll take satisfaction in knowing that I've at least tried."

Borilli left the papers he'd brought with him with Smith. When he was gone, Brixton sat with Smith in the attorney's office.

"He's a really nice guy," Brixton commented.

"I almost feel guilty taking his retainer when the possibility of achieving legal satisfaction is negligible."

"You've been straightforward with him about that," Brixton said. "And who knows? Maybe something good will come from it. I'll take a look at the papers he gave you, and get hold of Will Sayers to see if he's aware of this Bright Horizons."

"I hope this pays off in something positive for Mr. Borilli."

"Let's assume it will, Mac. I'll catch up with you later."

When Brixton returned to his office adjacent to Smith's Mrs. Warden had just finished wiping his telephone, doorknobs, and desktop with disinfectant wipes.

"Thanks, Mrs. Warden," Brixton said. "I've always been afraid of catching the bubonic plague."

She cast him a look that said she understood his humor and didn't appreciate it. "You've had a call from Mr. Portland," she announced over her shoulder as she left. "He said he'd be in his office at the embassy."

Brixton reached his British friend. "What's up?" he asked.

"I've had an interesting meeting with my supervisor," Portland said.

"Don't tell me he fired you."

"Very funny, Robert, and no, he didn't dismiss me. But you'll be eager to hear what came out of it."

"I'm listening."

"No, in person. A drink later, say at five?"

"Sure. The bar in the Watergate?"

"Sounds like a plan," Portland said.

Brixton's phone call caught Will Sayers as the journalist emerged from the shower.

"You're alive," Sayers said.

"Why would you think otherwise?"

"Just a nasty rumor that your Miss Flo had had enough of you and laced your dinner with cyanide."

"If she wanted to get rid of me she wouldn't use poison. She'd just take my handgun and shoot me."

"Women dislike shooting people, Robert. Too messy. Poison is a female's preferred means of murder. But now that I know that you're alive, what can I do for you?"

"I'm doing work for one of Mac Smith's clients, a guy named Borilli. His father got caught up in one of those Nigerian money scams and lost a fortune before he blew his brains out."

"A sad story, but how can I contribute to your investigation?"

"You've spent a year learning about Nigeria, haven't you?"

"Nigeria along with other places like Afghanistan and Iraq, where private security companies get rich protecting our military." He laughed. "Imagine that, our mighty military having to be protected by armed civilians."

"Yeah, I know the book that you're writing deals with private security firms, not Nigerian scam artists, but I figured that you'd run across information about them."

"And what if I admitted that I had?"

"Then I'd want to pick your large brain."

"Well, I have learned a great deal about how those infamous Nigerian scams work."

"I knew you would. Let me ask you a question. Has your research touched upon a Nigerian charitable organization here in D.C. called Bright Horizons?"

"That sounds familiar. Tell me more."

"I don't know any more except that Mac Smith's client's father mentioned them in notes he left behind and Mac has done some preliminary looking into it. I thought you could fill in a few blanks."

"Happy to, Robert, provided you're offering to buy lunch."

"Do I have a choice?"

Sayers's laugh was hearty. "No, you don't. I'm in the mood for some authentic British grub. Despite the bad rap British food has always gotten, pubs here rise above it, especially The Queen Vic on H Street, Northeast. Know it?"

"No."

"Then you're in for a treat. Their sticky toffee pudding is sublime. See you there. Oh, I'll wear a name tag to help you recognize me."

"What the hell does that mean?"

"I'm a shadow of my former self thanks to a special diet I've been on. *Ciao!*"

Brixton had to laugh when they ended the call. For as long as Brixton had known Sayers—which went back to Brixton's days as a detective in Savannah, Georgia, when Sayers edited the local paper—the journalist had been grossly overweight, a whale of a man. Although Sayers had never told Brixton how much he weighed, it had to be in excess of three hundred pounds, give or take twenty or thirty. Sayers had toyed with various diets over the years, but they'd been quickly abandoned. If the corpulent journalist was serious this time about shedding weight Brixton was all for it. Sayers was a heart attack waiting to happen, or was inviting a terminal case of diabetes. "Good for you, Will," Brixton said aloud as he read through the papers that Borilli had left.

Sayers was already at the bar when Brixton arrived, a mug of stout from the tap in front of him. While Sayers's weight loss wasn't immediately apparent, what the journalist wore was different. Instead of his usual wrinkled chino pants secured by multi-colored striped suspenders, striped shirt, oversized sport jacket that looked as though it had just gone through the wash cycle, and leather boots broken down from having carried too much weight, his friend sported a new wardrobe, not exactly high fashion but a cut above his usual garb—a plaid blazer, gray slacks, and an open-neck white button-down shirt.

"Well?" Sayers said after Brixton had taken an adjacent barstool.

"Well what?"

"Me. My new svelte look."

"It's ah—it's impressive, Will. How much have you lost?"

"As of this morning, my scale says that I'm down eleven pounds."

"That's great, Will. What does that represent, two, three percent of your weight?"

"I don't think in terms of percentages—*Bobby!*—and if you meant it as a snide attack on my valiant effort to slim down you've succeeded in hurting my feelings."

He let Sayers's use of his nickname pass despite how much he disliked being called it and said, "No, no, no, Will, I'm really impressed at what you've accomplished." His eyes went to the large mug of stout. "Is *that* on your diet?"

"In moderation. All things in moderation. That's the key to healthy living. Join me? I'm having Wells Bombardier. Oh, say hello to Noel, the establishment's extraordinary bartender."

"Hello, Noel," Brixton said, shaking the barkeep's hand. "Will you whip me up a cold, dry Beefeater martini with a twist, straight up, and shaken, please."

"You never change," Sayers said.

"Change is bad," said Brixton. "So, you say you know something about this Nigerian group Bright Horizons."

"I had run across them in my research on private security firms, nothing extensive unfortunately, but maybe enough to pique your appetite. Speaking of that, let's take a table. I'm in the mood for chicken tikka."

"Sounds like a kid's dish."

"Hardly," Sayers said, motioning to Noel for a check. "It happens to be an Indian creation that was voted the UK's most popular restaurant dish, a bit like marsala only spicier. You'll love it."

As Brixton ascended to an upstairs dining room behind the slow-moving Sayers he was able to get a better look at the allegedly slimmed-down journalist. *You've got a long way to go*, he thought.

After Sayers had been served a second stout—Brixton declined a refill—Sayers pulled a folded sheet of paper from his sport jacket and laid it on the table.

"What's that?" Brixton asked.

"Everything I know about Bright Horizons. First of all, Robert, the Nigerian Bright Horizons is not to be confused with a wonderful organization here in the States that provides early education, preschool programs, and employer-sponsored child care. That such a sterling educational endeavor shares the same name as this Nigerian outfit is unfortunate."

"Who came first?"

"Oh, the educational group by far. The Nigerian Bright Horizons was established here only four years ago."

"What does it do? The Nigerian one."

"What it purports to do and what it actually does are not necessarily one and the same. Its mission, according to its Web site, is to raise money for Nigerian orphans and the impoverished."

"Motherhood and apple pie. Sounds like a worthwhile goal."

"Yes, doesn't it? The problem is that no one can be certain where the money goes. That's not unusual for many alleged charitable organizations. I'm inundated with requests for money from dozens of groups who hire professional fundraisers and end up with a small percentage of what they raise going to the charities they claim to support. But Bright Horizons has an additional layer of opaqueness. Although they claim to be a private agency, their ties with certain powerful interests in Nigeria say something else."

"What powerful interests? Government?"

"Probably not officially but connected in some way. I recently read a survey about the most dangerous places in the world to visit. Nigeria ranks number one on that list."

"From what I read in the papers this fellow Borilli left behind," Brixton said, "a lot of the money he squandered was sent to Bright Horizons. He listed those payments as charitable contributions."

Sayers guffawed. "'Charitable contributions'? The only charity benefiting from suckers like this Borilli fellow is some warlord. Speaking of warlords, Robert, I have managed to trace where Bright Horizons is located in Nigeria. It's a city called Port Harcourt, in the Niger Delta."

"Where David Portland's son was murdered."

"I thought about your British friend while I was looking into it."

"I'm seeing him later today."

"I'd like to get together with him again. I'm just starting writing about a security firm called SureSafe. As I recall, your Brit pal worked for them."

"That's right. It's also the firm that provides security for the oil companies in the Niger Delta in Nigeria. There's a Frenchman there who runs things, name's Alain something-or-other."

"Alain Fournier. Quite a controversial figure."

"You've learned a lot."

"I have to learn a lot, Robert, if my book is to have any credibility. Let's eat, shall we? Order the chicken tikka."

Brixton didn't ask how two large steins of stout and an exotic Indian dish fit in with Sayers's diet but kept the question to himself.

He was pleased when Sayers eschewed dessert and finished off the meal with black coffee.

"I appreciate what you've told me," Brixton said. "Anything else you've dug up about Bright Horizons?"

Sayers replied by handing Brixton another piece of paper. On it was written: **Ammon Dimka**.

"What does this mean?" Brixton asked.

"It's a name."

"Okay, so it's a name. Who does it belong to?"

"Ammon is a Nigerian who lives in Arlington. He's a nice guy, educated, married, two little tykes."

"So?"

"Note that I refer to him by his first name. We've recently become friends. He's been a useful source in my research."

"About private security firms?"

"About security firms as well as Nigerian money scams. Ammon returned to Lagos after receiving his degree in economics and landed an important post with the so-called Economic and Financial Crimes Commission (EFCC). From what he's told me, the commission is more interested in *committing* financial crimes than riding herd over them."

"A whistle-blower."

"And not a popular one back home. He bucked the system too many times and his request for a transfer to the United States was happily granted, anything to get him out of their bureaucratic hair."

"What's he do here in the States?"

"Right now he's working for a construction company in Virginia. But what should pique your interest is that when he was transferred here he was put in charge of—ready for this?"

"Bright Horizons."

"Among many things I admire about you, Robert, is your quick uptake. Ammon didn't last long at Bright Horizons. According to him, the charity it purported to represent was a complete sham. The agency reports to a warlord in Port Harcourt and is a handy conduit for funds illegally generated by the scam masters. Don't misunderstand. It's but one of a number of Nigerian organizations that prey on desperate, naïve people, like your Mr. Borilli."

Brixton sat back and speared the last piece of chicken on his plate.

"There's another aspect of Bright Horizons that you might find interesting," said Sayers. "I don't have anything to prove this, at least not yet, but certain evidence indicates to me that Bright Horizons might have a function besides stealing life's savings from widows and the mentally feeble. It's said that the agency has also been known to provide—how shall I say it?—to provide *muscle* when needed."

"Muscle? You mean they can play rough?"

"Exactly. A Nigerian gentleman working for the embassy here in D.C. six months or so ago was allegedly telling tales out of school about his government's involvement in political assassinations in Nigeria. Poor chap. He was found garroted to death in his apartment."

"Bright Horizons was behind it?" Brixton asked.

"They didn't make the decision, Robert, but it's rumored that someone from that organization carried out the deed." Sayers wiped his mouth with his napkin and discreetly belched behind it. "You do realize what a bargain this lunch has been," he said.

"Yeah, it's been helpful," Brixton said, "but how about giving me more for my bucks."

"Such as?"

"Put me in touch with Mr. Ammon Dimka."

Sayers pondered the request. "I'm not sure I should do that," he said. "Ammon has crossed many people, Robert, and I'm confident that there are some who would like to see him—well, see him eliminated. His discussions with me have been strictly off the record."

"But you've shared it with me," Brixton said.

"A testimony to my faith in your discretion. I will, however, contact him and see if he's willing to speak with you—off the record, of course."

"Of course."

"And now that you know his name you won't do an end run around me and contact him yourself."

"You know me better than that, Will."

Brixton paid the tab and they parted in front of The Queen Vic.

"Your Ms. Flo is well?" Sayers asked.

"Doing fine. We'll have to get together soon for dinner."

"A splendid idea, hopefully with your friends the Smiths."

Brixton watched Sayers waddle up the street and disappear around a corner. As annoying as the overweight journalist could be, Brixton always knew that he was someone he could always trust, a man who stood by his friends.

"Ammon Dimka," he said to himself as he went to where he'd parked his car.

This was getting interesting.

CHAPTER 13

WASHINGTON, D.C.

Like most people, Brixton couldn't set foot in the Watergate complex without thinking of the scandal that shares its name, the infamous break-in and the resignation of President Nixon, the only time in our history that a president has resigned from office. He entered the bar, took a seat at a small table, and waited for Portland to arrive, who bounced into the room moments later. Their orders given, Brixton asked his British friend what had transpired during his meeting at the embassy.

"First, let me say that your snarky remark about my being fired was also on my mind when Conan summoned me to his office, saying that he had something urgent to discuss."

"Conan's your boss, right?"

"That he is, a prince among men. I never would have been hired at the embassy were it not for Conan Lester's insistence that my checkered background be ignored by the higher-ups."

"It's always good to have someone like that in your corner," Brixton said.

"Indeed it is. Anyway, Conan closed the door after I arrived at his office. He had a grim expression on his face, and I had the sense that he wasn't sure what to say first, so I broke the ice. I straight out asked him, 'What is this urgent thing you want to discuss?' "

"And he said?"

"He said . . ."

CHAPTER 14

You're well?" Lester asked after Portland was seated across the desk from him.

"Quite," Portland replied.

Conan Lester was a few months shy of sixty. He'd had a long, unblemished career in British security and intelligence, the quintessential British civil servant who wore that badge with honor. He'd been stationed in a variety of overseas assignments during his years serving the Crown; his posting to the embassy in Washington was considered a plum position for someone nearing retirement. Married, their children grown and off on their own, Lester and his wife, Celia, had accepted the transfer to Washington with enthusiasm. He was aware, of course, from having spoken to others who'd served on Massachusetts Avenue, that little happened to challenge the embassy's security staff, which was okay with him. His overseas postings had provided enough excitement to last the rest of his days. Slender, and with an angular face beneath an impressive shock of snow-white hair, he didn't fit the popular conception of someone who'd spent his life in the intelligence and security game—call it the spy game if you wish.

He nodded wearily. “You do know, David, the high esteem in which I hold you.”

“Which I’ve always appreciated.”

“When they approved you coming here to join the security team I was delighted.”

Portland now began to worry about what would come next. It smacked of the time-honored technique of issuing praise before lowering the boom.

“Take a look at this,” Lester said, handing Portland a communiqué labeled: “TOP SECRET.”

Portland rearranged himself in the chair, crossed his legs, and read. It was a message written to MI6, the British Secret Intelligence Service (SIS) in London, from someone named Paul Goad in the British High Commission in Lagos, Nigeria. While the text included the usual amount of government jargon, it was the underlying message that jumped out at Portland. He pressed his lips tightly together and handed the paper back to Lester.

“An interesting coincidence, wouldn’t you say, David?”

“ ‘Shocking’ would be a more apt term,” Portland said.

The communiqué reported on the killing of the son of a high-ranking executive at Great Britain’s Shell-BP refineries in the Niger Delta.

“Similar to the situation in which your son found himself.”

Portland could only nod. Reading the message brought back vivid memories of Trevor, his golden boy, allegedly slaughtered by members of Nigerian’s MEND, the Movement for the Emancipation of the Niger Delta.

“This piece of correspondence says that the son was killed by members of MEND,” Portland said.

It was Lester’s turn to nod.

“That’s what they said about *my* son.”

“Which you have good reason to challenge,” Lester said.

Portland had previously filled Lester in about having come across the bracelet worn by Trevor, and how the French boss of SureSafe's operation in Nigeria had lost it to a Nigerian security guard in a poker game.

"Thanks for sharing this with me, Conan," Portland said, "but I'm not sure why you did."

"MI6 wants you to look into the death of this young lad."

"Me? Why me?"

"It should be obvious, David. You have a direct connection with what has happened to the young man because of your own experience with your son." He sighed. "There's more to it than that, however. This message from SIS is only the latest of correspondence I've had with them. They're keenly interested in what's going on with our oil interests in Nigeria, including the role of SureSafe, the private security firm charged with protecting our citizens there."

"SureSafe?" Portland spit out. "I worked for them. So does the Frenchman Alain Fournier who ended up with my son's bracelet."

A small smile crossed Lester's lips. "Precisely," he said. "They want you back in London to tell them what you know about how SureSafe operates in the delta."

"I just recently got settled here," Portland protested. "Besides, I never worked for SureSafe in Nigeria."

"But you have firsthand knowledge of some of its activities there. Look, David, I certainly don't want to lose you. But let's be frank, shall we? While having you as part of my security team pleases me, you can't deny that it's—well, let's just say that it doesn't tax your brain and draw from your experience in security matters."

"Which is why I like it," said Portland. He managed a small laugh. "You've said it yourself, Conan. After years on the run in godforsaken places where you get up every morning hoping that you'll manage to get through the day, keeping people safe here at the embassy is a welcome change."

"True, but this situation in Nigeria has captured the interests of our friends back in London."

Portland chewed on his cheek before asking, "How long would I have to be there?"

"Not long. They'll probe what you know about the Nigerian situation, perhaps ask that you help them create a task force to get to the bottom of it, and that will be that. Just a few days."

"And when I'm finished there I can return to this job?"

"You have my word."

"Your word is always good with me, Conan. When do I leave?"

"They want you there day after tomorrow."

They shook hands after some less weighty conversation and Portland left Lester's office buoyed by what had transpired. Being placed in a quasi-official position to look into SureSafe's operations would give him the opportunity to pursue the truth about what had happened to Trevor.

CHAPTER 15

So you're leaving Washington," Brixton said after Portland had finished his recounting of the meeting with Conan Lester.

"For a while."

"I'll miss you, David."

"It's always nice to be missed. But I'll be back before you know it, hopefully with some answers about what *really* happened to my son."

"Here's to a successful trip," Brixton said, touching the rim of his glass to Portland's. As he did his cell phone rang. He glanced at it and said, "It's Will Sayers. I'd better take it."

"Am I taking you from something important?" Sayers asked.

"As a matter of fact, I'm in the Watergate bar enjoying a drink with my friend David Portland."

"Ah, give him my best."

"He's heading back to London in a few days, a special assignment."

"Wish him God's speed and safe travel. I'm calling to let you know that I've made contact with Ammon Dimka."

"Oh?"

"It took considerable persuasion on my part, but he has reluctantly agreed to meet with you."

"That's great, Will."

Sayers gave him Dimka's phone number and address in Virginia.

"I'd like to bring Mac Smith with me when we meet."

"Not a good idea, Robert. Ammon is apprehensive enough without introducing another party."

"I hear you," said Brixton. "What's a good time to call him?"

"The evening. He has two adorable young daughters who he and his wife dote on. Try him about nine after the children are in bed. And Robert, I've given him my sacred word that he will never be mentioned by name in my book, nor will you reveal him as a source. He is strictly to provide background."

"Okay, Will. Many thanks. I'll let you know after I've spoken with him."

"Sounded serious," Portland commented after Brixton had clicked off.

"I'm getting together with someone who knows a lot about how Nigerian money scams work. I've told you that Mac Smith has a client who got caught up in one of them."

"Ironic, isn't it?"

"What is?"

"That both you and I are involved in something having to do with Nigeria."

That night Brixton replayed for Flo the conversation he'd had with Portland. He also filled her in on his phone conversation with Will Sayers and that he'd be making contact with the Nigerian expat in Virginia, Ammon Dimka. He considered mentioning what Sayers had said about people from Bright Horizons possibly being hit men for the Nigerian government but thought better of it. No sense in unduly worrying her.

"I'm not sure I like you becoming involved with a foreign government," she said, "especially one like Nigeria. These groups I read about every day in the paper, like Boko Haram that kidnaps and kills anyone in their path, and this MEND organization that David has mentioned, aren't exactly the sort of people you want to cross."

"Not to worry, Flo," he said as he sliced a fresh loaf of bread to accompany dinner. "All I'm doing is gathering facts for Mac."

Later that night as they lay in bed and prepared to sleep, Flo repeated her concerns about his making plans to meet with the Nigerian Ammon Dimka. Brixton kissed her lightly on the lips and repeated, "Not to worry."

Which didn't reassure her.

CHAPTER 16

VIRGINIA

Ammon Dimka walked in his house after a day of work and was met with shrieks of joy from his daughters, ages six and eight. The younger insisted on being lifted into the air, which her father accommodated while her sister wrapped her arms around his sturdy leg.

"Easy now," he said, joining their laughter. "Give Daddy a few minutes to get into some different clothes."

After disengaging he went to the kitchen where his wife, Abiola, called Abi by her husband and friends, was preparing dinner. Abiola and Ammon had earned college degrees, Ammon's in finance and economics from the University of Benin, Abiola's Master's Degree in social work from the highly competitive University of Ibadan.

After a kiss and hug, Ammon went up to the bedroom to change into jeans and a sweatshirt.

"Ready for a game?" he asked his daughters when he came downstairs. Although it was cold outside, their backyard was dry, perfect for an impromptu game of soccer to work up their appetites. After a half hour of kicking a ball back and forth they were called inside for dinner. Ammon helped Abi clear the table and clean the kitchen, and then sat with his daughters to help them with their homework. When bedtime was announced the girls uttered their usual protests, but their pleas were disregarded and both parents got them ready for bed, tucked them in, joined them in prayers, and returned downstairs, where they settled in matching leather recliners to pick up where they'd left off in books they'd been reading.

At a few minutes past nine Ammon's cell phone rang.

"Mr. Dimka?"

"Yes."

"My name is Robert Brixton. I believe that a mutual friend, Will Sayers, mentioned me to you."

"Yes, he did, Mr. Brixton."

"Will told me that you'd be willing to speak with me—strictly off the record—about how money scams originating in Nigeria are conducted, and to what extent an organization like Bright Horizons might be involved."

Ammon glanced over at Abi, whose expression mirrored the displeasure she'd voiced when he'd told her about his conversation with Sayers.

"Mr. Sayers said that you are a private investigator, Mr. Brixton."

"That's right. I work with a leading attorney in Washington, Mackensie Smith. He has a client whose father was caught up in one of these schemes, and took his own life as a result after having sent hundreds of thousands of dollars to Nigeria, some of it through Bright Horizons."

Ammon checked his wife again before saying, "I suppose it will be all right for us to get together, but you do understand that I'm in a delicate position."

"I certainly do understand, Mr. Dimka, and I can only hope that you believe me when I say that whatever you tell me will be strictly off the record to help me and Mr. Smith get a handle on how these things work. There's no reason for your name to ever be raised."

"When would you like to meet?"

"Would tonight work for you? I'll be happy to come to your house. I don't want to take up too much of your time, but—"

"When can you be here?"

"In an hour?"

"That will be fine. You have directions?"

Brixton asked for more detailed directions than Sayers had given him and headed for Virginia.

"I wish you hadn't agreed to meet him," Abiola said. "You don't know him."

"I didn't know the journalist Mr. Sayers either," Ammon countered, "but he seems like a trustworthy person. So does this Mr. Brixton."

"I just don't like to see you involved with telling tales out of school, Ammon. They were very upset when you left Bright Horizons after six months and told them that you were disappointed in the way it was being used."

"I still feel that way, Abi. I accepted the job and the relocation it involved to the States because I believed what they told me. It was a lie, and innocent people are being bankrupted because of them. Besides, it's not as though I'm going public and condemning them. I just want the right people to know the truth."

They returned to reading for another half hour until Abiola announced that she was going upstairs. He kissed her good night and watched her leave the room.

He wished that she understood his need to share what he knew about Bright Horizons with those who would benefit from that knowledge.

At the same time he was respectful of her concerns.

They'd moved to Virginia from Lagos, Nigeria, in search of better opportunities for themselves and their children, and it had worked out after a rocky start. Upon graduating from college Dimka had accepted a post in Lagos with the Economic and Financial Crimes Commission. He'd soon become disenchanted with the agency, whose stated mission was to ferret out and bring charges against those in government or industry who manipulated the financial system for their own gain. It was an agency in name only, and he launched a series of complaints with high-ranking members of its hierarchy. He was soon branded a troublemaker, and meetings were held to discuss what to do with him. It was decided that to fire him from his position would only fuel his apparent need to expose the agency's misdoings. One of the top officials, who'd become friendly with Dimka and his family, knew that he harbored a dream of relocating to the United States. That's when Ammon was offered the job of running Bright Horizons, which he eagerly accepted.

But after less than a year with that alleged charitable group he saw that it was no better than the EFCC. He resigned and became the chief financial officer for the construction company, drawing upon his degree and experience in economics. It paid well, and Abiola's position as social media director for a nonprofit also produced a decent paycheck. Things were good, so much so that they were able to buy their home in Virginia and send money to their families in Nigeria, not large sums but enough to help assure that they could live a decent, albeit modest, life.

But despite her husband's perpetual positive outlook, fear lurked in the back of Abi's mind that their newfound success would one day come crashing down around them.

Brixton found the Dimkas' tract home in a Virginia subdivision and was greeted at the door by Ammon. After preliminary banter and the shaking of hands Brixton was invited to join Ammon in the home's small study, whose walls contained multiple photographs of the Dimkas' extended family in Nigeria. Brixton also saw, to his surprise, a framed color portrait of former U.S. president Franklin Delano Roosevelt. He asked about it.

"I've always been interested in history," Dimka said, "including the history of the United States. President Roosevelt did remarkable things to create a stronger, fairer nation, the sort of leadership that I wish was at work in Nigeria."

"FDR had a lot to overcome," Brixton said.

"And so does Nigeria, unfortunately. Please, sit. Coffee? A cold drink?"

"Got a Coke?"

"I have Pepsi."

"That'll be fine."

Ammon disappeared to fetch their sodas, and Brixton took the opportunity to peruse a collection of carved wooden African masks, fetishes, and animal figures proudly displayed on shelves. A photo of Ammon and his wife at their wedding in Nigeria showed the handsome young couple beaming while other family members and wedding guests stood behind and shared in their joy. He was more closely examining one of the wood sculptures when Ammon returned.

"*Salud!*" Dimka said, raising his glass.

Brixton returned the toast.

"Now," Dimka said after they'd taken chairs, "what would you like to know about the now infamous financial scams that originate in Nigeria, and the role Bright Horizons plays in it?"

Brixton had decided while driving to Dimka's home that he wouldn't take notes or use a recorder. He didn't want to give the appearance of amassing information that might be traced back. He started by asking who controls the scams in Nigeria.

Dimka thought before answering. "There isn't one person," he said. "As you may know, Nigeria is a fragmented nation, with various tribes controlling specific areas of the country. The south and southeast are primarily Christian; the northern part is Muslim. That's where Boko Haram has been slaughtering men, women, and children. They consider the only legitimate form of Islam is one ruled by Sharia law."

"They're like this MEND group that attacks people working for the oil companies in the Niger Delta?" Brixton asked.

"No, not really. MEND has a just cause. It fights for the thousands of natives who are kept in poverty while the oil companies—as well as too many government officials—reap the financial rewards while raping and polluting the land. Boko Haram's only cause is to create a society in which Sharia law is not only practiced, it is used as an excuse to brutalize its citizens. ISIS is much the same."

Brixton listened carefully as Dimka gave him a capsule explanation of the situation in Nigeria. He waited until the Nigerian paused to finish what was left of his drink to ask, "But what about these financial scams? Is the government involved, or is it a bunch of freelance operators who see a way to make a quick buck?"

"Freelance operators?" Dimka repeated, smiling. "I suppose you could call them that. A better term is 'warlord.' "

"What the hell *is* a warlord? Sounds to me like a high-ranking military guy."

Dimka shook his head. "No," he said, "a warlord is simply someone—almost always in a nation in chaos—who commands a group of people, usually a militia or a gang of thugs. Bright Horizons ostensibly reports to a Christian-led charity group connected with the government, but the real power behind it is a man, Agu Gwantam."

"He's Nigerian?"

"Yes. He functions in the south, in the Niger Delta where the oil fields are located. He controls other financial scams besides Bright Horizons and has become rich in the process. He's headquartered in Port Harcourt."

Brixton continued to take in Dimka's explanation of how the scams work, and the role that Bright Horizons has played in them. "Don't get me wrong," Dimka concluded. "Some of the money that Bright Horizons raises actually goes to its Christian charity in Lagos. But the majority of it is funneled straight into

Agu Gwantam's pockets. I wasn't aware of that when I accepted the post with Bright Horizons and uprooted my family and moved to Washington. Had I known I never would have accepted the offer. Once I discovered what was going on I voiced my objections to those in the Nigerian government."

"I bet they must have loved that," Brixton said, laughing.

"They suggested that I find work elsewhere. Fortunately, I'd made friends with a man who runs a construction company here and was looking for someone with my financial background. I have a good job with him, and my wife is happy with her position with a nonprofit agency in the city. She's not pleased that I've told these tales to Mr. Sayers, and now to you, but I suppose it's a way for me to cleanse my conscience."

"I'd say that you're a gutsy guy, Mr. Dimka."

Brixton shifted conversational gears and asked whether Dimka knew anything about the security firm SureSafe, which provided security for the oil companies in the Niger Delta. He also mentioned his friend David Portland.

Dimka's expression told Brixton that Dimka did know something, but he didn't respond.

"That's really not my reason for being here," Brixton said, "but David is a close friend. He's going back to London to help investigate the murder of the British son of a well-placed executive with Shell-BP. His own son was murdered in the Niger Delta while working there for a different oil company, XCAL."

Brixton had the feeling that Dimka was debating whether to say what he was thinking. He finally decided to and said, "You mention SureSafe, the security firm."

"Right," said Brixton. He went on to explain how Portland had come into possession of his son's prized bracelet that was being worn by a Nigerian who worked for SureSafe in Nigeria. "This Nigerian told my friend that he'd won it in a card game from the head of SureSafe's operation in the Niger Delta."

Dimka shook his head. "I really know little about SureSafe—

except that it is involved in providing security for Agu Gwantam, the warlord I mentioned. Bright Horizons is also involved with SureSafe."

"How so?" Brixton asked.

"I've been led to believe that Bright Horizons has been known to function as an extension of SureSafe here in the United States."

Brixton thought back to what Sayers had told him about the agency possibly functioning as an enforcer for Nigerian interests. He asked Dimka about that but received a reply similar to what Sayers had said, that it was only an unsubstantiated rumor.

The men talked for another half hour before Brixton sensed that he might be outliving his welcome and decided to call it a night. Dimka walked him to his car in the driveway.

"I really appreciate your time, sir," Brixton said.

"I'm happy to share what I know," the Nigerian said.

"You have a nice house," Brixton said.

"Thank you. We're fortunate people, Mr. Brixton."

And nice, Brixton thought. "Please say hello to your wife," he said.

"I'll be happy to do that, and give my best to Mr. Sayers."

Brixton got behind the wheel and drove away. He'd enjoyed the conversation with the proud Nigerian and hoped that his relocation to the United States would be all that he and his family hoped for. He also understood why Dimka was gun-shy about exposing Bright Horizon's role in Nigerian money scams, especially if the agency was capable of playing rough, and was determined to honor his pledge to keep Dimka's name out of whatever steps Mac Smith might take for his client Anthony Borilli.

CHAPTER 17

As he drove home, two men sat at a small desk in a cramped office tucked away at the rear of Bright Horizons' suite of offices in downtown D.C. One of them rewound the digital recorder to a predetermined spot on the recording and listened.

"Mr. Dimka?"

"Yes."

"My name is Robert Brixton. I believe that a mutual friend, Will Sayers, mentioned me to you."

"Yes, he did, Mr. Brixton."

"Will told me that you'd be willing to speak with me—strictly off the record—about how money scams originating in Nigeria are conducted, and to what extent an organization like Bright Horizons might be involved."

"Mr. Sayers said that you are a private investigator, Mr. Brixton."

"That's right. I work with a leading attorney in Washington, Mackensie Smith. He has a client whose father was caught up in one of these schemes, and took his own life as a result after having sent hundreds of thousands of dollars to Nigeria, some of it through Bright Horizons."

"I suppose it will be all right for us to get together, but you do understand that I'm in a delicate position."

"I certainly do understand, Mr. Dimka, and I can only hope that you believe me when I say that whatever you tell me will be strictly off the record to help me and Mr. Smith get a handle on how these things work. There's no reason for your name to ever be raised."

"When would you like to meet?"

"Would tonight work for you? I'll be happy to come to your house. I don't want to take up too much of your time, but—"

"When can you be here?"

"In an hour?"

"That will be fine. You have directions?"

The man turned off the recorder.

"First the reporter Sayers, and now this investigator," the other man, a Nigerian in charge of security at Bright Horizons, muttered. "Dimka has a bigger mouth than we thought."

The man operating the recorder stood to leave.

"There is no way that Dimka can become aware that his telephone has been tapped into?" the Nigerian asked.

The white man shook his head.

"And the recorder will record every conversation made on his phone?"

"Right again," the other man said as he slipped on a leather jacket with a patch on the sleeve that read: **SureSafe**.

"I want to be kept informed of other calls this investigator Brixton might make or receive regarding this matter—with anyone!"

PART TWO

CHAPTER 18

LONDON

Portland went directly from Heathrow Airport in the UK to his flat, where he stripped off the clothing he'd worn on the flight, stood under a hot shower, and put on a pair of shorts to wear while pedaling his exercise bike. The flight had tired him, but he felt that a brief workout would alleviate his fatigue better than a nap.

He sat at his desk and opened the package of Trevor's belongings that Elizabeth's mother had FedExed to him in Washington, which had arrived just prior to his leaving for London. He spread out the contents on the desk and stared at the artifacts that represented what was left of his son's life—a small notebook computer with a label with Trevor's name printed on it, two thumb drives, a wallet, his high school graduation ring, his passport, some loose change and a twenty-dollar bill, and a diary with handwritten entries. Portland sat silently, images of Trevor's face flashing through his mind like an out-of-control slide show.

"Enough of this," he muttered, and placed the items on a shelf in an open bookcase.

After checking e-mails on his laptop he dressed in a blue sweatshirt, jeans, sneakers, and safari jacket and went for dinner in the same pub where he'd encountered the big Nigerian wearing Trevor's bracelet. The owner greeted him as Portland took what had become his usual spot at the bar and ordered a glass of Chardonnay, and steamed cockles and leeks for openers. Business was slow; he was one of only a half-dozen customers.

"The last time I was here," he told the owner, who was busy drying glasses, "there were three Nigerians who had a pretty good snootful of booze."

The owner, a gruff but not unpleasant man, laughed. "It was you, wasn't it?" he said, tossing his towel on the bar and leaning closer.

"Me? What did I do?" Portland said playfully.

"Beat that big black bloke up in the men's room, that's what you did. My God, he came down the stairs from the loo all bloody and sputtering about how somebody had mugged him and broke his arm and stole a bracelet from him. He threatened to call the coppers, but his pals talked him out of it and they left, didn't pay their goddamn tab."

"Sorry," Portland said. "I owe you."

"Forget it, mate," the owner said. "They were looking for trouble, that's for certain. Glad they took a walk without breaking up the place. Had a hell of a time, though, cleaning his blood off the tiles."

"Adds character to the loo," Portland quipped.

The owner laughed and walked away.

As Portland finished his wine and meal, fatigue caught up with him. He paid, apologized to the owner for the problems he'd caused during his last visit, and went directly to his flat where he took from the shelf Trevor's handwritten diary. He idly thumbed through the pages, some of which contained humorous comments about things that Trevor had experienced while working in the Niger Delta. But other pages were angrier in tone. He railed in those entries against the plight of native Nigerians who lived in squalor in the midst of the oil companies' immense and visible wealth. In some of the entries he was especially upset at the rampant pollution the companies had inflicted on the land and water: "They poison the Nigerians who live and work there," he wrote, "and don't give a damn about their impact on individual lives. I'm embarrassed to be part of it."

He devoted one page to having been introduced to a few members of MEND, the movement dedicated to driving the oil companies from the Niger Delta, by a Nigerian he'd befriended, Barke Chukwu. According to Trevor's notes, Chukwu managed to make a living in Port Harcourt as a guide for visitors to the city. "Barke is a good man like most average Nigerians," Trevor wrote. "He's dedicated to seeing that the fortune in oil being brought up from the swamps benefits his people instead of making the oil company executives and corrupt Nigerian politicians rich."

His son's concern for the residents of the delta brought tears to Portland's eyes. He closed the diary, replaced it on the shelf with the other items, and climbed into bed, wondering whether he would be able to sleep. His snoring minutes later answered the question.

CHAPTER 19

He felt refreshed the following morning. He bounded from bed and went to the window. Everything was gray outside, typical of London in winter. He showered, dressed in the dark blue suit he'd brought with him—his only suit—and left the flat. After a quick breakfast at a local eatery he hailed a taxi and was transported to the location of his scheduled meeting at the headquarters of SIS on Albert Embankment in Vauxhall, in London's southwest corner. He went through a security checkpoint and waited until a woman arrived to escort him.

"Ah, Mr. Portland," a man seated at a conference table said, getting up and extending his hand. "So pleased that you were able to join us. I'm Fred Tompkins. MI6. Please call me Freddie." Tompkins was a short, barrel-chested man with a ready smile.

Portland took in the other two people at the table, a middle-aged man and woman who sat close to each other. The man, nondescript personally, balding, and with a paunch, but wearing an expensive Savile Row suit, stood and shook Portland's hand as he was introduced. His name was Brian Leicaster, who Tompkins explained was an executive with Shell-BP. His wife, Agnes, managed a smile and said to Portland, "I'm pleased to meet you."

Tompkins took the lead. He said to Portland, "As I'm sure you're aware, Mr. and Mrs. Leicaster have recently suffered a terrible tragedy. Their son, Nigel, was murdered in Nigeria."

Portland said, "Yes, I've been told about your loss. My condolences."

"Thank you," Mr. Leicaster said. His wife sniffled; he handed her a tissue.

"And, of course," Tompkins continued, "Mr. Portland's son met a similar fate in the same place."

"How terrible," Mrs. Leicaster said. "How old was your son?"

"Early twenties," said Portland, who wasn't eager to talk about Trevor's death.

"Mr. Portland works in security at our embassy in Washington, D.C.," Tompkins said. "Because he also has some experience with the situation in Nigeria I've asked him to aid in our investigation of situations such as the one you've experienced. Perhaps you would be so good as to fill him in on the circumstances of your son's demise."

Mr. Leicaster cleared his throat and adjusted his posture in the chair. "Well," he said, "Nigel went to work for the oil company XCAL as a geologist. He'd obtained his degree in geology from the Imperial College of London and—"

"He was such a bright boy," Mrs. Leicaster said.

"Yes, he was a bright young chap," her husband agreed. "When he decided to go to Nigeria to work for XCAL his mother and I were firmly against it. XCAL is a Yank company and I'm sure he could have gone to work for them in the States, or here in the UK. But Nigel was always headstrong, wanting adventure. Young people are like that."

"I urged Brian to find him a post with his company, Shell-BP, in a more civilized place, but—" Agnes said.

"But Nigel overruled that," said her husband. "He wasn't about to take a post where his daddy works."

"What do you do with Shell-BP?" Portland asked.

"Finance. I've been with them for more than thirty years."

"How did you learn that your son had died?" Portland asked.

The Leicasters looked at each other before he answered. "A phone call, a bloody cold phone call from someone who works for the security firm that's supposed to keep people safe in that godforsaken place." Anger had crept into his otherwise soft voice.

"Who called you?" Portland asked.

"A man. I forget his name. I've probably deliberately done so."

"Someone from SureSafe?" Portland asked.

"Yes, that's it," Leicaster replied. He snickered. "They certainly don't live up to their name, do they?"

"Was it a Frenchman?" asked Portland.

"Frenchman? No. At least he didn't sound French. Why do you ask?"

"No reason. I assume that he told you that your son had been killed by members of MEND, the renegade group that's waging a war with the oil companies."

"Precisely."

"That's the way *you* learned of your son's death, isn't it, Mr. Portland?" Tompkins said.

Portland nodded.

The meeting lasted another half hour. Portland had become antsy and wanted to leave but knew that he couldn't just walk out. Eventually Mr. and Mrs. Leicaster said their good-byes. As they were leaving, Mr. Leicaster said, "I hope you get to the bottom of how our son died, Mr. Tompkins. I don't believe for a moment that this MEND organization, whatever it is, singled out Nigel as a victim, and I trust that whatever investigation you undertake will find the answer."

"We'll do our best, Mr. Leicaster. Thank you for sparing us

time during the grieving that you and the missus are going through. My deepest sympathies."

With the Leicasters gone, Tompkins's demeanor became less cordial. "Tell me what you know about this SureSafe organization, Mr. Portland. Tell me *everything*."

CHAPTER 20

Portland spent the better part of the day at SIS, most of it with Fred "Freddie" Tompkins. Portland liked him, appreciated his straightforwardness, a welcome respite from the usual banal banter of government servants and politicians. They were now on a first-name basis.

Tompkins explored with Portland the possibility of leading a small task force to Nigeria, the mission to garner evidence about SureSafe's activities there.

"I know that SureSafe is a controversial company," Portland told Tompkins, but I'm not sure why SIS would be interested in them. As far as I know, they aren't involved in anything that threatens national security."

Tompkins leaned back in his chair and put his hands behind his head. "It depends, David, on how you define national security," he said. "SureSafe might not be involved with threats to the extent of the sort posed by ISIS, Al Qaeda, or Boko Haram, but the killing of British citizens in a foreign nation certainly qualifies as a national security threat. I might also mention that two

British citizens working for Shell-BP were recently kidnapped by MEND, which we've kept under wraps. They want a high ransom for their release. Shell-BP is vitally important to the UK, David. It provides us with a major presence in Nigeria, and I might add that the economic ramifications are substantial."

Portland digested what Tompkins said. He was sure that the SIS officer was right in his assessment of the situation with British oil interests in Nigeria. It had political and economic ramifications for the UK. Besides, an active government couldn't stand by while its citizens were slaughtered while working in a foreign nation.

But Portland's focus was on SIS's decision to probe the workings of SureSafe in Nigeria. Did they know something that he didn't? Like Leicaster, he'd been told that Trevor had been murdered by members of MEND. He, Portland, had accepted that reason for his son's death until encountering the Nigerian security worker in the pub and coming into possession of the treasured bracelet given to Trevor by his grandmother. It had been lost in a card game by the head of SureSafe's Nigerian operations, the Frenchman Alain Fournier. That had dramatically changed Portland's analysis of what *really* had happened.

Leicaster hadn't offered such a concrete reason for not buying that his son, Nigel, had fallen at the hands of MEND, but he was skeptical nonetheless.

All eyes were now on SureSafe, and Portland wanted to know what evidence SIS had to point in its direction. He probed Tompkins without success until, at the end of the day, Tompkins opened up.

"There is a chap who once worked for SureSafe. He's a Brit, spent the majority of his adult life working for various security firms overseas, most recently SureSafe in Nigeria's Niger Delta."

"What's his name?" Portland asked. "Maybe I ran across him when I worked for them."

"Matthew Kelsey."

"Don't know him."

"Rather a sad case, I'm afraid. He was part of a security team charged with protecting one of the oil fields and was badly injured by MEND during an attack."

"You've been in contact with him?"

"Yes, in a manner of speaking. I've spoken with Mr. Kelsey on the phone, but he's refused to meet with us. Frankly, I think he was in his cups when we talked. He's a bitter man, quite unpleasant. I also sense that he's afraid that if he talks about his experiences in Nigeria with SureSafe it will put his life in danger."

"Maybe he's right," Portland said. "I'd like to take a shot at getting him to talk."

"Of course, and I wish you the best." He wrote Kelsey's number and address on a slip of paper.

"Anything else?" Portland asked.

"No, except that I appreciate you taking time to meet with us. We'll be gathering again tomorrow at ten for further discussion. You'll be expected to join us."

"That's why I'm here," Portland said. "You've left me with a lot to think about between now and then. Have a good night, Freddie."

CHAPTER 21

WASHINGTON, D.C.

It was a day of meetings.

While Portland conferred with SIS in London, Brixton was huddled with attorney Mackensie Smith in Smith's office. Brixton had made notes from his visit with Ammon Dimka in order to brief Smith.

"He's a nice guy," Brixton began, "a real gentleman."

"I'm sure it hasn't been easy for him and his family to assimilate to his new life here in the States."

"They'll always be some bigoted clown who'll give him a hard time because he's black," Brixton said, "but I'm sure he and his wife have learned to deal with it."

"Do they live in an integrated neighborhood?" Smith asked.

"Beats me. It was dark when I arrived. Looks nice, though, suburban, tract houses from what I could see."

"You say he works for a construction company in Virginia?"

"Right. He has a degree in economics or finance, a bright guy. Anyway, Mac, what I came away with was a confirmation that

Bright Horizons is involved in the sort of Nigerian money scam that your client's father got suckered into."

"Dimka told you that?"

"Right." Brixton consulted his notes. "He says there's a guy, a warlord in a town called Port Harcourt. His name is—let me get it right—Agu Gwantam. I think that's the way it's pronounced."

"What about him?"

"Dimka says that this warlord controls how Bright Horizons distributes the money it raises. He claims that some of the money goes to a Nigerian Christian charity in the country, but most of it ends up in this Agu character's pockets."

"What else did he say?"

"Catch this. He says that the security firm SureSafe provides protection for Agu Gwantam. And . . . Bright Horizons might be in the same arm-twisting business as SureSafe."

"SureSafe is the same security firm that David Portland worked for," Smith said.

"The same one that the Frenchman, who had David's son's bracelet, heads up in Nigeria."

"And lost it in a card game."

"Yeah."

"What do you hear from David?" Smith asked.

"Nothing since he went back to London."

"From what you've told me David's interest in Nigeria is confined to how his son died."

"And how this British kid died, too."

"But our interest is in Nigerian financial scams."

Brixton cocked his head. "And?" he said.

"I was just wondering if there's a link between the two."

Brixton pondered what Smith had said before replying, "David thinks that SureSafe was behind his son's murder, and SureSafe provides protection for this Nigerian warlord. You may be right about there being a connection."

"Do you think that Mr. Dimka could be persuaded to come

forward and testify about Bright Horizons and how it's used as a conduit for illegal money?"

"No way," Brixton said, shaking his head for emphasis. "I'm surprised that he even agreed to talk to Will Sayers and me."

"Without an insider like him to testify there's really nothing I can do to bring legal action against Bright Horizons."

"I'll get back in touch with Dimka at some point and see whether he might consider breaking his silence," Brixton said. "We got along pretty good."

"Keep me informed," Smith said. "And since SureSafe is involved with this Nigerian warlord and his role in the scams, you might ring Portland in on it, see what he knows."

"I was thinking the same thing," said Brixton.

CHAPTER 22

Cameron Chambers, former Washington, D.C., cop and head of investigations for the law firm of Cale, Watson and Warnowski, looked forward to the return from London of Elizabeth Sims. He was loath to admit that he'd developed a crush on the beautiful, recently minted partner. *A "crush"? How sophomoric,* he thought as he carefully trimmed the hair around his ears and examined his face in the bathroom mirror, turning left and right. He'd recently considered seeking the services of a plastic surgeon to see what could be done about his developing jowls, and a few brown spots on his right cheek. The thought of having plastic surgery was anathema to him, but that attitude was mitigated by the signs of aging that peered back from the mirror. He wondered if a procedure could be performed in such a way that no one would know that he'd had it done. Maybe he could do it while on vacation; two weeks were due him and he'd been pondering what use to make of them.

Still thinking of Elizabeth—and uneasy about her spending time in London with XCAL's UK chairman, Manford Penny, whom Chambers considered a predatory phony—he dressed and set off for another day that would begin meeting with the top partner at the law firm, Walter Cale, who'd left a message the previous evening that they needed to get together first thing in the morning. Chambers would have appreciated an indication of why Cale wanted to meet, but the attorney preferred to shroud meetings in mystery, a management style that Chambers found disconcerting.

Cale, who prided himself on his trim figure and taste in clothes, as well as restaurants, musical genres, and artistic exhibitions, was waiting when Chambers arrived.

"Come in, come in," Cale said, leading Chambers into his spacious office with floor-to-ceiling windows that afforded him a view of the Mall.

"So," said Cale, "what's new in your life?"

"Not a lot, Walter," Chambers said. "Things are under control. No emergencies on the burner."

Cale's question mark expression said to Chambers that the senior partner didn't necessarily agree with what he'd just said.

"Have you heard any more from our British friends?" Cale asked.

When Chambers didn't reply Cale added, "Concerning Elizabeth Sims's ex-husband."

"Oh, that. No. I spoke with Robert Brixton about it during Elizabeth's party, alerted him to the potential trouble that her ex could cause. He assured me that he would report back to me if he learned anything."

"Brixton?"

"One of two private investigators I have on retainer in the event I need their services. He's a friend of Elizabeth's former husband, David Portland."

"Don't you think we should be more proactive than that?" Cale said.

"I'm not sure what you mean."

"I received a call from one of Manford Penny's people in London. According to him, Elizabeth has been asking questions about the death of her stepson in Nigeria and whether XCAL might have been involved."

"That sounds far-fetched," Chambers said.

"Of course it is, but XCAL doesn't need this sort of fanciful rumor circulating, not in the midst of sensitive negotiations that are under way with the Nigerian government. She's raising the same question about the role SureSafe might have played in his death."

"Does Elizabeth—?"

Cale's raised eyebrows invited Chambers to continue.

"Does Elizabeth realize that her questions are raising these concerns?" he asked.

"I assume that the answer is no, and I'd like to keep it that way. But there's more to this, Cameron. I assume that you've heard the rumor that this law firm, by virtue of its close relationship with Nigeria acting on XCAL's behalf, might be involved in laundering money raised by certain unscrupulous types there."

"Yes, I have heard that rumor," said Chambers. "It's ludicrous."

"Of course it is, but rumors have a habit of gaining steam and developing legs, as they say. You're also aware that we've lent our legal experience to a few Nigerian charities including Bright Horizons. It doesn't bring in much money for us." He guffawed. "That's a gross understatement. We do it as a favor for our client XCAL, which is always looking for ways to cement its relationship with the Nigerian government. I'm telling you this because we need to ensure that nothing—that no person—do anything to cast aspersions on us, particularly with clients like XCAL."

Chambers told Cale that he certainly understood. At the same time he was becoming increasingly curious about where the senior partner was going. He didn't have to ask.

"It's obvious that I and the other partners hold Elizabeth Sims in the highest regard. She's a brilliant attorney, and those at

XCAL with whom she interacts are quick to praise both her legal mind and her ability to forge productive relationships. However, there is this damnable complication with the death of her stepson and her ongoing relationship with her former husband, who, from what I hear, has become obsessed with creating a link out of thin air between XCAL, our partners in Nigeria, and his son's unfortunate death."

Cale waited for a response. When there wasn't one, he continued. "Are you still in touch with your former colleague at the MPD, Marvin is it?"

"Marvin? Oh, yes, Marvin Baxter. I occasionally run across him," Chambers said.

"He did good work for us last year in the Abbott matter."

Chambers squirmed in his chair and cast a glance out the window that provided a dramatic scrim behind Cale.

"I'd like to engage his services again," Cale said.

"For what purpose?" Chambers asked, already knowing the answer.

"To make use of his expertise, of course."

The mention of George Abbott brought back unpleasant memories for Chambers. Abbott, a young attorney with Cale, Watson and Warnowski, had raised suspicion with Cale and other partners that he was colluding with the attorneys from another law firm that was pitted against CW&W in a tangled legal case. Chambers had been ordered by Cale to arrange for taps to be put on Abbott's work and home telephones, which Chambers had argued against, pointing out that tapping citizens' phones without a court order was illegal. Cale dismissed Chambers's concern out of hand, and hinted—no, it was more than a hint—that if he was to continue as the firm's chief investigator he was expected to do what was necessary to ensure that bad apples were lopped from the firm's tree as quickly as possible.

Chambers reluctantly agreed. He contacted Marvin Baxter, a former MPD computer and technological expert who'd gone into business for himself, hiring out his services to a variety of security firms, including SureSafe, and arranged through him for taps to be placed on Abbott's phones. The recordings of his calls proved the suspicions to be valid and Abbott was fired without ever knowing that his double-dealings had been immortalized on tape. Of course, when he was presented with myriad examples of what Cale and the others knew about his dealings it was obvious to him that conversations with his contact at the other firm had been intercepted. But he couldn't prove it, and was summarily dismissed.

That Cale's suspicions about Abbott had proved to be correct salved Chambers's conscience to a degree, and he'd put the episode behind him—until this day in Cale's office.

"What do you want Marvin to do?" he asked.

"Nothing dramatic. As I've said—and elevating Liz Sims to partner status certainly testifies to the high esteem in which I and the other partners hold her—it's my duty to make sure that no one in the firm do anything that might possibly taint our reputation. I simply want to monitor Liz's conversations with her former husband regarding the death of his son and her stepson. Only conversations specifically regarding that issue are of interest to me. I'm sure that there's nothing for us to be concerned about, but I have to be certain."

"You want Elizabeth's phones tapped?"

"And her former husband's phone, too."

"As with the Abbott matter, Walter, I'm uncomfortable doing this, especially to someone like Elizabeth."

"I understand, Cameron, but sometimes we have to do things for the greater good."

Greater good? Chambers silently mused. Spouting that familiar, albeit debatable, phrase struck him as pompous, as though Cale were sending troops into battle on a suicide mission. Hitler had rationalized slaughtering millions for Germany's "greater good." But of course Chambers kept these thoughts to himself.

"I'll see if Marvin can do it," he said.

"Good man," Cale said, coming around his desk and slapping Chambers on the shoulder. "It'll be short-term, just until we can be sure that Elizabeth isn't letting her personal feelings interfere in any way with our relationship with XCAL and the Nigerian government."

Chambers went to his office and pondered the order he'd been given. Tapping Elizabeth Sims's phones struck him as misguided, even stupid. What if she was to find out that the firm's top partner had ordered that her privacy be invaded? Had Cale become so paranoid that he suspected her of disloyalty? What would it matter if she and her ex-husband discussed the death of his son?

He busied himself for the rest of the day with a report generated by the MPD on a client of the firm; he'd maintained his contacts with the MPD, which came in handy.

At four he dialed Elizabeth's extension.

"Hello, Cameron," she said.

"Welcome back," he said. "Good trip?"

"Hectic."

"I was hoping we were still on for dinner."

"Oh, Cameron, I'm sorry, but I'm suffering from terminal jet lag and—"

"No need to explain."

"Rain check?"

"Absolutely."

"You're a doll for understanding. Oops, I have another call, someone from XCAL in Maryland. We'll reschedule dinner, and it'll be on me."

"Sure," he said.

He hung up and exhaled. He was glad that she'd begged off. He wasn't sure that he could sit with her in a restaurant and not inform her that everything she said on her phones would now be heard by him and Walter Cale. He knew one thing. If he wanted to keep his job he'd forget about the taps on her phones and let things take their natural course.

He just hated to see what that natural course would be.

CHAPTER 23

LONDON

Portland tried to nap when he returned to his flat after the meeting at SIS, but too many things kept ricocheting in his mind. He watched the latest news on the BBC. The Middle East was still a cauldron of hate and brutality fueled by the perversion of a major religion. The West Coast of the United States was on fire, literally. The Russians and Putin were pulling out all the stops to regain their position of influence in the world, and the two Koreas continued to toss provocations at each other. World business as usual.

The BBC wrapped up its coverage of world current events by reporting on an attack on British oil interests in Nigeria by the group MEND, resulting in major damage to a petroleum refinery.

Portland clicked off the set. He'd held the bracelet his mother had given Trevor in his hands throughout the newscast, turning and twisting it, watching the flickering light from the television dance off its gold and gems. Disgusted with what he'd seen on the tube, he went to his small kitchen, emptied a bag of Yorkshire tomato, basil, and mozzarella crisps into a bowl, popped the cap on a can of Old Speckled Hen beer, and returned to the living room, where he took the items that had been in the box Elizabeth's mother had sent him, spread them out on his desk, and began reading Trevor's handwritten entries, more slowly and carefully than his original cursory glance.

Trevor's anger at the treatment of the Niger Delta's natives became more strident and fiery as Portland turned the pages. He stopped at one point and wondered whether Trevor had expressed those feelings to SealCom, his employer, or to executives at SealCom's client XCAL. If he had, his views would not have been welcomed.

Portland continued reading. He reached a page on which Trevor had commented about the security firm SureSafe. There was a single mention of the firm's boss in Nigeria, the Frenchman Alain Fournier: ". . . he reminds me of a poisonous snake," Trevor had written.

Portland turned the page. The name Matthew Kelsey captured his attention. That was the same man that SIS's Fred "Freddie" Tompkins had mentioned as having worked for SureSafe in Nigeria, and whom Tompkins had characterized as a sad, bitter man now living in the United Kingdom. Portland dug Kelsey's phone number and address from his jacket and checked his watch. It was only a few minutes past nine, not too late to call. Kelsey lived in Barrow-in-Furness, a blue-collar working-class city close to the Lake District. It had been one of the UK's most important shipbuilding centers during the war.

Portland pulled out a map. Barrow-in-Furness was a five-hour drive from London, provided traffic kept moving on the A1 and M1. He'd sold his car when leaving London for his assignment with the embassy in Washington and would have to rent one, assuming that Mr. Kelsey would invite him to visit. Somehow, from what Tompkins had said about the man, Portland considered it unlikely.

He dialed Kelsey's number. It rang numerous times and Portland waited for a machine to pick up. Instead, a man's husky voice answered.

"Mr. Kelsey? My name is David Portland."

"What do you want?"

Kelsey's abrupt response took Portland aback.

"Mr. Kelsey," Portland said, "I've worked for SureSafe in the past and—"

"That was your mistake," Kelsey said with what passed for a laugh.

Portland matched it. "I know what you mean. Look, Mr. Kelsey, I'm calling because I had a son, Trevor Portland, who was killed in the Niger Delta. He worked for—"

"Portland was your kid?"

"Yes. You sound as if you knew him."

"Damn shame what happened to him and the others."

Portland sat up straighter. "You know what happened to Trevor? The others? What others?"

Portland heard Kelsey belch loudly, and it sounded as though he'd dropped the phone. He waited until Kelsey came back on the line.

"I don't know nothing," Kelsey said.

"Mr. Kelsey, what I'm asking for is a chance to come and meet you, maybe share a beer and talk about what happened in the Niger Delta."

"What? Come here to this place?" It was another coarse laugh followed by a coughing spasm. Portland waited until it had abated. When he'd regained control Kelsey said, "You don't want to come here. Nothing to see here. Overrun by foreigners, from every damn place on earth. Can't find anybody who speaks English anymore."

Kelsey's bigotry offended Portland, but he didn't state it. "Mr. Kelsey, I might not speak the King's English, but you'll understand me. How about giving me an hour or two? We can meet any place you say."

"Hah! 'Meet any place you say,' huh? Where the hell do you think I can go sitting in this goddamn wheelchair? Huh? Where do you think I can go?"

Portland hadn't expected that Kelsey was crippled. He asked, "Did your injuries happen in Nigeria?"

"You bet they did. Those MEND bastards shot me up good. Had to be evacuated back to the UK and spent too many bloody weeks in hospital."

"I'm sorry to hear it," Portland said. "What if I come to your home and we can spend a few hours swapping war tales about working for SureSafe? You tell me what to bring and I'll be there with it."

Portland waited for Kelsey to shoot down that suggestion. Instead, he said, "It might be okay. Where are you?"

"London."

"Be a hell of a trip."

"Not so bad, four, maybe five hours. How about tomorrow? I have your address."

"Where did you get that?" Kelsey rasped.

"A friend. Tomorrow. If I leave early a.m. I can be there in time for lunch. Sandwiches? Beer? Something stronger?"

"You bring me some good whiskey and fat sandwiches."

"Count on it. I'll see you tomorrow."

Portland reserved a rental car for six the following morning. Having connected with Kelsey and the promise that the crippled SureSafe veteran might be able to provide knowledge about Trevor's murder energized him. He knew that he should get to bed in anticipation of the early start, but he was too wired. He glanced at the day's newspaper and saw that the Jamaican jazz pianist Monty Alexander was appearing with a trio at Ronny Scott's club, an iconic London jazz venue. Brixton was a fan of the pianist and had played some of his CDs for Portland.

He hailed a taxi—one of the things he missed about London while living in Washington was the cabs, spacious and immaculate and driven by courteous drivers who'd spent years learning London's streets in order to qualify for a license. Once settled at a table at Ronny Scott's he nursed a glass of wine during one set, thinking of Brixton and how much he looked forward to telling his Yank friend that he'd caught the pianist in person. Brixton would be envious.

After a few hours' sleep and a fast shower, he was at the car rental agency and drove off in a sporty new red Renault Captur with a stick shift, which he always enjoyed driving. He'd packed a few items in a small bag in case he decided to stay overnight in Barrow-in-Furness, although he intended to drive back to London after the meeting. His early start avoided the worst of London's traffic and Portland was soon speeding on the highway heading north to the Lake District.

He stopped an hour outside of Barrow-in-Furness to top off his gas, stretch his legs, and enjoy a cup of coffee and a cinnamon Danish. An hour later he entered a section of the city not far from the sprawling waterfront. He popped into a food shop and ordered sandwiches, which he added to a bag containing a bottle of Scotch whiskey he'd picked up on his way home from Ronny Scott's. He drove slowly and took in his surroundings, the GPS's female voice directing him to Kelsey's address. As he neared Kelsey's street he became aware of people eyeing him and his fancy red car. A trio of young men slouched against a boarded-up building, dragging on cigarettes and assuming tough-guy postures. Portland was sorry he hadn't rented something less flashy; the Renault was an inviting target in such a neighborhood. He drove past Kelsey's four-story building and went around the block in search of a parking garage. There wasn't one. Resigned to parking on the street, he found a space not far from the street corner lobos, locked the car, and walked the short distance to Kelsey's address. The door was encircled with crude graffiti; the smell of urine from the foyer was noticeable even without opening it. Portland glanced back at the street toughs before stepping into the foyer and looking at crudely scribbled names next to flat numbers. Kelsey was on the first floor, Number 2. Portland tripped on the hallway's broken tiles as he went to the door and knocked. He heard noise from inside, as though someone had tipped something over. When the door wasn't opened he knocked again. A chain was disengaged. The door opened. Kelsey, in a wheelchair, rolled backwards to allow it to fully open.

"Matthew?" Portland said.

Kelsey glared at him through bloodshot eyes. He needed a shave; his whiskers grew haphazardly, mostly white, flecked with stray black ones. He was a heavy man dressed in a blue-and-yellow flannel shirt, stained chino pants, and sandals.

"David Portland. I called and—"

"Yeah, yeah, I know. Come in."

Portland entered the small room. It was piled with old newspapers, cardboard boxes, and heaps of clothing. The smells of burned grease and alcohol were strong. He noticed a bottle containing an inch of whiskey, as well as four stained water glasses lined up on a small table next to the room's only stuffed chair. The blue haze of stale cigarette smoke hung over everything.

"Welcome to paradise," Kelsey said. "It's not as posh as my digs in Nigeria, but it'll have to do."

Portland held out the bag containing the food and booze. "I bought these," he said.

"Good. Put 'em in the kitchen." He pointed to a door at the rear of the room.

Portland went to the kitchen and was appalled at its squalor. He opened a rusted fridge, which contained leftovers that had seen better days, and put the sandwiches in. He returned to where Kelsey sat in his wheelchair in front of the small TV set on which a rugby match was being telecast.

"I appreciate you taking the time to see me," Portland said, looking for a place to sit.

Kelsey sensed his confusion. “Throw the junk off that chair,” he growled.

Portland removed newspapers from it and placed them on the floor. He handed the bottle of scotch to Kelsey, who eagerly opened it and poured some in one of the used glasses. “Grab a glass,” he told Portland.

Portland eyed the stained glasses. “No thanks,” he said.

“Suit yourself,” Kelsey said, taking a long swig and wiping his mouth with the back of his hand. “So Trevor Portland was your kid, huh?” he said.

“That's right. You knew him?”

“Knew him? Nah. Not like we were friends or anything. But I knew about him, was there when he got it.”

Portland stiffened. He hadn't expected that Kelsey would be so quick to indicate what he knew about Trevor's death.

“You say that you were there when Trevor—when he ‘got it,’ ” Portland said, wanting to keep the conversation on track.

“You ever been to Nigeria, to the Niger Delta?” Kelsey asked.

“No. You were saying that—”

Kelsey poured more scotch into his glass. “Sure you don't want some?”

Portland shook his head.

“What sorta sandwiches did you bring?” Kelsey asked.

“An assortment,” Portland replied, frustrated at Kelsey's penchant for changing the subject. “You were saying that you were there—”

“In the delta. I sure as hell was, three bloody years in that hellhole.” He cocked his head and said, “You say you worked for SureSafe.”

“That's right, a few times, but never in Nigeria.”

“I signed on for two years but stayed an extra one. That was my mistake, it was, a big mistake. If I'd cut outta there after two years I wouldn't be sitting in this goddamn wheelchair on the dole from the bloody welfare agencies. You know what it's like to have your legs shot out from under you, Portland?"

"No."

"You never forget it when it happens, I'll tell you that. One minute you're walking around and the next you're laying in a bloody heap, your legs not moving because the bullets cut right through your spine. Happened just like that." He snapped his fingers. "Like that, Portland."

"I don't envy you," said Portland.

Kelsey lit a cigarette and directed a stream of smoke into the air. "My doc says I should quit smoking 'cause it'll kill me." His laugh was a snort. "Hope it does. Might as well be dead sitting in this damn chair." He leaned forward. "But I can still take any man with my arms. Come here. Put your elbow on the table."

"All right," Portland said, surprised that Kelsey wanted to arm wrestle. They clasped hands. Portland immediately realized that he could defeat Kelsey but allowed the disgruntled former security operative to win.

"See?" Kelsey said.

"I'm impressed," Portland said.

Kelsey dragged on his cigarette and exhaled, saying as he poured more scotch, "They knew not to mess with Matt Kelsey when I was in the delta."

"They?"

"MEND, that's who I'm talking about," he snapped, obviously annoyed that Portland had to ask. "Course, you could never tell who was with MEND and who was working for them. That's the way they operate, rake in money and hire local yobbos, gangs, to do the dirty work. Can't say that I blame MEND. Let me tell you something, Portland; the oil companies are the bad actors in what's going on there in the delta, polluting the streams and swamps so that any man in his right mind won't even dip a finger in them. The oil companies get rich. So do the government whores who get paid off by the oil companies to look the other way." He suddenly brightened. "I got me a few before they got me."

"Got who?"

"Some of those MEND bastards or the ones working for them. Not long before they shot me full a' holes they tried to sneak up on a post I was manning near a swamp, came in a speedboat—they've got dozens of those boats—but I saw them and was faster than they were. Nailed two of them before the rest took off like scared rabbits. Got a commendation for that, I did. Only commendation I ever got from SureSafe."

Portland grew impatient. "I'm sure that you deserved those commendations," he said, "but I've driven here from London to learn what you know about how my son, Trevor, died. You said that you were there when it happened."

Another cigarette, more scotch, his face scrunched in thought.

"I was told that he was killed by members of MEND, or others acting on MEND's behalf. Is that what happened?"

Kelsey sat in silence for what seemed an eternity. Finally, he ran a large hand over his scraggly beard, closed his eyes, opened them, and said, "Your son was like every young lad looking to make the world better. Hah! As if they could do that. Hah! Silly dreamers, that's what they are. You don't change the world. All you can do is watch out for yourself, get the bastards before they get you."

Portland quietly debated whether to share with Kelsey his having found the bracelet that Trevor had worn, and that had been obtained by the security guard in a card game with Alain Fournier. Instead, he said, "I really need to know how Trevor died, Mr. Kelsey."

"'Mr. Kelsey'! Do I look like somebody who likes formality? Can your 'Mr. Kelsey.' It's 'Matt.' Got it? 'Matt.'"

"Okay, Matt, how did my son die? Was it MEND that killed him?"

Kelsey slumped back in his wheelchair and vigorously rubbed

his face with both hands. He said through his splayed fingers, "Froggie killed him."

"Froggie?"

"Fournier. The frog. The Frenchman."

"Fournier killed my son?"

Kelsey lowered his hands and held Portland in a hard stare.

"You saw him do it?"

"I sure as hell did."

Portland was at a loss for words.

"What are you, shocked?" Kelsey said with disdain. "You know Froggie. Scum of the earth. Rotten to the core. That's what he is."

"What happened?" Portland asked angrily. "Everything, tell me everything."

"Have a drink," Kelsey said.

Portland grabbed a dirty glass, poured two fingers' worth of scotch, but didn't drink. "How did it happen?" he demanded again.

"Happened at night," Kelsey said, shifting to a more comfortable position in his wheelchair. "Your kid—"

"Trevor," Portland said, annoyed that Trevor was referred to as his "kid."

"Yeah, right, Trevor. You know that he was involved, right?"

"Involved in what?"

"The war. MEND's war against the oil companies."

Portland moved to the edge of his chair. "Trevor wasn't involved with that," he said.

"The hell he wasn't. I was there, mate, saw it go down. I was on post one night, worst shift to catch. Post Seventeen it's called, right in the middle of the swamp. Hot as Hades and the bugs'll eat you alive." He lit a cigarette; the smoke drifted in Portland's direction.

"You mind putting out that stinking cigarette?"

"Bother you, does it?" He took another drag but sent the smoke to the ceiling.

"You were saying you were on post the night Trevor was killed?"

"The night he was captured."

"Wait a minute," Portland said, unable to keep pique from his voice. "Trevor was captured? Who captured him?"

"The boys who work for SureSafe, like me, like you. Hired guns."

"Who was he with when he was captured?"

"Some of the MEND boys. They slithered in that night intending to blow up one of our pipelines at Seventeen." He took a ragged map of XCAL's facility from the table next to his chair and tossed it at Portland. "See that red mark? That's where it happened. Post Seventeen. Hell of a gun battle took place, Portland, hell of a gun battle. That's when I got cut down, took three slugs in my belly and groin, damn near cut my spine in half."

Kelsey went into a coughing spasm and Portland used the distraction to pocket the map. "What about Trevor?" he asked after Kelsey's coughing fit had subsided.

"They took him in, delivered him to the floating barracks a hundred feet or so from where the battle happened."

"SureSafe took him in?"

"Dragged me there, too, all bloody and screaming in pain. Took us both there along with a couple of MEND savages."

Portland reached into the pocket of his safari jacket and withdrew a color photo of Trevor, and the bracelet the boy's grandmother had left him. He held them out for Kelsey to see.

"Is that the young man you saw captured by SureSafe?" Portland asked.

Kelsey nodded.

"You ever see this bracelet before?"

Kelsey became more animated. "That's what the kid was

wearing when they grabbed him. I remember it, wondered why he was wearing some fancy woman's bracelet. I figured maybe he was—"

Portland was glad that Kelsey didn't finish his thought. He replaced the picture and bracelet in his pocket and looked absently around the room, swimming in confusion, waylaid by what he'd just heard.

"What say we have some of those sandwiches you brought?" Kelsey said.

Portland returned to the here and now.

"How did Trevor, my son, die?"

Kelsey shrugged. "They roughed him up some. Maybe 'tortured' is more like it."

Portland shuddered.

"Who killed him?" Portland yelled.

"Froggie."

"Fournier?"

"Yup."

"He what, shot him?"

"Yup."

"Just like that? He decided to shoot Trevor?"

"He got a call on his mobile. After he took the call he shot him. Not the first time Froggie got rid of people he thought was against him and the oil companies."

"Who gave the order?"

"Beats me. I never heard who he talked to. He took the call, muttered something, clicked off, turned, and shot the kid in the head."

Portland had to fight against a welling up of bile, and tears.

"What did they do with his body?"

"Dumped it along with the MEND savages they killed, out in the swamp. They don't do proper burials in the Niger Delta, no sir, they do not. How about those sandwiches? All this talk works up an appetite."

Portland was furious with the callous way Kelsey had recounted what had happened to Trevor. At the same time he was grateful for the information the former SureSafe security guard had given him.

Now he knew. Trevor hadn't been murdered by MEND, no matter what he'd been told during the phone call from SureSafe's CEO. It had all been a lie.

He looked at Kelsey, who'd poured more scotch into his glass. Portland's glass remained untouched. He steadied himself before saying, "I appreciate everything you've told me."

"Not sure I should have," Kelsey said, now tipsy. "Those bastards at SureSafe and XCAL wouldn't take lightly me shooting my big mouth off like this. They're not a pretty bunch."

"No one will know what you've told me, Matt," Portland said, "at least not from me."

He went to the kitchen, found a reasonably clean plate, unwrapped two sandwiches and put them on the plate, and brought them to Kelsey, who was focused on the TV screen.

"I'd better be going," Portland said.

"Stay awhile, Portland. I don't get many people to talk to these days."

"No, I have to get back to London."

Portland shook Kelsey's hand and started for the door.

"You wouldn't have a couple of quid you could spare, would you?" Kelsey asked.

"Sure," Portland said, handing Kelsey some pound notes. "You take care, Matt. Thanks again."

He left the building. As he approached his rental car two of the yobbos were sitting on its hood.

"Get your asses off that car before I shoot them off," Portland said.

They looked at each other deciding whether to take him seriously. His tone of voice, and his hand stuck into his belt at the rear of his safari jacket, convinced them. They muttered four-letter words as they slid off the hood. Portland got in, started the engine, and knew that if he did have a handgun he might have been tempted to use it.

He roared away and headed for the highway leading back to London. A year earlier he would have checked into a cheap hotel, bought a bottle of gin at an off-license shop, and drunk himself into a boozy oblivion.

But this was a year later. All he wanted to do was get back to London and to his flat, away from Barrow-in-Furness, and decide what to do next.

CHAPTER 24

WASHINGTON, D.C.

Mackensie Smith was an inveterate tennis player. Not that he had any illusions about his performance level. He'd aged, although was still in decent shape for a fifty-plus-year-old man whose job was mostly sedentary; brief workouts on the treadmill and lifting light weights in his Watergate apartment mitigated that. He was also the proud owner of a bad knee; bone-on-bone the orthopedist said after the most recent X-ray. "You ought to consider a replacement," the doctor counseled.

"I'll think about it," Mac said.

"Piece of cake," the doctor said.

"I'll think about it," Smith repeated.

He left the physician's office with his usual conflicted reaction. He knew that knee replacements had become almost "routine," although he questioned whether any surgery was ever "routine." His knee hurt, especially when he was on the tennis court, but not to the extent that he was eager to go under the surgeon's knife. Annabel had subtly urged him to consider having his knee replaced, but whenever she did he announced that it was feeling better, especially after having received a steroid shot, and the topic was shelved until the next time.

After leaving the orthopedist's office he'd spent two hours in court representing a woman who'd sued a department store in which she'd tripped on the escalator and injured her shoulder. Smith would have preferred a different judge than Mitchel Junke, who, the saying went, never met a plaintiff in a personal injury suit he believed. A year from mandatory retirement, and with a shock of hair that he'd dyed a hideous orange color, he ruled his courtroom with an iron fist. Smith knew to keep his briefs short and to the point lest he receive a stern admonition from Junke. It went well. The attorney for the department store lacked Smith's insight into the judge's personality and did everything wrong, which pleased Smith while simultaneously activating his sympathy gland. The judge ruled in Smith's favor. The woman, his client, gave him a cursory thank-you and walked from the courtroom, a satisfied, smug look on her face. Smith decided while gathering up his papers that the next time a personal injury client appeared at his office he'd claim he was too busy to take the case. Life was too short.

His victory in court was soon forgotten as he drove to the Rock Creek Park Tennis Center, where he was scheduled to meet an infrequent, but favorite, tennis partner in one of that facility's indoor courts, Joe Stanko, a top official at the U.S. Department of Commerce's International Trade Administration. Stanko and Smith had met a few years earlier at a conference and had hit it off immediately, bound by a mutual love of many things—including tennis. Their busy schedules precluded them getting together often and Smith made time whenever Stanko could carve out a few hours to meet for a match.

Stanko, a few years older than Smith but who worked at staying young, was waiting when Smith arrived.

"Ready for a good workout, counselor?" Stanko asked as they left the locker room and stepped onto the court.

"I just came from one," Smith said, laughing.

"Judge gave you a hard time?"

"Actually, he was surprisingly pleasant this morning, at least to me, but my young opponent took it on the chin."

"All part of a lawyer's learning curve," Stanko said. "Ready for a good match?"

Smith started strong, his backhand more effective than usual, and his serves had good velocity on them. But as he and Stanko finished the first set with Smith the winner, and started their second, Smith's knee began to ache whenever he put pressure on it. He compensated for it, which threw off the rest of his body's motions, and Stanko won handily. Smith could have mentioned his aching knee but refused to use it as an excuse.

They retreated to a juice bar within the complex and sat at a table, their exotic liquid concoctions in front of them.

"Aside from your client's case that you won this morning," Stanko said, "what other cases are you involved with?"

"Actually, Joe, things are slow these days, although I am involved with a man whose father got caught up in one of those Nigerian financial scams. The father blew most of his money. When he finally realized that he'd been scammed he killed himself."

"He was that embarrassed?"

"Evidently. His son says that he'd begun to lose his mental faculties, which I suppose could help explain how he fell for the scam."

"Hard to understand," Stanko said, running a towel over his shaved head and sipping his juice. "You ought to talk to Ralph Cleland."

"Who's he?" Smith asked.

"He heads up a small office in my division at Commerce. He spent four years posted to our trade office in Lagos, Nigeria, as part of the consulate general's operation there. He's our expert on Nigerian financial scams, probably knows more about them than anyone else in D.C."

"I wasn't aware that you had such an office."

"It was inevitable that we'd end up with one. No matter how long they've been around, Nigerian financial scams are still big business. I forget the exact number—Ralph can give you an accurate figure—but the Financial Crimes Division of the Secret Service receives hundreds of calls and a ton of letters from American citizens who receive bogus letters offering big payoffs in return for sending large sums of money to the hustlers. Incredibly, some of these people actually follow through. People assume that these scams only impact a few gullible people, but hundreds of millions of dollars are squandered every year by folks like your client's father."

"I'd appreciate being put in touch with Mr. Cleland," Smith said.

"I'll have Ralph call you," Stanko promised.

Smith hadn't been back in his office for more than a half hour when Cleland called. "Joe Stanko suggested that we get together," he said.

"I'd like that very much," said Smith. "Buy you a drink?"

"Sounds good to me," Cleland said. "How about Mastro's Steakhouse on Thirteenth Street?"

They met at five thirty at the bar. Cleland was a roly-poly sort of man with a ruddy complexion. After initial getting-to-know-you chatter Smith told Cleland about his client Anthony Borilli and what had happened to his father. He ended with, "There's a Nigerian charity, Bright Horizons, here in D.C. that I'm led to believe is involved in the scam that Mr. Borilli got caught up in. My problem as Borilli's attorney is finding someone here in the States to sue on his behalf. I was hoping that this Bright Horizons might be the key."

Cleland, who'd ordered a Jack Daniel's neat, laughed. "Ah," he said, "good old Bright Horizons. Did your client's father go to Nigeria?"

"I don't believe so. His son never mentioned that he did."

"Just as well. Of course the father ended up dead anyway by his own hand, but the same thing might have happened if he'd made the trip."

"Do people caught up in these scams often go to Nigeria?" Smith asked.

"They certainly do, and some don't come back. That's what prompted us to set up an office to deal with the situation. The Nigerians who run these scams like to entice their marks to not only send money; they lure them to Nigeria supposedly to meet with the government officials or the ones who run the fake charities, you know, to give them a sense of legitimacy, shake the hands of these so-called important figures. Some of them bribe officials to let them use a room in a government building to add authenticity. What sometimes happens is that the sucker is told that no visa is necessary, and the perpetrators of the scam pay off airport personnel in Immigration or Customs to allow them in the country without one."

"I have a feeling I know how this story ends," Smith said.

"You're probably right," Cleland said. "Entering Nigeria without a proper visa is a crime. Once the sucker is there, he or she is told that they'll be arrested unless they come up with additional money."

"And if they balk?" Smith asked, anticipating Cleland's response.

"Some of them are never seen again. If they make a fuss they're—well, you can imagine. We've had some American citizens disappear there, poof, gone, no trace, no explanation. It's a serious problem, Mac, damned serious. I keep tabs on it through my office, but our hands are tied when it comes to bringing pressure on the Nigerian government to clamp down. Too many government officials, big and small, profit from allowing them to continue."

"My private investigator Robert Brixton has come up with the name of a warlord in Nigeria who might be involved with Bright Horizon's role in the scams. Agu something-or-other."

Cleland gave out with a hearty, knowing laugh. "Agu Gwantam, good old Agu. I knew him well when I was on the ground in Nigeria. He's headquartered in Port Harcourt, down south in the Niger Delta. That's oil country. Agu is one of those bigger-than-life characters, weighted down in gold chains and rings, gregarious, speaks good English with a British accent, dresses to the nines, and always has a bevy of beautiful females hanging on him. He tried to get me into bed with one of them, but I was too savvy to get snookered into that situation. There had to be cameras in the hotel room recording every minute. Hell, I was tempted. She was beautiful, but so's my wife. Besides, my wife has one hell of a temper and is a good shot."

Smith laughed. "Another drink?" he asked.

"Thanks, no. I've got to get home. As I said, my wife, the sweetheart that she is, has a temper. We have family coming for dinner." As he downed what was in his glass, he said, "You know, Mac, it's sad what's happening in Nigeria. I enjoyed my time there, had the best of everything, terrific quarters, household staff for my wife, and we made some really lovely friends. Nigerians for the most part are good people, gentle and generous. The oil they're bringing up makes it Africa's strongest economy, stronger even than South Africa. Oil is forty percent of Nigeria's GDP, eighty percent of what the government takes in. But it's also corrupt as hell. Damn near everyone in the government has his hand out."

"This has been quite an education," Smith said as they left the restaurant. "I appreciate it."

"Any time. One last word about Mr. Agu Gwantam. He comes off like a hail-fellow-well-met, million-dollar smile, give you the shirt off his back if he likes you."

"And if he doesn't like you?" Smith asked.

"He'll kill you. By the way, Mac, Bright Horizons is into more than bilking millions from suckers. They can get physical when told to. Thanks for the drink." He pulled a sheet of paper from his suit jacket and handed it to Smith. "Here's a copy of a letter someone recently received. Her daughter intercepted it and sent it to us." He laughed. "See how it's all in capital letters? They seem to think that gives it more clout. Give a yell if you want to know more."

Smith went directly home and sat with his wife, Annabel, on their terrace at the Watergate apartment. He'd read the letter given him by Cleland; now Annabel read it.

It started with: DEAR SIR: CONFIDENTIAL AND BUSINESS PROPOSITION.

"I thought you said this was sent to a woman," Annabel said.

"It was. The Nigerian who sent it obviously didn't know who his intended sucker was."

> I HAVE THE EXTREME PRIVILEGE TO SEEK YOUR ASSISTANCE TO TRANSFER $25,000,000.00 (TWENTY-FIVE MILLION DOLLARS UNITED STATES CURRENCY) INTO YOUR ACCOUNT. THE ABOVE SUM IS THE RESULT OF AN OVER-INVOICED CONTRACT, EXECUTED, COMMISSIONED, AND PAID FOR APPROXIMATELY FOUR YEARS AGO BY A FOREIGN CONTRACTOR. THIS ACTION WAS HOWEVER INTENTIONAL AND THE FUNDS HAVE BEEN IN A SUSPENDED ACCOUNT AT THE CENTRAL BANK OF NIGERIA APEX BANK.

"What's an 'over-invoiced contract'?" Annabel asked.

"Beats me," said Mac. "Go on. It gets even better."

> WE ARE READY TO TRANSFER THE FUNDS OVERSEAS AND THAT IS WHERE WE NEED YOUR MOST ABLE ASSISTANCE. IT IS IMPORTANT THAT WE INFORM YOU THAT AS CIVIL SERVANTS WE ARE FORBIDDEN BY LAW TO OPERATE A FOREIGN ACCOUNT.

WITH YOUR GRACIOUS HELP THE TOTAL SUM WILL BE SHARED AS FOLLOWS: 70 PERCENT FOR US, 25 PERCENT FOR YOU, AND 5 PERCENT FOR LOCAL AND INTERNATIONAL EXPENSES INCIDENTAL TO THE TRANSFER.

Annabel continued reading. The letter went on with increasingly flowery language to request the recipient's bank account information and account number, private telephone and fax numbers, and Social Security and other personal information.

She handed it back to Mac.

"Amazing," she said.

"I know what you're thinking," he said. "How could anyone be stupid enough to fall for it?"

"According to your Mr. Cleland, people fall for it all the time."

"Including Tony Borilli's father."

"You said that Mr. Cleland personally knew this warlord who runs such a scheme in Nigeria."

"Yeah. He sounds like quite a character, and not a very nice one."

"I think I'll get dinner ready," she said, standing.

"Good. I'm hungry. While you're busy in the kitchen I'll respond to this letter, give them the information they want, and send them whatever we have in our savings account."

"Not funny, Mac."

Later that night as they sat reading, Mac mentioned that he'd asked Brixton to contact Ammon Dimka in Virginia again to see whether he'd be willing to go public about his knowledge of how the Nigerian charity Bright Horizons fits into the scam that caused Borilli's father to commit suicide.

Annabel's attorney training kicked in. "Are you sure you want to pursue this, Mac? Suing a foreign government, especially one like Nigeria, is usually a waste of everyone's time. Its Bright Horizons might be U.S. based, but I'm sure it's wrapped in many layers of diplomatic immunity."

He started to respond, but she continued.

"I might also mention that the people who run these scams are not gentle, loving types."

"So I've been told," Mac said, thinking of what Cleland had said about Agu Gwantam killing people.

"I get your point, Annie," Smith said, "and you're undoubtedly right. But maybe if a suit is brought—even if it has little chance of succeeding—it will raise awareness and spare some other poor man or woman from turning over their life savings to these crooks."

The subject was dropped for the rest of the evening, but neither Mac nor Annabel stopped thinking about it before going to bed and falling asleep.

CHAPTER 25

PORT HARCOURT, NIGERIA

Agu Gwantam was in a festive mood as he oversaw preparations for that evening's dinner party. He entertained often in his large, expensively furnished gated home in an upscale neighborhood on the fringe of the city, and looked forward to that evening's guest list—government officials, wealthy neighbors, executives from XCAL Oil, a budding Nigerian actress and her entourage, a visiting British journalist who'd arrived in Port Harcourt a week earlier to write articles about the Nigerian oil boom, and a few Nigerian courtesans whom Agu liked to keep on tap in case one of the men felt sexually frisky after imbibing his top-shelf liquor. Alain Fournier, head of SureSafe's Niger Delta security force, a frequent guest at Agu's home, would also be attending. Two members of SureSafe's armed militia stood guard at the front gate, Russian-made AK-47s slung across their chests. Another SureSafe armed guard had followed Fournier's car in his own and waited outside the compound for him to emerge.

Inside the sprawling home the kitchen staff was busy preparing that evening's fare, the centerpiece a large goat that would be roasted over an open flame on the patio. There were platters of king prawns, scallops, and mussels, freshly baked bread, and a special banana dessert from a recipe that Agu's wife had imported from a South African friend. Two bars had been set up, one inside, the other on the patio, from which Champagne would flow freely, as well as more potent alcoholic beverages. Members of a popular four-piece Nigerian band, known for its melding of traditional Nigerian music with jazz and funk, laughed while setting up their instruments and amplification equipment on a raised wooden platform.

Agu showered in anticipation of his guests' arrival. Naked, he observed his large physique in the mirror and approved what he saw. He was a vain man. Although he was married, his sexual dalliances were numerous and ranged far and wide in Port Harcourt and beyond. His wife, Fayola, was well aware of her husband's extracurricular sex life but didn't complain. He treated her well; he was rich and made sure that she had every modern convenience and a room-size closet filled with the latest fashions. Too, her husband's status in the community rubbed off on her; she was a popular figure in town and at the Episcopal church that she and Agu regularly attended.

It wasn't any secret in Port Harcourt that the primary source of Agu Gwantam's money was generated by the financial frauds he oversaw, and he wasn't reluctant to brag how so many stupid people around the world fell easy victim to them. While the United States had been especially fertile ground, Agu had more recently found gold in the Soviet Union and other countries where the lure of easy money was equally enticing.

He personally greeted his guests as they arrived, most in fancy rented cars driven by Nigerians. Jaguars, Rolls-Royces, and high-end Mercedes were allowed to enter through the gates and park in front. The drivers of lesser vehicles were allowed to drop their passengers inside the compound but were required to park outside the high fence bordered along the top with razor wire.

Alain Fournier arrived with a paid escort, Carla, a strikingly beautiful brunette whose stunning figure was shown to its fullest by a tight red silk dress with a plunging neckline, and spike heels. She was slightly taller than Fournier, a dapper, slender man with a black pencil mustache and brown hair pasted to his head with some sort of gel. His beige three-piece suit was custom-made by Port Harcourt's leading tailor. His tan shoes came from London.

Agu greeted them warmly. "Things are good with you?" he asked in his British-tinged accent.

"Things are very good," Fournier said. "And you?"

Agu flashed a wide smile, his teeth a dazzling white against his dark skin. He indicated his house with a sweep of his hand. "Everything is wonderful, as you can see. Come, have a drink and enjoy yourselves." He added, "As usual we are declaring surplus," a familiar Nigerian term for enjoying the excesses of life.

All the invited guests had arrived and the band started playing as the bartenders dispensed drinks. The three executives from XCAL and their wives tended to bunch together, as did some of the government officials, but guests eventually mixed more freely as the alcohol greased the conversational skids. The senior member of the government contingent at the party, Blyds Okafor, area commander of the Economic and Financial Crimes Commission—and a frequent beneficiary of Agu Gwantam's largesse—wore his lofty title with pride. Educated in London, he carried himself self-assuredly, half-glasses perched on the tip of his surprisingly aquiline nose, a seemingly permanent bemused grin on his lips. He beckoned for Agu to join him in a secluded portion of the expansive property.

"I hesitate injecting something unpleasant into this festive day, Agu, but I've received a message from a colleague in Washington, D.C., that is troubling."

"Oh? This is not a day for troubles, Blyds."

"I would prefer that no day brings troubles, but that is wishful thinking."

"What is this trouble you mention?"

"Bright Horizons."

Agu's smile evaporated. "What about it?"

"You know, of course, the trouble we have had with Ammon Dimka."

"Oh, yes, Dimka. But he is no longer involved with Bright Horizons. He is now—as I recall—he works for an American firm, some sort of construction company?"

"Exactly. But that is not the issue. Dimka was encouraged to migrate to the United States to head up Bright Horizons, a move to get him out of our hair. You're aware of that."

"Yes, of course. And he resigned from that post because he was unhappy with certain aspects of that most worthwhile charity."

Okafor adjusted the glasses on his nose as he ensured that they were not being overhead. He leaned closer. "It seems that Mr. Dimka has been telling tales out of school to not only an American journalist; he's done the same with a private investigator."

"That *is* troubling," Agu agreed. "How does your colleague in Washington know this?"

Okafor looked across the yard to where Alain Fournier chatted with other guests. "SureSafe has recorded Dimka's calls," he said.

Gwantam also looked to where Fournier stood.

"Does Alain know this?" Okafor asked.

Agu hunched large shoulders beneath his pale blue blazer. "We should ask him," he said, "but later. I have things to attend to for my guests."

The band started playing, its infectious rhythms ramping up the party atmosphere. A few couples danced to the beat of the hybrid music. The actress danced by herself to admiring male glances, hips swaying, a sultry smile on her red lips.

Waiters passed trays loaded with the evening's pre-dinner treats while Agu and his wife mingled, making sure that each guest was having a good time. Alain Fournier did as he usually did at social gatherings. He stayed mostly to himself, a drink in his hand, his narrowed eyes taking in everyone as though searching for a missing person, or someone who shouldn't be there. His date had left his side and engaged in raucous conversation with others, opening flirting with a young government official who'd already had too much to drink.

Agu approached Fournier. "Are you enjoying yourself, Alain?" he asked.

"Of course," Fournier said, his accent reflecting his French origins. "You always provide the best parties."

"Thank you," said Agu. "I need to speak with you—in private."

Fournier said nothing as he followed Agu into Agu's private study, a large room at the rear of the home filled with trophies he'd garnered on frequent hunting trips. He closed the door, went to the window, and looked out at the revelers. Fournier took a chair upholstered in zebra skin next to the oversized desk. The mounted heads of wild beasts looked down on him.

"What do you hear from your people in Washington, D.C., about Ammon Dimka?" Agu asked without turning from the window.

"Nothing new that I am aware of."

"Blyds Okafor has told me that he received word that Mr. Dimka has been talking with people in Washington about Bright Horizons."

"What people?"

"A journalist and a private investigator."

"I have not been told this," said Fournier.

Agu now faced Fournier. "I am surprised that I am the one who must inform you of such news," he said sternly. "After all, security—*my* security—is in your hands, and you are paid handsomely for it."

Fournier started to respond, but Agu continued. "Yes, Alain, I not only pay you handsomely for your security services; I have generously cut you in on a percentage of the money that my enterprises generate."

"And I have expressed my gratitude on many occasions," the slender Frenchman said.

"Which I appreciate, of course, but I would also expect that you and your people stay abreast of matters that are of a direct concern to me."

Fournier twisted in his chair. He resented being lectured by the big Nigerian, and for a moment envisioned shooting him with the Beretta he carried. He'd often had such a vision. While his posting by SureSafe to the Niger Delta had reaped him substantial financial rewards—he was paid by SureSafe, was paid by Gwantam for personal security services, and received a cut of Gwantam's income from his financial scams—he deeply disliked the black men for whom he worked, considered them lesser human beings, men who lacked the sophisticated European upbringing that he, Alain Fournier, had enjoyed. But he expressed those feelings only to a few select European friends with whom he worked in the delta and who shared his views. The executives at XCAL Oil, whose security and safety had been entrusted to him and SureSafe, were gentlemen. Agu Gwantam and others like him were thugs in Fournier's estimation.

Agu forced a smile and turned to the window again. "We're missing the party, Alain," he said pleasantly. "I know that you will take care of this matter in due haste. Come, have a drink. It is too good a day to be indoors."

Fournier stayed for as long as he felt it was politic. As guests prepared to sit down for their roasted goat dinner, he grabbed his date and told her they were leaving. She'd had a lot to drink and protested but knew better than to make a scene. After apologizing for having to leave—something to do with an emergency at SureSafe—he hustled her through the front door and into the car that had delivered them to the party, his armed guard falling in behind. Fournier instructed the driver to take them to his apartment, told him to wait, and herded Carla into the bedroom, where he threw her on the bed. "You're drunk, you *chienne*! Sober up, take a shower, and be here when I return." She started to say something, but he slapped her. "Don't challenge me, Carla. Don't ever challenge me!"

He told the driver to take him to SureSafe's headquarters, a concrete two-story building on the shore of one of the delta's many swamps. He stormed into the first-floor offices where two Germans on duty that day watched a soccer game on a small TV set. They snapped to attention as he entered.

"Have you heard anything from our people in Washington about that fool Ammon Dimka?" he snapped.

One of the Germans rifled through a pile of communiqués on the desk and handed a sheet to Fournier. It was a report of SureSafe's monitoring of Dimka's telephone. Fournier seethed as he read it. He threw it at the German and snarled, "Why wasn't I informed of this the minute it arrived?"

One of the men mumbled an excuse in German about Fournier having been at a party, but Fournier brought his fist down on the desk, sending papers flying. He delivered a scathing diatribe laced with French four-letter words, turned, and left the building, his words trailing behind. His driver returned him to his apartment, where Carla, showered and wearing Fournier's bathrobe, pouted on the couch. His anger at the Germans hadn't abated, and his lovemaking reflected it. She was left with a bruised cheek and breast, and a bloody lip where her teeth had bitten into it. Fournier fell asleep when they were through, his handgun on the table next to the bed, and Carla considered picking it up and blowing the nasty Frenchman's brains out.

But good sense prevailed. She quietly left the bed, splashed her face with cold water in the bathroom, dressed, and left, rationalizing that she was at least paid, something she couldn't always count on with Alain Fournier.

CHAPTER 26

WASHINGTON—LONDON

Elizabeth Sims prided herself on her physical condition, not only because of the way exercise made her look but also because it cleared her mind to tackle the complex legal issues she was called upon to sort through each day. She'd been a runner since her teen years, and had joined her husband, David Portland, for daily jogs whenever he was in London after returning from his many trips. She enjoyed those romps in the British countryside, and her stepson, Trevor, sometimes joined them.

Following their divorce and her return to the States with Trevor, she continued a daily workout regime, and on this early morning she went to Rock Creek Park, a favorite jogging place, where she logged an easy five miles according to the small device worn on the waist of her shorts. She'd started her run just as the sun appeared over the horizon, which provided a modicum of light. While she wasn't paranoid about jogging alone, she was wary enough to not venture into strange areas at night; a canister of Mace that accompanied the odometer provided a sense of security.

Back in her apartment, she discarded her running clothes and stood under a hot shower, enjoying the tingle the rush of water provided. Wrapped in an oversized pale blue towel, and with a smaller one on her head, she settled in her kitchen with a bowl of oatmeal, glass of orange juice, and black coffee and read that day's newspaper, which she'd grabbed from a pile in the lobby, a perk of being a resident in the expensive high-rise apartment building, high at least by Washington, D.C., standards. One article after another testified to the mayhem taking place around the globe, and she pushed the paper aside. The news was too distressing, not the way to start another demanding day at Cale, Watson and Warnowski.

But there also was unpleasant news closer to home. Her father hadn't been feeling well for months and had finally succumbed to his wife's urging to see a doctor. After a battery of tests, the diagnosis was a particularly aggressive form of lymphoma. He was to begin six courses of a potent chemotherapy recipe, followed by multiple sessions of radiation. Elizabeth had spoken with him the night before and he'd sounded upbeat, although she sensed that his positive tone was forced. How could it not be? He was facing treatments that would undoubtedly leave him drained, physically and mentally, including the loss of his full head of steely gray hair in which he took pride. She'd have to get to Boston to spend time with him whenever she found a break in her busy schedule.

She chose a new navy pants suit to wear that day, and spent the requisite time adjusting her makeup and hair. Satisfied at how she looked, she gathered up papers she'd been going over the night before and was about to leave for the office when the phone rang. It startled her. Ever since she had learned of her father's illness she was convinced a ringing phone could herald bad news. Silly, she knew, but understandable. It went with the territory of having aging parents.

"Liz, it's David," Portland said.

She checked her watch. Seven forty-five. Early afternoon in the UK.

"Hello, David. You're still in London?"

"I'll be coming back in a few days. Liz, we have to talk."

"All right," she said, not eager to prolong the conversation. "When you get back we can—"

"It's about Trevor."

What else could it be about? she thought.

"Why don't you call me when you get back?" she again suggested.

"Yeah, I'll do that. But look, I've come across information while in London that shouts loud and clear that Trevor wasn't killed by members of MEND. He was killed by Alain Fournier, the Frenchman in charge of security for XCAL in Nigeria."

"That's a serious charge, David."

"Yeah, it sure is. He shot him after talking on the phone with someone, and I'll bet that someone was with XCAL."

Elizabeth started to debate it with him but caught herself. "Call me when you're back in Washington," she repeated. "I have to run now."

"XCAL," Portland muttered into the phone. "Your precious client."

She hung up without saying more.

"Damn you!" she said to the empty room. He was at it again, flinging accusations around based upon God only knew where he'd gotten his latest "information." Had he been drinking again? Why couldn't he let go of it? His son, her stepson, was dead and buried. He'd put himself in harm's way by taking a job in volatile Nigeria, and while that didn't mitigate the pain of his murder and the brutality of it, it tended to create a filter through which it became more understandable.

Those thoughts stayed with her as she drove to the office and settled in for a hard day of analyzing two new contracts initiated by her client XCAL Oil. She practiced what she'd learned about compartmentalizing, which helped to some extent, but David's call, and her father's health issues, kept getting in the way.

CHAPTER 27

The phone call to Elizabeth, and the whirlwind of thoughts and emotions Portland had suffered since meeting with the pathetic Matthew Kelsey, also made concentrating difficult for him. He paced his London flat, Kelsey's words on a loop, gripping the bracelet that the big Nigerian had claimed had been anted up by Fournier in a card game, turning it over and over in his hands, picturing it on Trevor's wrist and envisioning his murder, a bullet to the head, his body left to rot in the Nigerian sun until someone did the right thing and arranged to have it shipped home.

Mostly he was frustrated. He now had the information he needed to back up his suspicion that Trevor had been killed not by MEND members, but by the man in charge of security for XCAL in the Niger Delta, Alain Fournier. Of course, he realized that the information had come from a disgruntled former SureSafe employee, a hard drinker and cynical man. Could he believe Kelsey? He had no reason to doubt what Kelsey had told him, but he wanted more, something tangible to back up the drunk's claim.

But where would he find it?

His initial call to XCAL's London office had achieved nothing. He'd been shunted off to a young man who said that he was Manford Penny's executive assistant, whatever that meant.

He called XCAL's number and reached the same young man who'd taken his earlier call. After explaining why he was calling again, he was put on hold until the man with the title of executive assistant reappeared. "Yes, Mr. Portland," he said. "I have the report right here. Trevor Portland, aged twenty-three, employed by the geological survey company SealCom, hometown Boston, Massachusetts, United States of America, the victim of native forces associated with the Nigerian rebel organization MEND—"

"Yes, I know all that," Portland said, unable to mask his annoyance. "What I'm looking for is someone who might have been there, someone who knows more than is in the official report you're reading to me."

"I'm sorry, sir, but that is all that is known here at headquarters. The report is official and—"

"Who wrote that report?" Portland snapped.

"It was sent to us from SureSafe in Nigeria—that is the security firm under contract to XCAL—and it represents the official report on what happened to Trevor Portland, age twenty-three, who—"

"Thanks for nothing," Portland growled. "Have a good day!" He slammed down the phone.

Elizabeth had mentioned during their lunch that among many things she'd be doing in London was meeting with XCAL UK's chairman, Manford Penny. Portland didn't know him, but Elizabeth spoke highly of him, which didn't mean much. What was she supposed to say about the British chairman of the firm's most lucrative client—that she detested him?

He pulled from a file the notes he'd taken when first informed of Trevor's demise by a phone call from SureSafe's London-based office. The news had been sufficiently impactful to cause

Portland to simply thank the caller and hang up, no questions, no probing the facts behind his son's brutal death, just a burst of exhaled breath—and tears, a torrent of tears that he hadn't experienced for as long as he could remember. He'd accepted the news as fact: Trevor had been murdered by members of MEND, the native organization dedicated to ridding the Niger Delta of foreign oil companies and the havoc they'd inflicted on the land and its people.

Now, thanks to Matthew Kelsey, he knew better.

He dialed SureSafe's London number and reached a woman, who asked what his call was in reference to.

Portland mentioned the CEO and explained that he'd been the one who'd called to inform him of his son's death in Nigeria. "I'd like to speak with him again," Portland added.

He was put on hold for a few minutes. Finally, the CEO came on the line.

"Yes, Mr. Portland," he said cheerily, "I recall having the unpleasant duty of informing you of what happened to your son."

"I'm sure it wasn't easy for you," Portland said, not caring whether it had been or not. "Look," he said, "I've recently learned something that contradicts the official line that Trevor, my son, was killed by members of MEND."

"Oh?"

"I've spoken with a man who was working for SureSafe in the Niger Delta when Trevor was killed. According to him, MEND wasn't behind his murder. He was shot in the head by your top guy there, Alain Fournier."

If the silence on the other end could be translated, it said to Portland that his accusation had hit home.

"I'm sorry, Mr. Portland," the CEO said, "but whoever told you that is very mistaken."

"I don't think so," Portland said. "Look, I've been in touch with XCAL here in London. I'm not looking to cause trouble, but I intend to get to the truth about my son's death. I'd like to sit down with you and talk about it."

"I don't know if that's possible."

"Why? You and your people aren't capable of sitting down and talking?"

"It isn't that, Mr. Portland. It's just that—well, I'll have to discuss this with others."

Portland knew that SureSafe's London office was small, no more than twenty people, mostly clerical types. He was talking to the CEO, the top guy. Who else would he have to "discuss" it with?

"I used to work for SureSafe," Portland said.

"Yes, I'm well aware of that," said the CEO.

Really? Portland thought. He hadn't signed on with SureSafe for an assignment in a long time.

"Can we meet?" Portland asked.

"Let me have your number and I'll call you."

"I'll be waiting," Portland said.

The call came an hour later, but it wasn't from SureSafe. It was from the young man at XCAL UK, Manford Penny's executive assistant.

"Mr. Portland, Chairman Penny was wondering whether you would be free later today to meet."

Penny? XCAL's UK chairman?

"Sure," Portland said.

He was given a time to be at the oil company's London offices. This had been easier than he'd anticipated. He certainly didn't expect to end up meeting with Sir Manford Penny. Why would *he* make himself available for a sit-down? He also wondered whether he would hear back from SureSafe. It didn't matter. Being able to ask questions of someone like Penny was more likely to produce useful answers than asking anyone from SureSafe.

Portland wasn't accustomed to meeting with the chairman of anything, and he wondered whether he should wear his suit. "The hell with it," he mumbled as he prepared to leave. "I'm not applying for a job. I just want to know what happened to my son."

XCAL's London offices were in a relatively new office building near Marble Arch. Dressed in his usual safari jacket, black T-shirt, and sneakers, Portland was escorted to a large, sparsely furnished conference room where a man greeted him.

"Ah, Mr. Portland. Rufus Norris, SureSafe."

Norris was the CEO of SureSafe's British office with whom Portland had spoken earlier in the day. That he was at XCAL's corporate offices came as a surprise.

"Sorry I didn't have a chance to ring you back, but things got a tad hectic. I'm pleased that we have this opportunity to meet."

"Same here," Portland said. What else was there to say? He took in the handsome room. "I thought I was meeting with Mr. Penny."

"Oh, yes, you will be. Manford's running late, but he should be here any minute. I understand that you're now working for our embassy in Washington."

"That's right."

"Quite a departure from your previous work, isn't it?"

Portland cocked his head. "A departure? I don't see it that way. I've been involved in security my whole adult life. Security is security, isn't it? Doesn't matter who you provide it for."

"I suppose you're right, but I was referring to the sort of assignments you undertook with SureSafe earlier in your career."

"If you mean they involved more danger, you're right."

Norris laughed. "And you've had your share of that danger."

Portland checked his watch. What sort of game was going on? He'd come expecting to meet XCAL's chairman and instead ended up making small talk with Norris from SureSafe. His patience was running thin and he decided to move things along.

"Do you know why I'm here?" Portland said.

"Of course. Your son."

"That's right. My son. What do you know about how he died?"

"Only what I've been told."

"Who told you?"

"The report I received. I don't know who wrote it."

"Maybe Fournier wrote it," Portland suggested.

Norris had started to respond when the door opened and Manford Penny entered, dressed in his double-breasted blue blazer, sparkling white shirt, and red-and-blue regimental tie. He glided across the room and extended a weak hand. "Mr. Portland," he said in his cultured voice, "this is indeed a pleasure. How good of you to come on such short notice."

"I'm glad you were available," Portland said.

"Of course I made myself available for *you*, sir. Please, have a seat. Tea? Something more alcoholic? I'll have it sent in."

"Nothing for me, thanks, but you go ahead."

Penny turned to Norris. "You and Mr. Portland have met, I see," he said.

"Yes, we have," said Norris.

"I am pleased that we have this opportunity to speak man-to-man about the dreadful events that led to the demise of your son."

"That's why I'm here," said Portland. "I've already told Mr. Norris that I've learned that my son wasn't killed by members of MEND, no matter what the so-called 'official' report claimed. He was killed by someone from SureSafe, that organization's top guy in Nigeria, Alain Fournier. Of course, SureSafe works for your company, XCAL Oil, which makes you a player in this."

Penny's expression said both that he was surprised at what Portland had said and that he found it outlandish, if not amusing.

The three men sat in silence until Penny broke it.

"The reason I've made myself available today," Penny said, "is that we must put this unfortunate episode behind us." Portland started to respond, but Penny continued. "By 'us,' I mean this corporation, the good chaps at SureSafe, and of course you, Mr. Portland, whose grief I can only imagine."

Portland had disliked Penny the moment he walked through the door, and his disdain for the foppish chairman of XCAL UK only grew with each passing moment.

"If I might say something," Norris said.

"Of course," said Penny.

"I can fully understand Mr. Portland's obsession with his son's death and the circumstance surrounding it, but it seems to me as someone who had spent considerable years in the field that lodging unsubstantiated charges accomplishes nothing. It certainly doesn't bring back his son."

"No, it sure as hell doesn't," Portland snapped, his anger level rising, "but that's not the point. My son was murdered. That's a fact. What *isn't* a fact is that he was murdered by MEND. He was shot to death by a guy from your organization, Mr. Norris, who killed him on orders from someone in this company." He fixed Penny in a hard stare. "My question, Mr. Penny, is not how to put it behind us, as you suggest, but how to achieve justice for my son. What are you going to do about it?"

"I must say, Mr. Portland, that I resent your tone."

"And I resent the whitewash that's going on."

Penny looked past Portland as though seeking an easy exit.

"How about this?" Portland said, directing it at Norris. "Bring Fournier here to London and let me question him face-to-face about Trevor's death."

Norris looked at Penny before responding. "I'm afraid that's out of the question," he said.

"Why?" Portland pressed.

"You're suggesting that Mr. Fournier be summoned to London based upon your *belief* that he was, in some way, involved in your son's murder."

"My belief? It's more than that, Mr. Norris."

"But only based on what you've been told by a former SureSafe employee. Who was that employee, Mr. Portland?"

"That's not important," Portland said, knowing as he did that Norris wouldn't put any stock in what some anonymous person supposedly said. He was tempted to mention Matthew Kelsey but didn't out of fairness.

Penny, who'd sat quietly during the back-and-forth between Portland and Norris, stood and said, "I had hoped that this little get-together might have cleared the air for Mr. Portland, and allowed everyone to go about their business free of baseless accusations. But since that doesn't seem to be possible, I suggest that we end this pleasant little gabfest and—"

Portland erupted. He slammed his fist on the table and shouted, "'Pleasant little gabfest'? That's what you call it, Mr. Penny? You've got a dead young man on your hands, *sir*!" He turned to Norris. "And you have a murderer working for you—*sir*!"

"If you can't calm yourself, Mr. Portland, and behave in a civilized manner, I'll have to—"

"What?" Portland yelled. "Have me arrested? Go ahead. But listen to this, Mr. CEO. I'm not going to rest until the person who killed my son is brought to justice, and I don't give a rat's ass if it takes you and your goddamn oil company, and SureSafe, down, too."

His sudden fury put both men on the defensive. Norris stood as though prepared to do physical battle. Penny moved smoothly toward the door. Portland, shaking with rage, willed himself under control.

Penny opened the door to reveal two men in suits. The CEO said to Portland, "You can leave now, Mr. Portland. This meeting is over."

Portland glared at both men as he crossed the room. He paused in front of Penny, his fists clenched at his sides. He saw fear in Penny's face, which pleased him. He flashed XCAL UK's chairman a big smile and said, "You'll hear from me again."

He left the conference room, saying to the two men as he passed, "You aren't needed. Your boss is still in one piece." He got in the elevator and rode it down to street level, where he drew in deep breaths. Although nothing tangible had been accomplished, he was glad they'd met. He could now put a face to Manford Penny, with whom his ex-wife spent considerable time, and the British head of SureSafe.

As Portland made his way back to his flat, Rufus Norris accompanied Manford Penny into his office suite. The chairman, while maintaining a sanguine posture, was internally shaken, and ordered his private secretary to bring him a Cognac from his private bar. Without offering a drink to Norris, he sat behind his desk and said, "The man is dangerous, a volatile loose cannon. Keep tabs on him, Rufus. Keep very close tabs on him."

CHAPTER 28

WASHINGTON, D.C.

Robert Brixton decided to take the day off and drive to Maryland to visit his surviving daughter, Jill, and his grandson, Joey. Jill was married to Frank, an ex-marine who'd gone to college on the GI Bill and worked as an administrator at Walter Reed Hospital. Brixton adored Jill, and liked his son-in-law, too. Frank was a tall, taciturn guy with a buzz cut who said little. But what he did say was usually appropriate and meaningful. Maybe that Frank openly liked his father-in-law helped endear him to Brixton. No matter. Brixton considered himself blessed to have a wonderful daughter who'd established a thriving accounting practice from their home, a strapping grandson, and an okay son-in-law. Missing, of course, was his younger daughter, Janet, who'd perished in a terrorist's bombing of a café in D.C. Nothing could ever fill that void.

He hoped that his former wife, Marylee, wouldn't be visiting Jill when he arrived. Following her divorce from Brixton Marylee had married Miles Lashka, an attorney with a dazzling set of white teeth and a smarmy personality, at least in Brixton's estimation. Brixton, originally from Brooklyn, had been a uniformed cop in Washington, D.C., when he married the socially superior Marylee Greene. It had been a tumultuous marriage from the first day, and the divorce wasn't any better, thanks to Marylee's haughty mother's interference. The old lady was deceased, bless her soul.

But that was then. Following the divorce Brixton had moved to Savannah, Georgia, where he put in the requisite twenty years until retirement, the last few as a detective with a bad knee, the result of an errant bullet from someone he'd arrested. He stayed in Savannah and opened a private investigator's office, a not especially successful venture. But while in that quintessential southern city he'd met Flo Combes, another New York transplant, and they'd been together ever since—with some notable contentious gaps. Now, at the urging of attorney friend Mackensie Smith and his wife, Annabel, Brixton operated a PI agency from an office adjacent to Mac Smith's law office, and Flo was the proud proprietor of Flo's Fashions in Georgetown.

Brixton was disappointed when he arrived at Jill's home that Marylee had taken the boy for an overnight visit and wasn't due to return him until later that evening.

"I should have mentioned it when you called," Jill said.

"No, that's okay," he said. "I'm glad Joey has a good relationship with his grandmother. By the way, how is she?"

He read the expression on Jill's face, and it wasn't happy. "She and Miles are having troubles," she said softly, as though not sure whether she was allowed to reveal it.

"I'm sorry to hear that," said Brixton. "What's the problem?"

"Miles is—well, he's been having affairs."

"Oh."

"Mom found out about it and is devastated."

"I'm sure she is."

As fractured as his relationship with Marylee was, he found himself becoming defensive of her and angry at Miles Lashka.

"Are they still together?" he asked.

"Sort of. I feel terrible for mom. She doesn't deserve this."

"Looks like a divorce is in the works," Brixton said.

"They haven't been married that long," Jill said.

Brixton started to say that he and Marylee hadn't been married long either but didn't. Instead, he said, "Mind some advice?"

"Of course not."

"Stay out of it, Jill. Stay above the fray. You've got a nice life going, a terrific husband and a super son. Don't let your mother's problems with Lashka drag you down."

Tears formed in her green eyes. She placed her hand on his and said, "Thanks, dad. I'll remember that."

He stayed an hour. She whipped up tuna fish sandwiches for lunch. He didn't like tuna fish but pretended that he did. She indicated that she had better get back to work, which he understood. They parted in the driveway.

"Give that big kid a hug for me," he said.

"Frank?" she asked, laughing.

"Yeah, that big kid, too," he said.

They embraced and he saw her waving good-bye in his rearview mirror. Once she was out of sight he pulled over, took a handkerchief from his pocket, and dabbed at his own tears.

He swung by the office, where Mrs. Warden was filing papers.

"Anybody call?" he asked.

"No," she said.

"Is Mr. Smith in?"

"No. He's gone for the day with Mrs. Smith."

Disappointed that no potential client had phoned, he settled in his office and rifled through a pile of correspondence he'd fallen behind in answering. Included in them was a note he'd written to himself: "Follow up on Dimka."

He dialed Ammon Dimka's number, expecting to reach a machine. Instead, Dimka answered.

"Mr. Dimnka, Robert Brixton here."

"Yes, Mr. Brixton."

"I wasn't sure I'd catch you at home."

"Your timing is good. I've taken off two personal days that I've been saving up."

"Good for you. I was wondering if we could get together again."

"I suppose so. When were you thinking?"

"Later today? Tomorrow?"

"It would have to be tomorrow. Abi, my wife, is leaving work early today and we're doing some shopping together."

"Good for you. Tomorrow it is."

"I assume it's about the same matter we discussed when you were here before."

"Yes, sir, that's right. My friend Mac Smith, the attorney I told you about, wanted me to explore with you the possibility of you coming forward with what you know about Bright Horizons and the financial scams. He has this client and—"

"I remember. I've been doing a lot of thinking since your last visit. Maybe it's time that I become a little more open about it."

"Would you be willing to sit down with Mac and tell him what you know?"

"I'm not sure I'd be willing to do that yet, but we can discuss it when you're here. Tomorrow, say at noon. I'll put out a lunch for us."

"I wouldn't want to—"

"It'll be my pleasure. See you tomorrow."

Abi Dimka arrived home from work in time to greet her two daughters when they got off the school bus. After snacks for the girls, the family set off to shop for a new bedroom set for the older one, which set her younger sister into a pout that didn't last long. "We'll buy you a new set next year," their mother said comfortingly.

They topped off their family shopping excursion with pizza at a local Italian shop, and large cones of chocolate gelato for the girls. On the drive home Abi asked Ammon how his day had been, and what he intended to do the following day. He almost mentioned his lunch date with Brixton but decided not to. He was well aware of her concerns about his telling people of Bright Horizons' complicity in Nigerian financial scams and didn't want to further upset her.

"Just planning to hang around," he said as they pulled into the driveway. "Maybe I'll finally get around to cleaning out that hall closet."

As the Dimka family settled in for the night, two men in Bright Horizons' back office listened again to the tap on Dimka's phone that had recorded Brixton's call to the transplanted Nigerian.

"I'll send this to Fournier in Port Harcourt," the man who'd recorded the conversation said.

"Good. Agu Gwantam will want to know about it, too."

"Of course."

"Dimka has to go."

"That isn't my decision," the second man said as he secured the recorder in a closet, slipped on his coat and a knit cap, and left the building.

It had started snowing.

CHAPTER 29

WASHINGTON, D.C.

David Portland's flight from London landed on time at Dulles International Airport despite snow squalls. He hadn't told Brixton that he was returning; he didn't want him to feel obligated to pick him up again.

His combative confrontation with XCAL UK's chairman, Manford Penny, and SureSafe's head guy in London, Rufus Norris, had unsettled him to the point of considering getting drunk, and maybe even taking up smoking again. But while those urges were born of emotions, his cognitive sense overruled and he contented himself with sipping a glass of beer in his flat, and eyeing a clean empty ashtray that he kept on his desk as a reminder of when he used to go through two packs a day.

Before booking his flight he'd called Freddie Tompkins at M16 to see whether he was free to leave, and to report to him the result of his meeting with Matthew Kelsey in Barrow-in-Furness.

Kelsey is a mess," Portland told Tompkins.

"I'm well aware of that," said Tompkins.

"He confirmed that Alain Fournier killed my son. He was there when it happened."

Tompkins's silence said something.

"You have doubts?" Portland asked.

"Don't you? You've spent time with the man. He's unbalanced, along with being a raging alcoholic."

"He is both those things," Portland agreed, "but that doesn't mean he'd lie about something this serious."

"Lie? Probably not. But all that alcohol eats away at the brain. Maybe his memory isn't what it should be."

Portland didn't buy Tompkins's reason for not giving credence to what Kelsey had told him about Trevor's demise but left his thoughts unstated. Instead, he said, "Let's just say that Kelsey has given me reason to believe that SureSafe was behind the murder of my son."

"And you may be right, David. Look, what you do with what Kelsey has told you is your call. But before you leave London have you given any thought to how we might proceed in establishing what happened in Nigeria to the Leicasters' son, and how we can better protect our citizens from meeting a similar fate? The situation there is deteriorating. British workers are being kidnapped, or worse."

"Don't think I haven't been thinking about it, Freddie. My heart goes out to the Leicasters. Know what I think?"

"What?"

"The answer to your question lies with SureSafe. British oil interests, along with others, hire SureSafe to protect their workers. They're security experts who are supposed to lay down their lives to protect their clients. Instead, they're a bunch of thugs headed by a French scum named Fournier. You want to protect your citizens, Freddie? Get rid of Fournier and SureSafe and bring in a legitimate security force."

"I appreciate your honest input, David, and I'll take what you've suggested under advisement. But I have one more question. Why would SureSafe, and especially this Frenchman you mention, kill your son and the Leicasters' son?"

"I don't know" was Portland's answer.

Matthew Kelsey had claimed that Trevor had joined forces with MEND in its war on foreign oil companies, and had been involved in a raid that led to his death. Portland thought back to having read some of Trevor's diary entries in which he expressed his anger at the oil companies for raping the Niger Delta and its people. Could what Kelsey had claimed be true, that Trevor had actually joined forces with MEND in an attack on XCAL? While that possibility existed, Portland couldn't accept it. Yes, his son had been a typical idealistic dreamer of making the world a better and fairer place, a youthful fantasy that Portland understood.

But would he have gone to the extent of joining with MEND and physically attacking an oil company's facilities and maybe killing people in the process?

CHAPTER 30

Portland called Elizabeth at home. The machine answered, and while he was disappointed at not reaching her he enjoyed the sound of her voice on the outgoing message.

A call to her office resulted in her secretary informing him that Ms. Sims was in a meeting and couldn't be disturbed.

"Thanks," he said. "Tell her that her former husband, David, called."

Having struck out connecting with Elizabeth, he called Brixton's office and had better fortune.

"David," Brixton said. "Great hearing from you. Where are you?"

"In Washington."

"You devil, sneaking back without telling me. How are things?"

"I decided at the last minute to catch a flight. What's new here?"

"Not a lot. Was your trip a success?"

"Yes, I'd say it was, although I'm still trying to figure out why. Free for dinner?"

"Sure. It's Flo's late night at the shop."

Brixton was glad that Portland was back in D.C. He'd bonded with the Brit, something that didn't happen often in his life. That the two men were engaged in roughly the same sort of vocation played a role in cementing their friendship, as did their shared cynicism of the world and its people. Both had lost a child in a dramatic, brutal way. But equally important for Brixton was Portland's unwillingness to compromise his values and beliefs in the interest of expediency. Taking the easy way out was anathema for both men.

Mac Smith had been away from the office taking a deposition. He returned at four.

"Got a few minutes?" Brixton asked.

"Sure. What's up?"

"I got hold of Ammon Dimka. He's agreed to see me tomorrow at noon."

"Did you raise with him the possibility of coming forth and telling what he knows about Bright Horizons and its role in Nigerian financial scams?"

"Yeah, I did. He didn't promise anything, but he didn't rule it out either."

"That he even agreed to discuss it with you is positive."

"That's the way I read it. I asked if he'd be willing to sit down with you."

"And he said?"

"He said he'd think about it. I'm a little leery about getting him too much involved."

"Why?"

"He's a good guy with a nice family. I'd hate to see anything bad happen to him."

"He obviously knows the risk of going public about Bright Horizons."

"Sure he does. I just hope it doesn't backfire on him."

Brixton checked in with Flo at Flo's Fashions before leaving the office to meet Portland at Legal Sea Foods on Seventh Street, N.W.

"When did David get back?" she asked.

"Earlier today. How's things at the shop? Selling lots of dresses?"

"No. The weather is keeping people from shopping."

Brixton laughed. "That's D.C. for you. A few snowflakes and everybody panics."

"Say hello to David for me."

"Shall do. See you at home."

Portland seemed edgy when he joined Brixton at a table in the bar area, and Brixton mentioned it.

"I suppose I am a little edgy," Portland said. "My time in London this trip was informative. It was also unsettling."

"How so?"

He told Brixton of his meeting with Matthew Kelsey, and Kelsey's claim that he saw Alain Fournier shoot his son.

"Just like that?" Brixton said. "He shot him?"

Portland sighed and picked at his crab cocktail. "According to Kelsey," he said, "Trevor had joined forces with MEND to attack an oil facility."

Brixton hesitated before asking, "Is that—well, is that a possibility?"

"It's possible." Portland went on to tell Brixton about Trevor's diary entries.

"You think your son was capable of joining the rebels?" Brixton asked.

Portland shrugged. "Trevor was an idealist like most young people. If he did join up with MEND it was the wrong way to make his point."

They fell silent and ate. Brixton's thoughts were with his daughter Janet, who'd been killed by a terrorist bomb in a D.C. outdoor café. She, like Portland's son, had navigated her young life on her own terms, although her premature death was not the result of a decision she'd made. She and her father had met for a drink after he'd left work at the State Department. She'd wanted financial support to launch a project with her current boyfriend, an idea that Brixton thought was stupid. But what did that matter? He'd sensed a problem was brewing and walked away. She remained just long enough to be blown up by a young Arab woman at an adjacent table.

What a world.

Brixton brought up his appointment with Ammon Dimka the following day and explained the reason for meeting.

"You think this guy is willing to blow the whistle on Bright Horizons?" Portland asked.

"Yeah, I think he might," said Brixton.

Portland sat back and shook his head.

"What's the matter?" Brixton asked.

"I was just thinking how we both have an interest in Nigeria. For you it's because some gullible people get suckered into a Nigerian financial scam. For me it's because my son was killed there."

"Maybe there's a way we can work together," Brixton said.

They ordered coffee and a slice of lemon cheesecake: "Two forks, please."

Before they left the restaurant Portland asked about Ammon Dimka.

"He's a nice guy, family man, couple of daughters."

"I'd like to meet him."

"I'll give him a call and see if he minds if I bring you along."

Brixton used his cell phone and reached Dimka. "I mentioned my friend David Portland the last time I was with you," he said, and reiterated why Portland had a vested interest in what was happening in Nigeria. "He'd like to meet you when we get together tomorrow."

Dimka's silence said that he was considering Brixton's request. Finally, he said, "Yes, please bring him. I'll make an extra sandwich."

CHAPTER 31

Dimka took the call in the small room that he used as his study, where he'd been reviewing bids for a prospective client. He was glad that his wife hadn't been present. As much as he hated being dishonest with her about his plans to meet again with Brixton—and now with his British friend as well—he was only too aware of her concerns, and had decided that it was better to keep her in the dark. He'd come to the conclusion that it was his moral obligation to expose Bright Horizons for what it really was, a conduit for millions of dollars bilked from naïve people around the world. It had also, he knew, functioned as an enforcer for various government interests, a strong-arm extension of warlords such as Agu Gwantam. But while he was aware that exposing these aspects of Bright Horizons carried with it a certain danger, he simultaneously felt that nothing bad could come out of it. He was no longer living in Nigeria, where violence was commonplace. This was the United States of America, a nation in which he'd been allowed to forge a decent life for his wife and daughters. If he could help in some way to right a wrong, it was his duty to do so.

He turned off the lamp on his desk and quietly went upstairs to join his wife where she'd fallen asleep in a chair while reading a book.

"Let's get to bed, sleepyhead," he said softly, kissing her cheek. "I love you."

CHAPTER 32

WASHINGTON—VIRGINIA

Mac Smith had spent a portion of the previous night researching means of bringing a lawsuit against a foreign government and its entities in the United States. It was complex, as one would imagine. Foreign governments enjoy immunity, and trying to bring legal action against them is like trying to slam a revolving door. As least that's how Mac characterized it to Annabel over breakfast that morning.

"But an organization like Bright Horizons is fraudulently bilking U.S. citizens of millions of dollars," Annabel offered, trading her chef's hat for her legal one.

"True," Mac said, "but the question is whether Bright Horizons is an official extension of the Nigerian government, or is run as a private enterprise. Trying to trace the organization's roots is like—well, it's like my revolving door analogy."

"From what you've learned it's basically run by some warlord in southern Nigeria," she said.

"That's also true," Mac said, finishing up his scrambled eggs, "but the government in Nigeria uses at least some of the money to fund various charitable projects." He patted his mouth with his napkin and sat back. "I haven't finished researching it, but I have the sinking suspicion that Mr. Borilli doesn't have a chance in hell of recouping any of the money his father sent them. Sad but true."

Annabel didn't say what she was thinking. While she wanted to help her husband forge a case for Borilli, she was, at once, not unhappy that he might choose to drop it.

"I'm also thinking that by bringing a case, no matter how weak it might be, we can raise public awareness of these Nigerian scams and head off other tragedies like the one the Borilli family has suffered," Mac said.

"Use the press?"

"Right."

"I'd think twice before doing that," she counseled.

"Or three times," he said.

He took his plate and coffee cup into the kitchen, rinsed them, put them in the dishwasher, and offered to do the same for Annabel.

"I have it," she said, "but thanks. You're off for the day?"

"Duty calls. I have a few things to go over with Robert this morning."

"What's he up to these days?"

"I'll find out when we meet."

Annabel's concerns about her husband's involvement with the Borilli case stayed with her as she left their Watergate apartment and headed to open her pre-Columbian gallery in Georgetown. That Mac would become immersed in what was obviously a losing battle didn't surprise her. Besides being an astute and savvy attorney, he was a man for whom injustice and human suffering dictated his approach to law, and to life in general. Lately, he'd been consumed with the growing gap between the haves and the have-nots in the country, which he often cited as having been the cause of the collapse of past societies.

But those thoughts were soon replaced by more pragmatic ones, on this morning preparing for the arrival of a potential buyer of two painted baked clay tripod plates from the Mayan culture, circa 600–675. She'd purchased the plates from a collector in San Salvador and was anxious to find a buyer. She felt that she'd paid too much for them and was anxious to recoup her investment. Knowing what to pay for pre-Columbian items, and setting a price for buyers, was always the most difficult decision she had to make.

As Annabel pondered how to price the plates, Mac Smith met in his office with Brixton.

"So you're going back to meet with Mr. Dimka," Mac said after his secretary had delivered coffee and a plate of freshly baked lemon cookies.

"Yeah," Brixton said. "I was surprised that he agreed. I was up front with him, said that I wanted to discuss his going public with what he knows about Bright Horizons."

"And he didn't balk?"

"No. I also asked if I could bring you along, but he nixed that idea."

"But he said okay for David Portland to accompany you."

Brixton nodded. "I think he's a very confused guy when it comes to revealing what he knows about Nigerian financial scams. He has family back in Nigeria; I saw them in his wedding pictures."

"What about his wife?" Smith asked.

"I've never met her, but I get the feeling that she might not be too keen on him talking to me. Can't blame her. She's got two little kids and is building a life here in the States. She doesn't need her husband getting involved in controversy."

"Interesting that he agreed for you to bring David with you," Smith said.

"I told him about David's son being killed in Nigeria, and that maybe the same people who killed him might be involved with the financial scams. Whatever the reason, he agreed."

Their meeting ended when Smith left for an appointment. Brixton went to his office and went over a list of questions he'd formulated to ask Dimka. An hour later Mrs. Warden announced that Mr. Portland had arrived.

As they drove to Virginia in Brixton's Subaru he was aware of the funk that his friend had fallen into. Portland said little while at Brixton's office and continued his relative silence during the trip. It was obvious to Brixton that his friend's recent trip to the UK, and his meeting with the man who claimed to have seen Trevor Portland gunned down, was occupying his mind, no surprise. Brixton, too, spent a portion of the drive thinking back to when his daughter had been blown up in the outdoor café by a young, misguided Middle Eastern woman, and he wondered as he drove whether that memory would ever fade far enough into the distance to not hurt anymore. Probably not. That sort of pain imbedded itself into your DNA, and you'd better learn to live with it.

They turned onto Dimka's street and Brixton pulled up to the curb. The driveway was empty. Brixton had noticed on his previous visit that the Dimkas had two vehicles and that both had been parked in the driveway. Why didn't they use the attached two-car garage? he wondered. Maybe, like many garages, it was chockablock full of things other than what it was designed to hold—cars. He assumed that Dimka's wife had taken one of the cars to work this morning. Did the absence of the second car mean that Dimka wasn't home, perhaps had forgotten the meeting?

"Tell me more about this Dimka character," Portland said, breaking into Brixton's train of thought. "You trust him?"

His question surprised Brixton. "Trust him? What's not to trust?"

"I don't know," Portland said. "I'm gun-shy when it comes to Nigerians. Maybe what happened to Trevor has turned me against anyone from that place."

"I can understand that, David, but Dimka is a really nice guy. He's evidently willing to use what he knows from firsthand experience to help put a stop to these Nigerian scams. I admire him."

"Then let's go," Portland said, undoing his seat belt and opening the passenger door. Brixton turned off the ignition and followed. They stood in the empty driveway and took in their surroundings. Portland commented on how every house on the block had a neatly manicured lawn and nicely trimmed shrubs. He peered around the side of the house and saw that the yard, with an elaborate yellow-and-red jungle-gym structure, abutted a small wooded area.

"Nice neighborhood," Portland commented.

"The American dream, huh?" Brixton said. "I hope he's home." He approached the front door and had just reached to ring the doorbell when a loud explosion came from the rear of the house.

"What the hell was that?" Portland said.

His question was answered by a ball of flame that rose into the sky from the site of the explosion.

"Jesus!" Brixton muttered as he tried the door. It was unlocked and he pushed it open. A cloud of dense black smoke rolled from inside and hit him in the face, forcing him back. The strong odor of gasoline accompanied the smoke, the combination gagging Brixton. He wiped his eyes, spit, and peered through the swirling black smoke to the rear portion of the house where he and Dimka had met in the Nigerian's study.

Portland pulled a handkerchief from his pocket and pressed it to his face as he pushed past Brixton and entered the foyer. Brixton did the same. He saw through the smoke that the door to the study was open. He took bold steps into the living room, crossed it, his eyes stinging, his breathing labored, and reached the study. The heat from the fire was intense; Brixton and Portland felt as though their faces were on fire.

"It's him!" Brixton shouted, pointing to the prone body of Ammon Dimka on the floor in front of his desk. Sheets of yellow-

and-red flames rising up from the rear of the room now ignited the ceiling tiles.

"Come on," Brixton said.

They entered the room, coughing, tearing up, and cursing under their breaths. The house's smoke alarms went off and emitted a constant beeping as Portland bent over Dimka.

"Let's get him out of here," Brixton said.

Portland grabbed Dimka beneath his arms and Brixton started to lift him by his legs. As he did his attention went to the desk on which a package rested. He could barely make out what was written on it through the smoke but managed to see that someone, presumably Dimka, had written in bold strokes with a marker: **For Mr. Brixton**.

Brixton released his grip on Dimka's legs and grabbed the package. Portland dragged Dimka from the study and across the living room. Brixton followed, stumbling blindly through the room and out the front door, where Portland fell to his knees next to Dimka's body. Brixton drew deep breaths, his lungs threatening to burst. Portland grabbed Dimka's wrist and felt for a pulse. He looked up at Brixton and shook his head. Brixton placed his ear to Dimka's chest. He heard nothing. His eyes went to the side of Dimka's head. "Look!" he said. Dimka's skull was caved in, his hair matted with blood.

"He fall and hit his head?" Portland conjectured.

Before Brixton could reply their attention was diverted by the sound of a siren and the voices of neighbors who'd rushed from their homes and gathered across the street. Brixton looked back at the house, now engulfed in flames.

A marked patrol car screeched to a halt at the foot of the driveway. Two uniformed officers jumped out and joined Brixton and Portland, who hovered over Ammon Dimka's lifeless body.

"What happened?" one of the officers asked.

"I don't know," Brixton managed. "The place blew up."

With that another explosion occurred, the house's natural gas supply igniting, the force of it sending everyone stumbling back onto the front lawn.

"Get Dimka!" Brixton shouted.

He and Portland dragged the Nigerian expat away from the building and down to the lawn. Other sirens were now heard in the distance, the local fire department responding to a 911 call. Another police car arrived, joined by a Fire Department ambulance manned by two EMTs who immediately tended to Dimka. But it took only a few seconds for them to announce that he was dead.

As firemen set about fighting the flames—"The place is a goner!" one yelled—a police officer beckoned for Portland and Brixton to follow him to his patrol car. Portland obliged, but Brixton, bent over, hands on his hips, his breath coming in spurts, broke off and made his way through the crowd to a neighbor's driveway from where he could see beyond the burning house and into the backyard and wooded area that separated the Dimka property from another house and suburban street. A flash of yellow in the trees caught his attention. A man wearing a yellow shirt stood on the perimeter of the trees watching the inferno. It meant nothing to Brixton at first. Many people stood gaping at the scene. But something caused him—call it intuition honed by years of police work—to start toward the man. As he did, the individual in the yellow shirt turned and ran through the trees to the street.

There was no confusion now for Brixton, no second-guessing. Despite his chronically painful right knee that throbbed, he hobbled off after him, swearing as he went. The yellow shirt emerged from the woods and got into a car parked at the curb. Brixton reached the street just as the man started the engine and pulled away, tires squealing and kicking up smoke. Brixton's training took hold. He focused on the car, a two-door black Mercedes sedan with a license plate whose last two numbers were 64 and that had the word "Representation" on the lower right portion.

"Hey, you!"

Two uniformed police officers headed in his direction.

"Don't move," one commanded.

"I'm not going anywhere," Brixton said.

"Why did you run?"

"Run? I wasn't running, at least not *from* anything. I saw this man—"

"Come with us," a cop said.

"Sure," said Brixton, accompanying them to where two other officers stood with Portland. The cacophony around them made conversation difficult, and they had to raise their voices to be heard.

"He's the one was with you?" Portland was asked.

"Yes. That's what I said. We came here to meet with the owner of the house and—"

"Why?"

"Why *what*?" Brixton said. "Like my friend said, we—"

"Why were you meeting with him?"

Brixton started to reach for his wallet to withdraw his P.I. license, but one of the officers stopped him.

"I'm a private investigator," Brixton said. "I have my I.D."

"You're armed?"

"Yeah." Brixton raised his arms to allow the officer to remove his handgun from its hip holster.

"Show me your I.D."

Brixton did.

"What about you?" Portland was asked.

"I already told you that I work in security for the British Embassy here in Washington."

"You were meeting with the homeowner because of your job?"

"No. You see—"

Brixton interrupted. "Look, Officer," he said. "Mr. Portland and I had an appointment to see the homeowner—his name is Dimka, Ammon Dimka—to discuss something having to do with his knowledge of Nigeria. What about his family? He has a wife and two kids. Has somebody contacted her so she doesn't come home to *this*?" He pointed to the house, which by now was almost totally destroyed despite the firefighters' efforts. The fire had reached the garage, where a single vehicle was now engulfed in flames and threatening to explode at any minute.

A woman with a youngster in tow came to them. "Oh, my God," she said, "this is terrible. Is Abi all right, her children? Is Ammon—?"

Brixton waited for the officers to reply. When they didn't, Brixton said, "We're sure that Mrs. Dimka and the children weren't here when it happened."

"Ammon?"

"I'm afraid that—"

She broke down and wept. "I can't believe this," she said. "They're such nice people, good neighbors, kind and considerate, and—"

Brixton remembered the package he'd taken from Dimka's desk and dropped on the front lawn. It was still there.

"You want anything else from us?" he asked the officers.

"We want your statements. We'll take them at headquarters. You were here when the fire started."

"When somebody torched the place, you mean," Brixton said.

"How do you know that?" asked a cop.

Brixton decided that he'd said enough. The officer started to repeat his question when a car pulled up with **ARSON** on its doors. Another officer announced that the owner's wife had been notified at her place of business and was on her way.

"Come with us to headquarters," a cop said.

"We'll follow you in our car," Portland said.

The two officers agreed. "That's your car at the curb?" one asked.

"Right," Brixton said. "Don't worry, we won't try to take off."

Brixton and Portland started toward the Subaru. They'd almost reached it when Brixton remembered the package on the lawn. "Give me a minute," he told Portland, and went to retrieve it, glancing back to be sure that he wasn't being observed. He picked up the package, secured it under his arm, and watched as Ammon Dimka's body, covered with a sheet, was carried to the ambulance and placed inside.

"How much do you want to tell them about Dimka and the reason we're here?" Portland asked.

"As little as possible," Brixton said, looking back at what was once the Dimka family home. "I never met Dimka's wife, but I feel like I should be here when she arrives."

"Maybe it's better that you aren't," Portland said.

They got in the car and waited for a patrol vehicle to lead them to police headquarters.

"That fire was deliberately set," Brixton said. "Did you smell the gas?"

"Couldn't miss it," said Portland.

"An arson investigation will confirm it. The question for me is whether whoever did it knew that I was coming to meet with Dimka. If that's the case, how would anyone know that we were scheduled to meet? Did that same person know about my first get-together with Dimka? What did they do, tap his phone? The only people who knew that I was coming here, aside from you, are Mac Smith, my receptionist, Mrs. Warden, and Flo."

"You spoke with Dimka on the phone," Portland said.

"Sure, a few times."

Maybe *your* phone is tapped," Portland muttered.

The squad car pulled up and an officer motioned for them to follow.

"I might have seen who set the fire," Brixton commented as they drove.

Portland turned in his seat. "When?"

Brixton told the Brit of the man in the yellow shirt and how he'd run away when he saw him approaching.

"Not an especially intelligent chap," Portland commented, "staying around after the deed was done."

"The plate on the black Mercedes he was driving is from the District. I got the last two numbers of it."

"Easy to trace."

"Maybe. We'll see."

"Somebody gave him a hell of a whack to the head," Portland said.

"That's what killed him," Brixton said glumly. "The fire was probably started to cover it up."

Portland noticed the package that Brixton had taken from Dimka's study and dropped on the floor between the seats. "What's in that?" he asked, picking it up.

"I'll know when I open it. I just want to get this over with and get back to my office, where I can take a look."

"These cops think that you and I might have had something to do with the fire."

"They'll get over it," Brixton said as he pulled into the local police department's parking lot. Brixton shoved the package beneath his seat, and he and Portland were led inside, where they were settled in a small, sparsely furnished interrogation room. One of the officers who'd come from the house fire was joined by another uniformed cop who was introduced as "the chief," a beefy, pleasant man with ruddy cheeks.

"I don't know why we're here," Brixton said. "Like we told the officers, we had a meeting scheduled with Mr. Dimka, who owned the house. We were at the front door when the explosion took place. We managed to get inside, spotted Dimka on the floor, and dragged him outside. We were too late."

"Overcome by the smoke?" the chief asked.

"Can't be," said Brixton. "His head was bashed in before somebody torched the house. The smoke had just started, not enough time to overcome anybody."

"'Torched the house'?" the chief said. "You're saying the fire was deliberately set?"

"Looked that way to me," Brixton said.

"Why would somebody do that?" asked the chief.

"It's a black family," the other cop in the room said. "Maybe—"

"A hate crime?" the chief said.

That possibility had crossed Brixton's mind, but it didn't play for him. As far as he knew, the Dimkas had settled comfortably into the neighborhood and were liked and respected. Of course there could always have been some racist nut who decided to play out his hatred, but Brixton didn't think so. It had to have been because Dimka was about to go public with what he knew about Nigerian financial scams.

The chief looked at Portland. "You're with the British Embassy?" he said.

"That's right."

"And you were meeting with the homeowner, too?"

"Right again."

The second officer said, "You told me something about meeting with him because of what he knows about Nigeria."

"About Nigerian financial scams," Portland said.

"Why would you be interested in that?" the chief asked.

"My son was—"

"Your son got caught up in one of those scams?"

"No, he—it doesn't make any difference. I came along with Mr. Brixton to meet Mr. Dimka. I'm sorry I didn't have the chance."

Brixton hesitated mentioning his spotting of the man in the yellow shirt. He'd made a decision while driving that because the plate on the Mercedes indicated that it was registered in the District of Columbia, he'd take that scant information to friends at D.C.'s MPD instead of leaving it with the suburban cops.

After another twenty minutes the chief thanked them for

being there, his only request that they be available should the investigation into the fire raise other questions.

"You have my handgun," Brixton said. "It's licensed."

The chief looked to the other officer, who left the room, returning moments later with the weapon. He handed it to Brixton without a word.

"Thanks," Brixton said. He gave the chief his business card, and Portland wrote his contact information on a slip of paper. They left the low brick building, got in Brixton's car, and headed back to Brixton's office.

"I want to see what Dimka left me in this package," he said.

"Mind if I tag along?"

"Hell, no. I'd be disappointed if you didn't."

CHAPTER 33

WASHINGTON, D.C.

Mac and Annabel Smith were in Mac's office when Brixton and Portland arrived.

"David, good to see you," Mac said.

"Always a pleasure." Portland shook Smith's hand. "And good to see you again, Mrs. Smith."

"How did your meeting with Mr. Dimka go?" Mac asked after they'd taken seats around a conference table.

Brixton and Portland looked at each other before Brixton answered, "It never happened, Mac."

"Oh? He wasn't there?"

"He was there all right," said Brixton. "He was dead."

Brixton's blunt statement brought a hush to the table.

"Dead?" Annabel said.

"Somebody killed him and torched his house," Portland said.

"My God," said Annabel. "How terrible."

"You say someone killed him?" Smith said. "Do you have any idea who?"

Brixton shrugged. "I saw somebody run from the scene and

got a partial reading of his car's tag, but I can't be sure he was the killer."

"You never got to speak with Dimka?" Smith asked.

"Not today," Brixton said, shaking his head. "Whoever did it started one hell of a fire. The house was damn near burned to the ground when we left." He went on to tell them of having been interviewed by a local Virginia police chief. "I grabbed this before it burned up along with everything else." He handed the package to Smith, who turned it over in his hands.

"He obviously wanted you to have this," Smith said, indicating Brixton's name on it. "Do you know what's in it?"

"We're about to find out," Brixton said.

He took it from Smith and peeled off the strip of tape that sealed it, removed the large envelope's contents, and spread them on the table. The piece on top was a letter that Dimka had written to Brixton in anticipation of their getting together. Brixton read the first of three pages and handed it to Smith, who did the same and passed it to the others. The letter was, in effect, a synopsis of what Dimka had intended to verbally tell Brixton when they met.

After the four of them had read the correspondence, Annabel said, "It's almost as though he had a premonition that you wouldn't have a chance to talk."

Brixton, who'd gone on to begin reading the next letter from the package, handed it to Smith. It was a letter Dimka had written about his wife, Abiola, in which he professed his undying love and acknowledged that what he was doing regarding the infamous Nigerian financial scams could—and he underlined the word "could"—anger some people sufficiently to seek retribution.

Brixton read that sentence aloud and slapped the letter on the table. "Damn it!" he growled. "He knew he was in trouble talking to me and wanted things on the record in case anything happened to him. He's dead *because* of me."

"Not because of anything you did, Robert," Portland said. "If he hadn't decided to confide in you it would have been someone else. He also talked to your newspaper pal, Sayers."

"Yeah, but that doesn't make me feel any better. What I want to know is who was aware that Dimka and I were meeting and knew the reason that we were getting together."

"You say that you got a partial read on the car the man running from the scene used," Smith said.

"It was a District plate. I know that. Last numbers were six and four."

"Want me to run it past Zeke Borgeldt at MPD?" Smith asked.

"I'd appreciate that," said Brixton. "It was a black Mercedes, four-door."

Annabel asked, "Is it possible it was a hate crime directed at a black family in a white suburb?"

"That's always possible," Brixton agreed, "but it's too much of a coincidence that it coincided with my appointment with him."

Smith said, "This letter that Mr. Dimka left doesn't pull punches. He ties Bright Horizons to the Nigerian financial scams, and even implicates SureSafe, the security firm. It almost sounds from what he's written that Bright Horizons functions as an enforcing arm for SureSafe at certain times."

"I'm not surprised," said Portland. "SureSafe is evil. The Frenchman who heads it in Nigeria, Alain Fournier, is the guy who killed my son."

Mac and Annabel exchanged glances before Mac said, "Dimka mentions this warlord in southern Nigeria, Agu Gwantam. He seems to be at the crux of much of this. You mentioned him to me, Robert, and a friend I had drinks with, Ralph Cleland—he's the Nigerian financial scams expert at the Commerce Department—also mentioned Gwantam."

"What's the next step?" Annabel asked.

"I'll get hold of Zeke at MPD and see if he can get a fix on the car," Mac said.

"I feel like I should try and make contact with Dimka's wife," Brixton said.

"It might be too soon for that," Annabel counseled.

Portland's cell phone rang. He excused himself and took the call in a far corner of the room. When he returned he said, "That was Conan, my boss at the embassy. He wants to see me. I'd better get over there. He's probably wondering where I've been."

Portland and Brixton left, Portland to meet with his superior, Brixton to tie up loose ends in his office.

Smith called Chief of Detectives Zeke Borgeldt. After some preliminary chitchat—they'd been friends for a long time and often enjoyed nights out with their spouses—he gave him the license plate information that Brixton had provided.

"Why does he want it?" Borgeldt asked. He and Brixton had butted heads on more than one occasion, and while he respected Brixton's work as a private investigator, their personalities often clashed.

Smith gave him a capsule recap of the burning of Dimka's house in Virginia, and how Brixton had caught sight of a man leaving the scene.

"How is my favorite private eye?" Borgeldt asked sarcastically.

"Robert is fine, Zeke. He sends his best."

Which wasn't true but it seemed the thing to say.

"I'll run the plate," Borgeldt said, "but tell me more about this house fire. You say Brixton claims it was torched deliberately?"

"Not only that," Smith said, "the owner of the house, a Nigerian expat, Ammon Dimka, was murdered before the house went up. Brixton and a friend of his were supposed to meet with Dimka. They arrived just as the fire started and in time to drag Dimka from the inferno. Somebody had bashed his head in."

"I'm glad it's Virginia's problem and not ours," Borgeldt said through a laugh. "I'll run the plate and call you."

Borgeldt phoned Smith an hour later.

"It's a rental," he said.

"Who rented it?"

"A phony name, phony license, paid cash."

"Can whoever processed the rental give a description of the man who rented it?"

"I already asked, Mac, knowing you'd want that. The agent says that she doesn't remember what he looked like, just that he wore a bright yellow shirt."

"That matches up with what Brixton saw," said Smith.

"Great. We can pull in every guy who owns a yellow shirt. Sorry, Mac."

Smith thanked him and turned to another legal matter on his docket.

In the meantime Portland went to the British Embassy, where his boss, Conan Lester, awaited his arrival.

"How are you, David?" Lester asked.

"Fine."

"The trip to London worked out?"

"It seemed to. What do you hear from across the pond?"

"Freddie Tompkins was impressed with you. He told me that you'd met with a former SureSafe operative named Kelsey."

"Right. Kelsey is a mess personally, but not so much that he wasn't helpful to me. He claims that he saw my son Trevor shot in the head by Alain Fournier, SureSafe's top guy in the Niger Delta."

"Yes, Tompkins told me. Look, let me be blunt. You know that I hold you in high regard and that I lobbied to have you join the staff here at the embassy."

"And I've appreciated what you've done for me."

"The problem is that we've had a series of incidents here at the embassy, protests of our government's actions in the Middle East, verbal attacks—at least they're only verbal at this juncture—about the festering problems between the UK and Ireland and Scottish oil." Portland started to speak, but Lester cut him off. "You obviously have something weighing heavily on you, David.

Your son's murder was horrific, and I can only wonder how I would react while trying to make sense out of it, bring those responsible to justice."

Portland knew where Lester was heading.

"I want you to take a leave of absence from your post. You can keep your apartment, and I'll be able to keep you on salary for a month, maybe two—but no longer." He held up his hand against what he assumed Portland was about to say. "I don't have any choice," he added, "aside from canning you, which I don't want to do."

"Conan," Portland said, coming forward in his chair, "you don't have to explain. I understand the situation you're in and the decision you have to make. Frankly, I considered asking you for a leave of absence. I need time to sort out this thing about my son. It's on my mind day and night and gets in the way of my job here. Hopefully, I'll get to the bottom of it a lot sooner than a month."

Portland left Lester's office feeling as though a massive weight had been lifted from his shoulders. He'd felt guilt about time away from his job at the embassy and was relieved that he was now free to pursue the circumstances of Trevor's murder.

He went to his apartment and called his ex, Elizabeth, at her office. Her secretary answered.

"This is David, her former husband. I need to speak with her."

"I'll see if Ms. Sims is available," the secretary replied imperiously.

"Free for dinner?" Portland asked pleasantly when Elizabeth came on the line.

"No. Why?"

He laughed. "Do I have to have some deep, dark reason for asking my ex-wife out to dinner?"

"What's this *really* all about, David?"

"Let's see. First, I'm on a leave of absence from my job at the embassy. I'm free to pursue what happened to Trevor full-time.

Second, I spent part of my day at an arson and murder scene in suburban Virginia that might tie in with Trevor's death. If that isn't enough, I'd enjoy sitting in a candlelit bistro with the lovely Elizabeth Sims."

She laughed despite herself.

"Seven? You choose the restaurant. Not only will I gladly pick up the tab; you'll benefit from what I've learned about what happened to our son."

She started to correct him—Trevor was *his* son, her stepson—but didn't.

"All right," she said. "But you pick a place."

He thought back to having had drinks with Brixton at the Watergate Hotel, and perusing the menu for its Aquarelle Restaurant. It was out of his price range, and the dishes sounded heavy on the sauces, but what the hell?

"The Aquarelle at the Watergate," he said.

Elizabeth's silence said much.

"You're sure?" she said.

"Hey, don't worry. I'll wear a suit."

"I'll meet you there."

"Sure you don't want me to pick you up?"

"No, I—I'll see you there at seven."

Had he been able to see Elizabeth following the phone call, he would have known that she was enthusiastic about dinner with her ex. Although there was nothing tangible to point to, she'd spent the day strangely apprehensive about what was going on at the law firm of Cale, Watson and Warnowski.

CHAPTER 34

WASHINGTON, D.C.

Cameron Chambers, CW&W's chief of investigations, prepared to leave his office. He'd met late that afternoon with Marvin Baxter, the tech expert, to pay him his fee for tapping Elizabeth's and David Portland's phones, and to receive Baxter's initial report of what the taps had produced. They rendezvoused at a fast-food outlet in downtown D.C.

Chambers had never liked Baxter. He considered him a devious nerd who'd carved out a living eavesdropping on unsuspecting people. Not that Chambers hadn't benefited from Baxter's expertise while with the Washington MPD. And, of course, there was the George Abbott case, concerning which he had to admit when it was over that Cale had been right about the young lawyer's treason. Still, there was something distasteful about tapping phones, especially that of someone like Elizabeth Sims, who, from everything Chambers knew, was a loyal member of the law firm's staff.

In Chambers's eyes Baxter looked like the weasel he was. He was short, slender, always dressed in a jacket and tie and wearing glasses with lenses the thickness of soda bottle bottoms, and his high-pitched voice matched his appearance. There was also an air of intellectual superiority about him that was off-putting. But his personal feelings about Baxter didn't matter. Walter Cale was Baxter's rabbi, and Cale called the shots.

"Here's your retainer," Chambers said as he handed Baxter an envelope containing cash he'd picked up from the law firm's accounting department on his way to the meeting.

Baxter took it without comment.

"So, what have your taps learned so far?" Chambers asked, not attempting to mask his indifference.

Baxter pulled a piece of paper from his jacket pocket and made a show of smoothing it on the tabletop. "There isn't much, of course," he said, "because I've just started, but Mr. Portland called Ms. Sims at her place of employment." He cited the precise time the call had taken place. "Mr. Portland has arranged to have dinner with Ms. Sims at Aquarelle, at the Watergate, at seven this evening."

Chambers felt a stab of jealousy.

"What else?" he asked.

"I have nothing as yet from Mr. Brixton's phone, but—"

"Brixton? I didn't ask for a tap on his phone."

"Mr. Cale ordered it."

"Why?"

"Mr. Cale said that Mr. Brixton and Mr. Portland are friends."

"So what?"

"I do what I'm told to do."

"Why are you talking to Cale? *I'm* your contact."

Baxter's smile was self-satisfied. "He called me and—"

"You take orders from *me*," Chambers said.

Baxter's small grin remained fixed. "I don't care who hires me," he said, "as long as I get paid."

Chambers glared at him. "I'll discuss this with Mr. Cale in the morning," he said.

"Sure. Thank you for the advance. I suggest that we meet here every day at this time."

"I'll set the time and place for us to meet," Chambers snapped. "Is there anything else?"

"I'll have more tomorrow when we meet."

Chambers got up abruptly, leaving his untouched soft drink on the table. He left the restaurant without another word to Baxter and went directly to his office, where he closed the door and pondered the situation.

His emotions and thoughts ran the gauntlet, from anger that Cale had usurped his authority with Baxter to a nagging displeasure that Elizabeth would be with her former husband at the romantic Aquarelle.

He considered calling Walter Cale and arranging a meeting at which he could voice his displeasure about being blindsided by Baxter. But after some reflection he abandoned that idea. The truth was that no matter how distasteful some of Cale's actions could be, he was the man in charge. He was the boss.

CHAPTER 35

Portland knew that his only suit needed cleaning and pressing, but there was no time for that before his dinner date with Elizabeth. He hung the suit in the shower and allowed the steam to eradicate the worst of the creases. Satisfied that the suit was presentable, he matched it with a clean white shirt and burgundy tie and headed for the Watergate complex, where he waited for Elizabeth to appear. He watched a succession of taxis discharge passengers, expecting each to have delivered her. Finally, at a few minutes past seven, she arrived.

"Sorry, David," she said as she pushed through the doors and crossed the lobby. "The driver got held up by an accident, just a fender bender, but you know how that can be."

"You're only five minutes late," he said.

"I like to be early."

"Yeah, you always were one of those people," he said, wondering whether it sounded judgmental. Her smile said it didn't.

"I was surprised that you chose Aquarelle," she said.

"I had drinks here with a pal," he said. "Maybe you've met

him. Robert Brixton. He does freelance work for the chap who heads up your investigative office."

"Yes, I did meet Mr. Brixton at the party they threw for me when I made partner."

"I'm impressed, you making partner and all."

"So you've said. We have a reservation?"

"I didn't make one," he said, "but I'm sure they can accommodate us."

The maître d' escorted them to a table for two in a corner of the candlelit, sedate room where he snapped open a white linen napkin and dropped it with a flourish on Elizabeth's lap after holding out her chair.

"Drink?" Portland asked.

He knew that she was wondering whether he would order something strongly alcoholic, considering his addicted past.

"White wine," he told the waiter.

She smiled and ordered a vodka gimlet, straight up. "I need to unwind," she said, as though justifying her choice.

"You used to drink scotch," he said.

"I still do on occasion," she said.

"I'm off the hard stuff," he said.

"That's good."

Had they been able to read each other's minds, they would have known that both were in a relaxed mood. The restaurant's seductive ambiance, flickering candles, comfortable chairs, and hushed noise level were conducive to relaxation. Behind them, visible through giant windows, was the Potomac River, the full moon's rays dancing on the river's ripples. The subdued lighting cast a particularly flattering glow over her naturally beautiful face and auburn mane.

Portland had decided after making the date that he would avoid, if possible, injecting topics into the conversation that might spoil what he hoped would be a pleasant, nonconfrontational evening. He was still in love with Elizabeth Sims, and harbored fantasies that they would one day be together again. She was, as far as he was concerned, the most beautiful female on earth. Adding to her natural beauty was a keen mind that saw through phonies and enabled her to make prudent decisions. He'd known from the earliest days of their breakup that he'd caused the marriage to unravel, and often questioned how it might have been different if *he'd* been different. He didn't suffer any illusions about the possibility of rekindling their romance, but it was nice to contemplate.

While he'd pledged to himself to keep the evening lighthearted and noncontroversial, he was, at once, eager to tell her what he'd learned from Matthew Kelsey about how Trevor had died, of his experience with Brixton at Ammon Dimka's murder and arson scene, and of his contentious meeting with Sir Manford Penny at XCAL's London headquarters. "Focus on her and be a good listener," he'd reminded himself on his way to the Watergate. "Don't make a mess of things like you usually do."

"So," he said, "what's new in your life, Liz?"

"Busy," she said. "The firm keeps me hopping, lots of travel."

"You're in London a lot."

"Yes."

"I just got back from there."

"I know. Manford Penny told me that you and he had—well, I suppose you could term it a discussion."

It hadn't occurred to Portland that Penny would have filled her in on their set-to.

Portland laughed. "That 'discussion' wasn't especially pleasant. I suppose he considers me a loose cannon."

"He had a few choice things to say."

"I'm sure he did. I'm surprised he reported it to you."

"It came up in conversation," she said.

"That's old hat," he said pleasantly. "Let's stick with Elizabeth Sims. How are things at the law firm?"

"As busy and complex as ever," she said. "The XCAL account

keeps me hopping. There are so many issues to be resolved, not only here in the States but wherever we have operations."

"Like Nigeria?"

"One of our biggest and most challenging operations," she said. "Manford—Manford Penny—has his hands full with all the upheaval going on in the delta."

It just came from his mouth.

"I don't like the guy," he said.

"Who?"

"Penny. Sir Manford or whatever he's called."

"He's XCAL's UK chairman," she said. "He's an important part of the company's management."

"Yeah, I know that, and I still don't like him. He's a fop, a quarter-inch deep." Portland winced. "But let's forget him. Tell me more about you and what you're doing."

Elizabeth cocked her head and leaned back in her chair. "Why would you be interested in my work, David?"

"Hey," he said, "I just want to use this evening as a way to get to know each other again. Naturally, I wonder what you're doing with your life, how things are going, whether you're happy. After all, you were my wife."

"Yes, I was."

"I loved you."

She adjusted herself in her chair.

"Maybe I still do."

She lowered her eyes.

"Don't get me wrong," he said. "I'm not trying to come on to you. I just want you to know that even though we split up I appreciated what I had, and I'll always be grateful for the way you and your folks brought up Trevor."

His words touched her. "I appreciate that," she said.

Satisfied that he'd diffused an uncomfortable scene over Manford Penny, he asked, "How's your love life?"

"Why would I discuss that with you?"

"Just curious."

"How's *your* love life?"

"Nonexistent," he said. "By the way, I've taken a leave of absence from my job at the embassy."

"Oh? Why? What do you intend to do?"

Since he'd led to that obvious question he replied, "Find out what happened to Trevor in Nigeria and right the wrong."

Their Caesar salads arrived in the nick of time.

"Nice salad," Portland said.

"Yes, very nice," Elizabeth said.

"So," he said, "we were talking about your work at the law firm."

She lowered her fork. "No, we weren't," she said. "We were talking about how you intend to right the wrong of Trevor's death."

Despite not wanting to spoil a quiet evening with her, he launched into what had transpired during his visit to Matthew Kelsey in Barrow-in-Furness. She listened intently. When he was finished he sat back and said, "That's it. Trevor was shot to death by the Frenchman, Alain Fournier, who heads up SureSafe in the Niger Delta, and he did it on instructions from someone I have to assume is with your client XCAL."

He expected a negative reaction from her for once again raising the contentious issue of Trevor's murder, and braced himself for it. To his surprise, her expression reflected not anger but concern. She said, "I understand why you feel the need to do this, David. I truly do. You may not think that it weighs heavily on my mind, too, but it does, day and night."

His readiness to defend himself was reduced to relief.

"I'm glad to hear you say that, Liz. I know that it puts you in an awkward position considering your role as XCAL's lead attorney."

Her laugh was rueful. "You've always been good at understatement," she said. "What I'd like to know is how far you've come in nailing down the who and why of Trevor's death, and your plans to right this wrong, as you put it. Let's say that this Frenchman, Fournier, did kill Trevor, and let's say that he did it upon orders from someone with XCAL in Nigeria. Are you planning some sort of legal action?"

His answer was interrupted by the waiter, who took Portland's order of a strip steak, medium rare, and Elizabeth's choice of John Dory. When the waiter had departed, Portland said, "There's nothing that can be done legally about it. From what I know the Nigerian legal system is broken beyond repair, like everything else in that country. But there's another aspect of this that I haven't mentioned."

"Mind if I have another drink?" she said.

"Of course not."

"You?"

"One's enough."

"You were saying?"

"I was saying that there's another aspect of this. My friend Robert Brixton and I went to Virginia to meet with a man who'd moved here from Nigeria with his wife and two children. Brixton made contact with him on behalf of his pal and attorney, Mac Smith, who represents a client whose father got caught up in one of those Nigerian financial scams and ended up killing himself. This Nigerian—his name was Dimka, Ammon Dimka—knew a lot about the scams and how they work, and was about to go public with what he knew. Unfortunately, someone killed him and set his house on fire just before we arrived."

"That's a terrible story, David, but what does it have to do with Trevor's death?"

"I don't have a definitive answer to that, Liz, but there is a connection." He went on to explain how SureSafe, the security company, provided protection for a warlord in the Niger Delta who controlled much of the money raised by the scams, and used a D.C.-based alleged "charity" to raise that money. "In other words," he said, "everything seems to involve SureSafe."

As though cued, the conversation changed to less weighty topics. They reminisced about their early days together, and laughter came easily. She told him about her father's illness, and he expressed his sympathy. By the time they'd shared a dessert and had finished coffee, the relaxed atmosphere he'd hoped the evening would create was very much in evidence. Although he couldn't read her mind and know what she was thinking, he was filled with loving thoughts to the extent that he wanted to hug and kiss her; it even crossed his mind to get down on one knee and propose marriage again.

They walked through the lobby and went outside, where a doorman hailed a taxi.

"Mind dropping me off?" he asked.

She hesitated before saying, "No."

As they climbed into the cab, Cameron Chambers, who'd decided to have a drink at the Watergate after dinner, left his seat at the bar and watched their departure. From what he observed they seemed comfortable with each other, too comfortable as far as he was concerned. He returned to the bar and stewed for the next half hour over his drink.

As the cabbie drove, Elizabeth said, "I'm glad we did this, David. Aquarelle is expensive but—"

"It doesn't matter," he said. "I can handle it. I'm just glad that we could enjoy an evening together."

The cab stopped in front of Portland's building.

"What's on your agenda tomorrow?" she asked.

"Haven't figured that out yet, Liz. I suppose I'd better start the process of leaving."

"Leaving? London again?"

"No, Nigeria."

"Nigeria? You're going there?"

"I have to if I'm ever going to put Trevor to rest, *really* put him to rest. I'll stay in touch before I go. Let's do this again, huh? It's great being with you."

She had more she wanted to say but didn't. Instead, she kissed him on the cheek and turned so he wouldn't see a tear that had run down her cheek. He got out, watched the taxi pull away, and gave it a halfhearted wave as it disappeared around a corner.

"I love you, Elizabeth Sims," he said aloud.

PART THREE

CHAPTER 36

WASHINGTON—VIRGINIA

Robert Brixton and Flo Combes had spent the evening at home, where she prepared a favorite of his, Welsh rarebit with bacon on English muffins, and a large green salad. Following dinner they flipped through channels on the television, catching up on what was going on in the world according to a variety of talking heads. Brixton eventually dozed in his chair, which prompted Flo to nudge him and suggest an early-to-bed evening. Brixton came alive the minute he was in bed and they enjoyed a spontaneous bout of lovemaking before turning off the lights.

Flo was up before the alarm went off the next morning. She was expecting a visit from an up-and-coming fashion designer from Los Angeles who was making the rounds of East Coast shops with the hope of persuading their owners to carry his designs. "He's very cutting-edge," she told Robert when he joined her at the kitchen table. "I'd be the first outlet in D.C. to carry his line."

Brixton was as interested in women's fashions as he was in home decorating and bird watching, but he feigned interest in what she said. He was immensely proud of what she'd accomplished in opening and managing the store, and lent a willing hand when it came to small construction projects and painting the walls. But the subtleties of what made for a winning design were lost on him. It was good that she knew.

"Busy day ahead?" she asked.

"Busy but dull. I'm back checking security clearances for the Justice Department. Not exciting, but it pays the rent. Any further thought about you going to L.A.?"

Flo had received an invitation the previous day to attend the Los Angeles Fashion Council's weeklong fashion show, which would kick off in a few days.

"I'd really like to go," she said. "It would give me a feeling of truly being involved in the fashion industry. Is it okay with you? I've already arranged for Cynthia to run the shop while I'm gone."

"It's fine with me as long as we repeat last night before you go."

She smiled. "Count on it," she said mischievously. She kissed him good-bye. "Tonight's a late night at the shop."

"Maybe I'll swing by and bring you some dinner."

"That'd be sweet," she said. "Bye."

He spent the morning querying neighbors of a job applicant in search of something nefarious in his background but as usual came up with nothing. He had visions when he signed on with Justice of uncovering and exposing a foreign mole seeking to worm his way into a sensitive position with the U.S. government, but that was what fantasies were made of. Everyone he investigated came up squeaky clean, which wasn't a surprise. You'd have to be really stupid to apply for a sensitive government position with your neighbors knowing that you're a devout Communist or member of ISIL.

After interviewing neighbors he decided to stop in a neighborhood bar and grill for lunch. He'd just ordered when his cell phone sounded.

"Mr. Brixton?"

"Yes."

"Mr. Brixton, this is Abiola Dimka."

Hearing her voice and her name stunned him. "Oh, yes, Mrs. Dimka," he said. "I—I'm surprised to be hearing from you. I'm so sorry for your loss and—how are you? " He knew after he'd said it that it was a stupid thing to ask of a woman whose husband and the father of her children had just been murdered. *How are you? Oh, I'm terrific, happy as can be.*

She said, "Thank you."

"Yeah, I mean it. Are you—well, are you okay, your kids and all?"

"Mr. Brixton, I'd like to meet with you."

He hadn't expected that.

"Sure. I intended to contact you after—well, after some time had passed."

"I understand."

"Where are you and the children living?"

"Ammon's employer has given us a house he built that he intends to sell. He's a fine man."

"He sounds it. Where and when would you like to meet?"

"Whenever it is convenient for you."

"I'm free this afternoon," he said.

"Can you come here?"

"Anywhere you say."

She gave him the address of her temporary quarters and they agreed to meet in two hours.

When the call was completed he stared at the phone. Her call had come out of the blue, and he tried to conjure a reason for it. Since Dimka's death he'd assumed that his wife would blame him for having enticed her husband into the situation that led to his demise.

But she didn't sound angry.

He canceled plans for that afternoon's work and geared up for the drive to Virginia. He was on edge and he knew it. His intended making contact with Dimka's wife had seemed the decent move to make. But she'd called *him*. Why? Did she intend to berate him in person for his involvement with her husband's decision to blow the whistle on Bright Horizons and the Nigerian money scammers?

He stopped by his office before heading for Virginia to pick up the material that Dimka had left for him in the envelope. He wanted it with him to show Abiola Dimka that her husband had trusted him with the information it contained and that he was not an enemy. Mac Smith was gone for the day, but Annabel was there.

"What's new?" she asked when he poked his head into the attorney's office.

He told her where he was going.

"I don't envy you," she said. "Any idea why she wants to see you?"

"Not a clue," he said.

It occurred to him that having a woman at his side might ease the trauma of spending time with Dimka's widow. He started to ask whether Annabel would consider accompanying him when she said, "Want me to go with you?"

"You read my mind," he said.

"That's me," she said lightly, "Annabel Lee Smith, seer and mind reader. I'm free this afternoon, Robert, nothing on the calendar that can't wait. I'll leave Mac a note."

Having Annabel with him brightened Brixton's mood as they went to where he'd parked his Subaru. He tossed things off the passenger seat into the back before Annabel climbed in and buckled her seat belt. Brixton got behind the wheel and maneuvered into heavy traffic on his way to the Theodore Roosevelt Memorial Bridge leading from the District to Virginia.

"What is Mrs. Dimka like?" Annabel asked.

"I've never met her," Brixton replied. "I got the impression from her husband that she wasn't happy that he was blowing the whistle."

"Worried for his safety," Annabel said.

"Can't blame her," said Brixton. "Looks like she had every right to worry considering how things ended up."

He enjoyed having Annabel with him. While he'd become close to Mac Smith and spent considerable time with him, his interaction with Annabel was basically limited to times spent socially. She spent little time at Mac's office; her pre-Columbian gallery in Georgetown kept her busy, including numerous trips in search of antiquities to offer her buyers. She was a stunning woman; in some ways she resembled Portland's ex-wife, Elizabeth, tall, nicely formed, and both women blessed with a rich mane of copper-colored hair that bordered on being red. She smelled good, too. Brixton had always been aware of the provocative scent of Annabel's perfume and cologne, label unknown.

They chatted amiably during the drive. It was when they neared their destination that conversation turned to the purpose of the trip.

"You probably should have warned her that I was coming with you," Annabel said.

"I thought about that," he said, "but I didn't want to spook her. Her husband balked at having Mac come with me, although he didn't object to David."

"What was the husband like?" she asked.

He gave her a capsule description of Dimka. "He knew he was treading on dangerous ground," he concluded. "I really admired the guy."

"Was Zeke Borgeldt any help in tracing the man you saw fleeing from the scene?"

"No."

"How do you want to introduce me?" she asked.

"Just that you're the wife of the attorney I wanted to bring with me the last time I came, and that you're my friend."

"I hope that having a woman along eases things."

"That's what I'm hoping, too," he said as they pulled up in front of the address Abiola had given him. "I'm not looking forward to this."

It was a small tract house that was in the final stages of completion. Landscaping hadn't been provided yet, and the upstairs windowpanes were still taped.

"Will her children be with her?" Annabel asked.

"I hope not," Brixton said.

Brixton was about to knock when the front door opened and he and Annabel were faced with a short, lithe woman with ebony skin, short jet-black hair, and the biggest brown eyes Brixton had ever seen. She wore blue jeans, a VMI sweatshirt, and rubber flip-flops.

"Mrs. Dimka?" Brixton said.

"Yes." She looked past him at Annabel, who'd stayed a few steps behind.

"This is Mrs. Smith," Brixton said. "She's the wife of the attorney Mackensie Smith, who I work closely with. I thought that—well, that you might appreciate having a woman with me."

Abiola managed a small smile as she said, "I'm happy to meet you, Mrs. Smith. Please come in."

They stepped from a small foyer into a living room. Brixton was surprised to see a fair amount of furniture—a sofa, two red director's chairs, and a folding table surrounded by four collapsible chairs. As far as he knew, everything the Dimka family owned had been consumed by the fire.

Abiola sensed what he was thinking. "The neighbors have been so wonderful," she said. "We lost everything in the fire, but people have been bringing furniture from their own homes, and food, plenty of food."

"It's always nice to see people rise to the occasion when tragedy strikes," said Annabel. "I'm so sorry about what's happened to you."

Abiola successfully stifled tears and invited them to sit.

"Your children?" Annabel asked.

"They're with friends," Abiola said. "I don't think the reality of what has happened has truly sunk in with them." She said as an afterthought, "Can I get you something to drink, soda, iced tea?"

"Please don't bother," Brixton said, impressed that she was concerned about them and their needs at such a time.

Brixton and Annabel sat on the couch; Abiola took one of the director's chairs. She seemed small in it, her arms wrapped around her, her face reflecting her struggle to maintain her composure. "First," she said, "thank you for coming. I'm sure that Ammon would appreciate it."

"I really liked and admired your husband," Brixton said.

"And he obviously felt the same about you, Mr. Brixton. Excuse me."

Abiola left the room, returning moments later carrying an envelope of the same size as the one that Brixton had rescued from the burning house. She handed it to Brixton.

"What's this?" he asked.

"Evidence that Ammon had been collecting."

"Evidence?" Annabel repeated. "Evidence of what?"

"Evidence to support what he'd been telling you about Bright Horizons and the way innocent people are robbed of their hard-earned money by unscrupulous people back in Nigeria."

Brixton looked at Annabel before saying, "Your husband had prepared an envelope for me the day he died, Mrs. Dimka. I took it from the house before it burned, too. In it he wrote the same things he'd told me when we met in person." He held up that envelope.

"I know," Abiola said, "but this envelope contains *proof* of what Ammon told you, e-mails, letters, names, addresses, information he'd saved while in Nigeria, and after coming here to the United States to work at Bright Horizons. He kept it in a safe deposit box at our bank."

Brixton didn't know how to respond. Here was a woman who'd

lost her husband only days earlier, the victim of a vicious attack. Her home had been burned to the ground by the same people who'd killed him. Her two children had lost both a father and a home, and would have to grapple with that for the rest of their lives. She had every right to be angry at the role Brixton had played in her husband's death. And yet she had gone to the bank to retrieve what she thought he would want to have.

"I don't know what to say," Brixton said.

It was Annabel who said, "What do you want Robert to do with this?"

"I want my husband's murder avenged," Abiola said sternly, steel in her small voice. "I want his children to know that he didn't die in vain. I want—"

For the first time since they'd arrived Abiola Dimka broke down in a torrent of tears. Annabel went to her, knelt, and wrapped her arms about her. Brixton watched, speechless, moved, and angry at whoever had so brutally destroyed the dreams of this family. Once Abiola had pulled herself together, he said, "I'll do everything I can to accomplish what you want, Mrs. Dimka."

"Thank you," she said softly. "Ammon trusted you." She paused. "I do, too."

"Have funeral plans been made?" Annabel asked after disengaging from Abiola.

"In Nigeria. His family and mine would want that."

Annabel asked whether the Dimka family was safe in Nigeria considering the reason for his murder.

"We aren't afraid," she answered.

"What about the investigation into your husband's murder and the arson?" Brixton asked. "Have the local police interviewed you?"

Abiola nodded. "They've been very nice, very considerate."

"That's good to hear," said Brixton.

He sensed they were outwearing their welcome and suggested that they leave.

"Thank you for coming," Abiola said.

"When will you be leaving for Nigeria?" he asked.

"There is much to be arranged. Hopefully in a few days."

"Travel safe," Annabel said, and gave Abiola another hug.

Abiola came to Brixton and embraced him. "Do right by my husband," she said.

"I'll do everything I can," he said.

Once in the car Brixton vented his rage.

"What's with these Nigerians?" he asked. "What are they, made of steel? She's just lost her husband and she takes the time to go to the bank, call me, asks me to come to where she's living temporarily, her kids parceled out to friends, and thinks about how to honor her husband's death."

"A remarkable woman. What will you do with what she gave you?" Annabel asked, indicating the envelope she held on her lap.

"For now? Let's go back and wait for Mac to return. I'd like for you and him to see what this evidence amounts to."

Brixton and Annabel had settled in Mac's office and started to peruse what was in the envelope when he arrived.

"What are you two conjuring up?" he asked through a laugh. "The overthrow of the government?"

"The Nigerian government maybe," Brixton said. He went on to recount their trip to Virginia and their meeting with Ammon Dimka's widow.

When Brixton and Annabel had finished, Mac said, "She must be quite a woman."

"She certainly is gutsy," said Annabel.

Brixton handed Mac a page he'd been reading. "Look at this, Mac."

Smith took the sheet and quickly perused it. "He's laid out in this document how oil bunkering works in Nigeria," he said. "I thought Dimka's interest was in the Nigerian financial scams."

"It was," Brixton said. "There's a lot of documentation on that subject in what he left in this envelope. But he also had been accumulating the goods on how Nigerian crooks siphon off oil from the major refineries and sell it on the black market." Brixton read further. "He also alludes to how some in Bright Horizons use muscle to keep people in check. Damn!" He brought his fist down on the arm of his chair. "How about *this*?"

He handed the papers to Smith, his finger pointing to a name.

"'Agu Gwantam,'" Smith read aloud.

"The infamous Agu Gwantam," Brixton said, "the so-called warlord who Dimka told me about. He seems to be involved in everything."

The three of them continued rifling through the contents of the envelope Dimka had left behind. A few of the papers contained statistical information about the extent of oil bunkering in the Niger Delta and its impact on the Nigerian economy. Brixton cited one statistic. "The oil companies lose up to two hundred thousand barrels of crude oil every day through theft."

"Here's one," said Annabel. "It's estimated that thirty thousand people in the delta are involved in stealing oil from the big oil companies. According to Mr. Dimka, most of it is sold by natives to foreign cartels, but some of it stays in the delta and is sold locally."

"How the hell do you steal that much oil every day?" Brixton asked.

"I'll have to do some boning up on the process," Smith said.

"Mr. Dimka certainly didn't pull any punches in these pages," Annabel said. "According to him, politicians, and even executives of the major oil companies, are involved in oil theft, taking bribes to look the other way. In some cases they even *help* the thieves."

"Total corruption," Smith commented.

"And I thought D.C. politicians were bad," Brixton added.

Smith sat back and exhaled. "The question is, Robert, what do you intend to do with all this information that his wife decided to share with you?"

"I'm not sure," Brixton said. "I'd like to take this stuff with me and read it carefully. There's plenty to digest."

"By all means," Smith said. "Let me know what conclusions you come to."

As Brixton started to go to his adjacent office for an hour of serious reading, Annabel asked him how Flo and her shop were doing.

"Doing fine, Annabel. She's about to head for L.A. for some fashion week celebration there. She's excited about it. It'll do her good to get away for a few days."

"Looks like we'll be having a dinner guest for a few nights," Annabel said lightly.

"Count on it," said Brixton.

He secluded himself in his office to digest the copious material left by Dimka, and made notes. As he prepared to leave, Mac Smith looked in on him.

"Making sense out of it?" Smith asked.

"Yeah , I think so," Brixton replied.

"And?"

"I think I owe something to Ammon Dimka's wife, Mac. I want to do right by her."

Smith wished him a good night and left for an appointment, leaving Brixton with his thoughts about Abiola Dimka. He was deep into them when the phone rang. It was Flo calling from her clothing shop in Georgetown. She sounded upset.

"Something wrong?" Brixton asked.

"Yes, there is. I just received a threatening call."

"Somebody threatened you? Who?"

"I don't know. It was a man, He didn't give his name. He had a deep voice."

"What did he say?"

"He said that if I cared about my life I'd better get you to stop sticking your nose where it doesn't belong."

"'Sticking my nose?' Where am I sticking my nose?"

"He wasn't specific, Robert, but he mentioned Africa."

"What about Africa?"

"He said—wait, I wrote it down—he said that you should butt out of African affairs."

Brixton sighed. "Mrs. Dimka," he said flatly. "I just left her."

He explained how he had responded to Abiola Dimka's call, and that Annabel Smith had accompanied him to their meeting. "Whoever these people are, they know about my connection with David Portland and the Dimka family. Obviously, they also know that you and I are a couple."

"That's easy enough for anyone to find out."

"Why don't you lock up shop and head home?"

"I can't. I have customers."

"It's not worth selling a couple of dresses, Flo. These guys mean business. Look what they did to Dimka."

"I'll be careful."

"Good."

"You be careful, too, Robert."

He assured her that he would be and the call was ended. He wanted to wave away the call she'd received as nothing but an empty threat.

But he couldn't. He knew better.

He spent an additional hour in his office before deciding to call it a day and head for home. Mrs. Warden had already left, her desk spotless, pens and pencils lined up like well-trained soldiers, her flowered coffee cup immaculately washed and ready for the next day's combination of organic tea, honey, and lemon juice. Brixton had to smile; while he would never feel close to his receptionist, he'd grown to admire her.

He locked up the office and went downstairs to the underground parking garage where his Subaru was parked in a reserved spot. He unlocked the door, slid in behind the wheel, inserted the key into the ignition, and turned it. Nothing happened. It was dead. That was when he noticed that the hood was popped slightly open. *Strange*, he thought. That had never happened before.

He got out, went to the front of the car, and felt through the opening for the latch that would allow him to fully raise the hood. He found it and used the metal rod to prop it open. Although he knew little about the mechanical workings of an automobile, he knew enough to note that the battery cables had been disconnected from the battery and flopped loosely into the engine compartment.

He straightened and looked around the garage in search of someone, anyone, who might have removed the cables from the battery. He was alone. Whoever had done it was long gone.

He mumbled four-letter words as he reconnected the cables, hoping that he'd attached the right ones to the proper terminals. Still cursing, and with greasy hands, he reentered the car and turned the key. It started with a roar, a welcome sound.

He drove home, where he washed his hands and poured himself a drink, thinking all the while about the call that Flo had received. Her caller had told her to warn him to butt out of anything having to do with Africa, and his battery cables had obviously been disconnected to reinforce that message. Although it had been a minor inconvenience, he had every reason to believe that the next warning would be issued to him personally, perhaps the way it had been so brutally delivered to Ammon Dimka.

CHAPTER 37

PORT HARCOURT, NIGERIA

Sir Manford Penny, XCAL's British chairman, settled in his first-class seat on an early morning British Airways flight from London to Lagos, Nigeria.

He was not happy.

He'd recently learned that the British High Commission in Lagos had requested that a team of auditors from London's Serious Fraud Office of the Attorney General's Office be dispatched to Nigeria to look into allegations of financial misconduct by XCAL in the Niger Delta. He'd pressed to learn more about what had prompted the audit but had come up against a bureaucratic stone wall. All he was told was that it involved the theft of oil from the company's exploration and refining operations.

This wouldn't be the first British government inquiry into oil bunkering. Those probes had been limited to the loss of revenue suffered by British oil interests and finding ways to mitigate it; no allegation of fraud had been leveled against any individual. It was an accepted fact that millions of pounds each year were lost as a result of MEND and other groups' cutting into the pipes, siphoning off what spouted from them, and selling the crude on the international black market, or refining it in makeshift facilities for local sale as diesel or kerosene.

But this governmental intrusion sounded different to Penny, and potentially more troublesome. The auditors evidently wanted to examine whether some employees of the oil company might have financially benefited from it.

Like Sir Manford Penny.

He had quietly enjoyed a steady flow of money from Nigeria over the years in addition to his salary as the company's UK chairman. This income was, of course, off the books, laundered through banks in the UK. Penny had been careful when setting up those accounts; they were labeled as income from land deals that his family had entered into many years ago. As far as the meticulous Manford Penny was concerned, no one could ever make the case that the funds in those accounts had come from his share of illegal oil bunkering, theft from the very company in which he held a leadership role.

Penny viewed Nigeria as a cauldron of violence and disease; his lifestyle in London and trips to other European nations and to XCAL's U.S. headquarters better reflected his genteel, civilized lifestyle, and he used any excuse to avoid travel to Nigeria. But after a troubling phone conversation with Max Soderman, XCAL's chief operating officer in the Niger Delta, Penny decided that the trip was necessary.

Soderman had been running XCAL's Nigerian operations for nine years. He was a big, burly man with a loud voice, and a tendency to disparage Nigeria and Nigerians whenever he was in the company of equally prejudiced executives. German by birth, his parents had immigrated to the United States when he was an infant, settling in Oklahoma, where his father was employed by a local oil company. The young man earned a degree in geology from Oklahoma State University, and a master's degree in business administration from the University of Texas. His intelligence and outgoing personality propelled him through a succession of managerial jobs until being hired by XCAL to manage its stateside extracting operations. He would have happily stayed in that job had a nasty divorce not impacted his financial status, as well as souring his views of the American legal system. When the job of COO for XCAL in Nigeria opened, he applied and soon found himself in Port Harcourt in charge of the company's sprawling, trouble-plagued extracting and refining efforts. The job came with a sizable salary and numerous perks, including a handsome home in the upscale town of Ikoyi.

Penny's phone conversation began with the two men's contrasting styles—Soderman blustery and matter-of-fact, Penny falling back on his familiar strained pleasantness—"Cheerio, old chap, not to worry." But Soderman didn't sugarcoat his concern for what was happening. He said, "I think you'd better get here to Port Harcourt, Manford, and get here fast. Our private business arrangement might be in trouble, *big* trouble."

"Why don't you come here to London, Max? I'm sure that you would enjoy a respite from Nigeria's heat and humidity."

Soderman's reply was a curt, "No! You're the one with the most to lose, Manford. *You* get on a plane."

"All right," Penny said, "but it will be a short visit. I'm overwhelmed with things back here in London."

Had the reason for the trip been official company business, Soderman would have been reluctant to make such demands of XCAL's UK chairman. But this wasn't company business. It was personal, pure and simple, and involved a business arrangement the men had entered into four years earlier.

Penny's flight to Lagos was uneventful. He took a liking to a British Airways flight attendant and tried to chat her up, but she would have none of it. Disgruntled, he deplaned and connected with an Arik Air flight to Port Harcourt International Airport, recently branded by an international passenger organization as "the world's dirtiest and most corrupt." He and other arriving passengers were herded into a tent lacking air-conditioning that had been erected next to the airport's single terminal building. Penny had traveled with one oversized carry-on bag, which allowed him to skirt the chaotic baggage claim area. Once outside he spotted the company car that Soderman had dispatched for him, the driver a Niger Delta native with a pleasant, chatty demeanor. But Penny wasn't looking for idle conversation. His mood matched the heat and humidity he faced when departing the airport. Among many things that Sir Manford Penny found unpleasant was sweating.

"Thank God your air-conditioning is working," he told Soderman when he arrived at the COO's house and had been ushered in.

"It doesn't always," Soderman said. "The Nigerians don't know how to do anything right, including providing electricity. I had a gas generator installed right after I arrived in this hellhole, had to use it plenty of times. Nothing works in this goddamn place."

Penny was used to Soderman's grousing about conditions in Nigeria and chalked it up to the sour disposition of a perpetual malcontent, although he certainly understood. He wasn't any fonder of the Niger Delta than his host.

They deferred serious conversation during pre-dinner drinks and dinner, served by members of the household staff. As much as Penny disliked being there, he was grateful that they weren't served typical Nigerian food. The last time he'd visited XCAL's Nigerian operations he'd been served what he was told was called *Nkwobi*, cooked cow legs smothered in a thick sauce of chili peppers and peanut powder. It had taken him days for his delicate stomach to recover. Instead, Soderman had ordered that dinner consist of filet mignon, mashed potatoes, salads, fresh bread, and French merlot that he stocked in a basement wine cellar.

They retired after dinner to the privacy of Soderman's study.

Dressed in his usual double-breasted blazer and gray slacks with a razor crease, Penny had at least surrendered to the sticky weather by removing his tie after dinner. Soderman had exchanged the suit he'd worn that day for meetings with Nigerian government officials for loose-fitting crinkled tan pants secured around his stomach with a drawstring, and a flowing Hawaiian shirt he'd bought while on holiday in Maui. Leather sandals flopped from large, calloused bare feet. His head was shaved; the stubble looked like a gray helmet.

After hearing more complaints from Soderman about conditions in the Niger Delta, Penny said, "Perhaps we had better discuss what brings me here, Max. It's obviously important or I wouldn't have elected to leave the creature comforts of London for Port Harcourt."

"Creature comforts, huh, Manford? Don't talk about creature comforts to me, pal."

Penny made a show of looking around the spacious, well-furnished room. "It appears to me," he said, "that you aren't lacking in creature comforts."

"As long as I stay inside this house. The minute I go outside I know I'm in a Third World country run by whores and savages. That's assuming the AC even works. Let's get down to business. What the hell is this fraud division of your Attorney General's Office?"

"I think its title speaks for itself," said Penny.

"Why would *they* be involved?" Soderman asked. "You told me when you called that they deal with domestic fraud."

"What does it matter?" Penny said. "What *does* matter is that they're coming to Nigeria to look at our books, and that only means potential trouble for you."

"*Me?* Hey, pal, you're in as deep as I am."

Penny allowed the comment to pass. "I recognize the potential problem this poses. You didn't mince any words during our phone chat."

"Let's start with our buddy Agu."

"Oh, him. Yes. I understand that he's a most unsavory chap."

"Call him what you want, Manford. The truth is that he runs

things in this part of the delta. Every thieving native who taps into our lines pays a fee to Agu Gwantam, and he spreads the money around where it does the most good."

"A good businessman," said Penny.

"A warlord, you mean. That's what good businessmen are called here, warlords. He's got his finger into every drop of oil that's stolen."

"And he's posing the sort of problem you eluded to when we spoke?"

"You're damn right he is. He wants a bigger cut of our oil-bunkering money."

"And he's a *greedy* man, too. I assume you've told him that he's already amply compensated for overseeing the poaching of the oil lines. Besides, as I understand it, he doesn't need more money. He's already rich from those dreadful financial scams he runs."

"Of course I've told him that," Soderman snapped, "but he's a conniving bastard like everybody else in this country, hands out, always with their hands out. 'Gimme more, gimme more,' is all they know to say, everybody, government officials, local warlords like Agu, *everybody*!"

"And what did he say when you reminded him that his request for a bigger cut is unreasonable?"

Soderman guffawed. "You want to know what he said, Manford? He insinuated that the authorities might be interested in how you and I benefit from the bunkering of crude."

"That sounds like blackmail to me," Penny said.

"Does it?" Soderman said. "I never would have known that if you hadn't pointed it out."

Penny ignored Soderman's sarcasm. "As annoying as this may be," he said, "I'm certain that you'll know how to handle this when dealing with the auditors."

"Handle it? How? Do you want me to increase Agu's cut? If I do it'll mean less for you and me. I'm way out on a limb with this as it is, Manford. I'm supposed to protect XCAL's interests in the delta. That's what XCAL pays me for. It wouldn't look good for you if people knew of your involvement."

It was obvious to Penny that Soderman was himself engaged in a bit of blackmail, but he resisted pointing it out. Instead, he said, "I fully understand."

"There's more," Soderman said. "I had drinks with Fournier."

"Our French compatriot."

"He's slime," was Soderman's response. "He says that other oil companies are putting pressure on SureSafe to stop MEND from poaching their oil. He's getting nervous about ignoring our activities, says it's being rumored that more than locals are profiting."

"So?"

"So, he wants more money from me in return for *continuing* to turn a blind eye on *our* activities."

Penny looked away from Soderman while considering what the big man had said.

He'd known from the first days of their moneymaking cabal that people like Max Soderman, Agu Gwantam, and Alain Fournier could become a problem. The fewer people involved in a nefarious undertaking, the less chance of someone fouling the works. He understood why Agu Gwantam had to be included. The warlord had control of myriad local tribes and gangs who siphoned off XCAL's oil to resell to a variety of shell corporations and local hoodlums, business as usual in the Niger Delta. These gangs and tribes stole as much as two hundred thousand barrels of oil a day, and government authorities, including politicians, had enriched themselves through the bribes they enjoyed, money passed from the gang and tribal members through people like Gwantam, who distributed the spoils to others, including Max Soderman and, farther up the feeding chain, Sir Manford Penny. Certain members of SureSafe were also on the receiving end of those bribes, paid for their willingness to look the other way while the crude oil was illegally sucked from the pipes, Alain Fournier among them.

Penny tired of the conversation. He made a show of yawning and stretching. "Is there anything else that we should be aware of, Max?" he asked.

"Plenty."

"You say you met with Mr. Fournier of SureSafe. What did he have to say aside from wanting more money?"

"He talked about that Brit Portland, the one whose kid was killed here."

"Yes, I've met with Mr. Portland. I wouldn't be surprised if he was diagnosed as a psychopath."

"He's been sticking his nose in lots of places, trying to pin his kid's death on somebody from XCAL. Fournier tells me that Portland met with a former SureSafe guard who told him that Fournier killed him."

"Did he?"

Soderman's lack of a response answered the question.

"Mr. Portland claims that Mr. Fournier shot his son upon orders from someone here at XCAL. Who might that be?" Penny asked.

"What are you looking at me for?" Soderman asked testily. "You know damn well who I got the word from to get rid of the kid and others like him. Christ, how can any white guy get in bed with MEND and the rest of the savages here?"

"What else did Mr. Fournier tell you?"

Soderman shrugged and uncapped another can of beer. "He claims that big-mouth rat from Nigeria, the one who left for the States to head up a charity there, is no longer a problem."

"That's good to hear," said Penny. "It's been a lovely evening, Max. Thank you for your hospitality."

"The guest suite is made up for you."

"I'll be leaving in the morning, the first flight out to Lagos and then on to London."

"So," Soderman said as Penny prepared to retire to his guest quarters, "what have we accomplished? The auditors will be arriving and—"

"I suggest that we both have a good sleep," Penny said. "When I get back to London I'll take care of things. Not to worry, old chap. There are many ways to handle this problem."

Penny thought of Elizabeth Sims and of her marauding husband, David Portland, and the unpleasant scene he'd had with him in London. What a shame, he thought, that people like that existed, uncouth, godless men who didn't understand the way things worked in the real world. What had Elizabeth ever seen in him? She'd obviously been a callow youth impressed by his macho, strutting self.

Oh, well.

Before dozing off into a deep sleep—Sir Manford Penny always slept well—he said his nightly prayers, which he'd done since a young student at the private boys' school he'd attended in England.

"Now I lay me down to sleep . . . I pray the Lord my soul to keep. . . ."

CHAPTER 38

That same night, Cameron Chambers, head of investigations for Cale, Watson and Warnowski, deplaned his British Airways flight at London's Heathrow Airport.

He hadn't expected when he'd arrived that morning at CC&W's corporate headquarters that he'd be on a plane five hours later. He'd just poured a cup of coffee and was settling in when Walter Cale summoned him.

"What's up?" Chambers asked the senior partner.

"I want you to leave immediately for London."

"Immediately?"

"That's right. Is there a problem with that?"

"Well, no, it's just that I hadn't planned for it."

"Throw some things in a bag and head for the airport. Here." He handed Chambers a coach ticket on British Airways. "The travel office made the arrangements."

Chambers's expression mirrored his confusion.

Cale also handed him two sheets of paper. The hotel at which he'd be staying, a smaller venue on Gerrard Street, was noted on one of them. The second contained a series of instructions for Chambers to follow up on, the first of which was David Portland's London address.

"I'd appreciate some explanation, Walter," Chambers said as he scanned the other comments.

"You'll be given all the information you need by Rufus Norris."

"SureSafe's London chief? Why him?"

"Because he's fully aware of the reason you'll be in London and can point you in the right direction."

Chambers worked hard to keep his frustration in check. This was typical of Cale, issuing orders without clarification, demanding compliance sans justification.

"Go home and throw a change of clothes into a bag. Don't miss the flight. Keep Norris informed of everything you uncover."

Uncover?

What was he supposed to uncover?

Cale stood and picked a dead leaf from one of many plants in his office, a signal that the meeting had ended. He said over his shoulder, "Travel safe, Cameron."

Chambers returned to his office and told his secretary that he'd be in London for the next few days. She wondered why the last-minute trip had been scheduled but didn't ask. He gathered up materials, took a taxi to his apartment, told the driver to wait, hastily packed an overnight bag, returned to the cab, and checked in at the British Airways desk at Dulles Airport.

It had all happened so fast that he didn't have time to process his thoughts beyond the practical demands of making the flight. But now, settled in his seat and waiting for takeoff, he was able to review the information contained on the papers Cale had given him.

It was obvious that the reason for the trip was Elizabeth Sims's ex-husband, David Portland. Not only was the address of his London flat mentioned; the name of his favorite pub and its location were also included. There was a name noted that was unfamiliar to Chambers, Matthew Kelsey, in a town called Barrow-in-Furness. "Check with Norris" was written in parenthesis next to his name.

What had Portland done to pique Cale's interest to the extent that he had dispatched the firm's chief of investigations to London? It occurred to Chambers that he didn't know whether Portland was in London or in Washington, D.C., although he assumed the latter. He'd see him leaving the Watergate's Aquarelle Restaurant with Elizabeth Sims the night before, which didn't mean, of course, that Portland hadn't caught a flight to London the following morning. He hoped that wasn't the case. Having Portland in London would complicate matters.

During the flight and the long, tortuously slow taxi ride from the airport into the city, his thoughts kept returning to Elizabeth Sims. Had this trip resulted from the tap on her phones? He'd done as Cale had ordered and engaged the tech-savvy, insufferable Marvin Baxter to tap not only Elizabeth's line but David Portland's and Robert Brixton's, too. What was especially galling was that Baxter felt free to deal directly with Cale and to bypass Chambers. What information had Baxter passed on to Cale that prompted this trip? He, Cameron Chambers, had been effectively cut out of the loop, and the more he thought about it the angrier he became.

The hotel he'd been booked into was clean and relatively Spartan, but Chambers wasn't interested in opulence. His pique at being told to travel to London at the last minute stayed with him as he unpacked his belongings and surveyed his surroundings. He splashed cold water on his face in the room's small bathroom in an attempt to wash away his growing resentment.

He'd called Rufus Norris upon arriving at Heathrow and they'd agreed to meet for a late dinner in a Chinese restaurant not far from the hotel. Despite not having met Norris, Chambers had had a number of phone conversations with him and came away with a negative impression of the man and the firm he worked for. Chambers had been on the receiving end of a number of stories about how SureSafe did business, none of them mitigating his view.

Norris arrived late at the restaurant, adding to Chambers's annoyance. He'd developed a mental picture of what Norris would look like based upon their phone conversations, which turned out to be wrong. He'd pictured him to be short and squat, balding, and possibly with a handlebar mustache. Instead, Norris was a tall, handsome man, expensively dressed and self-assured. His handshake was strong. "Good flight?" he asked as he joined Chambers at the table.

"It didn't crash," Chambers replied glumly.

"Not like flying used to be, hey? The airlines are in the cattle car business these days."

Chambers agreed, although he wasn't interested in Norris's take on aviation. He was there because he'd been ordered to be, and his only thought was to get the dinner over with, do what had to be done in London, and return home.

Norris ordered a glass of white wine: "I happen to prefer vodka martinis," he said, "but not the way Chinese restaurants make them. You?"

Chambers ordered the same.

"How much did Walter Cale tell you about why you're here?" Norris asked.

"Virtually nothing, although it's obvious that it has to do with David Portland."

"You are, of course, correct," Norris said. "Tell me, how do you like your post with the esteemed law firm?"

"I, ah—I'm quite happy with it," Chambers replied, wondering why the question was asked.

"The law firm is tied in quite tightly with XCAL."

"I'm certainly aware of that. XCAL is its biggest client."

"The law firm has a vital stake in whatever happens to XCAL, just as SureSafe does."

A waiter arrived to take their order, which Norris gave. Chambers nodded his approval of the choices, not caring what food would be served.

Norris continued. "Back to Mr. David Portland. Portland has become a royal pain in the bum, Cameron," he said. "The man is obsessed with what happened to his son in Nigeria and he seems hell-bent on pointing a finger at XCAL and SureSafe as the culprits."

"Cale has filled me in on that," said Chambers. "What I don't understand is why so much focus is being placed on what Portland believes. He claims that his son was shot in Nigeria by someone connected with SureSafe on orders from an unnamed person at XCAL. But that's all it amounts to, his misguided claim. As far as I know, he hasn't gone public with his charge, hasn't hoodwinked some newspaper reporter into writing a story about it."

"Are you aware that Mr. Portland plans to go to Nigeria to confront those he's convinced are behind his son's death?" Norris said.

"No. How do you know that?"

Norris's smile was catlike.

Their first course was served and Norris didn't waste time digging into the platter of spicy shrimp, transferring a sizable amount to his plate. "Don't let it get cold," he said. "Eat up."

Chambers put a small portion on his plate but didn't touch it. As Norris tasted the shrimp and grunted his approval, Chambers asked again how Norris knew that Portland planned to travel to Nigeria.

Norris looked up, a piece of shrimp halfway to his mouth. "You, of all people, should know the answer to that, Cameron."

"Phone taps," Chambers said bluntly.

"Handy little things, aren't they?"

"And against the law unless authorized by a court."

"If conducted by a government agency. Privately? Well, that's a different story, isn't it?"

Chambers had had enough small talk about the niceties of phone taps. He said, "What is it I'm to do while here in London? Cale told me that you'd be the one with the answer."

"We want you to find out everything you can about David Portland."

It was Chambers's first laugh that day. "What's to find out? And why me? You head up SureSafe here in London, a worldwide security firm. You have the resources to find out anything you want about Portland."

Norris's sour expression wasn't caused by the food. He leaned across the table and said slowly and deliberately, "It should be obvious that SureSafe must not be connected to whatever happens to Mr. Portland."

Norris's careful use of words emphasized the seriousness of his tabletop message. *Whatever happens to Mr. Portland*? It sounded to Chambers like a direct threat on Portland's life. Was it? He decided to not pursue an answer, certain that whatever Norris would say next would be couched in equally vague terms.

"You have information about Portland's flat here in London," Norris said, pushing back from the table enough to allow him to cross his legs.

"Yes."

"I suggest that you pay it a visit. My best information is that Portland is in Washington, so he won't pose a problem."

"You're suggesting that I break into his apartment?"

Norris laughed. "I assume that you've done that in your previous career as a Washington, D.C., policeman. Of course, you might be able to sweet-talk your way in with Portland's landlord. It doesn't matter how you do it—just do it!"

"And what am I looking for?" Chambers asked, feeling impotent at even having to ask.

"Anything that might indicate what evidence Portland has at his disposal to validate the absurd claim he's making."

"What about this Matthew Kelsey character? I was told that you'd fill me in on him."

Norris finished his wine before answering. "Matthew Kelsey," he said absently, as though saying the name would refresh his memory. "Portland paid Kelsey a visit recently, a psychopath visiting a drunk. Make contact with Kelsey and see what he told Portland about his son's demise. My information is that Kelsey claims to have been there when the son was shot. He's not to be believed, of course, but even drunken liars have credibility in some quarters."

"Anything else?" Chambers asked.

"I'd say that this should keep you busy for a few days, Cameron."

Norris paid the check and they parted in front of the restaurant. "Keep me informed on a regular basis," Norris said, shaking Chambers's hand. "Among many things I dislike are surprises."

Chambers said nothing as the London SureSafe head suddenly broke away and climbed into the back of an available taxi. He watched the cab disappear around a corner before walking to his hotel, where he had a drink at a small bar in its lobby. As he sat alone he reflected on the conversation that had just transpired.

In all his years on the Washington PD and during his tenure as Cale, Watson and Warnowski's chief investigator, Cameron Chambers had never fired a weapon at anyone other than dummies on the firing range. But he realized as he downed what was in his glass and asked for a refill that if he had possessed a gun during dinner he might have been tempted to use it. He found Norris to be obnoxious; he'd been finding more people these days to be obnoxious.

While he understood his obligation to the law firm to do its bidding—as long as he continued to cash their checks—his positive thoughts were not with the firm. Elizabeth Sims took center stage. Her phone calls were being recorded, as were phone conversations by David Portland and Robert Brixton. He mumbled a four-letter word into his glass. Trevor Portland's murder in the Niger Delta was a tragedy not only for his father. Elizabeth had been the boy's surrogate mother and had devoted a portion of her life to helping bring him up. She'd been devastated by the news, too, and didn't deserve the treatment she was receiving.

As he grappled with these thoughts a wave of fatigue washed over him, and he decided to go to bed. Once in his room he stripped to his shorts, performed the usual nightly ablutions, and climbed in between the covers. He'd decided to call Mr. Kelsey the following day in Barrow-in-Furness, wherever that was, and hoped to arrange to visit him. It probably would have been more efficient to first try and gain access to Portland's apartment, but he'd have to gear himself up for that unpleasant, potentially risky task.

Elizabeth!

Her face was the last thing he saw before dozing off.

CHAPTER 39

That evening Portland and Brixton had a long telephone conversation.

"I visited Ammon Dimka's wife this afternoon," Brixton told his British pal.

"Really? What brought that on?"

"She called me," said Brixton. "She wanted me to come to where she and the kids are temporarily staying to show me something her husband left for me in his safe deposit box. That envelope we rescued from the burning house only tells a small piece of the story, David. The one Mrs. Dimka handed me is filled with evidence of everything he'd been saying about Bright Horizons—and a lot more about the corruption in the Niger Delta, including damning material about SureSafe and its criminal role there. Annabel Smith went with me to see her. I spent an hour with Annabel and Mac Smith after we got back."

There was silence on Portland's end.

"David?"

"Right, sorry. I was just thinking how timely your call is."

"Why is that?"

"Well, to cut to the chase, I'm about to leave for Nigeria."

Brixton exhaled. "That's a bit of news I didn't expect. Why are you going there?"

"To settle accounts."

"With?"

"With the Frenchman, Alain Fournier, and anyone else involved in Trevor's murder."

It was Brixton's turn to fall silent.

"Robert?"

"Yeah, yeah, I'm here. I was just thinking about Dimka's widow and how much she's like her husband, willing to tell the world about the horror show that's going on in Nigeria. I told Mac Smith that I want to do right by her."

"I can understand that."

"When are you leaving for Nigeria?"

"Tomorrow night. I'm flying to London. I'll catch a plane the next day to Lagos."

"Want company?" Brixton asked.

"Company? What are you talking about?"

"Would you like me to go with you? Look, I'm driving Flo to the airport in the morning for her flight to L.A., some sort of fashion shindig out there. She'll be gone for a week, give or take a day or two. I'll be rattling around in the apartment and the office with not a hell of a lot to do. Business is slow." He laughed. "How's that for an understatement? Besides, I've never been to London."

"Hold on, Robert. This is not some tourist jaunt I'm making to jolly old England. I'm just stopping off there before catching a flight to Nigeria."

"I know that," Brixton said, "and I'm not looking for a tour of Buckingham Palace. The point is that you're not the only one who wants to settle a score. I don't know how to explain it—Flo always says my sentimental gene was missing when I was born—

but I have this need to avenge Ammon Dimka's murder." He paused. "And the way you lost your son resonates with me, too. My daughter Janet died at the hands of maniacs and I've never fully resolved that in my mind. I feel like Dimka and I are on a mission together to confront those who left his wife a widow and his kids without a father. Maybe I also feel there's a mission where you're concerned because of what happened to Trevor. But hell, David, it doesn't matter *why* I want to go with you. I've made up my mind and that's that!"

"In other words, you aren't suggesting a trip to London. You want to come with me to Nigeria."

"Sounds dumb, huh?"

"As a matter of fact, it does."

"It's not dumb to me, David. Look, you're going off to set things right, which I understand. But from what I hear Nigeria, especially the Niger Delta where all the oil is, can be a pretty scary place. Am I right?"

"From what I read," Portland said sarcastically.

"I read about Nigeria, too, David. Dimka left plenty of reading material behind. His wife told me she wanted her husband's murder avenged. She also told me that she wanted his kids to know that their father didn't die in vain. I take her seriously, David." He lightened his tone. "Besides, you can always use somebody to cover your back."

"Come on, Robert, you make it sound like I'm going to war."

"Aren't you? What are you going to do when you confront this Frenchman, Fournier, or his buddy Agu something-or-other, tell 'em that you're unhappy that your son was killed, ask 'em not to do that sort of thing again, shake your finger at them, and fly back to London?"

"I'll decide what to do when we're face-to-face."

"I've learned firsthand they're not nice guys," Brixton said.

"Not true, Robert. I'm sure they're good and decent folks who rescue kittens and make cakes for their mothers' birthdays."

"In other words, they'll shoot you without batting an eye."

"If you say so. Look, my friend, it's bloody decent of you to offer to ride shotgun with me, but your offer is impetuous at best, and impetuous people usually get in over their heads."

"You're telling me I can't go with you?"

"I'm telling you that this is my war, Robert."

"Do I need a visa?" Brixton asked, not being put off.

"You're serious, aren't you?"

"Dead serious. I need a change of pace, a change of scenery. With Flo away I'm liable to get myself in trouble, so you'll be doing me, and her, a big favor by letting me tag along. I didn't mention that Flo has received a threatening phone call about my involvement in the Nigerian financial scams, and somebody messed around with my car's battery to reinforce that warning."

"You're lucky that's all they did. Remember Dimka."

"How could I *not* remember him? That was the wrong move on their part. Tell me not to do something and it makes me want to do it that much more. A visa? Do I need one?"

Portland's sigh of resignation said volumes. "You're supposed to have one to enter the country. That's the law. But those who check passports at the Lagos airport are more than happy to look the other way for a price. At least that's what I'm told. You do have a passport, I assume."

"Of course I do. Flo insisted that I get one so we can take some trips abroad."

"And she'll be a very unhappy woman if you make this trip overseas without her."

"She'll understand."

Portland wasn't sure he agreed with Brixton's assessment of Flo's reaction but didn't debate it.

Brixton wasn't in a debating mood either. "When do we leave?" he asked.

"Tomorrow night."

"And we fly to Nigeria the next day?"

"Right."

"And what do we do once we arrive there?"

"We contact someone who can help."

"Who's he?"

"Jeffrey Gomba."

"A friend of yours?"

"Somebody at the embassy put me on to him. He does odd jobs, for a fee, of course."

"So, it's agreed. You and I go to Nigeria."

"Provided your Miss Flo doesn't steal your passport and break your leg. What about your friends the Smiths? What will their reaction be?"

"I'll finesse that," Brixton said. "Where and when do we hook up tomorrow?"

Portland suggested a time and place, and they ended the call after Portland suggested the sort of clothing Brixton should pack.

CHAPTER 40

It hadn't been difficult for Brixton to inject himself into Portland's travel plans. The Brit, despite his initial balking, seemed to welcome Brixton's involvement. At least that's how Brixton read it.

But announcing to Flo that he would be going to Nigeria with Portland would be a harder sell, a *much* harder sell. He decided to not break the news to her that night. Better to wait until they were on their way to the airport for her flight to Los Angeles. Which meant, of course, that he was laden with guilt as they went about preparing for her departure.

Flo packed, placing outfits in her suitcase, then tossing them and opting for different clothing. Brixton watched with amusement. As far as he was concerned, she looked good in anything she chose to wear, and he told her so numerous times. But she dismissed his flattery and continued her quest for the perfect outfits to wear in sunny California.

Her packing finalized, they dined on food brought in from a local restaurant, and watched the news on television before going to bed and making love. Flo thought that Brixton was unusually aggressive and enjoyed his ardor. As they basked in the afterglow of their romantic interlude, she asked, "So, what are you going to do with me away?"

"Do? Me? I don't know. Maybe get together with Mac and brainstorm how I can hustle up more business."

"That's a good idea," she said. "They've invited you for dinner. You should go."

"Yeah, I will," he said into the darkened room, experiencing the guilt that had been building all evening.

"I'll miss you," she said, her voice husky.

"I'll miss you, too, babe. Let's call it a night."

He was about to fall asleep when she said, "Is something wrong?"

"What? No, nothing's wrong. Why do you ask?"

"I don't know, it's just that you seem, well, distracted."

"While we were making love?"

"No, before that."

Brixton turned on the bedside lamp.

"Why did you do that?" she asked, sitting up in bed.

"Look, Flo, I *do* have some plans while you're gone."

"Plans? What kind of plans?"

"I'm going to London with David."

"You're *what*?"

"I'm going to London with David for a few days. Actually, I'm—"

She was out of bed before he could finish and stood over him.

"When did you decide *this*?" she demanded.

"It was last-minute, Flo. You see—"

"I can't believe I'm hearing this," she said, grabbing her robe.

Brixton, too, got out of bed. "Look," he said, "you're going to be away on business, so I figured it was a good time to, well, to spend a few days with him in London."

"*I've* never been to London," she said curtly.

"I know, and we should plan a trip there, just the two of us. But David has business there and . . . well, he's going on to Nigeria to confront the people who killed his son and—"

"*Nigeria?* Don't tell me, Robert, that *you're* going to Nigeria, *too.*"

"Maybe. I mean—"

Flo flounced from the bedroom and plopped down on a couch. Brixton followed.

"I know this is a lousy way to announce my plans," he said. Flo didn't interrupt as he tried to explain his decision and how it came out of his meeting with Ammon Dimka's wife. The more he talked the greater his resolve was mirrored in his voice. He sat on the edge of the couch, held Flo's hand, and searched for the words that would justify his decision. When he was finished, he released her hand and said, "That's it, sweetheart. That's why I'm going with David to London and Nigeria. It may not make sense to you, but it does to me. It's like when that suicide bomber blew up the café and killed my daughter. The scum behind it had to be brought to justice. I had to do it, no matter what it took. Sure, Ammon Dimka wasn't a family member, but he and his wife meant something, to me and to the world. David lost his kid the way I lost mine, to some warped, evil people who spend their lives hurting others for their own gain. Sorry, hon, but it's something I have to do." He delivered the final words with conviction.

Flo said nothing, but Brixton saw that her eyes had welled up. She grasped his hand and squeezed.

"You are a prize knucklehead, Robert Brixton," she said. "My question is what do you and David intend to do once you're there?"

Brixton expected that question and hadn't formulated a reasonable answer. He shrugged, extended his hands in a gesture of futility. "I don't know," he said. Then, realizing that it was a weak response, he added, "I want to see for myself what Dimka wrote about in the package he left for me. Maybe just putting a face to whoever was behind the torching of his house and his murder will satisfy me. Try to understand, Flo. I need you to understand."

"What does it matter?" she said. "You've made up your mind, and once you do that's it. Robert 'Don't Call Me Bobby' Brixton is off with his British pal on an insane trip to Nigeria, and I may never see him again." Now she wept openly.

"Hey," Brixton said, touching her moist cheeks with his fingertips, "what's all this talk about never seeing me again? You won't get rid of me that easy."

They returned to bed, where both slept fitfully until the alarm sounded the next morning. Flo disappeared into the bathroom without a word while Brixton put together what amounted to breakfast. With silence still reigning, they swapped places in the bathroom. Brixton emerged showered, ate hurriedly, and said, "Time to go."

They rode in icy silence to the airport.

"I'll park and come in with you," he said.

"No," she said, leaning across the front seat and kissing his cheek. "I'm sorry if I'm acting like a shrew, but I just know that what you intend to do will have a bad outcome."

"I'll make sure it doesn't," he said, forcing lightness into his voice. "I'll be back before you even leave L.A."

"Take care of yourself, Robert, and don't do something stupid that gets you killed," she said, quickly exiting the car before he saw the tears running down her cheeks.

As he watched her wheel her suitcase into the terminal he had the sinking feeling that his decision to accompany Portland to Nigeria had been a huge mistake that would have serious ramifications. It wasn't that he was worried about his physical well-being. He just wondered whether he'd driven a stake into his relationship with Flo Combes that could never be extracted.

He was good at that sort of thing.

CHAPTER 41

Cameron Chambers would have preferred to stay in bed. Nothing on his agenda motivated him; he wished he were back in Washington.

It was a bright, sunny day in London, a departure from the gray overcast that had recently dominated the weather. After showering and dressing, he stopped at a small food shop where he had breakfast and lingered at the table as he tried to put his thoughts in some semblance of order.

First on his agenda was a call to the former SureSafe employee Matthew Kelsey. According to Norris's terse instructions at dinner, Chambers was to visit Kelsey to ascertain what Portland might have told him about his son's shooting, and to determine what Kelsey had witnessed the day the shooting took place. The contemplation of spending time with a drunken ex-employee of SureSafe didn't please Chambers, and he hoped that a call to Kelsey wouldn't result in the need to actually see him.

He returned to his hotel and dialed Kelsey's number.

"Hello?"

"Mr. Kelsey, my name is Cameron Chambers. I work for the law firm of Cale, Watson and Warnowski in Washington, D.C."

"Oh, yeah, that fancy law firm that works for XCAL."

"Yes, sir, that's correct," said Chambers.

"Why are you calling *me*?" Kelsey asked in a voice that sounded as though his vocal cords had been rubbed with coarse sandpaper.

"I'm in London on assignment to investigate the death of the son of a gentleman named David Portland."

Kelsey guffawed, which generated a coughing spasm. "Portland? He's a bloody fool."

"Yes," Chambers agreed, not wanting to challenge him. "The reason for my call is to see whether you might be willing to share with me what Mr. Portland said to you during his recent visit."

When Kelsey didn't respond, Chambers suggested, "I thought that maybe we could chat about this over the phone."

"The hell we can," Kelsey snapped. "You want to pick my brain the way Portland did, you come here, and don't forget to bring decent grub and a few pints and some quid for me. Portland gave me a pittance for what I know. I don't come cheap no more. You hear me?"

Chambers wasn't sure how to respond. The contemplation of having to actually meet with this drunk almost caused him to thank Kelsey for his time, hang up, and falsify a report for Walter Cale about having seen him. But his pragmatism got the better of him. He said, "Will later today suit you, Mr. Kelsey?"

"S'long as you don't arrive empty-handed."

Prior to making the call Chambers had explored ways of traveling to Barrow-in-Furness. He ruled out renting a car. Driving on the "wrong" side of the road would be too nerve-wracking. He'd done it once before and hated the experience. He considered hiring a car and driver but shelved that notion; his inherent sense of financial propriety ruled. A check of train schedules indicated that there was frequent service between London's Paddington

Station and Barrow-in-Furness, with two changes of trains involved. The total travel time was four and a half hours.

Armed with a book he'd brought with him from Washington and two British newspapers, and after changing dollars into pounds—he hoped enough to satisfy Kelsey—he boarded an eleven o'clock Northern Rail passenger train, ignoring Kelsey's demand that he bring food and whiskey. He wasn't about to arrive like some long-lost relative bearing gifts. All he wanted was to find out what he could about Portland's visit and leave.

He dozed during the trip, waking when it was time to change trains. He waited in line with other passengers at the Barrow-in-Furness station looking for taxis, settled in one, and gave the driver Kelsey's address. It was a quick ride; before he knew it he had paid the driver and stood in front of the run-down four-story building in which Kelsey's flat was located. He felt ill at ease. He wasn't eager to linger there. The neighborhood reminded him of certain sections of Washington, D.C., that he assiduously avoided whenever possible. He checked himself in his reflection in a window and decided he looked official enough, possibly even authoritative. Seeing that he was alone on the street, he approached the building, paused at the entrance, drew a breath, and stepped inside. He found Kelsey's name on the tenants' list—flat number 2—and knocked. He heard sounds inside and cocked his head, leaning closer. The door suddenly opened and he was face-to-face with a young man with deeply pitted skin and wearing a black motorcycle jacket.

"Mr. Kelsey?" Chambers said.

"No, mate. Kelsey's inside. Go on in. He's expecting you."

The young man pushed past Chambers and quickly exited the building.

Chambers stood by the open door, unsure of what to do.

"Mr. Kelsey?" he called out. When there was no response he repeated it, louder this time.

He stepped into the flat and paused in the small foyer, took in his surroundings, listened for sounds. *Who was that young man?* he wondered. *A friend of Kelsey's? But why would he just walk away? He seemed in a rush to leave.*

Chambers raised his nose and took in the odors. There was a sour smell, mixed with the aroma of burned food. In front of him was a doorway leading to the living room. He called Kelsey's name again. Silence.

Another few steps took him to the doorway. He leaned through it and was about to announce himself again when he saw a figure in a corner shrouded in darkness. He squeezed his eyes shut, opened them, and advanced farther. Now the figure was discernible. It was a man in a wheelchair, his head drooping to one side.

"Kelsey?"

Chambers closed the gap and stood over the figure. That was when he saw the wide red stain on the man's shirtfront and the knife protruding from his chest.

"Good God," Chambers muttered, reaching to touch Kelsey's cheek.

He stepped back and forced rational thought. Had the young man in the motorcycle jacket stabbed Kelsey to death? If so, it had happened just moments before Chambers had arrived. Had it been a robbery gone awry?

It then struck him that Kelsey might have been murdered *because* of their plan to meet. Was Kelsey's phone bugged? It seemed that everyone's telephone was tapped these days, Portland, Brixton, Elizabeth Sims, God knew who else. *His own phone?*

His initial instinct was to call the police. He'd come upon a murder victim. Had it happened in the United States he wouldn't have hesitated, but this was Great Britain. Would they suspect that he had something to do with it and hold him for questioning? He didn't need that. He came to the conclusion that there was no reason for him to report the murder and become involved with the ensuing investigation. No one aside from the young man with the motorcycle jacket knew that he was there.

He stepped back to put distance between himself and the lifeless Kelsey. During his tenure as a D.C. cop he'd never had to directly deal with the messy business of murder. His career had been spent behind a desk. His hands were clean, no bloodstains on them.

As he prepared to leave, he noticed Kelsey's cell phone resting on a small table next to him. Had he taken Chambers's call on that phone? There was no landline telephone near the body, leading Chambers to assume that the dead man had used his cell. Chambers grabbed the phone, shoved it in his jacket pocket, and retraced his steps to the foyer, where he hesitated, looking through the smeared glass to the sidewalk. He saw no one. He opened the door to the building and peered up and down the street. Not a soul. *Good.* He left the building and walked briskly toward an intersection where there were other people, women with children, men minding their own business. A few blocks later he waved down a taxi and told the driver to take him to the train station. As he sat back he realized that his heart was beating rapidly and there was a film of perspiration on his face. He wanted no part of this, should never have agreed to come to London.

His cell phone sounded.

"Hello?"

"Hello, Cameron. Rufus Norris here."

"Oh, yes, Rufus. Hello."

"Having a productive day?"

"I, ah—I've been making plans to carry out my assignments."

"I like that, someone who plans before acting. But don't spend *too* much time planning, Cameron."

"Of course. I—I called this Kelsey character. There was no answer. I'll try him again, of course."

"Perhaps it would be best to simply pop in on him."

"I considered that but wanted to make contact first. If I'm still unsuccessful in reaching him I'll do what you suggest."

"Good. And what about Mr. Portland's flat?"

"That's on my agenda."

"Splendid. Get it done, Cameron, and keep me informed of your progress."

Chambers was aware during the brief conversation that he was tense, his shoulders hunched, his free hand drumming on his thigh. Electing to leave Kelsey's flat and pretending that he hadn't been there now seemed less prudent than it had while he was formulating it.

Still . . .

He forced himself to believe that he'd made the right decision. The hell with worrying about Matthew Kelsey and deciding not to report his death. Kelsey wouldn't be mourned by anyone, just another drunk murdered by some punk. All he, Chambers, had to do now was gain access to Portland's flat, gather up what he could in the way of information about Portland's son's murder, and wing back to Washington.

It occurred to him as he went through his mental process that he'd reached a point at which he had decisions to make about continuing to work for the law firm. He'd had inquiries from other employers about the possibility of joining them. It was time for a change.

The train ride back to London was consumed by these thoughts, and myriad others. Kelsey's cell phone felt heavy in his pocket, and he debated what to do with it. He decided that he would destroy it and dump it in a public trash receptacle, which he did outside Paddington Station, using the heel of his shoe to smash it.

The taxi deposited him at his hotel, where he went into the small bar and had a drink, and then another. He decided he needed a good night's sleep before accomplishing his second and last mission, gaining access to David Portland's flat and gathering up evidence to satisfy Walter Cale.

As the alcohol took effect, the absurdity of having been dispatched to London took center stage. So what if David Portland was on the warpath about his son's death? What was he, nothing but a crude soldier of fortune with a checkered background and a penchant for causing trouble? What had the beautiful and intelligent Elizabeth Sims ever been thinking to have gotten involved with such a distasteful character? She'd been young, too young to rein in her youthful sexual hormones, and Portland, swine that he was, had taken advantage of her. Chambers could forgive her for that. What bothered him more was that she'd maintained a relationship with Portland, dining with him at the candlelit, romantic Aquarelle and probably gazing at each other like long-lost lovers.

That final vision disgusted him. He signed for his drinks, sought out a British pub for dinner, and spent much of the evening watching British television, much of which he found silly. His plan for the next day was to use the cover of darkness to break into Portland's apartment. He'd carried with him a set of lock picks that he'd had since his cadet days at the Washington PD but had never used.

CHAPTER 42

Robert Brixton and David Portland settled in their coach seats for the flight to London.

Brixton was a cauldron of mixed emotions. Announcing to Flo at the last minute that he intended to accompany Portland to London and then Nigeria weighed heavily on him. She had every right to be angry, and he wondered what life would be like between them when they returned from their respective trips. Added to his angst was a fear of flying, which he didn't verbalize but that kept his stomach churning.

At the same time he felt energized, even exuberant to be off on an adventure. While he was grateful that Mac Smith had set him up in his own private detective agency and fed him a fair amount of business, he'd recently fallen into a funk; doing background checks on potential government employees didn't get his blood flowing. He was also aware that he'd never found closure for the terrorist attack that took the life of his younger daughter. Not that the people whom Portland intended to confront had anything to do with that directly, but they were of the same ilk, at least as far as what Portland had told him about SureSafe's Nigerian head, the Frenchman Alain Fournier, and others associated with that agency.

"I still can't believe that you're with me," Portland said after the flight had reached cruising altitude over the Atlantic and they'd purchased drinks from the flight attendant.

"I have trouble believing it, too," Brixton said, "but I'm glad I am."

"From what you've told me, your lady Flo doesn't share your enthusiasm."

"It came as a surprise to her, my fault. I should have been up-front the minute I decided to make the trip. What about your ex, Elizabeth? Does she know you're going to Nigeria?"

"Yes. I told her when we had dinner together. I really don't know how she feels about it." He laughed. "I'd like to think that she fears for my life, but that might be wishful thinking on my part."

"Maybe she agrees with what you're doing," Brixton offered, "wants your son's murder avenged, like Mrs. Dimka wants for her husband."

"Yes, women can be vengeful," was Portland's reply.

It was Brixton's turn to laugh. "You'll get no argument from me. Flo can be one tough lady and I have the scars to prove it. As for Abiola Dimka, she's made of steel."

They fiddled with their individual in-flight entertainment systems but found little of interest. Brixton turned to Portland. "So," he said, "tell me about this guy who'll be helping us once we get to Nigeria."

"Jeffrey Gomba? My friend at the embassy says that Gomba is a real hustler, has fingers into everything. He sells bunkered oil that's siphoned off from the refineries, provides weapons to anyone with the money to buy them, and even pimps for prostitutes."

Brixton said, "He doesn't sound like the sort of character you'd want to do business with."

"Yeah," Portland said, "Gomba would be behind bars in the States or the UK, but in Nigeria he's just a businessman. Besides, he hates SureSafe and the oil companies, which gives him a motive for helping me."

"Us."

"Right. Us. My friend assures me that Gomba can be trusted."

"For a price," Brixton said.

"Like most people," Portland agreed.

"So, what's our agenda when we arrive in Lagos?"

"We lay low for a few days, make contact with Gomba, and figure out our next move. Once we have we'll fly down to Port Harcourt, where the action is."

"The action," Brixton repeated. "What *is* the action once we get there?"

"I haven't figured that out yet. All I know is that I won't rest until I come face-to-face with that French bastard Fournier and get him to admit that he shot Trevor."

"And then?"

Portland shifted in his seat and shrugged. "I'll know the answer to that when the time comes."

Brixton had many more questions for his British friend, including the role of the Nigerian warlord Agu Gwantam. "What do you know about him?" he asked.

"Like everything else," Portland said, "I only know what I'm told about Mr. Gwantam. You probably know more about him than I do from your meetings with Dimka. They say that Gwantam is bigger than life. He controls the money that flows through that so-called charity Bright Horizons and SureSafe provides security for him."

"That's what Dimka claims in the material he left for me. Evidently, Gwantam doesn't hesitate to get rid of anyone who challenges him and Bright Horizons is always on tap to carry out an order from him."

"I've heard the same, which is why one of the first things we arrange for through Gomba is some self-protection."

"You told me to leave my handgun home," Brixton said.

"I left mine back in D.C., too," Portland said. "I have one at my London digs, but it's too much of a hassle to check a weapon when flying. I'd rather pick up fresh ones once we're on the ground. Besides, no one will be able to trace the weapons Gomba gives us."

"*Sells* us," Brixton corrected.

"Right you are, mate," Portland said, stretching his arms and legs and grunting with pleasure. "I think I'll watch a movie."

"You said you didn't like what they were offering."

"Exactly. A bad movie always puts me to sleep, which is what I need."

Portland was asleep ten minutes into the film. Brixton closed his eyes, but sleep was elusive. His mind had gone into overdrive, and as he grappled with his whirlwind of thoughts he came to the conclusion that accompanying Portland to Nigeria might have been an impetuous mistake.

It had all seemed so appealing, standing by his British pal's side as he sought to avenge his son's murder. Now, in the darkened cabin of the jet, its allure was fading fast.

He nodded off after they'd been served their coach-seat meals, and awoke when the plane was nearing London's Heathrow Airport.

"Smooth flight," Portland commented as they gathered up their belongings in preparation for deplaning.

"Can never be too smooth for me," Brixton said.

"That's right," Portland said. "Flying's not your favorite pastime."

"Let's just say that I prefer the ground under my feet."

"Man wasn't meant to fly?" Portland said as they joined other passengers in the aisle.

"Man wasn't meant to do a lot of things," said Brixton, "but they do it all the time."

It was a long, slow taxi ride into London, where Portland's flat was located. Brixton was impressed with the cab's spaciousness and cleanliness, and the driver's professional bearing, a far cry from taxis in New York and D.C. He mentioned it to Portland.

"It takes cabbies here in the UK years of training before they're licensed to carry paying passengers," Portland told him. "They have to know every street in London and environs, and prove it to inspectors. Most fail on their first, even second attempts."

They pulled up in front of Portland's apartment building. Portland paid in British pounds, dismissing Brixton's attempt to split the fare, entered the building, and Portland opened the door to his flat.

Brixton took it in. "Nice place you have here, David."

"Nothing fancy, but it suits me," Portland said, opening the blinds to allow in some light. "Drink?"

"Too early for me."

"Tea?"

"When in Rome, huh?" Brixton said lightly. "Sure, some British tea sounds good."

As Portland disappeared into the kitchen Brixton took the opportunity to more closely explore his surroundings. He was looking at the pile of Trevor Portland's material on a bookshelf when Portland reemerged. "That's all that's left of my son," he said glumly.

"I don't even have this much of Janet to remember her by," Brixton said.

"Feel free to read what's there," Portland said.

"Sure you don't mind?"

"Not at all. You're part of what I'm about to do, so no secrets."

Brixton sat at the table, his tea next to him, and began to read what Trevor had written in his diary about Nigeria, especially the Niger Delta, where he'd lived and worked under contract to XCAL. Portland sat on a couch, a mug in his hand.

"Your son didn't mince any words about how bad things were there," Brixton commented.

"Yes, and I'm proud of him for the way he viewed the plight of the natives in the delta. It really saddened him."

"And made him angry," Brixton said.

"That, too," said Portland.

Portland raised his mug to his lips, allowing the bracelet on his wrist that had been Trevor's gift from his grandmother to glisten in light from the window.

"You always wear that bracelet," Brixton said.

"And I always will," said Portland. "For me it symbolizes everything that was good and decent about Trevor."

"What about Elizabeth?"

"What about her?"

"You've told me that she was a damn good stepmother to Trevor."

"The best. I was the one who let everyone down. Maybe that's why I have to put it to rest, find closure, as people are fond of saying."

Brixton nodded. He'd never found that illusive thing called closure where Janet's death was involved and wondered whether he ever would.

"I need a nap," Portland said. "The couch is yours. It's quite comfortable, pulls out into a bed if that's your preference. We'll have an early dinner at a favorite pub of mine, the same one where I borrowed this bracelet from a Nigerian chap who had no business wearing it."

Portland went to the flat's bedroom while Brixton continued

to peruse the materials about Trevor, but eventually the long flight and restless attempts at sleep on the plane caught up with him. He closed the blinds, kicked off his shoes, sprawled on the couch, and was asleep in minutes.

CHAPTER 43

Cameron Chambers sat in a London pocket park a block from where Portland and Brixton slept off their jet lag. His eyes, too, were closed, although he was awake, his head tilted back to catch the welcome warmth of the sun that had broken through the city's grayness.

He'd made a conscious decision to relax and enjoy the day until dark, when he would let himself into David Portland's flat.

Rufus Norris had called Chambers at the hotel soon after he had arisen that morning to see what he'd gathered from Portland's flat.

"I'm waiting for nighttime to go there," Chambers replied.

"Why wait?" Norris asked.

"Because I'm not comfortable breaking into someone's apartment in broad daylight," Chambers replied curtly.

"And what about Matthew Kelsey?" Norris asked. "Have you made contact with him?"

"Not yet, but I'll call again. If I can't reach him by phone I'll visit him unannounced."

Norris's silence said that he wasn't pleased with what he was hearing.

"Anything else?" Chambers asked.

"I'll call again," Norris said curtly, and hung up.

Following that phone conversation Chambers left the hotel and found the park where he could enjoy solitude while deciding what to do next about Kelsey.

He had to assume that Kelsey's body had now been discovered and that a murder investigation was under way. Was there any chance that his visit to Kelsey's flat could become known to investigators? Although he'd physically destroyed the cell phone, he knew that there would be a record of his call with the cell provider. But he rationalized that there was no reason for the authorities to check those records. Kelsey's murder would be chalked up to some punk looking for cash or drugs, most likely the young man in the motorcycle jacket, whoever he might be.

He continued with his what-if line of thought.

What if they had identified the young man and arrested him for the murder? Would he be able to testify that he, Chambers, had arrived at the flat right after the murder had taken place? Impossible, he decided. The young man didn't know who he was and had left the building in a hurry, certainly without having taken time to scrutinize Chambers's face.

No, he decided, it was highly unlikely that the police in Barrow-in-Furness could place him at the scene of Kelsey's murder. Not that he would be accused of having taken part in the killing. It was just that he didn't need the inconvenience of having to partake in the investigation. Kelsey's death meant nothing to him.

But as much as he convinced himself that this was the case, fear would occasionally wash over him and render his self-assurances as just that, wishful thinking. The key was to leave the UK on the first available flight to the United States, where he would resign and put this sordid adventure behind him.

Walter Cale and Rufus Norris would be told that he had been unable to make contact with Kelsey, which, in an ironic sense, was true. They could learn of Kelsey's demise on their own.

He would go through with his instruction to break into Portland's flat, not only because he'd been dispatched to do that; there was the possibility that he would come up with something that would serve to put Portland in his place.

Portland!

His thoughts went to Elizabeth Sims.

As he strolled from the park and down a busy commercial street he fantasized that he was with her, enjoying a leisurely day in London, perhaps buying her something nice in one of the shops and then enjoying tea or a drink in the fancy hotel in which they were staying. With everything that was on his mind—stumbling upon Kelsey's murder, the phone taps ordered by Walter Cale through the smarmy Marvin Baxter, his being shut out of the decision-making loop—it was she who provided his pleasant thoughts, the beautiful, brilliant, radiant Elizabeth Sims.

CHAPTER 44

David Portland thought of Elizabeth, too, when he awoke in the bedroom of his London flat. Her smiling face was before him as he shook his head and rubbed his eyes to dispel the wispy remnants of his nap. He got out of bed and peered into the living room where Brixton, who'd awakened earlier, had resumed going through Trevor's things.

"You didn't sleep?" Portland said.

"Oh, yeah, I did, but not for long. Have a good nap?"

"As a matter of fact, I did."

"This desk chair is broken," Brixton said. "It damn near tipped me over."

"I keep meaning to get it fixed," Portland said as he went to the window. Darkness was setting in; he'd slept longer than intended.

"Up for dinner?" Portland asked.

Brixton checked his watch, did a calculation of what time it was in London. "A little early for dinner, isn't it?"

"I suppose it is but not too early for a drink at a favorite pub of mine. Run across anything of interest in Trevor's diary?"

"He talks about the Frenchman you always mention, this Fournier character. He sure as hell wasn't a fan."

"He certainly wasn't, and for good reason. Fournier is evil, Robert."

"And that's who you want to confront."

Portland nodded grimly.

"From what your son wrote, the oil companies are really ripping off the locals in the delta."

"It's a tragedy," Portland said. "The Niger Delta is a hellhole for Nigerians who work for the oil companies. They live in poverty while the companies pollute their land and drinking water and keep them in line with heavy-handed help supplied by security companies like SureSafe. That's why rebel groups like MEND are at war with them."

Brixton hesitated before saying, "I get the feeling that Trevor not only sympathized with the rebels; he might have joined them."

Portland's response was a growl. "That's the official line, Robert. That's what Fournier and his cronies wanted me and the rest of the world to believe. It's garbage, pure garbage. It's their way of shifting blame to others. No, it's a lie. Sure, Trevor was sympathetic to the rebels' cause, because he was a sensitive young man who responded to injustice when he saw it."

Brixton saw that Portland was becoming passionate and decided to drop the subject. Instead, he said, "So tell me about this favorite pub of yours."

"Nothing special," Portland said, "straight-ahead pub fare. I like that it's usually quiet." He laughed. "I'm sure the owner isn't happy about that, but it suits me fine. By the way, the food is better than in all the fancy pubs that have opened up for the tourist trade."

"David Portland, the purist," Brixton quipped.

"At least when it comes to pubs. Freshen up and we'll head over. It's a short walk."

CHAPTER 45

Chambers, too, decided to nap. While waiting for sleep to come he vacillated between going through with the illegal entry into Portland's flat and calling it off, the hell with what Norris and Cale would say. As far as he was concerned, he no longer worked for Cale, Watson and Warnowski. But there was a nagging need to delve into Portland's life, this man who had captured Elizabeth Sims's heart and mind years ago.

He eventually slept. When he awoke it had turned dark, and the fair weather of the day had become gloomy; occasional raindrops hit the windowpane. He showered, dressed in dark gray slacks, a blue button-down shirt, black sweater, black sneakers, and a forest green slicker, an outfit chosen specifically for becoming a second-story intruder. Satisfied with his reflection in the mirror, he went downstairs and had a drink in the bar.

Have dinner before going to Portland's flat?

He decided it was a good idea. There was no rush. The later he arrived at the flat the better, less chance of people getting in the way.

Fortified with a single-malt scotch, he ventured out onto the street and walked to the Chinese restaurant where he'd dined the previous night with Norris. He ordered another scotch and enjoyed a leisurely dinner, aware that he was putting off the inevitable.

CHAPTER 46

Brixton and Portland sat at the pub's bar, Portland's usual spot, and indulged in drinks—martinis for Brixton, which he had to admit weren't bad, and a glass of white wine for Portland. The owner had warmly welcomed the Brit and his American guest, insisting that an order of prawns was on the house to accompany their drinks. Brixton was relaxed. Although he hadn't seen any of London aside from Portland's flat and the pub, he felt as though he was part of the scene and felt surprisingly at home.

Portland had been chatty earlier in the evening but had now fallen silent.

"What are you thinking?" Brixton asked, hoping he wasn't intruding on a private thought.

"I was thinking about you, Robert."

"Should I be flattered?"

"Probably not. I was thinking—well, I was wondering whether you really want to come with me to Nigeria."

"Well, here I am, David. Are you having second thoughts about letting me tag along?"

Portland's response was a slight nod.

"Why?"

Portland drew himself up on the barstool. "It's my fight, Robert," he said.

"I know that. I've always known that. But it's a little late to question it now."

Portland faced him. "No, it's not," he said. "Look, I don't have a lot of friends. That's just the way I am. I've always been a bit of a loner. But every once in a while someone comes along who I like, *really* like, and you're one of those chaps."

"Now I *am* flattered, David," said Brixton, "but you're not the only loner on this earth. There's damn few people in this world who I care about, really care about. David Portland is one of them."

"I hope no one is listening," Portland said. "It sounds like we're lovers."

"A mutual admiration society, that's all," Brixton said, "but let's get back to what you said. If you really don't want me with you I'll have to decide whether to continue the trip."

"I'm giving you an out, Robert; that's all. Look, I don't have any idea how things will fall when and if I get to face Fournier. It could be—well, it could get nasty."

"Nasty? You mean somebody's liable to get killed?"

Portland's lack of response answered Brixton's question.

"Last chance," Portland said.

"Last chance for *what*?"

"To bail on me. Our flight to Lagos leaves Heathrow in the morning. You can decide to go back to Washington, no questions asked, or get on the Nigerian flight with me. Either way, Robert, I appreciate your friendship."

Before Brixton could answer, the pub's owner, who'd been chatting with other customers at the opposite end of the bar, came to them. "You blokes having dinner?" he asked.

Brixton looked at Portland, grinned, and said to the owner,

"David and I need a good meal before we head to Nigeria in the morning."

"You heard the man," Portland said through a smile. "We'll start with cockles and leeks and both have bangers and mash. Oh, and my American friend needs a drink refill."

CHAPTER 47

Cameron Chambers deliberately lingered at the restaurant until the owners hinted that they would like him to leave.

He paid his bill, stepped out onto the street, and walked slowly in the direction of the small, nondescript building that housed Portland's flat. He felt conspicuous, as though his every step was being observed. You'd think that as a former cop he would be able to set aside such thoughts and simply get on with the job, no matter what it entailed. But his years with the Washington MPD had been spent behind a desk, giving orders to others who did the heavy lifting.

He paused across the street from the building and stood in shadows. He knew where Portland's flat was located, second floor, front, left side. A faint light was burning in the room, which concerned him. Portland, as far as he knew, was still in Washington. Would he leave a lamp burning while away, perhaps to discourage thieves? Maybe he had a lamp on a timer; Chambers had three lamps in his apartment rigged to come on once darkness set in.

He took in the street. There weren't many people on it at that hour, an occasional couple, a man walking a shaggy dog, and a young woman whom Chambers thought might be a prostitute.

Fortified by a few deep breaths, he stepped from the darkness, crossed the street, and stood in front of the building. Confident that he wasn't being watched—as confident as his paranoia would allow—he tried the front door. It was locked. After another series of furtive glances he pulled his set of sixteen lock picks of various sizes from his pocket and tried a few until one worked. The door swung in, exposing a neat, dimly lit foyer. Chambers closed the door behind him and started up the stairs, slowly, quietly, his ears poised for any sound indicating that he was not alone. He heard a dog bark from one of the apartments; a TV set (owned by someone with a hearing problem?) blared from another. He reached the landing and went to Portland's door. This time the first pick he chose worked and he was inside.

He went to the lamp that was on. There was no timer attached to it. *What a waste of electricity*, he thought, *leaving it on day and night*. He debated turning on other lamps, or the overhead fixture, and opted for the overhead. But first he went to the windows that faced the front and looked down at the street. No one looked back up at him. He lowered the blinds, partially raised them, rechecked the street, and closed them again.

Now that the room was more brightly lit he was better able to survey it. It looked as though someone had recently slept on the couch, which he chalked up to Portland's lack of housekeeping skills. Chambers was an obsessive-compulsive when it came to neatness; his bed was made every morning, and a soiled dish or cup in the sink was inconceivable.

His eyes went to Portland's desk. Folders that Brixton had been perusing were there; one labeled "Diary" was open. Chambers sat in the tilting, swiveling chair and had to grab the desk's edge to keep from falling backwards. He silently cursed and repositioned himself. Confident that he wouldn't end up on the floor, he focused on the open file folder and began to read.

Fifteen minutes later he closed it and processed what he had been led to believe about how Trevor Portland died.

The official line, at least from XCAL's British head, Manford Penny, was that Trevor had joined forces with the rebel group MEND and was killed during a raid on the oil company's facilities by members of SureSafe. That explanation had obviously rung false to Trevor's father, David Portland, and had fueled his campaign to prove otherwise. Entries in Trevor's diary fed into that official scenario—the young man *had* expressed his agreement with MEND's goals. He'd been disgusted by the way the oil companies violated the basic human rights of Nigerian citizens. The situation was deplorable. The oil companies raked in millions while the natives scrambled to survive. Chambers took from Trevor's correspondence with his father that it was *possible* that the idealistic young man had joined forces with a rebel group such as MEND, a decision that led to his untimely death.

But had he actually joined MEND and attacked the XCAL oil facility? Espousing agreement with a cause was one thing; taking action on behalf of that cause was another.

He pulled himself close to the desk and turned to the contents of a folder containing a series of handwritten notes that Portland had made following his meeting with Matthew Kelsey.

From what he read, Kelsey had claimed to Portland that the French head of SureSafe in the Niger Delta, Alain Fournier, had shot Trevor point-blank after receiving an order from an unnamed person, most likely someone working for XCAL. Kelsey confirmed that Trevor had been with members of MEND when he was captured.

But if Kelsey was right, Trevor hadn't been killed during the raid. He'd been taken prisoner, and instead of being treated like one he'd been *executed* by Fournier.

In terms of his professional allegiance, the theory that Trevor had joined forces with MEND and was killed by SureSafe played into the hands of XCAL, and by extension Chambers's employer, Cale, Watson and Warnowski, whose major client was the giant oil company. He could return to Washington carrying with him that rationale for Trevor Portland's death and be viewed as a hero, his efforts in London having substantiated XCAL and SureSafe's claim.

But what he read about Kelsey and his meeting with Portland cast a different light on the subject.

If Kelsey was correct in his assertion that Trevor had not been killed during the raid but, in fact, had been murdered following it upon orders from someone at XCAL, the official line was just that, dishonest and self-serving.

It was a lie.

CHAPTER 48

Brixton and Portland were finishing their desserts, trifle for Brixton, plum crumble for Portland. It had been a relaxed evening, the two men enjoying each other's company and their deepening friendship. The owner had offered free after-dinner drinks, but they passed. Despite their naps, they were still feeling the effects of the plane ride; the thought of a good night's sleep before leaving in the morning for Nigeria was appealing.

"Let's call it a night," Portland said as the owner placed the bill in front of them.

"I'll get it," Brixton said, grabbing it before Portland had a chance. "You got the cab fare from the airport."

"We'll have to pick up some Nigerian naira at the airport," Portland said.

"Local Nigerian currency?"

Portland nodded. "This character Gomba prefers British or U.S. money," Portland said, "but there'll be others to pay, like the passport inspectors when we arrive in Lagos."

"They're that corrupt?" Brixton asked. "Everybody's on the take?"

"Hey," Portland said as he scooped up his last bit of his plum crumble, "I only know what I'm told. Remember, I've never been in Nigeria."

"And you think we can get into the country without the proper visas?"

"We'll find out soon enough."

Once outside, Portland drew in a deep breath of the chilly air. "Enjoy this weather," he told Brixton. "It'll be hot in Nigeria."

They walked to Portland's street, where they paused to allow cars to pass before crossing.

"It's clear," Brixton said, stepping from the curb, mindful that he was in the UK, where traffic approached from a direction opposite from in the States. He was aware that Portland wasn't crossing with him, stopped, and turned. "What's the matter?" he asked, retracing his steps to the curb.

"The window," Portland said absently.

Brixton looked up at the apartment building. "What window?"

"The one facing the street. The blinds are drawn."

"Uh-huh."

"They were open when we left."

"They were? You're sure?"

"Yeah, I'm sure. Looks like the overhead lights are on, too. It's bright behind the blinds."

Brixton grunted.

"Come on," Portland said, checking traffic before quickly crossing the street, with Brixton at his heels. Portland paused at the front door.

"You think somebody's up there?" Brixton asked.

"Maybe, maybe not, but somebody's sure as hell has been there since we left."

Portland unlocked the door and he and Brixton stepped into

the foyer, silently pausing to better hear. The only sound was the barking dog.

"That dog barks all night," Portland said, slowly starting up the stairs, one by one, with Brixton close behind. They reached the second-floor landing and Portland pressed his ear against the door.

"Hear anything?" Brixton asked in a whisper.

Portland shook his head, put his finger to his lips, and pressed his ear closer. He heard someone move inside, as though whoever it was had stumbled and uttered a muffled curse. Portland pulled the key to his flat from his pocket and said to Brixton in a muted voice, "Somebody's in there."

"They might be armed," Brixton said.

"Let's hope not."

With that Portland slid the key into the lock, paused, turned it, flung open the door, and barged into the room. Chambers, who'd been struggling with the broken desk chair, pulled back in shock at the unexpected intrusion and flailed his arms to regain his balance. Portland was the first to reach him. He grabbed an arm and twisted it behind Chambers's back while Brixton did the same with the other arm.

"What the hell are *you* doing here?" Brixton snapped, recognizing Chambers.

"What?" Portland said, looking to Brixton.

"I know this guy," Brixton said. "Cameron Chambers. He heads up the investigation unit for the law firm your ex works for."

"Take it easy," Chambers said weakly. "You're breaking my arm."

Portland echoed Brixton's question as to why Chambers was in the flat.

"Let go of me and I'll tell you," Chambers said.

"You armed?" Portland asked.

"No."

They released their grips and allowed him to stand, giving Portland a chance to pat him down. "He's clean," he told Brixton.

"How did you get in?" Brixton asked as Chambers manipulated his arms and shoulders.

"I used a—what difference does it make?" Chambers asked.

"What I want to know is *why* you're here," Portland said.

When Chambers didn't respond, Portland asked, "Who sent you?"

"I—look, I apologize for having broken in, but I wasn't looking to steal anything, nothing like that."

"Then why?" Portland said, bringing his face closer to Chambers's. "The law firm you work for send you?" Brixton added.

"Can we sit down and discuss this?" Chambers asked.

"Sure," said Portland, "but your explanation had better be bloody damn good."

CHAPTER 49

Portland launched a heated interrogation.

"I could call the police and have you arrested," Portland said. "You realize that."

"I know that," Chambers said quietly.

"You broke in here and went through my personal things, including papers my son left me. What were you looking for?"

"I was looking for—does it really matter?"

"It matters to me," Portland said.

"Who sent you?" Brixton chimed in.

"My—my former employer," Chambers replied.

"*Former* employer?" Brixton said. "You don't work for that law firm anymore?"

"I did work for them when I came here. I don't now. What I mean is I intend to resign when I get back to Washington."

"You mean you'll resign *after* you deliver to your employer what they're looking for," Portland said.

Chambers didn't answer.

"What *were* you looking for?" Portland pressed.

"They—the senior partner, Walter Cale, wants to know what proof you have that Trevor Portland, your son, wasn't killed by a Nigerian rebel group."

"Why is that important to him?" Portland asked.

"He's protecting his client XCAL and the security firm that works for them in Nigeria, SureSafe. He knows that you've been going around claiming that the Frenchman who heads up SureSafe murdered your son on orders from someone at XCAL. He wants to disprove that."

"And did you find anything that disproves it?" Portland asked.

"No. I mean, your son obviously had sympathy for the rebel groups that are fighting the oil companies, but I didn't see anything that indicates he joined them on a raid."

"It doesn't matter whether he did or not," Portland snapped, "but even if he did he was captured and *executed.* You want proof? Talk to a guy named Matthew Kelsey. He lives in a town a few hours from here and was there when my son was shot by the Frenchman, Alain Fournier, on orders from someone who, by the way, I'm convinced worked for XCAL."

"I never got a chance to speak with Mr. Kelsey," Chambers said.

"You intended to see him?" Brixton asked.

Chambers said, "I was told to get together with him but never did. He was dead when I got there."

Portland and Brixton looked at each other before Portland said, "That's news to me, Chambers. You say he's dead?"

"Murdered, stabbed to death."

"Who killed him?" Brixton asked.

"How would I know?" Chambers replied with more energy than he'd exhibited earlier. "He was dead when I got there. A young punk was leaving just as I arrived, so I suppose it was him. Frankly, I don't care who did it."

"A robbery?" Brixton asked.

"I assume so," Chambers said.

"You called the police?" Brixton asked.

"No. I didn't want to get involved."

Brixton wanted to criticize him for not having reported the murder but decided to not bother. He hadn't liked Chambers from the first time they'd met, and the past half hour hadn't changed his opinion. He sized him up as a weak, ineffectual man lacking a moral and ethical compass.

Chambers turned to Portland. "I'm sorry about what happened to your son," he said.

"Yeah, thanks," Portland said.

"I know how much his murder affected Elizabeth."

The mention of Elizabeth Sims brought Portland up short. "What about Elizabeth?" he said.

"I was just thinking about her," Chambers answered. "She's a lovely woman—and a good lawyer, too."

"Tell me about it," said Portland.

"I think it's terrible that—"

"What's terrible?" Portland asked.

"That the firm—well, look, Walter Cale—he's the senior partner at Cale, Watson and Warnowski—he arranged to have her phones tapped."

"Elizabeth? Her phones are tapped?"

Chambers nodded. Two thoughts had entered his mind. The first was that since he intended to resign anyway, there was nothing to be lost by revealing the phone taps ordered by Cale and installed by Marvin Baxter.

But along with that decision, it also occurred to him that since Portland's and Brixton's phones were also tapped, Cale must have known that they would be in London at the same time that he, Chambers, was breaking into Portland's apartment. Why hadn't Cale or anyone else warned him? The more he pondered it the greater his disillusionment and anger with the law firm.

"Your phones are tapped, too," he said flatly.

Brixton said, "Cale ordered taps on *our* phones?"

Another nod from Chambers.

"Did you arrange for the taps?" Portland asked.

"I was the liaison with the man who did the taps, a former cop named Baxter."

"And you knew about the taps on Elizabeth's phones and didn't do anything about it, never told her?" Portland asked.

"I'm afraid not," said Chambers. "I've spent lots of sleepless nights over it."

Portland fought the urge to scoff at Chambers. Instead, he said, "So, you've broken into my flat, read everything that my son left me, and are salving your conscience by admitting these things to me. Why? Do you think that by telling me you'll make me let you walk out of here like nothing has happened?"

Chambers stared at the floor while gathering his thoughts. Finally, he said, "Look, Mr. Portland, and you, Brixton, you can do with me whatever you like. I never wanted to come to London, didn't want to contact Mr. Kelsey, and certainly wasn't keen on breaking in here and violating your personal space. But that's irrelevant. It's been done. It's over with. There's nothing to gain by holding me here, or turning me over to the local police. But that's out of my hands. It's your decision what happens next."

They'd been talking for two hours and everyone was tired. Brixton knew that the next move was up to Portland. It didn't matter to Brixton what Portland decided to do. Chambers's candor about phone taps, and having walked away from the scene of Kelsey's murder without notifying the authorities, hadn't mitigated Brixton's negative view of the former Washington MPD cop. But he *was* surprised at what Chambers said next.

"Is there anything I can do to help you get to the bottom of your son's death?"

Neither Portland nor Brixton had a ready answer, but Portland said, "Robert and I are leaving tomorrow morning for Nigeria."

"To find out more about how he died?"

As far as Portland was concerned, he already knew all he needed to know about Trevor's murder. But he answered, "Yes."

"Does Elizabeth know that you're going?" Chambers asked.

"Yeah, she does," Portland said.

"I'm sure she wants to get to the bottom of it as much as you do," Chambers said.

"I assume so," said Portland.

"And you're going, too?" Chambers asked Brixton.

"That's right."

"What if I joined you?" Chambers said.

The questioning expressions on Portland's and Brixton's faces mirrored their confusion.

Portland asked, "Why the hell would you want to come to Nigeria with us?"

Chambers made a show of gathering his thoughts before answering. "Maybe I want to make amends for coming here and breaking into your apartment," he said. "Maybe I need to prove that Cale and the law firm are not only wrong about the way your son died; they're lying to cover up the truth. Maybe—well, maybe I'd like to do it for Elizabeth."

Portland cocked his head. "You sound like you have a thing for my ex-wife," he said.

"A thing? Let's just say that I admire her greatly."

When neither Portland nor Brixton responded, Chambers said, "Well? Can I come with you?"

"Sure," Portland said. "Why not?"

PART FOUR

CHAPTER 50

Are the three of you traveling together?" the Arik Air ticket agent asked Portland at London's Heathrow Airport.

"Yes, we are. Mr. Chambers is a last-minute addition to our group."

She glanced at Chambers, who had just scored the last coach seat on the Arik flight to Lagos.

"You each have one bag to check?"

"Just Mr. Chambers," Portland said. "Mr. Brixton and I each have a carry-on."

The agent pulled Chambers's checked bag from the scale and deposited it on the moving belt behind her. She flashed a wide smile and said, "Welcome to Arik Air. Have a good flight."

Chambers subscribed to a service called Priority Pass, which allowed him access to a wide variety of airport lounges. He and his two traveling companions found one not far from where they'd checked in, and after signing the guest book they settled by a large window overlooking one of Heathrow's active runways.

"What does it cost you to join a club like this?" Brixton asked after returning from a coffee bar with a steaming cup.

"Not much," muttered Chambers, his attention focused on planes landing and taking off.

There had been little conversation between the men since awakening that morning. After showering and dressing they'd taken a taxi to the airport, stopping on the way at Chambers's hotel for him to retrieve his belongings. It was obvious that the decision Chambers had made the previous night after a long discussion with Portland and Brixton weighed heavily on him, and the other two men wondered whether he'd change his mind at the last second.

CHAPTER 51

The boarding of the Arik Airbus A330 at Heathrow, destination Lagos, Nigeria, was chaotic. The Nigerian airline's gate agents did their best to maintain order, but a large contingent of XCAL oil workers in Nigeria's Niger Delta, who'd spent their vacation days in Europe blowing their salaries on wine, women, and song, especially wine, were already in their cups and had become boisterous.

Brixton and Portland sat together in a section of the waiting area far removed from the noisy oil workers. Chambers had chosen a chair away from his new traveling companions, which suited Brixton.

"I don't like him coming with us," he said to Portland.

"Why?" Portland asked.

"Why? Because I don't trust him. He's like a supervisor I had when I was a cop in Savannah, all talk, no action. He's a quarter inch deep."

"He's all right," Portland said. "Besides, it can't hurt to have an extra body with us. The more the merrier, I say."

Brixton grunted and turned away, his glum expression mirroring his mood.

Portland's embrace of Chambers accompanying them disappointed Brixton. He considered his British friend a pragmatic, no-nonsense kind of guy, which was part of his appeal. He wasn't a man who did things on a whim, and accepting Chambers's suggestion that he accompany them to Nigeria smacked of that, an inexplicable whim. It didn't make sense to Brixton. After all, Chambers worked for those who were determined to undermine Portland's claim about how his son had actually died, and here was Portland inviting him to join forces. Brixton didn't like it any more than he understood it.

But while he was critical of Portland's decision to invite Chambers, he had to admit to himself that his own decision to accompany Portland to Nigeria had also been rash and impetuous, certainly not well thought out. He'd joined hands with Portland as a commitment to their friendship and to feed into his own emotional need to take a stand on behalf of Ammon Dimka's wife and her murdered husband. On top of that there was the visceral need to do something proactive to honor the death of his own daughter at the hands of people who, he felt, were represented by those in Nigeria who'd murdered Trevor Portland.

Terrorists! It didn't matter where they lived or who they killed; they were all the same.

He was deep into his retrospection when Portland said, "Lighten up, Robert."

When Brixton didn't respond, Portland added, "Not too late to change your mind about coming with me."

Brixton started to say something, but Portland cut him off. "Look, Robert, I never did understand why you insisted upon coming with me to Nigeria, but I didn't argue. Frankly, I welcomed your company. I like *you*, consider you a good friend. You seemed determined to make the trip and I understand why. But Trevor was *my* son, and I'm going to Nigeria to make those responsible for his murder come clean, look me in the eye, and admit what they did. I appreciate you joining me, but it's probably better that you don't."

Brixton looked to where Chambers sat reading a newspaper. "You tell me I can bail out," he said, "but you'll travel with the guy who works for the ones who killed Trevor."

Brixton hesitated to add what he'd started thinking moments earlier: Was Portland taking Chambers with him with the goal of making *him* pay, too, for Trevor's demise? Could Portland be that Machiavellian? That train of thought was interrupted by a gate agent's announcement that boarding was about to commence.

"It's your call," Portland said, standing and picking up his carry-on. "I'm happy to have you with me, Robert, but I'll understand if you change your mind."

Brixton considered shaking Portland's hand, wishing him well, and walking away. Instead, he said, "Time for us to board."

They found their seats in the coach section of the Nigerian Arik Airbus A330, the aisle for Brixton, Portland at the window. Chambers's assigned aisle seat was four rows away. The man occupying the middle seat between Portland and Brixton was an XCAL oil worker with bloodshot eyes and alcohol on his breath who quickly made it known that he didn't like being squeezed in between them.

"We have a friend with an aisle seat," Portland told the man in the middle. "Maybe he'll swap with you."

"Sounds good to me," said the man.

"Leave him where he is," was Brixton's comment, referring to Chambers. He wasn't eager to sit next to him on the long flight.

Portland ignored Brixton, got up, and went to Chambers. Brixton hoped that Chambers would balk at giving up a more comfortable aisle seat for a middle one, but Chambers got up and accompanied Portland to where the man in the middle struggled to his feet and took the seat Chambers had vacated.

Chambers settled in and searched for his seat belt. Brixton ignored him and perused printed material in his seat pocket. His innate fear of flying had begun to fester on the way to the airport and had now intensified to the point where he had started to perspire and his heart beat faster. The cramped, confining coach seat didn't help, nor did the raucous banter and laughter coming from the many XCAL oil workers surrounding him, some of whom had broken out miniature bottles of booze. Adding to his discomfort was being on a Nigerian plane. Did Nigerians know how to fly and maintain their aircraft as well as American or British airlines did? That question remained there along with imagined scenarios of crashing.

He squeezed his eyes tightly shut as the aircraft taxied into position for takeoff, received clearance, and roared down the runway, smoothly lifting into the air and climbing to its assigned cruising altitude, destination Lagos, Nigeria's largest city. He ignored Chambers during the early portions of the flight but was aware that Portland and Chambers had engaged in what sounded like a pleasant conversation, which galled him. He tried to occupy his time by going through the airline's in-flight magazine but found little of interest. Even the crossword puzzle failed to provide distraction. He was never very good at doing them; Flo invariably came to the rescue.

But while he struggled to take his mind off his fear of flying and the easy rapport that Portland and Chambers had forged, he was also acutely aware of what was going on around him. The oil workers had become increasingly raucous, and some were overtly drunk. They'd abandoned their seats and congregated in the aisle; one kept bumping into Brixton's shoulder with his hip. Brixton tried to ignore him, but after another particularly hard bump he tapped the man on the leg. "Hey, take it easy, okay?" he said.

The man glared at him.

"You keep bumping into me," Brixton said.

"You got a problem?" the man asked.

"I just don't like to be hassled," Brixton said. "Why don't you sit down and—?"

The man said in a loud voice to his buddies, "Hey, this guy wants us to sit down."

"I don't care whether you sit or not," Brixton said angrily, "but stop hitting me."

"I got a right to stand here," the man said. "Who the hell do you think you are tellin' me to sit down?"

"I didn't tell you to sit," Brixton said. "I just said—"

The man laughed and swigged down what was left in a miniature bottle of whiskey. Brixton looked to a flight attendant who was busy placating another male passenger and decided she was too busy to intervene. As the large man in the aisle continued to crowd into Brixton's space he considered challenging him more forcefully. But a flight attendant asked over the intercom that passengers resume their seats to allow the meal to be served, and the oil workers obeyed.

Portland and his two traveling companions ate in silence, Portland's attention on a film on the small screen in front of him, Chambers juggling a paperback book for space on his crowded meal tray. Brixton silently stewed. His anger bubbled near the surface, exacerbated by the passenger in front of him who'd reclined his seat into the already cramped quarters.

Chambers turned to him. "Airline food leaves a lot to be desired, doesn't it?" he said.

"I thought it was pretty good," Brixton replied, not meaning it. He wasn't about to agree with Chambers about anything.

"We never had a chance to work together," Chambers said, "even though you and your agency are on the payroll."

"That's okay by me," Brixton said.

"I just meant that—"

"Look," Brixton said, checking that Portland was engaged in his onboard film and wore earphones, "I'm not happy that you're here with us and I've made that clear to David. It's his trip, so he's the one to make the decision, but as far as I'm concerned it was a mistake."

"Why do you feel that way?" Chambers asked in his pinched voice. "What have I ever done to you to make you angry? You didn't express those feelings when you signed the agreement that put money in your agency's pocket every month without having to do anything to earn it."

"This has nothing to do with money," Brixton countered. "It has to do with you working for the same people who killed David's son, and who thought nothing of breaking into his apartment to find ammunition for those people."

"I understand why you feel that way," Chambers said. "I would, too. But people change. I asked to come on this trip because I want to help David achieve peace with his son's death and I assume that's your motive, too. I'm sorry that you think so poorly of me, but maybe you'll have a change of mind when it's over."

He turned from Brixton, adjusted his small pillow beneath his head, and closed his eyes.

Brixton wasn't in the mood to accept anything that Chambers said, nor was he interested in establishing a bond with him. But he put his attitude toward Chambers aside and thought of Flo, wondering how she was doing at the fashion shindig in Los Angeles. He should have offered to go with her instead of signing on with Portland to travel to Nigeria. He'd made many rash decisions in his life but couldn't shake the feeling that this one might have been the worst of them all.

He eventually fell asleep and awoke when they were about to land in Lagos, a bumpy arrival due to crosswinds. There wasn't any conversation as the three men—The Three Musketeers, he mused—gathered their belongings and joined the line of other passengers heading for the exit. The international terminal at Murtala Muhammed International Airport was teeming with people, the noise deafening; Brixton's stomach was already upset by the aircraft's bumpy landing, and the din made it worse. Portland led them into a line at the head of which uniformed men, military or perhaps law enforcement officers—their uniforms didn't indicate—checked passports of arriving passengers. As Brixton pulled his from his jacket pocket a pen came with it and rolled away. By the time he'd picked it up the passenger behind him in line, the XCAL worker with whom he'd had a verbal altercation on the plane, had taken his place.

"Excuse me," Brixton said as he tried to slide in ahead of the man.

"Wait your turn," the man said.

"I was there, but I dropped something and—these are my friends I'm traveling with and—"

"Shut the hell up," the big oil worker growled.

"Watch your mouth," Brixton said as he pressed his attempt to rejoin Portland and Brixton.

The man pushed his bulk against Brixton, forcefully shutting off his attempt to move ahead of him. Brixton placed his hand against the man's chest and pushed, sending him off-balance. He righted himself and swung at Brixton, who eluded the blow and raised his fist to the man's face.

"Hey, stop it!" someone behind them shouted.

The man grabbed Brixton by the neck.

Another oil worker wedged himself between them. Portland, too, interceded by coming up behind Brixton and wrapping his arm around his neck. "What the hell are you doing?" Portland said into his ear. "Cool it. We don't need trouble."

Chambers stepped out of line and joined Portland and Brixton. Two uniformed Nigerian security guards suddenly appeared and led the men from the fracas and into a small room with windows overlooking the terminal.

"What is this about?" one asked.

"Just a misunderstanding," Portland said, smiling. "The other fellow had too much to drink on the plane and—"

Another Nigerian officer entered the room. Judging from the array of insignias on his uniform, he was of higher rank. "What is the problem here?" he asked in a deep voice tinged with a British accent.

"Just a misunderstanding with another passenger," Portland repeated.

The ranking officer responded by dismissing the other two. Their superior took a seat behind a small, bare desk, looked up at the three men, and smiled. "Your passports, please."

Portland handed his document to the officer and Brixton and Chambers followed suit. The officer made a show of carefully scrutinizing each one, his only comment an occasional grunt. When he'd finished he laid them on the desk and asked, "What is your purpose for coming to Nigeria?"

Portland had anticipated the question. "We're looking for work with one of the oil companies in Port Harcourt," he said.

"I see. You have job interviews scheduled?"

"Not yet," Portland answered, "but we expect to set up appointments soon."

"I see," the officer said, running his fingers over his chin. "You have visas, I presume."

Brixton was surprised when Chambers entered the conversation. "We left at the last minute, sir," he said, "and didn't have time to apply for visas. But we don't intend to stay in country long, just a few days."

Chambers, Brixton, and Portland waited for the response.

"It might be possible to allow you to enter Nigeria without the proper visas for a short stay," he said, "but there is paperwork to be done, a great deal of paperwork." He sighed deeply to reinforce how difficult it would be. "Of course," he continued, "there is a cost involved in preparing that paperwork, a cost that you will have to pay. It is the law."

Brixton started to protest, but Portland shot him a look that would have silenced a chorus. He said to the officer, "We understand perfectly, sir. How much will it cost?"

The officer frowned and mumbled to himself as he did the calculation. Finally, he came up with a figure.

"That's a lot of money," Portland said.

"It's too much," Chambers chimed in.

Portland ignored Chambers, pulled what Nigerian naira bills he had from his pocket, and handed them to the officer. "That should be enough," he said.

The officer carefully, slowly counted the money. He scowled.

"I have British pounds, too," Portland said, extracting some of that currency from his jacket.

The officer counted those bills, too. When he'd finished, he said, "I will allow you to enter the country for a limited time and for the purpose of applying for work with the oil companies."

"That's generous of you," Chambers said.

The officer stood, shook their hands, flashed a wide smile, and left the room.

"What a rip-off," Brixton muttered.

"Yeah, it is," agreed Portland, "but we're here." To Chambers: "Let's grab your bag and get the hell out of here before he changes his mind and wants more."

As they left the room and headed to the baggage claim area they saw the officer hand some of the money to the two officers who'd preceded him, and who laughed heartily as they pocketed the bills.

Portland exchanged more British pounds for Nigerian naira while Chambers retrieved his luggage. They navigated the crowd to the front of the terminal, where a line of taxis waited.

"Where are we going?" Brixton asked.

"A hotel ten minutes from here," Portland said, "depending on traffic. Gomba recommended it."

"What about this guy Gomba?" Brixton asked. "You trust him?"

"For now," Portland said.

Chambers waved for the first cab in line to approach, but Portland said, "No, no taxi. There's the shuttle van from the hotel." He waved it down.

A sign on the side of the van read: **GrandBee Suites**.

"GrandBee Suites?" Brixton said. "Is that a chain like Marriott or Hyatt?"

"Beats me," Portland said as the van came to a stop and the driver opened the door. "You're paying guests?" the driver asked.

"That's right," Portland replied, leading the way onto the van.

The ten-minute drive took a half hour because of a clot of traffic that crawled slowly along the rutted road leading from the airport to the hotel. Portland tipped the driver, and they entered the brightly lit, attractively decorated lobby. A pleasant young African woman behind the desk welcomed them and asked if they had a reservation.

"Mr. Gomba reserved for us," Portland said, and gave their names.

"Yes, I see that you do have a reservation but only for Mr. Portland and Mr. Brixton. I don't see a Mr. Chambers here."

"I was a last-minute addition," Chambers explained.

"I'm sorry," she said, "but we have only two available rooms. The hotel is full."

"Gomba didn't know you'd be with us," Portland said.

"But they are executive rooms," the clerk said, "with a bed and a pullout couch. Two people will be quite comfortable."

Portland looked to Chambers, who shrugged. "Whatever you say," he said.

Now Portland looked to Brixton, his question obvious. Would Brixton be willing to bunk in with Chambers?

Brixton picked up on Portland's intent and said, "You two will get along fine in the same room. Like the lady says, it's an *executive* room."

Portland put aside the question of who would room with whom and said, "That sounds fine. We'll take both rooms."

He slapped an American Express card on the counter and they were registered.

"Let's drop the luggage and get something to drink," he said, looking past the lobby to the busy bar. "Can you recommend a good restaurant?" he asked the clerk.

She reeled off a half dozen, including a Domino's Pizza.

"Pizza," Brixton said.

"That steak place appeals to me," Chambers said.

"No, I want pizza," Brixton said, unwilling to subject himself to an unknown Nigerian restaurant. "They can't screw up pizza."

CHAPTER 52

PORT HARCOURT, NIGERIA

Pizza wasn't on the menu at Max Soderman's house that night.

The XCAL COO hosted his weekly poker game for a few select executives from the oil company, men who shared his jaundiced views of the Niger Delta and particularly its native inhabitants. It was a gathering of like-minded bigots; "The Klan's got nothing on us," one quipped.

Soderman had enjoyed a solitary dinner of lobster tails, a salad, and fresh-baked bread before the others arrived, its dishes lovingly prepared by household servants. Now, in his den, he and four others sat around a custom poker table with green felt, and channels for their chips. The stakes were high for a seemingly friendly neighborhood game. Some pots exceeded five hundred dollars.

One of the players was William Jessup, Soderman's vice president of purchasing. He was the youngest man at the table and had become Soderman's most trusted lieutenant. The tall, lithe Brit with an affable personality had become Soderman's eyes and ears within the company, his antenna always up to intercept someone's disparaging remarks about his boss and his ironfisted running of XCAL. The executive rank and file were well aware of Jessup's allegiance to Soderman and knew that whatever they said in Jessup's presence at the water fountain or in the cafeteria would be dutifully reported back to him. It was office politics as usual, practiced in every company and corporation in the world. But the ramifications of someone spouting negative thoughts about Soderman in front of Jessup were sometimes harsh, resulting in a denial of promotions and raises, and in certain instances termination.

The game was less spirited than most had been, thanks to Soderman's sour mood. He usually reveled in the hands he was dealt and didn't attempt to disguise his glee at taking the other players' money. But he was noticeably glum this night, going through the motions and anxious for the game to end. His mood didn't improve as one of the executives had a run of good fortune and pocketed much of Soderman's stake. The game broke up at eleven; the players stayed behind for a while to continue their bashing of Nigeria and its people. "They have to take off their shoes to count to twenty," one particularly prejudiced man said with a hearty laugh.

Finally, Soderman and Jessup were alone in the den after the other players had departed and staff members had cleared away their food and glasses.

"Sorry you're in a foul mood," Jessup commented.

"You'd be, too, if you had these clowns from London descending on you," Soderman grumbled, pouring another shot of bourbon. "What do *you* hear about the audit?"

"Not a lot, Max. I saw a communiqué from the high commission in Lagos that the contingent from London is expected any day."

Soderman guffawed. "That bunch of weak-kneed bureaucrats should stay the hell away from here. They come from their cozy lives in the UK and think they can understand what's going on in Nigeria. This is a hellhole, Bill, a real hellhole. MEND hit another of our facilities this morning."

"So I heard. I was told that they overran the SureSafe chaps and killed two of them."

"So much for security. Penny and I talked about that."

"Fournier was part of that discussion?"

"Of course. I wouldn't mind if the Frenchman did his job and kept the facilities safe, but his people are idiots. Not only that, most of them are on the take, too." He muttered something under his breath. "And while all this goes on Agu Gwantam sits back and keeps collecting his vig. I've had it."

"Are you still talking about packing it in and getting out of here?" Jessup asked, hoping the answer would be negative.

"I think about it all the time. Christ, you'd think that my benefiting from the siphoning of some of their damn oil was like holding up a bank. How much do I benefit from it? Chump change, that's how much. It's not worth it. And now I have to deal with the auditors."

"It'll be just like the other probes," said Jessup. "They'll arrive, make a show of their so-called investigation, and hightail it back home. What's new with Sir Manford Penny?" He spoke his name with exaggerated awe.

"He's a real weak sister, Bill."

Jessup finished his drink. That his boss, Soderman, had benefited from Agu Gwantam's largesse in spreading around the money that oil bunkering produced was no secret. He knew it because not only had Soderman taken him into his confidence; he'd also begun to cut him in on the spoils.

Jessup had taken the job in the Niger Delta with XCAL after having spent a half-dozen years as a buyer of auto parts for a major British automobile manufacturer. As with Soderman, a romantic relationship gone bad had propelled his decision to leave the UK and to experience the adventure of living in a country whose culture was vastly different from his. He hadn't been on the new job long before the opportunities to enhance his already generous salary became evident. In Nigeria few business transactions were conducted without bribes being included in the bottom line, and he became adroit at eliciting them.

"This will all blow over," Jessup said, hoping it would raise his boss's spirits.

"Will it?"

"You need a night out on the town," Jessup said.

"I need a lot of nights away from here."

"How about tomorrow?" Jessup suggested. "We can go down to the beach, suck up a few cocktails, and maybe hook up with a pretty *ashawo*," he said, using the Nigerian slang for "prostitute."

"Yeah, maybe. Let's see how tomorrow goes. Another drink?"

"Thanks, no, Max. Time to get to bed. See you in the morning."

Jessup left Soderman but didn't go home. Instead, he drove to the posh neighborhood in which Agu Gwantam, the Nigerian warlord, lived. Gwantam welcomed him warmly and led him to a secluded patio where a servant served cordials. Their meeting resulted from Jessup having called Gwantam a few days earlier to inform him that London's Serious Fraud Office of the Attorney General's Office was in the process of dispatching auditors to the Niger. Gwantam had thanked Jessup profusely and invited him to the house for a drink after the poker game.

Jessup didn't like Gwantam—he didn't like any of the black Nigerians with whom he interacted—but he recognized the warlord's power to distribute his share of the profits from oil bunkering and bowed to that power, especially since he benefited from it.

"And how was your card game?" Gwantam asked the young executive. "I hope you left it a richer man."

Jessup laughed. "I'm afraid not," he said. "I'm not a very good poker player."

"Perhaps you should take up a game at which you excel," said Gwantam, smiling.

"I'm sure you're right," Jessup said.

"I appreciate very much, Mr. Jessup, your confiding in me things in which I am naturally interested."

Jessup found Gwantam's studied correct English annoying.

"And I appreciate your generosity, Mr. Gwantam."

The big Nigerian shrugged. "It is just a matter of rewarding those who do favors for others. Knowing what Mr. Soderman is thinking and feeling is important to me. I'm sure you understand that."

Jessup nodded.

"And I must admit that I have grown tired of Soderman's complaints about the size of his share from the oil bunkering. To be truthful, his lack of gratitude for the money I have provided him distresses me."

"Of course," said Jessup. "He should be grateful."

"So," Gwantam said, "what came out of your regular poker evening?"

Jessup dutifully recounted what had been said about things that might interest Gwantam, ignoring, of course, the racist comments that had passed around the table along with the cards.

They spoke for another half hour before Jessup took his leave and returned to his home in Ikoyi, considerably smaller and less opulent than Soderman's but perfectly suitable for a single young man. On his way out of Gwantam's house the Nigerian warlord handed him an envelope filled with Nigerian naira notes. "Remember, Mr. Jessup, that Agu Gwantam is always ready to reward his friends," Gwantam said, his smile wide and bright enough to light the path to Jessup's car.

CHAPTER 53

LAGOS, NIGERIA

They'd agreed to meet for breakfast at eight.

Brixton, who'd had trouble sleeping, arrived at the hotel restaurant at seven and perused the buffet in search of simple dishes that didn't involve Nigerian culinary creativity. He'd heard about that nation's fondness for hot, spicy ingredients and wasn't eager to start the day with heartburn. He'd wondered at dinner whether the Nigerian penchant for spicy foods would extend to pizza. It hadn't. His sausage slices tasted the same as they did back in D.C.

After a glass of orange juice, a buttered bagel, and coffee, he strolled outside and scoped out a patio at the side of the hotel, away from the main entrance where a succession of cars came and went, and street hawkers had begun to gather. Portland and Chambers found him.

"Sleep well?" Portland asked cheerily.

"So-so," Brixton said.

"Looks like a nice buffet in there," said Chambers. "I think

I'll make a pass at it. I'll catch up with you later. I have an errand to run after breakfast."

"What errand?" Brixton asked Portland after Chambers had left.

"He wants to buy some new clothes before we head for the delta. He's hardly dressed for an expedition into the bush."

"Yeah, I noticed," said Brixton.

"There's a men's clothing store a few blocks from here. I'm sure he'll find something to wear there." He laughed. "Maybe he'll come back dressed like the great white hunter. Let's go inside. I need something to eat."

As they came around to the front of the hotel, street vendors and beggars harassed them before they could reach the entrance, selling everything from watches ("Genuine Rolexes") to a small white puppy cradled in the arms of an old, toothless woman. Some hawked crude hand-carved figurines, others fruit from burlap bags. A few simply begged, their cupped hands shoved in front of passersby. Portland waved them off and navigated the throng, Brixton close behind. But Brixton stopped when confronted by a young girl he judged to be no older than twelve or thirteen. She had a board around her neck on which crude letters said: **Deaf-Dumb**. She looked at him with large, brown eyes and gestured toward her mouth with her fingers, which he took to mean that she was hungry. He fished in his pocket, pulled out some Nigerian naira notes, and handed them to her. Portland watched the exchange with interest. When the girl had bowed repeatedly to Brixton and left to find another person willing to respond to her plight, Portland said, "I didn't know you were an easy touch, Robert."

"I felt sorry for her," Brixton said defensively.

"I thought you might buy the puppy," Portland said.

"I would if I knew what to do with it."

When they were settled in the restaurant and Portland wolfed down the dishes he'd chosen from the buffet, he said between forkfuls, "You still have a thing about Chambers, don't you?"

"It doesn't matter," Brixton replied, peeling a banana. "He's here. You wanted him here. End of story."

"Mind a suggestion?" Portland asked.

Brixton cocked his head.

"I don't know what the next couple of days will bring," Portland said, "but it could get uncomfortable. Carrying your dislike for our friend on your sleeve won't help matters."

"'Our friend'?'He's *your* friend, David, not mine. Sorry, but I'll never understand why you took him up on coming with us."

"It doesn't matter why I did," Portland said, "but I know one thing. Your animosity toward him had better not get in the way of why I'm in Nigeria."

Had he continued with his thought he would have said that he was sorry that he had allowed Brixton to accompany him, and was second-guessing having bent to Chambers's wish that he, too, join them. What was happening to him? Was he turning soft? Had he lost his ability to analyze a situation and take a stand based upon pragmatic conclusions? It didn't matter. They were here, and he'd better make the best of it.

"I hear you," said Brixton. "You don't have to worry about me."

"Good."

Portland checked his watch. "Our flight to Port Harcourt leaves at two. Mr. Gomba will meet us when we arrive. I left a message on his cell phone in response to one of those outgoing messages recorded by a professional announcer. I said that we had a third party traveling with us."

"Why should it matter?" Brixton asked.

"He should know how many items to bring with him."

"What items?" Brixton asked. Then, realizing what Portland meant, he said, "Weapons?"

"That and a few other things."

"What's the drill when we get to Port Harcourt?" Brixton asked.

"First we meet up with Gomba," Portland said. "He'll take us from the airport to a group that he works with."

"That rebel group MEND?" Brixton asked.

Portland shrugged, said, "Maybe."

"I don't understand why MEND would be involved," Brixton said. "I thought you wanted to confront the Frenchman Fournier about your son's death."

"Look," said Portland, "I don't know if Gomba is involved with MEND, or how he plans to put me in touch with Fournier. We're just visitors here. He knows the territory and how to navigate it. That's good enough for me. Let's get ready to leave."

As Portland signed the check, Chambers arrived wearing the clothing he'd purchased, two typical African outfits, a dashiki pants set in shocking blue with ornate white and yellow embroidery, another set in plain white, and what he said was called a *buba*, a loose-fitting pale green shirt that went halfway down his thighs. He wore his blue ensemble.

"Look at you," Portland said. "You've really gone native."

"When in Rome," Chambers said. "Comfort. It's all about comfort."

Brixton thought that Chambers looked foolish but kept his thought to himself.

"It does look comfortable," Portland agreed.

They packed their belongings and went to the lobby, from which they intended to take the hotel's van to the airport, but were told it wouldn't be available for an hour. "Let's grab a cab," Portland said after having exchanged British pounds for Nigerian naira.

A lineup of taxis of various types waited outside the entrance. They chose a Mitsubishi minivan driven by a young man who looked to be in his teens. There was no meter in the cab, so they haggled over a price until they'd reached an agreement. The driver, who announced that his name was Tom, pushed through the knot of street sellers, reached the road in front of the hotel, and roared away, the vehicle's wheels digging into the road's ruts and tossing his passengers against one another in the backseat. They were flanked right and left by *okadas*, motorbike taxis whose drivers seemed oblivious to other vehicles and the mass of pedestrians crossing the road. Tom lit a cigarillo with one hand while navigating the traffic and pedestrians. A man herding a solitary goat with a stick crossed in front of them and Tom came to a screeching halt, swearing in pidgin English.

They eventually turned onto the road leading to the terminal at Murtala Muhammed International Airport and pulled up in front of the domestic terminal. Tom took the bills that Portland handed him, smiled, pointed to his wristwatch, and said, "Very fast trip, yes? You pay extra for the fast trip."

"No, nothing extra," Portland said as he and the others pulled their baggage from the cargo area.

"Everybody's got his hand out," Brixton grumbled.

"Don't give him anything extra," Portland said as Brixton fumbled in his pocket for money.

They pushed through the legion of people inside the terminal and stood in a long line for the Arik Air flight to Port Harcourt. The line moved slowly, causing Portland to frequently check his watch.

"This is taking forever," Chambers said. "We're liable to miss our flight." He'd received many stares because of what he wore, the tall white man dressed in typical Nigerian native garb. He seemed to enjoy the attention.

They eventually reached the ticket agent, and twenty minutes later were strapped in the seats of an aircraft considerably smaller than the one they'd taken from London. This flight, too, was filled with oil workers from the delta, and Portland hoped that Brixton wouldn't get into another tussle with one. He didn't. After waiting a half hour for takeoff clearance they were airborne, and an hour later were on their final approach into the Port Harcourt International Airport, ranked by frequent fliers as one of the world's dirtiest and most chaotic.

Portland looked out the window and felt his stomach muscles tighten. Until now the idea of confronting Alain Fournier had been just that, an idea, a goal that was with him day and night, waking him from sleep, stabbing him at odd moments. He'd had moments of doubt since leaving Washington and setting out on this revengeful venture but never to the extent that he considered canceling his plans. He wouldn't let Fournier go unscathed for having murdered his son. He couldn't, not if he intended to live with himself for whatever days he had left.

For Brixton, their arrival at Port Harcourt spawned an intense feeling of wanting to be home with Flo, in bed with her, enjoying her feminine charms and protective embraces. He glanced at Chambers in the middle seat and wondered what he was thinking.

Their thoughts were interrupted by the flight attendant who announced over the PA, "Welcome to Port Harcourt, ladies and gentlemen. Enjoy your stay."

CHAPTER 54

WASHINGTON, D.C.

Walter Cale, senior partner of the law firm Cale, Watson and Warnowski, made a series of phone calls. The first was to Rufus Norris, SureSafe's British chief.

"Have you heard from Cameron Chambers?" Cale asked.

"No, I haven't," Norris replied. "He was supposed to stay in touch but hasn't."

"The hotel he was staying at says he checked out," Cale said.

"That's news to me," said Norris.

"You were supposed to keep a tight rein on him."

"I can't babysit him day and night," Norris countered. "He's probably on his way back to the States."

"He would have called. Go by the hotel and see what you can learn."

Norris's sigh reflected his annoyance. "All right," he agreed.

"And what about this Matthew Kelsey character?"

"What about him?"

"Did Chambers make contact with him?"

"The last time I spoke with Chambers he was in the process of doing that."

"And?"

"And what?"

"Did he? Make contact with Kelsey?"

"I assume that he did."

"Assume?"

"I'll check out Kelsey and see if Chambers spoke with him."

"You do know that Portland intended to go to Nigeria," Cale said.

"Yes, I heard that."

"Can you ascertain whether he has?"

"I suppose I can try and check airline records, but that won't be easy."

"And while you're at it check out David Portland's apartment in London. Chambers was supposed to do that. Maybe there's something there that will indicate where he's gone. Get back to me!"

Norris took a minute or two to get over his pique at the way Cale had spoken to him. He called the phone number he had for Kelsey in Barrow-in-Furness. It didn't ring. He then called a friend in the City of London Police force.

"What's up, Rufus?" his bobby friend said.

"I need a favor," Norris said. "Can you check with the police in Barrow-in-Furness to see if there's been any report concerning a man who lives there, Matthew Kelsey?" He provided the address.

Fifteen minutes later his call was returned.

"Your Matthew Kelsey is no longer with us," he said.

"What does that mean?"

"He was murdered. He's the subject of a homicide investigation."

"Who—are there any suspects?"

"Not at the moment. He was knifed to death. Probably some

addict looking for a few quid. He was a down-and-outer, a cripple in a wheelchair. Nasty business, these murders. An addict will do anything for his fix. What else can I do for you, Rufus?"

"Nothing at the moment," Norris said. "Thanks. I owe you one."

The officer laughed. "Got me less than a year till retirement, Rufus. I'll be looking for a job once I turn in the uniform."

"Call me when that time comes," Norris said. "I might be able to find you a spot here at SureSafe."

"Much obliged, Rufus. Much obliged."

Norris was not eager to try to persuade the various airlines serving Nigeria from the UK to reveal their passenger manifests. As far as he was concerned, Walter Cale's obsession with David Portland and Cameron Chambers was just that, an obsession. His time spent with Chambers, which was minimal, caused him to dismiss the law firm's investigator as ineffectual, a lapdog for his employer. Still, XCAL was an important client of the law firm, which meant that it was also an important source of income for SureSafe. He'd go through the motions.

But as he pulled up contact information for the airlines he wondered whether Chambers had, in fact, made personal contact with Matthew Kelsey. It was a devious thought. Was it possible that Chambers had killed Matthew Kelsey? Couldn't be. It was too far-fetched.

But contemplating it gave him his first smile of the day.

CHAPTER 55

PORT HARCOURT, NIGERIA

Portland, Brixton, and Chambers deplaned into the Port Harcourt airport and were immediately immersed in a sea of people. Shrill voices cut through the general din competing with a constant series of PA announcements, crying babies, rhythmic music coming from boom boxes, and shouts in a wide variety of languages.

"I have to get my suitcase," Chambers said as they skirted two men selling T-shirts with photos of Hollywood actresses on them.

"Your suitcase is a pain," Brixton said. "You should use a carry-on."

"But I didn't," Chambers said sharply. He turned to Portland. "Where is this Gomba fellow we're supposed to meet?"

"He said he'd be just outside the main entrance," Portland replied, leading the way in that direction through throngs of other passengers, and peddlers selling everything from trinkets to medicine guaranteed to cure all ailments known to man, and some that weren't.

"I'll meet you there," Chambers said.

"Yeah, you do that," Brixton said.

"Lay off him, Robert," Portland said.

Brixton ignored the admonition and asked, "Do you know what Gomba looks like?"

"He sent a text message saying that he'd be wearing a yellow hat with a big brim."

Brixton snickered. "Great. So all we have to do is find a black guy in a yellow hat."

They managed to reach the entrance to the terminal and stopped for a moment to get their bearings before going through the doors to the front of the building, where they encountered as many people as had been inside. Portland stood on his toes and searched for Gomba.

"There he is," he said, pointing to where a long line of cars waited, their engines running, owners standing by them.

"Jeffrey Gomba?" Portland said to the person in the yellow hat leaning on a silver Mercedes. *He* wore a black suit, and an open-necked white shirt with decorative folds on the chest, a tux shirt. Bare feet were encased in sandals. But the moment he said it he realized that the wearer of the yellow hat was a woman, a stunningly beautiful one with a perfectly chiseled cinnamon-colored oval face and a female body that was barely contained by what she wore.

"You're Portland?" the woman asked.

"Right. This is Robert Brixton, a close friend."

Gomba extended her hand, whose nails were tipped in a vivid red nail polish. "I appreciate you picking us up," Portland said, "but I have to admit that I'm surprised that—"

"My pleasure," Gomba said. She looked beyond Portland. "Where is the third person?" Her voice had a discernible cultured lilt to it.

"He's getting his checked baggage," Portland said. "You're . . . you're a woman."

Her laugh was guttural. "I was when I got up this morning."

"Your name is Jeffrey?"

A lighter laugh this time. "Thanks to my daddy. I'm the youngest of five daughters. My father always wanted a son, but that wasn't to be, so he gave me a boy's name." She looked beyond Brixton and Portland. "Big mistake checking baggage," she said. "Takes too much time."

"Tell me about it," Brixton groused. He'd found the conversation between the beautiful woman with a male name and Portland amusing.

Gomba lit a cigarillo and offered one to them. "Lino cigarillos," she said. "The best."

They declined.

"Welcome to Nigeria," Gomba said, taking in the chaos surrounding them. "There are lots of problems here."

"So I've read," Portland said. "You—you act as a guide?"

"I do whatever I must to make a living in this crazy land. You need something? Gomba will get it for you. You have a problem? Gomba will solve it."

"A jack-of-all-trades," Brixton said.

"What is that?" Gomba asked.

"Just a saying," Brixton said. He looked at his watch. "Where the hell is Chambers?"

Gomba, too, checked her watch. "We must leave," she said. "It is difficult to drive at night where we are going."

"Where *are* we going?" Brixton asked, searching for Chambers in the crowd.

"To meet my friends who will help you," Gomba answered.

"Who are they?" Brixton asked over the din.

Gomba's answer was interrupted by a uniformed Nigerian police officer who ordered Gomba to move her car. Gomba smiled and said something in one of Nigeria's myriad native languages. The officer responded in kind. The confrontation was resolved when the officer accepted naira notes from Gomba and walked away without saying another word.

"You bought him off," Brixton said.

Gomba laughed. "It is just a business transaction. It was easy. Usually they want more, always more."

"Everybody in Nigeria seems to be involved in these so-called business transactions." As Brixton said it he thought of Flo in Los Angeles and wished that he were there with her. He wished he were anywhere but Port Harcourt, Nigeria.

Chambers eventually emerged from the terminal carrying his suitcase.

"It's about time," Brixton said.

Gomba greeted Chambers, who also displayed surprise that the person they were meeting was a woman. She commented on his African dress.

"It's comfortable," Chambers said.

"You look like a Nigerian," Gomba said, "except for—"

"I know," said Chambers. "I'm the wrong color."

"A little makeup will fix that," Gomba said cheerily. "Come. We're losing time." Gomba threw Chambers's luggage in the trunk with the other bags and urged them to get in the car. Once they were—Portland took the front passenger seat—Gomba pulled away from the curb, cut off a panel truck and two cars, and drove across a median divider, the right wheels digging into the grassy strip.

"Whoa!" Brixton exclaimed.

"Not to worry," Gomba said over her shoulder. "I am a very good driver, only had a few tickets."

Darkness began to set in as they rode in silence, Chambers and Brixton wincing each time Gomba had to navigate multiple tie-ups on the roads she chose. She once had to skirt a crater that slowed traffic to a crawl, bringing forth a string of curses from her. They seemed always to be surrounded by *okadas*, motorbikes whose reckless drivers caused Brixton to mutter, "They're nuts, like the Japs and kamikaze."

"Do you mind telling us where we're going?" Chambers asked,

hoping his question wouldn't result in Gomba taking her eyes off the road.

"You will soon see," their guide said. "You need help? Jeffrey Gomba is here to help you. Patience! It is a virtue." A loud laugh followed. "You can call me Jeffy," she added. "Sounds more feminine, doesn't it?"

They eventually left the more populated areas between the airport and the city of Port Harcourt and were now on narrow dirt roads. To their left and right were the waters of the Niger Delta's twisting streams, rivers, and lakes, sparkling in the moon's rays. The roads narrowed even more, causing Jeffy to drive slowly to avoid hitting rocks that were strewn everywhere. As they progressed, a feeling of unease permeated the car.

Chambers kept asking where they were headed, to Brixton's annoyance, although he, too, had become edgy. He knew that Portland had engaged Gomba on the advice of someone at the British Embassy in D.C., but he couldn't help but wonder whether they'd ended up in some sort of trap. Who was this woman who called herself Jeffy, this beautiful Nigerian wearing a black suit, tux shirt, and yellow floppy-brimmed hat? For all Brixton knew she might be driving them to their demise.

"Tell me a little about yourself!" Brixton yelled over the seatback to her, suffering the same anxiety as Chambers.

"Almost there," was Jeffy's nonresponsive reply. "Almost there."

There was a jetty perched on the edge of a small waterway. She stopped the car, left the headlights on, got out, and walked to the edge of the rickety wooden dock. Her passengers joined her, their every step causing the dock to sway. There was a sour smell in the heavy humid air, an oppressive odor of gasoline or motor oil coupled with human excrement.

"What are we doing here?" Chambers asked, his voice belying his nervousness.

Portland, who'd remained silent for most of the trip, now spoke up. "He's right," he told Jeffy. "What the hell *are* we doing here in the dark?"

The silence was broken by the sound of an approaching motorboat. Jeffy waved to it before going to her car to turn off the lights and to lock it. When she returned, the boat, which had been shrouded in darkness, now came into view. It was an older craft, wooden, with a makeshift patterned bedsheet stretched over its occupants. Jeffy trained a flashlight on it. The paint on the hull had flaked off in large swatches. It had once been blue. Now its sides were weathered gray.

Three men in the boat exchanged greetings. The young man operating the engine throttled back, causing the motor to burp and balk, with sounds occasionally resuming a low rumble. His two colleagues were also young. They were black, of course, their faces coming and going in the erratic motion of Jeffy's flashlight. One, who was bare-chested, wore a bright orange band on his head that almost obscured his eyes. Another was dressed in a one-piece camouflage outfit and cradled an AK-47 in his arms. The boat's operator had an unusually elongated face that never changed its stoic expression. Brixton's take on him was that the smile gene had been absent at his birth.

"Get in, my friends," Jeffy told Portland, Brixton, and Chambers.

"Why?" Chambers asked.

"Where are we going in that thing?" Brixton demanded.

"As I have told you, to meet the people who will help you," Jeffy said. Her pleasant, friendly tone was now replaced by a stern voice. "You must trust me," she said. "If you do not trust me I—"

"I just don't want to be kept in the dark like this," Portland said.

Jeffy laughed. " 'In the dark,' "she said. "Very clever. Come on, man, all of you get in. We don't have all night."

Portland was the first to scramble aboard, followed by

Brixton. Chambers appeared to be deciding whether to join them. "Come on, man," Jeffy said. "Wasting time is not good."

"Are we going to a hotel?" Chambers asked.

"Later, man," said Jeffy. "First we make our plans."

As the boat's operator advanced the throttle, the engine protested and grumbled before catching and propelling them away from the dock. Chambers looked back at Gomba's car and wondered whether he'd ever see his suitcase again. He was also aware of the way the man with the AK-47 stared at him. He forced a smile and indicated his African garb with his hand. The man's stony stare never changed, the whites of his large eyes his only discernible feature in the darkness of the swamp they'd entered.

Jiffy pulled a flask from her inside jacket pocket and offered it to Portland, who sat beside her on one of the boat's four bench seats.

"What is it?" Portland asked.

"*Ogogoro*, man," she said. "Very good gin. My father makes it from the juice of the raffia palms. Very powerful, good for your stomach and your sinuses. You listen to Dr. Gomba."

"You're a medicine man, too," Portland commented.

"Medicine woman," she corrected. "I am a registered nurse among other things. Doing many things is the only way to survive in Nigeria unless you work for the oil companies." She spit over the side. "I would rather die than do *that*!"

The boat's pilot made a sharp left turn into a channel flanked by mangroves, their branches hanging low over the water and forcing everyone to crouch in their seats to avoid being hit by them. Minutes later they broke free of the mangrove canopy and were in a cove with a small, sandy beach.

"This is it?" Portland asked as the boat's pilot ran it full throttle up onto the sand.

"What is this place?" Chambers asked.

"We are among friends," Jeffy said, "good friends who will help you."

"Who are these friends?" Portland asked.

"Men who share your vision of how our people have been raped by the big oil companies, their land polluted and destroyed, their families torn apart by greed."

"What is this, some MEND operation?" Brixton asked. "That's what it's called, isn't it, MEND?"

Gomba answered with a simple nod as the young men in the boat hopped out and manually pulled the boat as far up on the beach as possible. Portland, Brixton, and Chambers climbed from the beached boat and were soon surrounded by a dozen men carrying weapons of various types, some of whom greeted Jeffy Gomba warmly. Their chatter was indecipherable to Brixton, Portland, and Chambers, who stood awkwardly on the perimeter of the knot of people. Jeffy eventually introduced them to the Nigerians, not by name but by "my good friends."

Most eyes were on Chambers, whose African garb had garnered attention, but the others were also acknowledged. Brixton's expression mirrored his confusion at why they were there, and where they would go next. His question was answered when the group moved from the beach to a campground of sorts, a series of ramshackle huts fronted by a makeshift sidewalk made of wooden slats lashed together. Beyond the huts was a larger building, a one-story partially completed structure made of cinder blocks and wooden panels that had been haphazardly fitted together. Old clothing was wedged into gaps to keep out the elements. A porch sagged in front of the building. Above it a flag made of white bath towels waved in the evening breeze. They would later learn that the flag was in honor of Egbesu, who, Jeffy explained, was a mythical spirit worshiped by her Ijaw ethnic group. The odor of oil and human waste was even stronger now. They passed what served as an open-air latrine, a mud flat containing human feces and urine. Chambers gagged but managed not to vomit.

If there was any doubt that the encampment housed fighters,

two pits surrounded by sandbags contained machine guns manned by members of the group. A half-dozen other men, their automatic weapons and rifles propped at their sides, lolled about on mattresses that had long ago been discarded from the beds they'd serviced.

Gomba led her three guests up onto the porch and indicated they were to take seats on barrels that served as chairs.

"What's going on?" Brixton whispered as he sat next to Portland.

"Beats me, mate," Portland replied.

Jeffy disappeared inside, returning minutes later accompanied by a tall, slender older man with white hair, dressed in purple coveralls and sneakers, and a young man carrying a battered black director's chair. Jeffy didn't introduce them by name. All she said was, "The commander wishes to welcome you."

The three men stood. The commander smiled and indicated that they were to resume their seats. When they had, the young man set down the director's chair. The commander took it and instructed his young aide to bring refreshments for his guests.

"Jeffy says you are good men to be trusted," he said in almost flawless English. Brixton, Portland, and Chambers looked at one another before Portland said, "Thank you for your hospitality, sir."

The commander looked down from the porch at a dozen members of his ragtag army who'd gathered to witness the meeting. "I am afraid that I do not have much to offer in the way of hospitality," the commander said, "but we do our best. Jeffy tells me that you have come to Nigeria on a mission. Is this correct?"

"A mission?" Portland said. "Yes, I suppose you could call it that."

"A mission to avenge the murder of your son," said the commander.

"That's right," Portland replied.

"A terrible thing when a son is murdered."

Portland said nothing. But Brixton spoke.

"You're right, sir," he said, "about why we're here. But I have to admit I don't have any idea why we've ended up in the middle of a swamp." He batted away a mosquito that attacked his face. "My friend David wants to confront the man who shot and killed his son, a Frenchman who heads up a security force here."

"Alain Fournier," the commander said flatly. "SureSafe."

"You know him?" Brixton asked.

The commander smiled. "Of course we know him," he said. "He is known to every Nigerian who lives and works in the delta—and is hated by all."

"Your people have had run-ins with him?" Chambers asked, wanting to be part of the conversation.

Another knowing smile from the commander. "You might say that, sir. Run-ins? Yes, we have had many of those with Mr. Fournier." He turned his attention to Portland. "What do you wish to accomplish by confronting Fournier?"

It was a question that Portland had been grappling with ever since he'd made the decision to come to Nigeria. His stab at formulating an answer was postponed by the arrival of the commander's aide carrying a tray containing a plate of small fried balls of food of an unknown origin, and small glasses of an equally mysterious beverage.

"Please," the commander said. "Enjoy."

"What is it?" Chambers asked.

"Dough balls," said the commander. "Quite tasty. The drink is *paraga*, a specialty of Nigeria, a mix of herbs and spirits."

Portland and Chambers took glasses as a courtesy to their host. Brixton didn't. He'd had enough of this macabre nighttime gathering in a swamp with a bunch of Nigerian militants. That wasn't why he'd accompanied Portland to Nigeria. He said, "Look, Mr. Commander, we appreciate all this, but the reason we're here is for my friend David to confront the man who killed his son. That's it, pure and simple. I thought that your friend Ms. Gomba would pick us up, take us to a hotel, and help plan how the confrontation would take place. I have to admit that we were shocked that she was a woman. I mean—"

"Jeffy Gomba may be a woman," said the commander, "but she has the heart of a warrior."

"Yeah, I don't doubt that. She's good-looking, too. But I'd like to know why you and your friends got involved."

His question coincided with his first swallow of the potent *paraga*. It assaulted his sinuses. His eyes watered and his throat felt as though a scalding liquid had been poured down it. Chambers, his glass poised at his lips, put it down. Portland wheezed and gasped, returned his glass to the tray, and managed to say, "It's—it's very strong."

"But good, yes?" the commander said.

Brixton ignored the banter over the drink and pressed his concern about why they were there. "What are you going to do to help my friend face the guy who killed his son?"

The commander thought for a moment before saying, "Mr. Fournier is not an easy man to confront. He controls a powerful security force that protects him at all times. I know of what I speak. Not that we are friends. I detest the man and everything he stands for. He and his security forces have killed many of our people, gunned them down, threw their bodies away in the swamp like fetid meat, all in the interest of the oil companies that pay their bloated salaries and further line their pockets with bribes, dirty money stolen from our people. Yes, sir, I know the Frenchman Alain Fournier, well enough to want to see him dead."

When Brixton and the others didn't respond, the commander added, "You see, sir, Fournier murdered my son, too."

CHAPTER 56

PORT HARCOURT, NIGERIA

Portland, Brixton, and Chambers spent an additional hour with the commander of the militia unit, who seemed to enjoy having them as an audience and took advantage of their presence, railing against the oil companies and the destruction they'd inflicted on Nigeria. He was especially incensed about the culture of graft and greed that permeated the nation, particularly in the Niger Delta where the abundant oil made the companies and their backers rich while impoverishing his people. He frequently downed shots of *paraga*, which fueled his rhetoric. His three guests pretended to join him in consuming the potent beverage but left most of what was in their glasses untouched. Brixton was hungry. He'd tasted the food on the tray but decided to forgo it. It was like biting into a tennis ball.

They were interested, of course, in the commander's tale of how his son had been murdered by Alain Fournier. While he wasn't certain that it had been Fournier who'd pulled the trigger, he was adamant that the Frenchman had been present when it happened and whoever wielded the weapon did so upon Fournier's orders.

"My son had been part of a unit that attacked one of the oil companies' refining operations," the commander said. "He had taken part in many such raids."

"MEND raids," Portland said.

"We are not MEND," the commander explained. "We are one of many independent groups that act on behalf of MEND when it is necessary to take action."

Hired guns, Brixton thought. *Don't take these guys lightly no matter how scruffy they are.*

"It's been a long day," Portland said to the commander during a lull in his diatribe. "Where's Ms. Gomba? Time for us to leave."

The commander dispatched his aide to round up Jeffy, who appeared from inside the building.

"We're ready to go," Portland told her.

"Whenever you say," she said. She'd applied makeup that enhanced her natural beauty. Brixton noticed her ample bosom, which pressed against the tux jacket she wore, but quickly averted his eyes, not wanting to offend her by staring. He was glad that they'd finally be heading for some hotel where he could take a shower and get something to eat. Mosquitoes had become increasingly aggressive and plentiful and he'd been bitten a half-dozen times—*Did they carry some sort of rare African terminal disease?* he wondered.

It occurred to him that the meeting with the so-called commander hadn't enlightened anyone on how his militia would be helpful to Portland's need to confront Fournier. That was on Portland's mind, too, and the Brit asked directly, stressing that his only motive was to challenge the Frenchman and his role in Trevor's murder.

The commander said in response, "Alain Fournier is a formidable man, sir. The SureSafe security forces he leads are ruthless, criminals without a conscience who think nothing of murdering our people who dare to challenge the oil cartels. Fournier is never without armed guards. They are with him day and night." He paused, and the hint of a smile crossed his chiseled face. "Except, of course, when he is with one of the many *ashawos* he enjoys." His guests' blank expressions prompted him to add, "Prostitutes. Whores."

"So you're saying that you'll help me confront Fournier?" Portland said.

"I have already discussed it with Jeffy," said the commander. "She will talk more specifically with you about it." He stood. "Thank you for visiting us. You are, of course, not to discuss anything about this meeting, including its location."

"You don't have to worry about that," Portland said, offering his hand.

The three men and Jeffy were escorted back to the boat. They said nothing to one another as they sat hunched over during the trip back to the jetty where she had parked the car. The three Nigerians manning the boat were effusive in their farewell to Jeffy, who was obviously well known and respected.

"Where to now?" Brixton asked once they'd settled in the car.

"To your hotel," Jeffy said.

A half hour later, after turning onto the Port Harcourt–Aba Expressway, they pulled up to a white building surrounded by a high white wall. An armed guard stood sentry duty at a gate leading into the complex.

"This is it?" Chambers asked.

"You will be comfortable here," Gomba said, "and quite safe."

"I need a bathroom," Chambers said.

"Yes, of course," Jeffy said.

She got out, opened the liftgate, and they retrieved their luggage. She reached into the cargo area's recesses and emerged with a large package wrapped in brown paper, which she handed to Portland.

"What's this?" Portland asked.

"Things you will need," Jeffy said. "I will return at ten tomorrow morning to brief you."

"Brief us?" Brixton asked. "Brief us about what?"

"How we will dispose of Mr. Fournier."

"Hold on a second," Portland said. "Who said anything about disposing of him? I just want to—"

She held up her hand. "Please, sir, I know what you are saying. We can discuss it further tomorrow. Have a good rest. I will see you at ten."

They watched her get back into her Mercedes and drive away.

"What do you figure is in it?" Brixton said, referring to the package.

"Let's check in and we'll find out," Portland said, leading the way to the gate where, after explaining that they were guests, they were allowed to enter the lobby. Registering was quick and easy, and they soon found themselves in their assigned rooms, small by U.S. standards but not unpleasant. This time Portland ensured that each would have his own room in deference to what he knew Brixton was thinking.

They later met in the hotel's small bar next to a swimming pool. They were the only patrons. After ordering drinks, Portland held up the package.

"Open it," Brixton said.

In it were three compact Pamas-BU9 Nano handguns, magazines holding eight rounds of 9mm ammunition, and ankle holsters.

"Boy, it's small," Brixton commented as he examined one of the weapons.

"Put it away," Chambers said. "We don't need people seeing it."

"Guns make you nervous?" Brixton asked.

"Put it away," Portland told Brixton, sensing another conflict brewing with Chambers.

"I'd think that a cop would—"

"Put it away, Robert," Portland repeated, steel in his voice.

Brixton rewrapped the three handguns and placed the package on an empty chair next to him.

They sipped their drinks without saying much until Chambers broke the silence.

"I know that this isn't my business," he said, "but I get the feeling that we're going beyond why David wanted to come here in the first place. That commander makes it sound like we're about to become part of his group's assault on the Frenchman and his people. If that's the case, count me out. I didn't come here to end up in a war."

"Why *did* you come?" Brixton asked.

"Because—because I believe in what David is trying to do here and . . ."

"And what?" Portland asked.

"And—and because I came to realize that the people I work for aren't interested in the truth about what happened to your son. They're trying to cover up the truth by tapping phones and sending me to spy on you. Look, deciding to give up my job wasn't easy. It was a good job, paid well, came with lots of perks. But when Walter Cale told me to have Elizabeth Sims's phones tapped, too, that went over the line as far as I was concerned. I know that the killing of your son affected her deeply, too. After all, she was his stepmom and raised him by herself for the most part." Portland stiffened and Chambers sensed it. He said to him, "You decided to come to Nigeria to face the man who took your son's life. I guess it was important to me to be able to tell her that I was a part of it."

"Tell Elizabeth?" Portland said.

"Yes."

"You sound like you're in love with David's ex," Brixton said, glancing at Portland, whose expression was blank.

Chambers ignored the comment and continued. "Look," he said, "I know that neither of you particularly likes me, especially you, Robert, and I understand why. I wish it were different. I just want to see a wrong righted, that's all. I haven't had many opportunities in my life to do that."

Brixton and Portland took in Chambers and saw that he was on the verge of tearing up.

"Let's see what the restaurant is serving and get some sleep," Brixton said. "Tomorrow's shaping up to be busy and I'm beat."

They went to their rooms following dinner, and Chambers was relieved to be away from them. He feared that he'd offended Portland by his comments about Elizabeth, and Brixton's animosity toward him was becoming wearing. He sat by the window and reflected on what his life had become.

His decision to accompany them to Nigeria might have been a boneheaded one, but now that he was here he'd rise to the occasion and help Portland achieve his goal.

His final thought as he turned off the light was that Elizabeth would be proud of him.

CHAPTER 57

PORT HARCOURT, NIGERIA

After dropping her wards at the hotel, Jeffrey Gomba, aka Ms. Jeffy Gomba, drove to her house on the outskirts of Port Harcourt, where she whipped up a late supper. She had the house to herself. Her sisters were seldom there; their busy social lives occupied their time away from the various office jobs they held, as well as having to keep their husbands happy.

Jeffy had shared the house with her aging father until his death. It was one of the better homes in the modest neighborhood, purchased and maintained with money that Jeffy earned from her variety of ventures, supplemented by what her sisters and father could contribute. He was a poorly educated but intelligent man, who had worked hard at myriad jobs to provide a better life for his family, his efforts appreciated by his now-deceased wife and their daughters. He'd been brought up in poverty. The first house in which they'd lived lacked indoor plumbing; the better ones featured outhouses, others open ditches. Their current home had all the amenities, including a flush toilet.

The Gomba family's patriarch had succumbed to a terminal

lung condition. He'd made his living on the streets of Port Harcourt after having dropped out of the Catholic school he'd attended until the eighth grade. Although uneducated, he was naturally bright and ambitious and always seemed to find a way to generate income, even when some of those ways involved illegality. Some said it was his charm that carried him. Others pointed to occasional contacts he'd managed to nourish in high places. But the reasons for his modest success weren't important. Jeffrey Gomba knew his way around the system, and his street smarts had rubbed off on his daughter Jeffy.

Unlike her sisters, Jeffy had followed a rebellious path since her teen years. No one debated that she was the most beautiful of the Gomba sisters; it had been suggested more than once that she pursue a career as a model or actress, and she had entered a teenage beauty contest when she was sixteen. After coming in second she announced to her family that she felt humiliated at parading in front of drooling male judges and would never debase herself that way again.

She'd turned down a scholarship to college and proceeded to forge a life with various anti-government groups, which turned out to be surprisingly profitable. Her activities were of concern, of course, to her father, but at the same time he admired her dedication to righting wrongs in the Niger Delta and being paid for those efforts. In a sense he lived vicariously through her, enjoying her tales of clashes with government or oil company security forces, and wishing that he were a young man again. At the same time he feared for her life and hoped that her activities wouldn't result in her premature demise.

After cleaning up she settled at a table in a small room and went over notes she'd been making since agreeing to sign on with the project involving the Brit David Portland. She'd enjoyed meeting his friends Robert Brixton and Cameron Chambers but had found herself especially drawn to Portland, whose rugged good looks appealed. She'd never spoken directly with him until their meeting at the airport; initial planning had come through his friend at the British Embassy. That phone call had been fortuitous, and Jeffy immediately recognized what it could mean not only to her but also to certain friends, especially the militia commander with whom she'd forged a close relationship.

Portland's embassy friend had made it plain during that initial phone conversation that his pal's sole interest in coming to Nigeria was to confront Alain Fournier about the death of his son. He needed a pathway to gain access to the Frenchman and had asked if Jeffy could help bring that about.

"Yes, I think so," she had replied, "but it will not be easy. Fournier is well aware of how much he is hated, and is never without armed men to protect him."

"I understand," said Portland's friend, "but our mutual friend at the embassy in Washington assured me that if anyone could come up with a plan, it was you."

Jeffy Gomba feigned embarrassment at the compliment but quietly concurred. She prided herself on being a problem solver of the first order—provided the price was right.

They ended the call with Jeffy agreeing to meet Portland's flight in Port Harcourt and act as his guide, put him in touch with the right people, and see to it that he and his friends had everything they would need.

"Your friends will need handguns," he said, "unless they will have brought weapons with then."

"Carrying them on their flights will be too difficult," Jeffy said, "so, yes, they will need handguns. I assume that Mr. Portland's colleagues will want them, too." She gave Portland's friend the price for three handguns and added it to the fee she was charging.

Later that night two of Jeffy's sisters stopped in and toasted Jeffy's new lucrative assignment.

"You'd never before met this Brit Portland?" Jeffy was asked.

"No, nor the two men he is traveling with."

"He certainly is generous," a sister commented after being told the fee Jeffy was charging.

"He gave me half when we met at the airport," Jeffy said, "and the other half will be mine after I have put him in touch with the Frenchman."

"You trust he will pay the second half of the money?"

Jeffy grinned. "Of course he will. The commander's people will make sure that he does. More scotch? It is very tasty."

After refilling their glasses, Jeffy said, "It is a fair price he is paying, but there is more to it."

"Oh?"

"My friend the commander has wanted to rid the country of the Frenchman for a long time, ever since his own son was killed by Fournier's people. I have no doubt that he will happily join this Portland fellow in accomplishing that goal."

"Portland wants to *kill* Fournier? You said he wanted only to talk to him about what happened to his son."

"Talk to him?" Jeffy said mockingly. "Everyone I know wants to see Alain Fournier dead and buried. The commander has been planning an attack on him since his son was shot but has not found the right moment. Now, with this British fellow leading the way, the time might have arrived."

"You will not be involved in any killing, Jeffy?"

"Of course not. I will only work with the Brit and the commander to help them achieve their goal. That is what I do, yes? I help others do what they need to do."

She smiled and grasped her sister's hand, who said, "And you are so good at doing that, Jeffy. You are so good."

CHAPTER 58

WASHINGTON, D.C.

Walter Cale received a call from Rufus Norris in the UK.

"What have you learned?" he asked SureSafe's British head.

"A great deal. Portland has gone to Nigeria."

"Chambers?" Cale said. "What about Chambers?"

"Are you ready for this?" Norris asked.

"What does that mean?"

"It means that Chambers has also gone to Nigeria. He's traveled there with Portland and with that American private detective Brixton."

"Chambers went to Nigeria with them?" Cale said, his voice mirroring his disbelief.

"That's right," said Norris. "You'll also be interested to learn that Matthew Kelsey, the former SureSafe operative who was shot up in the delta, has been murdered, stabbed to death."

"Chambers?"

"What about him?"

"Did he make contact with Kelsey before he was killed?"

"I have no idea," replied Norris. He was tempted to express

his fanciful thought that Chambers might have killed Kelsey but thought better of it.

"Does Manford Penny know this?" Cale asked.

"Yes. I called him just before I called you."

Cale's silence allowed him time to process what he'd been told.

"That's all I have," Norris said.

"Do you know why Portland has gone to Nigeria?" he asked.

"It has to do with the death of his son," Norris said. "The phone taps confirm this."

"You'd better let that French guy in Nigeria with SureSafe know that Portland will be there."

"Alain Fournier? I've already alerted him, too."

Cale muttered, "Chambers! Damn fool!"

"What?" Norris asked.

His question was met with the sound of a phone being slammed down.

Cale called the tech expert Marvin Baxter.

"Has there been anything of interest on Ms. Sims's line?"

"No," said Baxter.

"She hasn't received any calls from her former husband, David Portland?"

"No. There are lots of other calls. I was going to bring you a list later today."

"Don't bother, but if there are calls from Portland I want to know about it immediately."

CHAPTER 59

Elizabeth Sims had been putting in her usual long days at the law firm, but she'd found that her ability to concentrate on legal issues had been compromised.

On this morning a rumor circulated around the law firm that Cameron Chambers, its head of investigations, had traveled to Nigeria with David Portland, Elizabeth's ex. Could it be? Why would he do that? She knew that David intended to go to Nigeria because he'd told her after their dinner at Aquarelle, but she'd had no idea that Chambers would be with him. The scuttlebutt was that Chambers wouldn't return to his job. Some said that he'd probably be killed in Nigeria, a few of those doomsday types not masking their pleasure should that happen.

CHAPTER 60

Brixton's decision to accompany Portland to Nigeria had blindsided Mac and Annabel Smith.

"Why the hell would he do that?" Smith asked his wife over breakfast.

"You know Robert, Mac. He shoots from the hip."

"Yeah, but Portland has a good motive for going there. Well, at least he has a reason, his son's murder. What's Robert doing, riding shotgun for him?"

"Maybe he saw it as an opportunity to cement their friendship," Annabel offered. "Besides, he was really impacted by what happened to the Nigerian in Virginia, Mr. Dimka."

"Impacted is one thing," Mac countered, "but—"

"Don't forget how Robert's daughter died," Annabel said. "He's been looking for a way to avenge her death ever since the day it happened."

"The terrorist who blew up his daughter wasn't Nigerian."

"That doesn't matter," said Annabel. "He's been seething with anger since that day. The people who killed David Portland's son represent to him the same sort of people who blew up his daughter. I wish he hadn't gone, and I hope he comes back in one piece, but I do understand."

"Do you think Flo understands it?" Mac asked.

"I hope so," Annabel said. "I hope so."

CHAPTER 61

LONDON

Rufus Norris's call to Sir Manford Penny, chairman of XCAL UK, had upset the UK chairman and he pondered how to react before calling Max Soderman, XCAL's COO in Port Harcourt, Nigeria.

"Max, it's Manford."

"Calling from jolly old England."

"David Portland is in Nigeria."

"Who? Oh, right, Portland. What's he doing here?"

"I don't know. He's traveling with an American private detective named Brixton and a Cameron Chambers."

"Who's that?"

Penny explained.

"So, what do you expect me to do?" Soderman asked, his voice gravelly from having had little sleep after a night of carousing.

"I just thought that you should be aware."

"Thanks. Does SureSafe know?"

"Yes."

"Anything else, Manford? I'm due at a meeting."

Penny was sorry that he'd bothered to call. Soderman had worn thin on him, and his recent visit to Port Harcourt had been anything but pleasant and productive.

"No," he said, and hung up.

CHAPTER 62

PORT HARCOURT, NIGERIA

Alain Fournier was also bleary-eyed from having had too little sleep the previous night. On this morning he was forced to sit through what seemed an endless meeting with executives of XCAL to discuss the recent escalation of raids on their facilities by members of MEND or its surrogate militia groups.

The meeting was chaired by Max Soderman, who'd had a brief talk with Fournier before the meeting started.

"You heard from Penny in the UK that David Portland is here in Nigeria?" Soderman said.

"Yes. Do you know what he plans to do?"

"No, I don't, but I suggest that you keep your guard up."

Fournier's laugh was dismissive. "I am not worried about someone like Portland," he said.

"It has to do with his son."

Fournier shrugged. "That is old news, Max. I forgot about it long ago."

"Suit yourself, Alain. Let's start the meeting. I want to get it over with."

Soderman's foul mood extended into the conference room. He berated Fournier for not having stopped recent assaults by MEND on XCAL's facilities, and chastised members of his staff for what he considered a gross dereliction of their duties. The gathering droned on, and Fournier had all he could do to not leave in a huff. Soderman's comments infuriated him; murderous thoughts came and went. Eventually the meeting was concluded and its participants departed. Fournier buttonholed Soderman in the hallway.

"I resent what you said in there about me," the Frenchman said.

"I'm under a lot of pressure to stop the losses the rebels are inflicting."

"It is impossible to stop every raid," Fournier said. "The rebels come from all directions, in their speedboats, on land, impossible to predict. The black bastards are well armed and seem to know everything about us. They have their people working at the company who tell them where and when to attack."

"Then identify these people and root them out," Soderman said. "That's what you and your people are paid for." He walked away, leaving an irate Fournier stewing in his anger.

CHAPTER 63

Agu Gwantam had a meeting that morning with Blyds Okafor, the area commander of Nigeria's Economic and Financial Crimes Commission. The subject was the arrival of a contingent from London's Serious Fraud Office of the Attorney General's Office.

"They flew into Lagos last night," Okafor told Gwantam over breakfast on the warlord's patio. "One of the inspectors called me at my home."

"How many are there?" Gwantam asked between bites of toast slathered with marmalade.

"A half dozen at least. They want to meet with me in the morning."

Gwantam took another piece of toast from the basket and buttered it as he said, "This does not concern me, Blyds. You say that they are here to investigate whether executives at XCAL benefit from the oil bunkering. I am not employed by the oil company."

"But you *are* involved in the oil bunkering, Agu. Their investigation will certainly trace payments paid to XCAL executives by you and your people. There is Soderman and Penny in London . . . and all the others."

Gwantam tossed the toast on the table and stood. "Enough of this," he growled. "These high-and-mighty bureaucrats from England come here and investigate how things are done in Nigeria? How dare they? They know nothing except their comfortable lives in London. This is Nigeria! I spit on them and their arrogance."

Gwantam's outburst took Okafor by surprise. He picked up his teacup and raised it to his lips, but his hand shook and some dribbled on his gold tie. He put the cup back down and asked, "What do you suggest I do about them, Agu?"

Gwantam composed himself and smiled. "I trust that you will do whatever is necessary to keep them away from me and my businesses. Finish your breakfast and join me in the house."

Thirty minutes later Okafor left Agu Gwantam's house with an envelope containing five hundred dollars' worth of Nigerian naira, and a pat on the back. "Do what you must, Blyds," Gwantam said as he showed him to the door. "Send the Brits back to London with their self-righteous tails between their legs."

CHAPTER 64

Jeffy Gomba arrived precisely at ten to pick up Portland, Brixton, and Chambers. She'd substituted a black SUV for the silver Mercedes she'd driven the previous day. She'd also changed from her black suit and white tuxedo shirt to a bright yellow African dashiki.

"What do you have, an auto dealership, too?" Brixton asked as they exited the hotel and approached the car.

"I have friends," Gomba replied. "Some of my best friends have nice automobiles, yes?"

"Evidently," said Brixton. "Where did you get the handguns? Your friends sell firearms, too?"

She grinned. "The guns are nice, yes? Very small, easy to carry."

Portland pulled up his pant leg to display the ankle holster he'd strapped on. "Impressive," he said.

Chambers handed her an 8 × 10 envelope. "I put my weapon in here," he said. "You can leave it in the car."

Brixton and Portland glanced at each other but said nothing

as Jeffy slid the envelope containing the weapon into the glove compartment. "Ready?" she asked her passengers.

"Let's go," said Portland, "but *where* are we going?"

"To find your French friend."

As they drove, Jeffy launched into a travelogue, pointing out sites they passed and giving a capsulated history of Port Harcourt. Whether she felt it was necessary to do this as their paid guide or because she was naturally proud of her city, her running commentary began to rub Brixton the wrong way and he tuned it out.

He was moved by the abject poverty that lived side by side with overt examples of wealth. As they drove through neighborhoods it occurred to him that the concept of architectural planning was absent from Nigeria. Some blocks had hastily constructed buildings that seemed to lean on each other; some faced other structures with only a narrow slit of land between them. The streets were filled with sidewalk vendors hawking their wares, some of whom approached the car and banged on the windows when Jeffy was forced to stop. Brixton occasionally looked over at Chambers, who was visibly uncomfortable with the chaos surrounding them. At one point three young toughs stood in front of the car and demanded money for it to proceed. Jeffy waved them off. When they didn't move, she leaned heavily on the horn and allowed the SUV to creep forward until it bumped the young men, who grumpily moved out of the way, extending their middle fingers. Jeffy laughed it off and said, "Doing business. Everybody is doing business in Nigeria."

"We'd call it a crime back in the States," Brixton grumbled.

"But this is Nigeria," she said.

"Everybody's got their hand out," Brixton said.

"Because everyone must eat and feed their families," was her reply.

The conversation ended when Gomba turned onto a narrow road that left the more populated areas and led into the swamps and rivers that defined the Niger Delta.

Portland asked where the road would take them.

"To where the Frenchman has his headquarters," she said.

"Why are we going there?" Chambers asked Portland. "You don't intend to simply walk in and ask for an appointment, do you?"

Portland didn't answer, but his mind was racing. The truth was that while he had a clear vision of why he'd decided to travel to Nigeria, he hadn't formulated a plan about what he'd do once he got there and confronted Alain Fournier.

Jeffy answered Chambers. "I want you to see where he works, where his headquarters are. What is the word? We *reconnoiter*, yes? I show you everywhere the Frenchman and his people are and where they go. You must know these things."

She came to a stop on the fringes of a grove of baobab and obeche trees six hundred feet from a two-story concrete building perched on the edge of one of the delta's myriad swamps. A sign above the front door read: **SureSafe**.

"This is it?" Brixton said, surprised at the Spartan appearance of the building. He'd expected something grander based upon all he'd heard about SureSafe and its global reach.

"It is where Mr. Fournier has his office," Jeffy said. She reached beneath her seat, came up with a set of binoculars, and handed them to Portland, who trained them on the front entrance.

"What are you looking for?" Chambers asked.

Portland ignored him and continued to peruse people coming and going from the building. He was about to abandon it when Jeffy, who was also looking at the entrance, said, "There he is."

"Who?" Brixton asked.

"The Frenchman."

Everyone focused their attention on the slight figure of Alain Fournier, who'd just exited the building and paused to light a cigarette. He wore a green double-breasted blazer, shirt, and tie and carried himself like men short in stature often do to appear bigger.

"That's *him*?" Brixton said.

"You're sure?" Portland asked Jeffy.

"Yes. That is the Frenchman. You have never seen him before?"

"Never," said Portland, the binoculars still raised to his eyes.

"Who are *they*?" Chambers asked, referring to two men carrying AK-47s who'd also emerged from the building and now flanked Fournier.

"His armed guards," Jeffy said. "See the one on his left? He is a friend of mine, a good friend. His name is Chimamanda. His friends call him Chima." She pronounced it "Cheé-ma."

"Your friend protects that slimy Frenchman?" Brixton said.

"He is paid well to do it," Jeffy said. "It is better for Chima than working on his family's farm."

"Everything here is about the money, huh?" Brixton said.

"Is it not the same where you come from?" Jeffy said, annoyance in her well-modulated voice.

Portland had to smile. Jeffy was right; money fueled almost everything, not only in a place like Nigeria but in more advanced nations, too.

"How close a friend is this Chima to you?" Portland asked.

Her smile was sly and knowing. "Let me just say, Mr. Portland, that Chima will do anything for me if asked."

They watched Fournier and his escorts walk to a SureSafe company car, get in, and drive away.

"So," said Jeffy, "now you have seen the man you must meet."

"He doesn't look like much to me," Brixton said.

"No," she agreed, "but he is evil, a very evil man."

"So, what do we do now?" Chambers asked.

"See where he is going," Jeffy said, slipping the transmission into Drive and falling in behind Fournier.

Fournier, who drove the company car, was still in a combative mood after his meeting with Max Soderman and other executives from XCAL. Following that meeting he'd gone to his office at the SureSafe building, handled some paperwork, and was now returning to XCAL's Niger Delta headquarters. Jeffy kept a safe distance to avoid alerting Fournier that he was being followed. Eventually the SureSafe car pulled into a parking lot in front of an imposing three-story white building with a large sign emblazoned across its façade—**XCAL**. Gomba chose a vacant parking space facing the main doors, turned off the engine, and they watched as Fournier got out and strode into the building, nodding at armed guards manning the entrance. The security men who'd accompanied him leaned on the car's hood and lit cigarettes, their weapons propped up against the vehicle.

After a half hour Chambers groused, "Are we just going to sit here for the rest of the day?"

"What *are* our plans?" Portland asked.

"That is up to you," said Jeffy.

As he said it Fournier reemerged from the XCAL building with another man, heavyset, with a sizable paunch and a shaved head.

"You know him?" Portland asked.

"Soderman," Jeffy said.

"Who's he?" Brixton asked.

"He is the big man at XCAL here in Nigeria, the boss."

"How do you know all these people?" Brixton asked.

"It helps in my work to know such people."

"Your work," Brixton said sarcastically. "Just what *is* your work?"

Portland waved Brixton off and concentrated on Soderman and Fournier, who climbed into the car that had brought Fournier. His two guards took the backseat.

Jeffy started her engine and after waiting a prudent minute fell in behind.

"I really don't see why we're doing this," Chambers said, "following cars like in some grade-B movie."

"Shut up," Brixton said.

"Wait a minute," Chambers said. "Who do you think you're talking to?"

"Just stop complaining," Brixton said. "I'm tired of your complaining."

Chambers mumbled a curse before saying aloud, "I never should have come here."

Brixton's laugh was forced. "Finally!" he said.

"Will you two stop it," Portland snapped.

"Ah," said Jeffy.

"What?"

"Look where they are going."

Fournier had pulled up to the gate of a property on the outskirts of Port Harcourt surrounded by a high concrete wall topped with razor wire. She stopped on the well-tended suburban street far enough away to not be noticed.

"What's this place?" Portland asked.

"Agu Gwantam's home."

"The warlord?" Portland said.

"Right," said Jeffy. "A very powerful man here in the Niger Delta."

"Why would Fournier and this guy Soderman be coming to *his* house?" Brixton asked.

"Gwantam has his finger in everything," Portland said, thinking back to what he'd been told by Ammon Dimka and others about Gwantam's grip on virtually everything that transpired in the delta, including benefiting from funds channeled through the bogus Nigerian charity Bright Horizons. "Fournier provides security for him, too."

They watched as an armed guard approached the SureSafe company car. Fournier rolled down his window and exchanged words with the guard, who nodded and activated the gate, causing it to slowly swing open to allow them entrance to the grounds.

Chambers looked at his watch. "I wonder how long we'll have to sit here," he said.

An angry look from Portland cut off what else Chambers was about to say.

Although Portland didn't express it, his sympathy began to shift to Chambers's attitude. They waited for an hour, which turned into two. Growling stomachs announced that hunger had set in.

"Let's get something to eat," Brixton said.

"No," Portland said. "I want to see where they go next."

They didn't have to wait much longer. Fifteen minutes later the SureSafe car exited Gwantam's grounds and passed where they were parked. Jeffy gave them time to disappear around a bend before making a U-turn and again tailing Fournier and his passenger, Soderman. This time the destination was the XCAL headquarters.

Chambers started to suggest something, but Portland, anticipating his thought, said, "Okay, let's call it a day and get something to eat."

They lingered in a small Nigerian restaurant. When they'd finished, Portland suggested to Jeffy that they return to the hotel and come up with a plan of action. "I appreciate seeing them go about their daily routines, but I need to decide what I'm going to do."

As they returned to their hotel, Fournier and Soderman huddled in the COO's XCAL office. Conversation during their lunch with Agu Gwantam had concentrated on knowing that David Portland and his two friends were in Nigeria. The unanswered questions were why Portland had made the trip and what he intended to do while there. Fournier had expressed that concern; Gwantam had dismissed them.

"The man poses no threat," the warlord said.

"But Alain is right," Soderman said. "There can be no other reason for Portland to have traveled this far than the death of his son."

"And what can he do about it?" Gwantam said. "It happened more than a year ago. Two years ago. You know how the British can be. They're sentimentalists. Chances are he has come here out of some warped belief that in doing so he will be closer to his son." He waved his large black hand for emphasis. "Forget about him."

Fournier put the brakes on what he was thinking—that Gwantam was a typical black fool lacking an understanding of the way more sophisticated men think.

"From what I understand the man is mentally unbalanced," Soderman said.

"All the more reason to ignore him," said Gwantam. He asked Fournier, "The two men he travels with. Who are they?"

"One is an American private detective named Brixton, Robert Brixton. He and Portland are friends. The other man, whose name is Chambers, works for the law firm in the United States that represents XCAL."

"Why is this law firm involved in his trip?" Gwantam asked.

"I heard from a colleague in London," Fournier said, smug that he had a direct source of information, "that this man Chambers works for the law firm as an investigator. He was dispatched to London to look into Portland and his accusation that SureSafe played some role in his son's death." He guffawed. "It is nonsense, of course, but as you say, this man Portland is mentally ill. Why Chambers is accompanying Portland to Nigeria is a question to be answered."

"Do we know where Portland and his friends are staying in Port Harcourt?" Soderman asked.

"It will not be difficult to find out," Gwantam said. "I will see to it immediately."

It took Gwantam only two hours for his wide group of loyalists to identify the hotel in which Portland and his traveling friends were staying, which he reported to Alain Fournier.

CHAPTER 65

I must go to an important meeting," Jeffy told Portland, Brixton, and Chambers when she dropped them at the hotel, "but I will be back in a few hours."

"I thought we were going to come up with a plan of action," Portland said.

"We will, we will," she said, "but first I must attend this meeting. It has to do with the steps we will take next."

"Who are you meeting with?" Brixton asked.

"Those who will be able to help you. Trust me. You must trust me."

She drove away, leaving them to ponder their situation.

Chambers, who'd had little to say all day, announced that he wasn't feeling well and intended to rest.

"You go ahead," Portland said. "We'll meet up for dinner if you're up to it."

Portland and Brixton took advantage of Chambers's absence to get together in Portland's room.

"So," Brixton said, "here we are in scenic Port Harcourt. Do you know what's going on? I sure as hell don't."

"I know as much as you do, Robert. We're in this Jeffy woman's hands, which might be a good thing, maybe not. I still don't know how she plans to get me together with Fournier."

"Don't look to me for an answer," Brixton said. "You're the one who hired her."

"My contact at the embassy vouched for her, no reservations," Portland said defensively. "He told me that if anyone can arrange for me to confront Fournier, it's Jeffrey Gomba."

"Who turns out to be a woman. I don't trust her," Brixton said. "I don't trust anybody in Nigeria. What's she done for us besides taking us to that cesspool of a militia camp? Speaking of that, what did we accomplish by meeting with the so-called commander of that group? 'The commander'! We don't even know his name."

"Maybe she introduced him to us to make the point that there are other people who'll be happy to get rid of Fournier."

"Is that what you intend to do, David, 'get rid of Fournier'?"

"I don't know *what* I intend to do."

"Well, David, let me make it plain that if you're here in Nigeria to kill the guy, count me out. I don't need to end up in some stinking Nigerian jail."

"Nobody asked you to come," Portland said.

"Yeah, I know that. I decided to tag along for reasons of my own, none of which are important. What *is* important is that we're here. Okay. We've seen Fournier. What's our next step?"

Portland searched for a sensible answer. Lacking one, he shrugged.

"Mind a suggestion?" Brixton asked.

"Shoot."

"Maybe it's time to call it a day and head home. You've now seen Fournier, know what he looks like, know how much he's hated by people like Jeffy and that so-called commander. What's to gain by hanging around hoping to talk to him? What are you going to do when and if—and I stress 'if'—you have the chance to confront the Frenchman, vent your spleen about your son, cuss him out, ask for an apology?"

"Are you suggesting, Robert, that I cut and run? No, Fournier owes me an explanation about Trevor. I want to know who gave him the order to shoot my son, and why he followed through on it. I didn't come this far to call it quits. I need to talk to him and I can't leave until I do that."

"Who do you think you're kidding, David? You don't intend to *talk* to him. You want to see him dead before you leave Nigeria. Right?"

"It's crossed my mind," Portland said. He rubbed his eyes and yawned. "Chambers has the right idea. I need a nap, too."

"Jeffy said she'd be back in a few hours," Brixton said. "Let me know when she arrives. I'll say one thing about her."

Portland cocked his head.

"She's a knockout."

Brixton went to his room and tried to sleep, but his mind was too active. He realized that he'd put himself in a tough spot. If Portland intended to take some sort of physical action against Fournier he wanted no part of it, no matter how close his friendship with the Brit had grown. It wasn't that he didn't understand his friend's need to inflict some sort of retribution on the man who'd murdered his son. He'd had the same vengeful thoughts countless times about the people behind the suicide bomber who'd taken the life of his daughter Janet. But he wasn't about to take part in an assassination.

He grappled with the decision he knew he'd have to make: continue on with Portland in his quest to confront Fournier and be supportive or bail out and head for home. Both options made sense to him, and he was left with the same quandary as when he'd initiated his internal debate. He couldn't make a decision—

which meant, he realized, that the decision had been made for him. He'd continue at Portland's side and hope that his presence might influence him.

Portland knocked on Brixton's door three hours later.

"Jeffy's back," Portland said. "She wants to meet."

"It took her long enough," Brixton groused, checking his watch.

"She says she's worked out a plan."

"Then let's hear what she has to say. You want to get Chambers?"

"No, let him sleep. We'll tell him what we're doing after the decision's been made."

Jeffy suggested that they talk outside the hotel. "Too many eyes and ears inside," she explained.

They walked from the hotel grounds into a dense kapok grove, where they came upon a small, rust-pocked black metal bench on the edge of a swamp. Jeffy had changed clothes; she now wore an olive green sport jacket over a white T-shirt, and jeans.

"You have a big wardrobe," Brixton commented after he and Portland had sat on the bench.

Jeffy remained standing. "What is that saying? Clothes make the man, huh?" she said through a wide smile.

"Maybe," Brixton grumbled. "Okay, you said you'd have a plan when you got back. What is it?"

Jeffy's smile was now smug as she turned to Portland and asked, "What would you think about meeting your French friend tonight?"

Portland looked at Brixton before replying, "That depends on how and where it's done."

"Of course, of course," Jeffy said. "The meeting I have just come from was very valuable."

"Who did you meet with?" Portland asked.

"Friends who have many connections here in the delta. Friends are the most important thing in life. Am I right?"

"Who are these friends?" Brixton asked, his impatience showing.

"It would not be prudent of me to tell you their names. Let me just say that they are able to help you accomplish your mission."

"You said that I could meet Fournier tonight," Portland said. "All right, lay it out for me."

As she started to elaborate they became aware of two black men who'd stepped from the grove of kapoks and approached. They wore khaki pants and shirts. The shirts had emblems on the sleeves, which they couldn't read from their vantage point. But holstered revolvers on the men's belts were plainly visible. They positioned themselves at either end of the bench. Now the emblems on their sleeves were readable: **SureSafe Security**.

"Hello, brothers," Jeffy said pleasantly.

"Your passports please," one of the men said.

"Why?" Brixton asked.

"Your passports," the man repeated, more sternly this time.

"Who are you?" Portland said, standing. "SureSafe is a private security firm. You don't have any legal right to—"

"I think you are making a mistake," Jeffy said to them. "These men are my guests." She pulled a business card from her pocket and held it out.

Brixton slowly got up from the bench and moved to the side. With the men's attention focused on Portland and Jeffy, he quickly and smoothly came up behind, pulled his weapon from its ankle holster, and pressed it to the neck of the man closer to him. Jeffy was wide-eyed; Portland acted immediately. He held out his hand and said, "Give me your gun."

The men looked at each other, confusion written on their faces. "Come on," Portland said.

He was handed the weapon. Brixton reached from behind and removed the other from its owner's holster.

"Now," said Portland, "get lost. Go back to your boss Fournier and tell him he should have sent smarter guys. You hear me? Go on. Leave!"

The men backed away and disappeared into the trees.

"That was a dumb move," Portland said to Brixton.

"It worked, didn't it?" Brixton said. "What do we do now?"

"We get out of here," Portland said, handing the weapon he'd confiscated to Brixton. "Fournier must have found out where we're staying and sent these clowns. They'll be back, more than two next time."

Brixton asked Jeffy where they could go.

"No problem," she said.

"Go rouse Chambers," Portland told Brixton. "I'll check out. Ten minutes, no more."

It took Chambers more than ten minutes to wake up and gather his belongings. He asked Brixton what was going on but didn't receive more than, "Come on, move it. We're out of here."

Twenty minutes later they were in Jeffy's car, this one a forest green SUV that matched her jacket.

"Where are we going?" Brixton asked.

"Not to worry," she said. "I have friends."

"You said I'd be meeting up with Fournier tonight," Portland said.

"I will tell you about it soon," was the lovely, shapely Nigerian's reply.

"What did you do with those two goons' guns?" Portland asked Brixton.

"I left them in my room," Brixton said. "We don't need to carry an arsenal."

Chambers, who'd been awoken from a deep sleep, took in what the others were saying and tried to make sense out of it. He finally asked, "What is all this about guns and goons and having to leave in such a hurry?"

Brixton filled Chambers in on what had motivated the quick getaway.

"And what about meeting this guy Fournier tonight?" Chambers asked.

"That's what Ms. Gomba says," Brixton said. "Relax, Chambers. We'll find out soon enough."

Jeffy turned down a street lined with dilapidated houses and continued until reaching one at the end of the road. She pulled into a weed-choked area next to it and cut the engine.

"What's this place?" Portland asked.

"A good friend lives here," said Jeffy.

"Another good friend, huh?" Brixton said. "Who is it this time, the general?"

She ignored him. "Wait here," she said before she got out of the car and went to a door at the rear of the house. After conferring with someone, she returned to the car and told the men to follow her.

"I don't like this," Brixton said to Portland.

"I don't either," Chambers agreed. "It could be some sort of a trap."

"You have your gun, Robert?"

"Yeah, but Chambers doesn't. It was in the glove compartment of the other car."

Jeffy overheard the conversation. "I have your gun," she told Chambers. "I transferred it to this glove compartment. Come, come. Everything is fine. My friends in this house will help you."

The three men exited the SUV and fell in behind Jeffy as she approached the rear door. It opened and a man bearing an automatic weapon was framed by it. He stepped aside as Jeffy entered. When the others didn't follow she turned and motioned for them to join her.

The room they'd entered was a kitchen, although it appeared that it hadn't been used for its intended purpose for some time. A bare bulb hanging on a cord from the ceiling provided the only light. Voices could be heard from another area of the house. Jeffy motioned for them to wait as she left the kitchen. A few moments later she returned with two men, one of whom was "the commander" who'd been at the jungle outpost when Portland and crew had been taken there.

"Welcome," the commander said.

"What's going on?" Portland asked.

Jeffy answered. "I will explain everything to you."

"That'll be nice, getting an explanation," Brixton said.

Chambers, wearing his blue African dashiki outfit, stood a few steps behind Portland and Brixton, as though using them as shields.

"Are you involved in my meeting Fournier?" Portland asked the commander.

"I will be," was his terse response as he turned and left the kitchen. The man who'd been with him placed a bottle on what had been a countertop, accompanied by four glasses. He turned and left.

"What are we doing here?" Chambers asked. "I don't like this at all," he said. "There's something fishy about it."

"Have a drink," Jeffy said. "It's good *ogogoro.* It will help you relax."

"No thanks," said Portland. His colleagues also declined.

Although it was no more than ten minutes, it seemed much longer before Jeffy returned to where she'd left them in the kitchen. "Everything is arranged," she said. "Come. It is time to act."

C H A P T E R 66

Jeffy drove away from the house and navigated the clogged streets until escaping the impoverished neighborhood.

"Where is Fournier?" Portland asked.

Until that moment, actually confronting the Frenchman had only been a goal for him, a concept. But Jeffy had indicated that the time had come for the meeting to take place, and Portland's nerve ends were sputtering with anticipation. Brixton, too, reacted to the heightened tension. For him it was like when he was a detective in Savannah, Georgia, and a sting was about to go down.

Chambers sat stoically, which didn't mirror what he was feeling. Deciding to accompany Portland and Brixton to Nigeria had been the result of an impetuous need to break away from his life and the law firm back in D.C. That there would actually be a collision between Portland and the man who'd killed his son seemed fanciful. Now it was real. He considered asking Jeffy to retrieve his gun from the glove compartment but didn't want to break the silence. Would he need it? Would he be called upon to use it? If so, it would be the first time he'd used a weapon aside from mandatory sessions on the MPD firing range.

Jeffy answered Portland's question. "The Frenchman will be at his apartment," she said.

"How do you know that?" Portland asked.

A smile crossed her cinnamon face. "A friend told me," she said.

"What friend?" asked Brixton.

"Her name is Carla, but that is not important."

"'Her'?" Portland said. "Another woman?"

"And a very pretty one," Jeffy said. "*Ayana*, the African word for 'beautiful.'"

"What does this other woman have to do with this?" Brixton asked.

"Your French friend has an eye for beautiful women," Jeffy said. "He will be with her when we arrive. She has arranged it."

They entered an upscale suburb of Port Harcourt, with homes set on manicured grounds. Ahead was a relatively new two-story apartment building, its circular driveway bordered by flowering plants and mature trees. Jeffy pulled to the curb across the street and turned off the engine and lights.

"He's in that building?" Portland asked.

"Yes," Jeffy said. She took a slip of paper from her pocket and read from it: "'Apartment number six, second floor, end of the hallway, largest apartment in the building, two bedrooms, a kitchen, two baths, a small terrace faces woods at back.'"

"Where did you come up with this?" Brixton asked.

"Friends. I have friends."

"Oh, right, I forgot. You have lots of friends," Brixton said.

"And you know that Fournier is in there now?" Portland asked.

"He is there."

"Who's with him?" Brixton asked.

"The beautiful woman."

"Just them? They'll be alone?" Portland asked.

Jeffy said, "There will be one of the Frenchman's bodyguards. He will be sitting outside the door to the apartment. I will call him before you enter the building and he will find another place to be for as long as is necessary."

"Another friend of yours?" Brixton said.

Jeffy ignored him and checked her watch. "It is time," she said. "I suggest you do what you have to do, and do it quickly."

"Will Fournier be armed?" Portland asked.

"I doubt if he will have his weapon with him. He will be busy doing other things." She grinned. "It is difficult to possess a weapon when you are naked."

"What about the door?"

"It will be unlocked. Go now. Hurry. It has not been easy to arrange this."

"You'll wait for us here?" Brixton asked.

She nodded.

" 'Us'?" Portland said to Brixton. "This is my fight."

"Sorry, pal, but I wouldn't miss it for the world," said Brixton.

"What about him?" Brixton said, referring to Chambers, who'd sat silently during the conversation.

"You stay with Jeffy," Portland told the former law firm investigator, which didn't elicit a protest.

Jeffy placed a call on her cell phone as Portland and Brixton left the car and approached the main entrance to the building; Portland was surprised that they were able to simply walk into the lobby without being challenged. A flight of stairs led to the second level.

"Ready?" Portland asked.

"Let's go," Brixton replied.

They pulled the handguns from their ankle holsters, ascended the staircase, and quietly walked down the carpeted hallway to apartment six. An empty chair stood next to the door. Portland turned the door handle. The door swung open slowly, silently.

They stepped into a foyer, focusing their attention on noise coming from a room at the end of the hallway whose door was partially open. Brixton looked at Portland and grinned. It was the sound of a couple making love, loud and urgent.

Portland led the way to the open door, Brixton close behind. They stopped and looked into the bedroom where a naked man and woman were coupled. Neither Portland nor Brixton said anything, but the man, Alain Fournier, whose attention wasn't totally consumed by the sexual act, sensed their presence. He climbed off the woman and turned to face them. Brixton and Portland leveled their handguns at him. He swore something in French and pushed himself up against the headboard. The woman scrambled from the bed and grabbed a blouse from the floor.

"Who are you?" Fournier demanded.

The woman scooped up the rest of her clothing and headed toward the bedroom door.

"Carla!" Fournier yelled. "You bitch!"

She went to the living room, finished dressing, and fled the apartment.

Fournier called out again. "Chima!" he shouted to the young man who'd been standing guard just outside the apartment door. There was no response.

"Get dressed," Portland commanded.

"You have no right," Fournier said. "I will have you arrested and—"

"And what, have me shot like my son?" Portland said.

"Portland?" Fournier said.

"Get dressed before I kill you here and now," Portland said.

Brixton, who stood behind and to the side of Portland, wondered what the next step would be. Here they were, confronting a helpless Alain Fournier. What would Portland do? Would he shoot Fournier on the spot? But that didn't seem to be on the Brit's agenda.

Fournier rolled off the bed and slipped on his boxer shorts, accompanied by a string of French curses. He reached for a weapon on a night table, but Brixton was quicker. He grabbed the handgun and shoved it in his waistband. They watched as Fournier finished putting on his clothes. Portland came around behind him and pressed his Pamas handgun to Fournier's temple. "You make one stupid move and you're dead," he said into his ear.

"What do we do next?" Brixton asked.

Portland responded, "Check out the hall and stairs."

Brixton did as instructed and reported that the way was clear. Portland placed a hand on Fournier's shoulder while keeping his weapon pressed against his head and pushed him through the door to the hallway. With Brixton leading the way they retraced their route out of the apartment building to where Jeffy waited.

The beautiful Nigerian's large, wide eyes mirrored her surprise at seeing Fournier alive. She'd expected Portland to kill the Frenchman in the apartment, and had planned to drive him, Brixton, and Chambers to a safe place until they could be spirited out of the country.

"Get in," Portland told Fournier, indicating the backseat where Chambers sat.

Fournier slid in next to Chambers, who moved away and pressed himself against the door. "Why is he here?" Chambers asked. "What are you going to do with him?"

Portland sat next to Fournier, his gun still trained on him. Brixton took the front passenger seat; he was as confused as Chambers.

"Where do we take him?" Jeffy asked.

"Position Seventeen," Portland said. "Here." He handed her the map he'd taken from Matthew Kelsey. "Where that red mark is. Position Seventeen. We're taking this slimy bastard to where he killed my son." He pushed the gun hard against Fournier's head. "That's where it happened, right, Fournier? Position Seventeen?"

Fournier swore.

"Come on, let's move," Portland told Jeffy.

She pulled from the curb and headed in the direction of one of XCAL's extraction facilities, known as Position Seventeen. She drove faster than usual, her eyes fixated on the road.

Fournier, who'd been verbally combative, shifted gears. "Why are you doing this to me?" he asked, his voice less angry.

"*Why?*" Portland guffawed. "Because I want to take you to where you gunned down my son, that's why."

"You are wrong," Fournier said. "I didn't kill your son. I am told by many people that you claim I did, but you are wrong. I swear on my mother, I did not kill him."

Portland's reaction was to ram the muzzle of his gun against the side of the Frenchman's head. "You're a lying bastard, Fournier."

Fournier noticed that Chambers was wearing an African outfit. "Who are you?" he asked.

Chambers responded by turning from him and staring out the window.

They ended up on a winding dirt road leading through mango groves and low-hanging bushes, the road's ruts filled with stagnant rainwater. Jeffy had opened some of the windows and the oppressive, heavy humid air filled the car as it slowed to accommodate rocks and tree branches. Ahead was a dock that served one of the oil company's extraction units. A single light affixed to it provided an eerie modicum of light. Jeffy came to a stop, allowing the vehicle's headlights to provide additional illumination.

"Why are we here?" Fournier asked, his voice belying his fear.

"This is where my son died?" Portland asked.

When Fournier said nothing Portland repeated his question, this time emphasizing the question with a nudge from his handgun.

Fournier said, "You don't know what you are talking about. I know nothing about your son."

"What about *this*?" Portland said, holding his wrist wearing Trevor's bracelet in front of Fournier's eyes.

"What? What is it? I know nothing about it. A bracelet."

Fournier's lies fueled Portland's anger. "You took it from my dead son and lost it in a card game." He took a series of deep breaths to calm himself. "Get out!" he said, opening the door on his side and sliding from the car. The Frenchman followed.

Brixton and Chambers also exited. Jeffy, who'd remained behind the wheel, said to Portland, "I must speak with you."

"Make sure our French friend doesn't get frisky," Portland said to Brixton through the driver's window. "Shoot him if he does."

"I must go now," Jeffy said.

"Go?" Portland said. "What, and leave us stranded out here in the middle of nowhere?"

"You will be all right," she said. "You will be picked up soon."

Portland peered into the vast darkness of the delta's swamp. "Who's picking us up?"

"The commander. He and his men will arrive soon in their boats."

"Why are they coming?"

"To do what they must. Please, no more questions. Everything will be fine."

"I owe you money," Portland said.

"You have my card," said Gomba. "You can wire it to me at my address. But if you do not, it is all right. I am just happy to see the Frenchman dead."

"Wait a minute," Portland said. "I'm not sure that—"

"You are a good man, Mr. Portland. It has been my pleasure to have been of help to you." She opened the glove compartment, took Chambers's weapon from it, and handed it to Portland before rolling up the window, shifting into reverse, backing away, turning, and disappearing into the hot, humid night, her red taillights fading in the swamp's murkiness. The sudden absence of her headlights cast the dock and the people on it into virtual darkness.

"Where did she go?" Chambers asked when Portland returned to the dock. "She's leaving us here?"

"Home, I suppose," Portland said, handing Chambers his handgun. "She did what she said she'd do, brought me face-to-face with our French friend here. Don't sweat it. Everything will be fine." One of his thoughts at that moment was that he would have enjoyed spending more time with Jeffy Gomba. Her radiant beauty cut through the tense scene in which they were embroiled, and he wondered whether he would once again meet up with her. He hoped so.

Fournier had returned to his earlier bravado. He sneered at Portland and said, "So, what do you intend to do, Mr. Portland, shoot me? It will not bring back your precious son. I suggest that you and your friends walk away and be grateful that the Niger Delta hasn't become your final resting place. I hold no grudge toward you."

"Who gave you the word to kill my boy?" Portland asked.

When Fournier didn't answer, Portland said, "Was it that so-called warlord Agu something-or-other, or that British fop Penny in London? Come on, Fournier. I'm losing patience."

"Talk to Penny," Fournier said. "He's the boss."

"Penny gave you the word to shoot Trevor?"

Fournier's expression confirmed to Portland that it had been Sir Manford Penny, XCAL's UK chairman, who'd issued the order to execute Trevor.

Neither Chambers nor Brixton knew what Portland was thinking at that moment. Had they, they might have attempted to dissuade him from the decision he'd made to shoot Fournier and achieve the closure he so desperately needed. His hatred for the Frenchman was all-consuming, enhanced by Fournier's defiant stance and the scornful expression on his face. But as he raised his weapon to aim at Fournier's heart, he was distracted by a noise coming from the swamp. He and the others looked into the blackness in search of its origin but could see nothing. Then, the noise became louder. It was an engine, more than one. A moment later two speedboats appeared from the recesses of the delta.

Simultaneously, behind them, headlights appeared. SureSafe's headquarters had been alerted that people were at Position Seventeen and had dispatched three security guards to investigate. As they came to a stop and the security guards piled out of the vehicle, rifle shots rang out from one of the speedboats. Brixton and Chambers flung themselves to the deck as bullets flew over their heads. Fournier turned and ran toward the SureSafe vehicle, his hands in the air. But he had gone only a few feet when one of the bullets caught him in the back and sent him tumbling face-first onto the deck. Portland's initial reaction was to go to him, but that lasted only a few seconds. He was about to join Chambers and Brixton, who'd remained prone on the dock, when a shot from one of the SureSafe security guards tore into his abdomen, bringing him to his knees. He clutched at his wound before pitching forward.

"David!" Brixton said, crawling to his fallen friend.

Portland looked up at him. "Fournier," he rasped. "Where is he?"

"He's dead, David," Brixton said.

"Who?"

"Who killed him? The rebels."

A dozen fighters from the two speedboats poured onto the dock. They'd killed one of the security guards; the remaining two managed to get back into their vehicle and sped away, bullets ricocheting off it and smashing the rear window. Members of the militia group came to where Brixton and Chambers hovered over Portland.

"He needs a doctor," Brixton said, "and fast."

Portland was lifted by the rebels and carried to one of the boats. Brixton and Chambers stayed with him while two rebel fighters rigged an explosive device on an XCAL pipeline. When they'd finished, they joined the others in the boats. One detonated the explosive charge. It wasn't a terribly loud explosion, but the explosives were sufficient to blow a gaping hole in the pipe, and oil poured from it. There were celebratory cries as the boats left the dock and headed back into the dark cover of the Niger Delta's swamps.

It didn't surprise Brixton that their destination was the rebel camp they'd visited upon arriving in Port Harcourt. He didn't care where they went as long as Portland could receive medical attention. He asked a rebel who seemed to be in charge whether a doctor was at the camp.

"One will come," the rebel replied, "a very good doctor. He helps us many times."

Brixton sat during the trip with Portland's head in his lap. His British friend kept trying to speak, but his words were swallowed in coughing, which brought up blood.

"Hang on, David," Brixton said over and over. "We'll get you a doctor and you'll be good as new."

"I did it," Portland managed to say.

"You did what, David?"

"I got Fournier. I got him."

"You sure as hell did, David."

"It was Penny, the XCAL boss in London, who gave Fournier the word to kill Trevor."

"I'll remember that, David," said Brixton. "We'll figure out a way to make him pay, too."

Portland's breathing became shallower as they neared the rebel encampment and he suffered a coughing spasm, his blood spattering on Brixton. The Brit struggled to lift his hand.

"What is it, David?" Brixton asked.

"The bracelet," Portland said. "Take it off."

Brixton had trouble opening the clasp but eventually succeeded.

"Give it to Liz," Portland said.

"I'll hang on to it, David, but you can give it to her yourself."

The boat's pilot revved the engine and ran the boat up onto the small beach adjacent to the camp. As he did, Portland let out a loud groan. He grasped Brixton's hand with surprising strength, then let go.

"David," Brixton said. "Come on, buddy, a doctor is coming and—"

But Brixton knew that it was too late for any physician. His British chum, a man he'd grown to love and admire, was dead.

CHAPTER 67

Brixton had assumed that he'd seen the last of Jeffy Gomba, but he was wrong.

Brixton and Chambers spent the night with rebels at their remote outpost. It wasn't what Brixton would have opted for, but they didn't have a choice. They lay awake most of the night swatting at mosquitoes and trying to find a comfortable position on straw mats that served as mattresses.

David Portland's body had been carefully wrapped in oilcloth by members of the rebel group and placed in a ramshackle house in the middle of the encampment. Brixton and Chambers were fed a dinner of rice and beans, washed down by *ogogoro* gin.

Following dinner they met with the commander.

"We will make arrangements for you to leave the country," he said.

"Not without David," Brixton said.

The commander nodded. "Yes, I understand that. It will be done. Gomba will handle things."

"Ms. Gomba? Her? What *can't* she do?" Chambers asked.

The commander laughed, exposing yellow teeth. "Yes, the person we know as 'Jeffy' Jeffrey can do almost anything."

"I don't doubt it," Brixton said, this time without sarcasm.

Brixton and Chambers spent the following morning biding their time while preparations were made for them to leave the camp with David Portland's body. They bathed in a portion of the swamp that was relatively free of oil slicks, and joined members of the rebel force for a meal. Eventually they, along with Portland's body, were loaded into a panel truck driven by Jeffy and driven from Port Harcourt across the border into the small neighboring African nation of Benin and its international airport at Cotonou. Brixton and Chambers bought one-way tickets on an Air France flight to Paris, where they would connect with another Air France flight to Washington. Jeffy had arranged through a Nigerian undertaker friend to properly prepare and document Portland's body to accompany them—she had more friends than a D.C. lobbyist.

"I hope you know how much I appreciate everything you've done for us," Brixton told her before entering the terminal.

"I am only sorry about what happened to Mr. Portland," the Nigerian said. "I hope that you and your friend will come back one day," Jeffy said.

"I'd like that very much," said Brixton. "Oh, before I forget." He reached into a tote bag that contained Portland's belongings and withdrew the three Pamas handguns she had given them. "Here," he said. "You take them. I don't need them anymore. Besides, they won't allow them on the plane."

"They will be here for you when you return," Jeffy said.

"I know that David owes you money," Brixton said. "I have your card and will find a way to pay you."

"It is not necessary," she said, checking her watch. "I must go now. Travel safe, Mr. Brixton." She shook hands with Brixton and Chambers, got in the van, and drove away.

"That's one hell of a woman," Brixton said to Chambers.

"Someone *I'll* never forget," Chambers said. "Tough as nails and beautiful, too."

Although the contentious relationship between Brixton and Chambers hadn't thawed, Portland's death served to mitigate Brixton's negative view of the former D.C. cop. They'd shared a traumatic experience, a memory that both men would carry with them forever.

When they arrived in Washington a mortician who'd been engaged before their arrival was on hand to take possession of Portland's body. "What funeral plans have been made?" he asked Brixton.

"There aren't any plans yet," Brixton replied. "I'm sure that his former wife will want to take charge of his remains. She'll be in touch with you. She lives here in D.C."

Brixton had intended to call Elizabeth Sims from Africa to inform her of David's death, but he resisted the urge. Somehow, it seemed too callous and impersonal to break the news to her long distance, and he decided to wait until he was back in Washington. The bracelet that Portland had given him was in his pocket and seemed to weigh far more than it actually did; he found himself constantly fondling it. It had meant so much to Portland.

He and Chambers left the terminal in D.C. and joined a line of people waiting for cabs. Brixton had considered calling Mac and Annabel Smith to let them know that he'd be arriving but decided not to. He needed time for himself when he got back, a chance to go to his apartment and decompress.

"Where are you headed?" Brixton asked.

"Home," Chambers said. "I'll have to spend time at the law firm to wrap up details of my leaving. I'm sure it won't be pleasant." He'd told Brixton during their flights about the role that Cale, Watson and Warnowski had played in trying to whitewash XCAL and SureSafe in the killing of Trevor Portland, and how Walter Cale had dispatched him to London to try to neutralize Portland's quest for justice.

"You're better off away from them," Brixton offered.

"I feel the same way," said Chambers. "Do me a favor?"

"If I can."

"You said you'd be getting together with Elizabeth to give her the bracelet and tell her how David died."

"I don't look forward to it."

"I'm sure you don't. Look, please tell her for me that I'm sorry about what happened to David, and that I'm thinking of her."

Brixton caught the catch in Chambers's throat. He smiled and slapped him on the back. "I'm happy to do it, Cameron, but maybe you should call and tell her yourself."

"I will at some point." He shook his head. "The truth is I've had a crush on Elizabeth Sims from the first day I met her."

" 'A crush'?" Brixton said, laughing. "I haven't heard anyone say that in a long time."

"Pathetic, huh?"

"No, not pathetic, Cameron. Human. It's just being human. I've had a few crushes myself."

The next vacant cab pulled up.

"You take it," Brixton said.

Chambers opened the taxi's door but paused before getting in. "I know how much you were against me coming with you and David to Nigeria, but I'm glad I did. I learned something about myself and want you to know that I appreciated the opportunity. You and David made quite a team."

Brixton watched Chambers's taxi get swallowed by the traffic.

The cab that Brixton took delivered him to the apartment he shared with Flo Combes. He'd tried to block her from his thoughts over the past few days, but now that he was there the reality of her absence hit him hard. He went in the kitchen and looked at her travel itinerary, which was secured to the refrigerator door by two small decorative magnets. She was due back the following day. They hadn't spoken since she left for Los Angeles, and no arrangements had been made for him to meet her plane. He poured two fingers of scotch, sat at the kitchen table, dialed her cell number, and braced for what he was certain would be a cold welcome.

"Flo? It's Robert."

"Where are you calling from?"

"The apartment. I just got back."

"You're—you're okay?"

"Yeah, I'm fine. I'm sorry I didn't call earlier, but cell service in Nigeria isn't the best and—well, I was busy, too. How are you? How's the fashion show going?"

"It's been wonderful. I've met some great designers and will have a terrific new line to show in the shop. Is David with you?"

"No, David is—David is dead, Flo."

She gasped. "Oh, no. My God. What happened?"

He gave her a capsulated version of the events leading up to Portland being shot. "I'll tell you more when you get back tomorrow. I'll pick you up at the airport."

"Robert, are you sure you're all right?"

"I'm fine, Flo, just a little shaken by what went down in Nigeria. I have to call David's ex-wife, Elizabeth. She doesn't know."

"Can you wait until I'm back?" she asked. "We can do it together. It might be easier on you that way and—"

"No, I have to get it over with. I'll be okay."

"Why don't you call Mac and Annabel and see if they can go with you?"

"Maybe I will," he said, not intending to. "Look, Flo, I'm sorry the way things fell the day you left. I should have told you the minute I decided to travel with David and—"

"It's okay, Robert. I understand. I really do. Please take care of yourself until I get back. You've been through an ordeal."

"I'll be fine," he said, "and you enjoy your last day in L.A. Just don't let any sleazy Hollywood agent get you to sign a long-term movie contract."

"Very funny, Robert. I love you. I miss you. Take care."

He made himself crackers and cheese to go with the scotch and summoned the courage to call Elizabeth Sims. He first tried the law firm of Cale, Watson and Warnowski. The woman who answered tersely informed him that Ms. Sims was not available.

"She's busy?"

"She isn't here."

"Lucky her. Thanks."

He called her home number.

"Hello?"

"Elizabeth?"

"Yes."

"It's Robert Brixton, David's friend."

"Oh, hello. You and David are back from Nigeria?"

"Yes, but . . . You see—"

"Has something happened to David?"

"He's dead, Elizabeth. He was shot and killed in Nigeria."

There was a long silence on her end, followed by uncontrolled sobbing. Brixton waited until her emotions had ebbed before saying, "I hate to be the one to have to tell you this. Look, could we get together? I can be anywhere you say, your place, mine, a bar, restaurant, you name it."

She fought to compose herself. "Could you come here?" she said. "I'm afraid I'll make a scene in a public place."

"Sure."

She gave him her address and ten minutes later he was on his way.

CHAPTER 68

Liz Sims was dressed in a teal sweat suit when Brixton arrived. She'd pulled herself together, and he saw that she'd applied fresh makeup. She greeted him at the door and led him into the living room.

"Would you like a drink?" she asked.

"Are you having one?" he asked.

She pointed to a half-consumed glass of an amber liquid on a coffee table.

"Good," he said. "I wouldn't want you to drink alone."

They settled on a couch in front of a picture window that afforded a view of downtown Washington.

"Sorry I'm the bearer of bad news," Brixton said.

"I understand," she said. "I know how close you and David were."

"He was a special guy."

She drew a breath before asking, "How did he die?"

Brixton, too, inhaled before launching into the story of how Portland had been gunned down on the dock in the Niger Delta.

Elizabeth listened quietly, never interrupting to ask for a clarification or to comment on what he'd said. It took Brixton fifteen minutes to provide all the background.

"That's it," he said.

"And the security man that David went to Nigeria to confront, Fournier? Was he also killed?" she said.

"Yeah, but not by David."

"Did David have a chance to question Fournier before he died about who gave the order to shoot Trevor?"

"Yes, he did."

"And?" she said.

"It was the British guy in London, the chairman of XCAL, Manford Penny. He's got a 'Sir' in front of his name."

Elizabeth's expression turned hard. "That bastard," she said.

Brixton reached in his pocket and pulled out the bracelet that Trevor's grandmother had given him, and that had set into motion everything that had occurred over the past few days. He handed it to Elizabeth.

"Trevor's bracelet," she said, twisting it in her fingers.

"David gave it to me as he was dying," Brixton said. "He told me to be sure that you got it."

"Thank you," she said, slipping it onto her slender wrist. "I'll wear it everywhere I go."

She refreshed her drink; Brixton declined her offer.

"So," he said, "how are things in the D.C. legal world?"

She returned to the couch, pressed her lips together, and said, "Everything is fine, I suppose, but I'm not part of it any longer."

"Oh?"

"I've resigned from the firm."

"I didn't know."

"I love the law, Robert, always have. I just don't like the games the firm has been playing with XCAL, SureSafe, and Trevor's murder."

"Gutsy move. You were a rising star. David was proud of you."

"David would agree with my decision," she said. "You knew him as well as anyone. He didn't have patience with BS."

Brixton laughed. "That's an understatement," he said.

"I'll be moving to Boston," she said. "There's an attorney I graduated with who's established a firm there. It's small, of course, but I'm looking forward to small. My dad has cancer and is undergoing treatments. I'd like to be closer to him."

"I wish him well," Brixton said.

They spent another half hour talking about David and those aspects of him that they'd admired and enjoyed. Finally, Brixton stood, thanked her for letting him share thoughts about David, and promised to stay in touch. He drove back to his apartment and called Mac and Annabel Smith at their Watergate apartment.

"Welcome home," Mac said. "How was Nigeria?"

Brixton told him about Portland's death and what had led up to it.

"That's a hell of a story, Robert," said Smith. "I'm sorry about David."

"Yeah, I am, too. Flo comes home tomorrow. I was wondering whether you and Annie can put up with a last-minute dinner guest tonight."

"If his name is Robert Brixton he's always welcome. Be here in an hour?"

"I'll be there."

CHAPTER 69

Brixton slept soundly after dinner with the Smiths. He got up later than usual the following morning, enjoyed a large breakfast at a favorite coffee shop, and waded into a collection of unanswered correspondence that had arrived during his absence. His receptionist, Mrs. Warden, had separated it into individual piles based upon subject matter, and had left a stack of phone messages written in her precise hand.

He ordered lunch in and ate in his office before heading for the airport to meet Flo's flight from Los Angeles. It was on time, and collecting her checked luggage went smoothly.

"It is so good to see you," Brixton said after they'd settled in his Subaru and were headed back to the District.

"I've been worried about you the entire trip, Robert. Nigeria! I read while you were away that it's considered one of the most dangerous places in the world to visit."

"Worse than the streets of our nation's capital?" he asked.

She hit his arm. "Don't make light of it. You could have been killed—like David."

"It wasn't my time," he said. "I had a nice visit with the Smiths last night. They want us for dinner this week."

"Sounds good."

He read a magazine in the living room while Flo unpacked. When she joined him from the kitchen she carried a tray of snacks, two glasses, and a bottle of white wine she'd opened. They toasted her return, and his, too.

"I'm glad your trip was successful," he said, raising his glass.

"And I'm glad you're back safe, although the news about David is terrible. I'm so sorry. I know you've lost a good friend."

"Yeah, I miss him a lot. It's good of Elizabeth to arrange for him to be buried in her family's plot in Massachusetts. He'll be with his son again." He looked away from her and became reflective. "I don't know how David would view it, but I'm glad he wasn't the one to kill Fournier. Better that one of the rebels did. At least David didn't die a murderer."

"But the Frenchman did. He'd murdered David's son."

"Yeah. Justice was served, I guess. It's good that David knew before he died that Fournier was killed. Maybe it brought him some peace of mind."

"What did Mac say last night about that client of his, the son whose father committed suicide after falling for a Nigerian money scam?" Flo asked.

"Just that the son, Anthony Borilli, has decided not to pursue any legal action. It was a losing proposition for everybody. That phony Nigerian charitable organization, Bright Horizons, packed up in the middle of the night and closed its doors. Mac thought that he might be able to bring a suit against it on Borilli's behalf, but that was a long shot at best. Nothing changes where Nigeria is concerned. They'll keep pumping oil out of the ground, the execs and government bigwigs will continue to get rich, the poor natives will keep on suffering, and there'll always be people who'll buy into the Nigerian financial scams. Same old, same old, Nigerian-style."

"There's nothing you can do about that, Robert."

"I know. I just wish there was. The only thing that came out of this past week was David's death."

"It wasn't worth it," she said.

"Yeah, except maybe David wouldn't view it that way. Even though he didn't get to personally pull the trigger on Fournier, he got his revenge." He grunted. "Will Sayers gets something out of it, too. I called Will and told him everything that had happened while we were in Nigeria. He can use it in the book he's writing."

"What are we doing for dinner?" she asked.

"I'm in the mood for Chinese," he said.

"Good," she said. "I was afraid you'd want to go to some exotic African restaurant."

She stood and started to carry the tray inside.

"I want to run something past you," he said.

She resumed her seat.

"I got to travel to London thanks to David Portland, but all I saw was his apartment—they call it a flat there—Heathrow Airport, and David's favorite pub. I was thinking that *we* should plan a trip there, you know, the two of us, take a week and enjoy ourselves."

She leaned over and kissed his cheek. "What a nice idea," she said. "I'm ready to go whenever you say."

"Yeah," he said. "I'd really enjoy seeing more of London than I did this past week. Besides, there's some business I need to take care of."

She looked at him quizzically, head cocked. "Business? What business?"

"Not a big deal. I promised David that I'd look up a guy there."

"What guy?"

Brixton's shrug was deliberately nonchalant. "His name's Penny, Manford Penny. *Sir* Manford Penny."

"Who's he? He sounds important, like a member of Parliament."

"He's a big-shot businessman. Not important. I just want to keep my promise to David." He got up, grabbed Flo's hand, and pulled her to her feet. "Come on," he said. "Time for some wonton soup and Peking duck. It's good to be home, Flo. It's *really* good to be home."